What the Tides Ask of Us

The Tides Between Us, Book 2

Written by Diane Kann

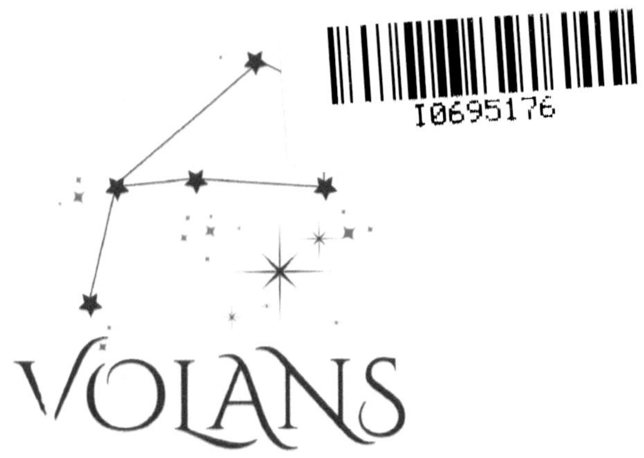

Brought to you by Volans Galaxy Press

Published by Kannceptual Creations LLC

An imprint of Volans Galaxy Press

ISBN: 978-1-971356-30-3

Printed in the United States of America

First Edition, January 2026

Contents

CHAPTER ONE

Echoes of the Summer Tide

The salt-laced air, once sharp with the urgency of a crisis, now carried a gentler, more familiar scent. One year. A full cycle of seasons had spun since the churning, chaotic moments that had irrevocably bound Mara Ellison and Eli Carter. The coastal town, a constant presence in Mara's life, had undergone a subtle metamorphosis in her perception. Its rugged beauty, the steadfast lighthouse, the weathered storefronts – they were no longer merely landmarks, but intimate witnesses to a shared history. The beach where she'd first seen Eli, his strength a stark contrast to the helplessness she'd felt, now offered a different kind of solace. As she walked along the tide line, the sand cool beneath her bare feet, a phantom sensation would sometimes ghost across her arm, the memory of his firm, steady grip. It was a sensation so fleeting, so ephemeral, it was like a whisper from a past life, a summer storm that had long since passed, leaving behind a sky of clearer, albeit more complex, hues.

The feverish intensity of that initial connection had undeniably receded, dissolving into the steady, predictable rhythm of everyday life. Yet, what remained was not a void, but a quiet current, a subtle undercurrent of possibility that Mara observed with the practiced, if slightly hesitant, gaze of someone who had learned to tread carefully. She was a woman who understood the power of currents, both in the ocean and in the human heart. Her instinct was to navigate, to observe the flow before committing to a direction. The marine rescue center, the crucible where their intertwined destinies had been forged, now hummed with the predictable, vital rhythm of its daily operations. The familiar clang of equipment, the hushed urgency of radio transmissions, the purposeful stride of staff members – it was a symphony of routine, a stark contrast to the seismic personal shifts that had occurred between her and Eli. The center, once a place of unexpected collision, had become a space of quiet, shared purpose, a constant reminder of how far they had come, and how much had changed, not just around them, but within them.

Mara found herself revisiting moments from that transformative summer not with a pang of regret, but with a burgeoning curiosity, a gentle probing into the present state of their connection. Eli's presence, which had once arrived like a sudden, astonishing calm amidst a tempest, had woven itself into the fabric of her days. It was no longer a dramatic intervention, but a steady, reassuring hum in the background of her life, a melody she'd come to recognize and, in quiet moments, even anticipate. She acknowledged the tangible evolution of their bond, the subtle yet undeniable shift from casual interactions, marked by necessity and shared experience, into a realm of unspoken understandings. It was in the way he'd learned to read the subtle shifts in her posture, the almost imperceptible tightening around her eyes when she was wrestling with a difficult decision. It was in the way she, in turn, had learned to anticipate his need for quiet solitude after a particularly taxing rescue, or the way she instinctively knew when a shared meal was more about comfort than sustenance.

This phase was Mara's introspective landscape, a quiet acceptance of this new, gentler reality. It was a space where she allowed herself to acknowledge the subtle ways Eli's influence had become a part of her routine, like the comforting warmth of a mug of tea on a cool morning, or the familiar scent of the sea that permeated her home. Even as she maintained her characteristic emotional reserve, a carefully constructed edifice built over years of self-reliance, she felt its gentle erosion, not through force, but through the steady, patient presence of Eli. He didn't demand access; he simply created an environment where the doors felt safe to open. He was a constant, not in an overwhelming way, but in a way that provided a sense of grounding, a stable anchor in the often unpredictable currents of her own emotions.

Eli, on the other hand, experienced a quiet satisfaction, a deep-seated readiness to invest more fully in the burgeoning relationship. The man who had once felt adrift, buffeted by uncertainties and the echoes of his past, now felt a new sense of anchor. The rescue, and by extension, Mara's integral role within it, had provided him with a purpose that resonated deeper than any career aspiration. He observed Mara with a gentle, unyielding persistence, a quiet understanding that the walls she'd meticulously built over a lifetime wouldn't crumble overnight. He respected the strength that lay beneath her guardedness, recognizing that it was a testament to her resilience, not her unwillingness to connect. His perspective was one of patient cultivation, a deliberate intention to nurture what had begun. There was a quiet confidence in him, not arrogance, but a steady belief in the strength of their burgeoning bond, a bond that, while still delicate, felt intrinsically right. He saw the future not as a grand pronouncement, but as a series of carefully placed steps, each one building upon the last, solidifying their shared path.

The concept of commitment, once a distant, perhaps even daunting, shore, now loomed as a tangible, reachable destination. For Mara and Eli, in their separate reflections, the quiet hum of their connection began to carry the weight of intention, the nascent acknowledgment of the demands that an evolving relationship would inevitably place upon them. It was no longer enough to simply share stolen glances across the rescue center floor, or to encounter each other by chance along the familiar coastal paths. It was about the conscious, active choice to build something more, to invest not just emotion, but time and energy into its sustenance. This was the crucial shift, the subtle pivot from the realm of 'what if' to the nascent, yet potent, question of 'what now.' It was a quiet internal dialogue, a series of unspoken conversations that were beginning to take place in the hushed spaces between heartbeats, even if spoken words remained scarce. The ocean, in its vast and indifferent beauty, seemed to hold its breath, as if waiting for them to articulate the unspoken desires that stirred within its depths.

The rescue center, a nexus of their shared experience, continued its vital work, a constant in their lives that provided both a backdrop and a catalyst for their evolving relationship. Its operational challenges, the daily demands of saving lives and safeguarding the coastline, served as a mirror to the personal shifts that were unfolding between Mara and Eli. The external pressures, the unpredictable nature of their work, the constant need for vigilance and swift action, were a stark contrast to the deliberate, internal journey they were undertaking. Yet, it was within this shared environment, amidst the controlled chaos and the profound sense of purpose, that their connection had found its fertile ground. The rescue center, with its sturdy walls and its unwavering mission, had become more than just a workplace; it was the silent witness to the quiet unfolding of their love, a place where the echoes of a summer tide were slowly, surely, giving way to the steady pulse of a shared future.

Mara often found herself walking the familiar stretch of coastline, the same stretch of sand where the impossible had happened. It had been a summer storm, not just of wind and rain, but of circumstance, a tempest that had swept her from her feet and deposited her, shaken but whole, into the steady orbit of Eli's life. Now, a year later, the storm had passed, leaving behind a landscape transformed. The salt spray that kissed her cheeks felt different, no longer stinging with the raw aftermath of near-disaster, but caressing with the gentle familiarity of a season's turn. She'd learned to read the tides, not just the oceanic ebb and flow that dictated the rescue center's operations, but the subtler, more profound tides that moved within her own heart.

There were moments, when the late afternoon sun cast long shadows across the dunes, that the phantom sensation would return. The ghost of Eli's hand on her arm, a steadying presence during the terrifying moments of the rescue, would linger, a warm imprint on her skin. It was a sensation that spoke of strength, of unwavering calm in the face of chaos, a stark contrast to her own internal turbulence that had once threatened to capsize her. The summer's intensity, a period of raw vulnerability and unexpected connection, had faded into the everyday, replaced not by a void, but by a quiet current of possibility. Mara observed this current with a gaze that was both practiced and hesitant. She had built her life on a foundation of self-reliance, each stone carefully placed, each mortar joint meticulously sealed. The idea of allowing another to navigate these carefully constructed walls was a prospect that still stirred a tremor of apprehension within her.

The marine rescue center, their shared crucible, now pulsed with a different kind of energy. The clang of equipment, the hushed urgency of radio communications, the purposeful stride of the rescue teams – these were the sounds and sights of routine, of a well-oiled machine functioning with precision. It was a stark contrast to the personal shifts that had occurred between Mara and Eli, a quiet revolution that had taken place beneath the surface of their professional lives. The center, once the stage for a dramatic intervention, had become a space of quiet understanding, a testament to the enduring strength of their connection. It was here, amidst the calls of distress and the triumphs of rescue, that Mara felt the subtle recalibration of her world.

As she continued her walk, the rhythm of her footsteps syncing with the gentle whisper of the waves, Mara found herself replaying fragments of that transformative summer. It wasn't a process of regret; there was no longing for what had been lost, but rather a growing curiosity about what had been found. Eli's presence, once a sudden, vital calm amidst the roaring storm, had become a steady hum in the background of her life. It was a melody she'd unconsciously learned to anticipate, a reassuring presence that didn't demand attention but simply *was*. She acknowledged the tangible evolution of their connection, the way casual interactions, born of necessity and shared trauma, had deepened into unspoken understandings. The hurried exchanges of information had given way to lingering glances, the shared silences now imbued with a comfortable intimacy, the kind that spoke volumes without uttering a single word.

This was Mara's internal landscape, a space she navigated with a practiced, almost unconscious, grace. It was a quiet acceptance of this new phase, a gentle surrender to the unfolding of their relationship. She recognized the subtle ways Eli's influence had settled into her routine, like the comforting warmth of a well-worn blanket on a chilly evening. He was a constant, not in an overwhelming or intrusive way, but in a way that provided a sense of grounding, a stable anchor in the often unpredictable currents of her own emotions. Even as she maintained her characteristic emotional reserve, a fortress built over years of self-reliance, she felt its gentle, persistent erosion. It wasn't a demolition, but a gradual softening, an opening of carefully guarded gates, not through force, but through the steady, patient presence of a man who seemed to understand the value of waiting, of allowing things to unfold in their own time.

Eli, on the other hand, felt a different kind of shift. His was a sense of quiet satisfaction, a profound readiness to invest more deeply, to build upon the foundation that had been laid. The man who had once felt adrift, buffeted by the winds of uncertainty and the lingering echoes of his past, now felt a new sense of anchor. The rescue, and Mara's integral role within it, had provided him with a purpose that resonated deeper than any personal ambition. He observed Mara with a gentle, unyielding persistence, a quiet understanding that the walls she had meticulously constructed over a lifetime wouldn't crumble overnight. He respected the strength that lay beneath her guardedness, recognizing it as a testament to her resilience, not her unwillingness to connect. His perspective was one of patient cultivation, a deliberate intention to nurture what had begun. There was a quiet confidence in him, not arrogance, but a steady belief in the strength of their burgeoning bond, a bond that, while still delicate, felt intrinsically right. He saw the future not as a grand pronouncement, but as a series of carefully placed steps, each one building upon the last, solidifying their shared path.

The concept of commitment, once a distant, perhaps even daunting, shore, now loomed as a tangible, reachable destination. For Mara and Eli, in their separate reflections, the quiet hum of their connection began to carry the weight of intention, the nascent acknowledgment of the demands that an evolving relationship would inevitably place upon them. It was no longer enough to simply share stolen glances across the rescue center floor, or to encounter each other by chance along the familiar coastal paths. It was about the conscious, active choice to build something more, to invest not just emotion, but time and energy into its sustenance. This was the crucial shift, the subtle pivot from the realm of 'what if' to the nascent, yet potent, question of 'what now.' It was a quiet internal dialogue, a series of unspoken conversations that were beginning to take place in the hushed spaces between heartbeats, even if spoken words remained scarce. The ocean, in its vast and indifferent beauty, seemed to hold its breath, as if waiting for them to articulate the unspoken desires that stirred within its depths.

The rescue center, a nexus of their shared experience, continued its vital work, a constant in their lives that provided both a backdrop and a catalyst for their evolving relationship. Its operational challenges, the daily demands of saving lives and safeguarding the coastline, served as a mirror to the personal shifts that were unfolding between Mara and Eli. The external pressures, the unpredictable nature of their work, the constant need for vigilance and swift action, were a stark contrast to the deliberate, internal journey they were undertaking. Yet, it was within this shared environment, amidst the controlled chaos and the profound sense of purpose, that their connection had found its fertile ground. The rescue center, with its sturdy walls and its unwavering mission, had become more than just a workplace; it was the silent witness to the quiet unfolding of their love, a place where the echoes of a summer tide were slowly, surely, giving way to the steady pulse of a shared future. The air within its walls, thick with the scent of salt and diesel, held a new quality for Mara – the distinct aroma of possibility, a subtle perfume that mingled with the ever-present brine, promising something more, something lasting. She recognized the familiar, comforting weight of Eli's presence beside her as they coordinated the day's patrols, a silent understanding passing between them with a shared glance, a subtle nod. It was a language they were still learning, a dialect of the heart spoken in the vernacular of shared purpose and quiet regard. The rescue center, once a symbol of crisis, had become, for Mara, a sanctuary, a place where the unpredictable nature of the sea was met with unwavering human dedication, and where her own guarded heart was slowly, tentatively, finding its own safe harbor.

The late afternoon sun, a softened, diffused light through the persistent coastal haze, painted the familiar stretch of shoreline in hues of muted gold. Mara walked, her bare feet sinking slightly into the cool, damp sand, the rhythmic hush of the waves a familiar lullaby. It had been a year since the maelstrom, a year since Eli Carter had appeared like a beacon in her personal tempest, his presence a steadying force when her world had threatened to spin out of control. The memory of that initial encounter, sharp and visceral, had receded, the raw edges smoothed by the passage of time and the quiet accumulation of shared days. Yet, it hadn't vanished. Instead, it had transformed, like a piece of sea glass tumbled smooth by the relentless surf, its original form now softened, its essence preserved in a gentler, more polished state.

She found herself returning to those moments, not with a yearning for the intensity, but with a nascent curiosity, a desire to understand the quiet evolution that had followed. The storm had passed, leaving behind a landscape irrevocably altered. Where once there had been a chaotic churn of fear and adrenaline, there was now a profound calm, a stillness that Eli's presence seemed to radiate. He was no longer the unexpected savior, the answer to an urgent plea; he had become something more subtle, a constant, reassuring hum in the background of her life. It was the warmth of a shared glance across the bustling rescue center, the knowing nod exchanged when a difficult call was resolved, the comfortable silence that settled between them during late-night debriefs. These were the small, quiet affirmations, the tender seedlings of a connection that had taken root in the most unexpected soil.

Mara traced the line of the tide with her toe, watching as the foamy fingers of an incoming wave lapped at her ankles. She remembered the sheer physical imprint of his hand on her arm, a lifeline in the midst of the roiling sea and her own internal turmoil. The memory, once a jolt of pure relief, now felt like a gentle echo, a phantom touch that spoke of strength and unwavering presence. It was a sensation that underscored the tangible shift in their dynamic. The hurried, often terse, exchanges dictated by necessity had long since given way to something richer, something built on a foundation of unspoken understanding. She found herself anticipating his needs, recognizing the subtle signs of fatigue etched around his eyes after a grueling shift, or the way his shoulders would relax almost imperceptibly when he finally allowed himself a moment of quiet reflection. In turn, he had learned to read her, to understand the slight tightening of her jaw that signaled unspoken concern, or the way her gaze would soften when she spoke of the ocean's quiet power.

This was her internal landscape, a space she navigated with a practiced, almost unconscious, grace. She was a woman accustomed to self-reliance, her life a meticulously constructed edifice, each stone laid with care, each joint sealed against the unpredictable winds of circumstance. The idea of allowing another to navigate these carefully guarded walls still stirred a tremor of apprehension within her, a faint echo of the vulnerability she had learned to keep at bay. Yet, Eli's presence was not a force that battered down her defenses; it was more akin to the gentle erosion of a cliff face by the persistent tide, a slow, inevitable softening that made the stone more receptive to change. He offered a quiet steadiness, a grounding influence that didn't demand entry but rather created an atmosphere of safety, a palpable sense that here, within the orbit of his quiet strength, her carefully constructed world could afford to be a little less fortified.

The rescue center, their shared crucible, now pulsed with a different kind of energy. The urgent clang of equipment, the hushed tension of radio transmissions, the purposeful stride of the rescue teams – these were the familiar sounds and sights of a well-oiled machine functioning with precision. It was a stark contrast to the quiet revolution that had taken place between Mara and Eli, a personal shift that had unfolded beneath the surface of their professional lives. The center, once the stage for a dramatic intervention, had become a space of quiet understanding, a testament to the enduring strength of their connection. Here, amidst the calls of distress and the triumphs of rescue, Mara felt the subtle recalibration of her world. The air within its sturdy walls, thick with the scent of salt and diesel, held a new quality for her – the distinct aroma of possibility, a subtle perfume that mingled with the ever-present brine, promising something more, something lasting. She recognized the familiar, comforting weight of Eli's presence beside her as they coordinated the day's patrols, a silent understanding passing between them with a shared glance, a subtle nod. It was a language they were still learning, a dialect of the heart spoken in the vernacular of shared purpose and quiet regard. The rescue center, once a symbol of crisis, had become, for Mara, a sanctuary, a place where the unpredictable nature of the sea was met with unwavering human dedication, and where her own guarded heart was slowly, tentatively, finding its own safe harbor.

The sea itself, in its vast and indifferent beauty, seemed to hold its breath, as if waiting for them to articulate the unspoken desires that stirred within its depths. For Mara, this was a new terrain, a landscape of subtle emotions and nascent hopes that she was only beginning to explore. She had always been a woman of action, her strength forged in the face of immediate crises. The quiet, introspective work of understanding her own heart, and the heart of another, was a challenge of a different magnitude, a test of patience and a willingness to embrace a vulnerability she had long since learned to suppress. Yet, with Eli, it felt less like a daunting task and more like a gentle unfolding, a natural progression that felt... right. There was a quiet confidence in his demeanor, a steady belief in the strength of their burgeoning bond, a bond that, while still delicate, felt intrinsically sound. He saw the future not as a grand pronouncement, but as a series of carefully placed steps, each one building upon the last, solidifying their shared path.

She recalled a moment from the previous week, a shared dinner at a small, unassuming café overlooking the harbor. The conversation had flowed easily, touching on the mundane details of their days, the challenges of the rescue operations, the ever-present beauty of their coastal home. But beneath the surface, Mara had felt it – the deeper current, the unspoken acknowledgment of their shared journey. He hadn't pushed, hadn't demanded declarations or commitments. He had simply been present, his gaze steady and understanding, his quiet demeanor a balm to her sometimes restless spirit. It was in the way he listened, truly listened, not just to her words, but to the emotions that lay beneath them. He possessed an innate ability to sense her unspoken needs, to offer comfort or space with equal grace. This was the essence of his influence, not a forceful intrusion, but a gentle, persistent presence that created an environment where the doors of her heart felt safe to open, not in a sudden rush, but in a slow, deliberate creak, revealing glimpses of the carefully curated space within.

He, on the other hand, experienced a quiet satisfaction, a deep-seated readiness to invest more fully in the burgeoning relationship. The man who had once felt adrift, buffeted by uncertainties and the echoes of his past, now felt a new sense of anchor. The rescue, and by extension, Mara's integral role within it, had provided him with a purpose that resonated deeper than any career aspiration. He observed Mara with a gentle, unyielding persistence, a quiet understanding that the walls she'd meticulously built over a lifetime wouldn't crumble overnight. He respected the strength that lay beneath her guardedness, recognizing that it was a testament to her resilience, not her unwillingness to connect. His perspective was one of patient cultivation, a deliberate intention to nurture what had begun. There was a quiet confidence in him, not arrogance, but a steady belief in the strength of their burgeoning bond, a bond that, while still delicate, felt intrinsically right. He saw the future not as a grand pronouncement, but as a series of carefully placed steps, each one building upon the last, solidifying their shared path.

The concept of commitment, once a distant, perhaps even daunting, shore, now loomed as a tangible, reachable destination. For Mara and Eli, in their separate reflections, the quiet hum of their connection began to carry the weight of intention, the nascent acknowledgment of the demands that an evolving relationship would inevitably place upon them. It was no longer enough to simply share stolen glances across the rescue center floor, or to encounter each other by chance along the familiar coastal paths. It was about the conscious, active choice to build something more, to invest not just emotion, but time and energy into its sustenance. This was the crucial shift, the subtle pivot from the realm of 'what if' to the nascent, yet potent, question of 'what now.' It was a quiet internal dialogue, a series of unspoken conversations that were beginning to take place in the hushed spaces between heartbeats, even if spoken words remained scarce. The ocean, in its vast and indifferent beauty, seemed to hold its breath, as if waiting for them to articulate the unspoken desires that stirred within its depths.

The rescue center, a nexus of their shared experience, continued its vital work, a constant in their lives that provided both a backdrop and a catalyst for their evolving relationship. Its operational challenges, the daily demands of saving lives and safeguarding the coastline, served as a mirror to the personal shifts that were unfolding between Mara and Eli. The external pressures, the unpredictable nature of their work, the constant need for vigilance and swift action, were a stark contrast to the deliberate, internal journey they were undertaking. Yet, it was within this shared environment, amidst the controlled chaos and the profound sense of purpose, that their connection had found its fertile ground. The rescue center, with its sturdy walls and its unwavering mission, had become more than just a workplace; it was the silent witness to the quiet unfolding of their love, a place where the echoes of a summer tide were slowly, surely, giving way to the steady pulse of a shared future.

Mara continued her walk, the gentle ebb and flow of the tide mirroring the rhythm of her thoughts. She acknowledged the subtle shifts within herself, the gradual softening of her defenses, the nascent willingness to embrace a future that included another. It was a profound change for a woman who had so fiercely guarded her independence, so carefully constructed a life that was solely her own. Eli's presence had not diminished that independence; rather, it had enriched it, adding a layer of warmth and connection that had been missing.

He was not a part of her life; he was becoming a part of its very fabric, woven in with threads of shared experiences, quiet understanding, and a growing, undeniable affection. She realized, with a sense of quiet wonder, that the lingering spark of that summer storm had not extinguished itself but had, instead, transformed into a steady, enduring flame, one that promised to illuminate the path ahead. The shoreline stretched out before her, an endless horizon of possibility, and for the first time in a long time, Mara felt an eager anticipation for what lay beyond.

Eli found himself observing Mara with a quiet, unwavering attention, a habit he'd developed over the past year, and one that had only deepened with time. He'd always been a man who noticed details, a trait honed by his profession, but with Mara, those observations carried a different weight. It wasn't about assessing a risk or charting a course; it was about deciphering the subtle shifts in her posture, the flicker of emotion in her eyes, the almost imperceptible tension that sometimes settled in her shoulders after a particularly grueling shift. He understood, with a clarity that surprised even himself, that the carefully constructed walls around her heart hadn't been built overnight. They were fortifications, meticulously maintained, born of experiences that had taught her the harsh necessity of self-reliance. His approach, therefore, had to be one of patience, of gentle persistence, rather than any attempt at a forceful breach. He was acutely aware of the vulnerability that lay beneath her strength, a vulnerability she guarded fiercely, and he respected that. It wasn't a sign of resistance to him; it was a testament to her resilience, and he wouldn't jeopardize that hard-won fortitude for anything.

His own internal landscape had undergone a seismic shift, a transformation he still marveled at. There had been a time, not so long ago, when he'd felt like a ship without a rudder, adrift in a sea of his own uncertainties, the echoes of past mistakes and unresolved doubts a constant, disorienting swell. The rescue center, and Mara's integral role within its operations, had provided him with an anchor, a sense of purpose that resonated far deeper than any professional ambition had ever managed. It wasn't just about the adrenaline of a rescue, or the satisfaction of a mission accomplished; it was about the shared commitment, the unwavering dedication to a cause that extended beyond individual accolades. And woven inextricably into that purpose was Mara. Her presence had become a steadying force, a quiet constant that grounded him in a way he hadn't known he needed. He watched her navigate the complexities of her role with an efficiency and dedication that never ceased to impress him, her mind sharp, her actions decisive, yet always tempered with a deep well of compassion.

He recalled a recent evening, after a particularly demanding day. The air in the common room of the rescue center was thick with the lingering scent of salt and damp neoprene. Most of the team had dispersed, their energy reserves depleted, but Mara remained, meticulously going over incident reports, her brow furrowed in concentration. Eli, ostensibly tidying up, found himself lingering, content to simply be in her proximity. He didn't interrupt her focus, knowing that her need for quiet processing was as important as any need for conversation. Instead, he observed the way the lamplight caught the faint traces of exhaustion around her eyes, the almost imperceptible tremor in her hands as she turned a page. He resisted the urge to offer a comforting hand, knowing that such an gesture, premature and unsolicited, might inadvertently trigger the very defenses he was so carefully trying to help her dismantle. His intention wasn't to force a connection, but to create an environment where one could flourish organically, a space where she felt safe to lower her guard, not because she was pressured, but because she felt understood and accepted.

He had learned to read the subtle nuances of her moods, the unspoken language of her body. A slight tightening of her jaw, for instance, was often a precursor to her voicing a difficult truth. A faraway look in her eyes could signify a moment of deep introspection, or perhaps a memory surfacing from the depths of her past. He'd discovered that his own quiet presence, a steady hum of reassurance in the background, could sometimes be more potent than any outward display of affection or concern. He'd learned to offer his support in ways that felt natural to him, and, he hoped, unintrusive to her. It might be a carefully brewed cup of coffee placed silently beside her during a late-night shift, or a brief, affirming nod of acknowledgment when she accomplished a particularly challenging task. These were not grand gestures, but small, deliberate acts of tending, like a gardener carefully watering a delicate sapling, ensuring it had the best possible chance to grow.

The concept of commitment, once a distant, perhaps even daunting, shore, now loomed as a tangible, reachable destination. For Eli, in his own quiet reflections, the burgeoning relationship with Mara had begun to carry the weight of intention, a nascent acknowledgment of the demands that an evolving connection would inevitably place upon them. It was no longer enough to simply share stolen glances across the rescue center floor, or to encounter each other by chance along the familiar coastal paths. It was about the conscious, active choice to build something more, to invest not just emotion, but time and energy into its sustenance. This was the crucial shift, the subtle pivot from the realm of 'what if' to the nascent, yet potent, question of 'what now.' It was a quiet internal dialogue, a series of unspoken conversations that were beginning to take place in the hushed spaces between heartbeats, even if spoken words remained scarce.

He felt a deep-seated readiness to invest more fully, to nurture the fragile beginnings of what they shared. The rescue, and by extension, Mara's integral role within it, had provided him with a purpose that resonated deeper than any career aspiration had ever managed. He observed Mara with a gentle, unyielding persistence, a quiet understanding that the walls she'd meticulously built over a lifetime wouldn't crumble overnight. He respected the strength that lay beneath her guardedness, recognizing that it was a testament to her resilience, not her unwillingness to connect. His perspective was one of patient cultivation, a deliberate intention to nurture what had begun. There was a quiet confidence in him, not arrogance, but a steady belief in the strength of their burgeoning bond, a bond that, while still delicate, felt intrinsically right. He saw the future not as a grand pronouncement, but as a series of carefully placed steps, each one building upon the last, solidifying their shared path.

He found himself drawn to the quiet moments, the pockets of stillness that punctuated the demanding rhythm of their work. These were the moments where he felt he could truly see her, not as the skilled rescuer, but as the woman beneath the uniform. He'd noticed, for instance, the way her eyes would soften when she spoke of the ocean, a reverence in her voice that went beyond professional admiration. It was a deep, intrinsic connection to the sea, a force that both challenged and soothed her. He recognized a similar quiet strength within himself, a resilience forged in the crucible of his own past struggles. It was this shared understanding of weathering storms, both literal and metaphorical, that formed a silent, yet powerful, bond between them. He didn't need grand declarations or effusive displays of affection; he found profound satisfaction in the simple act of being present, of offering a steady hand when needed, a listening ear always ready.

He understood that their connection was still in its nascent stages, a delicate seedling pushing through the sandy soil of their shared experience. It required careful tending, a consistent supply of patience and understanding. He was not about to rush the process, to demand an immediate blooming. Instead, he was content to provide the ideal conditions for growth, to stand by and watch as the roots deepened, anchoring them more firmly to each other. He knew that Mara had a capacity for deep affection, a loyalty that, once given, was unwavering. He was willing to wait, to earn that trust, to demonstrate through his actions that he was a safe harbor, a constant presence she could rely on. This wasn't a passive waiting; it was an active investment, a conscious choice to be present, to nurture, and to believe in the potential of what they were building together. His own past had taught him the impermanence of many things, but the feeling he had for Mara, the quiet certainty that had settled within him, felt different. It felt solid, enduring, like the ancient cliffs that stood sentinel against the relentless tide. He was ready to commit to that feeling, to that potential, to her.

The air within the rescue center often held the lingering scent of brine and the faint, metallic tang of adrenaline, a perfume of purpose that had, over the past year, become as familiar to Mara as her own breath. Yet, lately, beneath the familiar hum of activity, a new frequency had begun to resonate, a quiet undertow pulling her towards an uncharted territory. The concept of commitment, once a distant, perhaps even intimidating, horizon, now seemed to be drawing nearer, not with the sudden force of a rogue wave, but with the steady, inexorable advance of the tide. It was a realization that settled upon her not with a dramatic pronouncement, but with a series of gentle, persistent nudges, much like the sand shifting beneath her feet as she walked the shore.

She found herself replaying moments, not with the analytical precision of a rescue debrief, but with a softening of focus, a lingering warmth that surprised her. There was the time Eli had simply appeared beside her during a particularly brutal storm surge, not with words of unsolicited advice, but with a thermos of steaming coffee, its warmth a silent offering against the biting wind. Or the way he'd instinctively known when to step back, when to grant her the necessary solitude to process the raw emotions that the job often dredged up, offering instead a steady, unobtrusive presence that spoke volumes more than any spoken reassurance could. These weren't grand gestures, she acknowledged, not the fireworks of a budding romance she'd only ever read about. They were subtler, deeper, woven into the fabric of their shared days with an almost imperceptible thread.

Her own carefully constructed walls, the fortifications she'd meticulously maintained against the buffetings of life, felt as though they were being gently tested, not by force, but by the persistent, unwavering light of Eli's regard. He saw her, she suspected, in a way that few others ever had. He saw the exhaustion etched around her eyes after a twenty-hour shift, but he also saw the quiet triumph that flickered there when a life was saved. He noticed the tension in her shoulders, a constant companion born of the weight of responsibility, but he also saw the grace with which she carried it. It was this seeing, this quiet acknowledgement of her whole self, that was slowly, tentatively, eroding the foundations of her self-imposed isolation.

The shift from 'what if' to 'what now' was a subtle one, a metamorphosis that happened not in a single, dramatic instant, but in the cumulative effect of countless small interactions. It was the way her gaze would unconsciously seek him out across the bustling operations room, the almost automatic tilt of her head when he spoke, as if attuned to a frequency only she could hear. It was the lingering warmth after their paths crossed on the coastal trails, the quiet understanding that bloomed in the shared silence as they watched the sun dip below the horizon. These weren't just chance encounters anymore; they were becoming deliberate moments, anchors in the often-turbulent sea of their work.

She found herself wondering about the future, not in the abstract, grand pronouncements of old, but in the quiet, practical terms of shared sunrises and comfortable silences. It was the dawning realization that a life without Eli's steady presence felt increasingly... incomplete. This wasn't a panicked thought, a desperate grasp for stability, but a gentle unfolding, a recognition that a new kind of richness was possible, a depth of connection she hadn't dared to believe in. The idea of commitment, once a daunting precipice, now beckoned like a welcoming harbor, a place of safety and shared purpose.

Eli, too, found himself caught in the gentle currents of this evolving understanding. His initial fascination with Mara, a quiet observation born of respect for her skill and dedication, had deepened into something more profound, something that resonated in the quiet spaces of his own introspection. He recognized the gradual shift within himself, the way his own internal compass had recalibrated, its needle now consistently pointing towards her. The rescue center, and Mara's integral role within it, had provided him with a sense of purpose that had filled a void he hadn't even realized existed. But it was Mara herself, her quiet strength, her unwavering compassion, that had truly anchored him.

He understood that the carefully constructed defenses she possessed were not barriers to him, but markers of her resilience, a testament to the storms she had weathered. His approach, therefore, had to be one of patient cultivation, of creating an environment where trust could bloom organically, not be demanded. He saw the future not as a grand edifice to be erected overnight, but as a series of carefully laid stones, each one reinforcing the last, creating a solid, enduring path. His own past had taught him the ephemeral nature of many things, but the steady, quiet certainty he felt for Mara, the burgeoning hope that intertwined with her very presence, felt different. It felt grounded, like the ancient rocks that bore the brunt of the ocean's fury, yet remained steadfast.

He was ready to invest more fully, to nurture the fragile beginnings of what they shared. The rescue, and by extension, Mara's integral role within it, had provided him with a purpose that resonated deeper than any career aspiration had ever managed. He observed Mara with a gentle, unyielding persistence, a quiet understanding that the walls she'd meticulously built over a lifetime wouldn't crumble overnight. He respected the strength that lay beneath her guardedness, recognizing that it was a testament to her resilience, not her unwillingness to connect. His perspective was one of patient cultivation, a deliberate intention to nurture what had begun. There was a quiet confidence in him, not arrogance, but a steady belief in the strength of their burgeoning bond, a bond that, while still delicate, felt intrinsically right. He saw the future not as a grand pronouncement, but as a series of carefully placed steps, each one building upon the last, solidifying their shared path.

He found himself drawn to the quiet moments, the pockets of stillness that punctuated the demanding rhythm of their work. These were the moments where he felt he could truly see her, not as the skilled rescuer, but as the woman beneath the uniform. He'd noticed, for instance, the way her eyes would soften when she spoke of the ocean, a reverence in her voice that went beyond professional admiration. It was a deep, intrinsic connection to the sea, a force that both challenged and soothed her. He recognized a similar quiet strength within himself, a resilience forged in the crucible of his own past struggles. It was this shared understanding of weathering storms, both literal and metaphorical, that formed a silent, yet powerful, bond between them. He didn't need grand declarations or effusive displays of affection; he found profound satisfaction in the simple act of being present, of offering a steady hand when needed, a listening ear always ready.

He understood that their connection was still in its nascent stages, a delicate seedling pushing through the sandy soil of their shared experience. It required careful tending, a consistent supply of patience and understanding. He was not about to rush the process, to demand an immediate blooming. Instead, he was content to provide the ideal conditions for growth, to stand by and watch as the roots deepened, anchoring them more firmly to each other. He knew that Mara had a capacity for deep affection, a loyalty that, once given, was unwavering. He was willing to wait, to earn that trust, to demonstrate through his actions that he was a safe harbor, a constant presence she could rely on. This wasn't a passive waiting; it was an active investment, a conscious choice to be present, to nurture, and to believe in the potential of what they were building together. His own past had taught him the impermanence of many things, but the feeling he had for Mara, the quiet certainty that had settled within him, felt different. It felt solid, enduring, like the ancient cliffs that stood sentinel against the relentless tide. He was ready to commit to that feeling, to that potential, to her.

The quiet hum of the rescue center often served as a backdrop to Mara's internal dialogues, a gentle counterpoint to the more significant shifts occurring within her. The word "commitment" itself, once a distant, theoretical concept, now felt like a tangible destination, a place she was consciously navigating towards. It wasn't a sudden epiphany, but a gradual recalibration, a series of small acknowledgements that accumulated like sea glass polished by countless tides. The stolen glances across the crowded common room, the serendipitous encounters along the windswept coastline – these moments, once mere pleasantries, now held a deeper resonance, a silent affirmation of a shared path.

She found herself archiving these interactions, not in a cold, analytical manner, but with a warmth that colored her memories. Eli's presence had become a steadying force, a quiet constant in the often-chaotic rhythm of her life. She remembered the unspoken understanding that passed between them when a particularly difficult rescue left them both drained, the way he would simply offer a cup of tea, its warmth a silent empathy that needed no words. It wasn't about grand pronouncements or dramatic declarations of affection; it was about the quiet, consistent demonstration of care, a steady hand offered in moments of vulnerability. This was the currency of true connection, she realized, a subtle exchange that built a foundation far stronger than any superficial attraction.

The carefully erected walls around her heart, once formidable defenses, now felt less like fortifications and more like a well-tended garden, where new growth was tentatively, yet surely, emerging. Eli's patience was the sunshine, his unwavering regard the water that nourished these delicate shoots. He didn't try to tear down her defenses; he simply created a space so safe, so accepting, that she felt compelled to, almost unconsciously, lower them herself. It was in his steady gaze, his quiet presence, that she found a reflection of her own strength, tempered by a compassion that reached deeper than she had ever allowed herself to believe was possible.

The transition from 'what if' to 'what now' was a profound internal shift, a silent evolution that had been subtly at play for months. It was the dawning realization that the possibility of a future with Eli wasn't just a fleeting wish, but a grounded, achievable reality. The question was no longer whether she was open to it, but how they would build it, brick by careful brick. This was the nascent stage of commitment, a quiet acknowledgment of the demands and rewards that such a shared journey would entail. It was about choosing to invest not just emotions, but time, energy, and a willingness to be vulnerable, in the unfolding narrative of their lives.

She found herself re-evaluating her own deeply ingrained need for self-reliance, not as a weakness, but as a strength that could now be shared. The idea of leaning on someone, of allowing another to bear a portion of the weight, was no longer a terrifying prospect, but a comforting invitation. Eli's quiet confidence, his own journey through past challenges, had provided her with a tangible example of resilience and hope. It was this shared understanding of weathering storms, both literal and metaphorical, that formed a silent, yet powerful, bond between them. He didn't need grand declarations or effusive displays of affection; he found profound satisfaction in the simple act of being present, of offering a steady hand when needed, a listening ear always ready.

He understood that their connection was still in its nascent stages, a delicate seedling pushing through the sandy soil of their shared experience. It required careful tending, a consistent supply of patience and understanding. He was not about to rush the process, to demand an immediate blooming. Instead, he was content to provide the ideal conditions for growth, to stand by and watch as the roots deepened, anchoring them more firmly to each other. He knew that Mara had a capacity for deep affection, a loyalty that, once given, was unwavering. He was willing to wait, to earn that trust, to demonstrate through his actions that he was a safe harbor, a constant presence she could rely on. This wasn't a passive waiting; it was an active investment, a conscious choice to be present, to nurture, and to believe in the potential of what they were building together. His own past had taught him the impermanence of many things, but the feeling he had for Mara, the quiet certainty that had settled within him, felt different. It felt solid, enduring, like the ancient cliffs that stood sentinel against the relentless tide. He was ready to commit to that feeling, to that potential, to her.

The steady rhythm of the ocean, a constant presence in their coastal town, seemed to mirror the quiet shift occurring within Mara. The concept of commitment, once a theoretical horizon, had gradually materialized into a tangible landscape, a place she felt an undeniable pull towards. This wasn't the sudden, overwhelming crest of a wave, but the subtle, persistent erosion of doubt, the gentle lapping of certainty against the shores of her heart. The days of merely exchanging polite greetings or sharing brief, professional interactions were fading, replaced by a growing awareness of shared moments imbued with a deeper meaning.

She found herself cataloging these exchanges, not as mere occurrences, but as building blocks. There was the quiet solidarity after a particularly harrowing rescue, the way Eli's hand had briefly rested on her shoulder, a gesture of shared exhaustion and unspoken pride that transcended words. Or the time he had simply appeared with a thermos of hot chocolate during a late-night patrol, the simple act speaking volumes about his awareness of her needs, his unspoken support. These weren't grand pronouncements or flamboyant displays; they were the quiet, consistent affirmations of a connection that was slowly, steadily, taking root.

The protective shell she had so meticulously crafted around herself, a necessary shield against past hurts, felt less like a prison and more like a home that was beginning to welcome guests. Eli's consistent presence, his unwavering respect for her boundaries, had created a sanctuary where she could tentatively begin to unfurl. He saw not just the capable rescuer, but the woman beneath the uniform, the quiet strength that had been forged in the fires of adversity. He recognized the depth of her resilience, not as a refusal to connect, but as a testament to her enduring spirit. His patience was a gentle rain, his steady gaze the sunlight that encouraged new growth.

The subtle but undeniable transition from 'what if' to 'what now' was a silent conversation she was having with herself, a dialogue woven into the fabric of her daily thoughts. The question of a shared future, once a distant and almost improbable dream, had begun to solidify into a more concrete possibility. It was no longer a matter of if, but of how they would navigate this evolving landscape together. This was the nascent stage of commitment, a quiet acknowledgment that the deepening of their bond would inevitably bring new responsibilities, new joys, and new challenges. It was about a conscious choice to invest not just emotion, but also time, effort, and a willingness to embrace vulnerability, in the unfolding narrative of their shared lives.

She had always prided herself on her self-sufficiency, a trait honed by necessity. But now, she began to see that strength could also lie in shared burdens, in the quiet comfort of knowing she didn't have to face every challenge alone. Eli's own journey, marked by resilience and a quiet understanding of life's complexities, provided a powerful example. Their shared understanding of overcoming adversity, of finding solace in the face of storms, had forged a silent, yet profound, connection between them. He didn't require grand gestures or effusive displays; he found profound satisfaction in the simple act of being present, of offering a steady hand when needed, a listening ear always ready.

He understood that their connection was still in its nascent stages, a delicate seedling pushing through the sandy soil of their shared experience. It required careful tending, a consistent supply of patience and understanding. He was not about to rush the process, to demand an immediate blooming. Instead, he was content to provide the ideal conditions for growth, to stand by and watch as the roots deepened, anchoring them more firmly to each other. He knew that Mara had a capacity for deep affection, a loyalty that, once given, was unwavering. He was willing to wait, to earn that trust, to demonstrate through his actions that he was a safe harbor, a constant presence she could rely on. This wasn't a passive waiting; it was an active investment, a conscious choice to be present, to nurture, and to believe in the potential of what they were building together. His own past had taught him the impermanence of many things, but the feeling he had for Mara, the quiet certainty that had settled within him, felt different. It felt solid, enduring, like the ancient cliffs that stood sentinel against the relentless tide. He was ready to commit to that feeling, to that potential, to her.

The rescue center, a beacon against the vast indifference of the ocean, continued its tireless work. Its walls, weathered by salt spray and time, held within them a constant hum of activity—the murmur of radios, the clatter of equipment being prepped, the quiet urgency that permeated every corner. For Mara and Eli, this was more than just a workplace; it was the very soil in which their nascent connection had begun to take root. The demanding nature of their shared profession, the constant call to action, had, paradoxically, created a space for something tender and real to grow. Here, amidst the scent of brine and the faint, ever-present possibility of crisis, their understanding of each other deepened with each shared sunrise and each hushed debrief.

The season had been particularly demanding. The currents seemed more unpredictable, the storms fiercer, pushing the center and its dedicated crew to their limits. It was a testament to their collective resolve, a shared grit that Mara had come to admire in Eli, and one she recognized mirrored within herself. Their work was a relentless reminder of the fragility of life, a constant dance with the unforgiving power of the sea. This shared understanding, forged in the crucible of life-or-death situations, was a silent language they spoke fluently. When a particularly taxing rescue concluded, leaving them physically drained and emotionally raw, a shared glance was often enough. Eli's quiet nod, the subtle softening of his gaze, conveyed a depth of empathy that words could never adequately express. Mara, in turn, found solace in his unspoken presence, in the reliable strength that emanates from him, a silent promise of steadfastness.

The operational realities of the center were never far from the surface. Funding had been a perennial concern, a constant undercurrent of anxiety that threatened to disrupt the smooth flow of their vital services. Grant applications had to be meticulously prepared, fundraising events organized, and every penny accounted for. It was a practical burden that weighed on everyone, requiring not just dedication to the core mission, but also a shrewd understanding of resource management. Mara, with her characteristic pragmatism, had always approached these challenges with a determined efficiency, seeing them as another problem to be solved, another obstacle to be overcome. Now, however, with Eli by her side, these burdens felt less isolating. He would often be found poring over spreadsheets with her late into the night, his focused presence a calming counterpoint to the inherent stress of their financial precariousness. He brought a different perspective, a calm analytical approach that often unlocked solutions she hadn't considered.

This shared struggle, the collective effort to keep the center not just operational but thriving, added another layer to their bond. It was a testament to their shared values, their unwavering commitment to the community they served. They were more than colleagues; they were partners in a vital endeavor. The late nights spent discussing budget projections or strategizing about the next donation drive were not just professional obligations; they were moments where their shared purpose solidified into a tangible force. Mara found herself looking forward to these discussions, to the easy camaraderie that developed as they tackled these complex issues together. Eli's quiet confidence, his steady reassurance that they would find a way, was a balm to her sometimes-anxious spirit.

The relentless rhythm of the rescue center's operations, the ebb and flow of calls for assistance, provided a constant, grounding presence. It was a predictable, if demanding, structure within which their own more unpredictable personal lives could unfold. The challenges the center faced – the perpetual need for funding, the demanding seasons that stretched their resources and their stamina – mirrored, in a way, the external pressures that could impact any relationship. But here, within these walls, those pressures often served to strengthen their nascent bond. They were a team, not just in the face of emergencies at sea, but in navigating the everyday complexities of life. The rescue center, with its steady pulse, was the heartbeat of their shared world, a constant reminder of the purpose that bound them together.

The increasing intensity of the rescue season had brought with it a palpable sense of shared exhaustion, but also a profound sense of camaraderie. After a particularly harrowing call – a small fishing vessel caught in a sudden squall, its occupants clinging precariously to life – the air in the center was thick with the residue of adrenaline and relief. Mara and Eli, having worked seamlessly together, their movements synchronized, their commands clear and concise, found themselves in the quiet aftermath, the storm passed but its echo lingering. It was in these moments, stripped of the immediate urgency, that their connection felt most profound. Eli would often find Mara by the large windows overlooking the choppy sea, her gaze fixed on the horizon, her shoulders still tense with the residual fight. He wouldn't intrude with platitudes, but simply stand beside her, a silent anchor in the vastness. Sometimes, he would offer a hand, not to pull her from the brink of exhaustion, but to simply be a steady, reassuring presence. Other times, a shared thermos of strong coffee, its warmth seeping into chilled hands, was all that was needed. These were not grand gestures, but the quiet, consistent offerings of mutual respect and understanding, the building blocks of something far more substantial.

The operational demands were relentless. The aging infrastructure of the center, a constant source of worry, required ongoing repairs and upgrades. The boats, though meticulously maintained, bore the scars of countless missions, each scrape and dent a testament to their hard-won victories against the elements. Securing adequate funding for these essential needs was a perpetual challenge, a task that often fell to Mara and Eli to champion. They spent countless hours writing grant proposals, attending local council meetings, and engaging with potential donors. It was a part of the job that was far removed from the immediate thrill of a rescue, requiring patience, persistence, and a deep well of resilience. Yet, even in the face of these often-frustrating administrative hurdles, their shared purpose provided a powerful motivator. They saw the direct impact of every successful grant, every generous donation, in the improved readiness of their equipment, the enhanced training of their crew, and ultimately, in the lives they were able to save.

Mara found herself increasingly drawing strength from Eli's steady optimism during these periods. Where she might feel the weight of the financial anxieties pressing down, Eli would offer a measured perspective, a focus on the achievable steps forward. He had a way of breaking down complex problems into manageable parts, of reminding her that progress, however incremental, was still progress. He never dismissed her concerns, but rather acknowledged them with a quiet understanding before gently guiding her focus towards solutions. This collaborative approach to problem-solving extended beyond the professional realm, bleeding into their personal interactions.

They learned to anticipate each other's needs, to offer support before it was explicitly asked for. During particularly stressful periods at the center, when the calls seemed to come in rapid succession and sleep was a luxury, Eli would often take it upon himself to ensure Mara had a moment to eat, a few minutes of quiet respite. These small acts of consideration, woven into the fabric of their demanding lives, were the silent affirmations of their deepening connection.

The rescue center was a microcosm of their shared life, a place where the external pressures of their demanding work and the internal stirrings of their hearts intersected. The constant need for vigilance, the unwavering commitment to their mission, provided a stable framework against which their own evolving relationship could be explored.

The center's steady pulse was, in essence, the steady pulse of their growing bond. It was a testament to the power of shared purpose, a reminder that in the face of life's unpredictable tides, a strong anchor, a steadfast companion, could make all the difference. The challenges of funding, of equipment, of the sheer relentless nature of their work, were the crucible in which their trust and affection were being tempered. Each hurdle overcome, each successful mission completed, served not only to reinforce the vital role of the rescue center but also to solidify the strength of the connection between Mara and Eli. They were, in every sense of the word, a team, facing the storm together.

CHAPTER TWO

Navigating the Currents of Doubt

The salty air, once a balm, now carried with it a subtle sting, a whisper of apprehension that Mara couldn't quite shake. It was a new sensation, one that pricked at the edges of the contentment she'd been cultivating with Eli. Their shared laughter, the easy rhythm of their days at the rescue center, the quiet comfort of his presence beside her as they navigated the complexities of their work – it was all beginning to feel... precarious. And the fear, a familiar phantom from her past, was starting to stir. It wasn't a fear of Eli himself, of his kindness or his strength. It was a fear of dissolution, of being absorbed, of losing the sharp, distinct edges of herself that she had fought so hard to define.

She watched him now, across the bustling operational room, his brow furrowed in concentration as he reviewed a weather report. The late afternoon sun, filtering through the grimy windows, caught the dust motes dancing in the air and illuminated the strong line of his jaw. He was so present, so grounded. And that, paradoxically, was what made her heart clench. Her independence had been a hard-won battle. Years of feeling overshadowed, of having her own needs and desires relegated to the background, had forged in her a fierce determination to remain her own person. She had built walls, not of brick and mortar, but of carefully cultivated self-reliance, and now, as Eli's presence wove itself so effortlessly into the fabric of her life, she felt those walls beginning to tremble.

The thought that commitment, that a deep and abiding love, might necessitate an erasure of self was a deeply ingrained one. It was a narrative she had unconsciously absorbed from her past, a quiet whisper that suggested love meant compromise to the point of self-negation. Her mother, well-meaning but suffocating, had always prioritized her husband's needs above all else, her own identity seemingly dissolving into his. Mara had witnessed it, absorbed it, and vowed, with the fierce certainty of youth, that it would never happen to her. She had learned to stand alone, to rely on her own judgment, to find her own strength. And now, this burgeoning happiness with Eli, this feeling of being truly seen and understood, felt like a dangerous siren song, luring her towards a shore she had sworn to avoid.

She found herself dissecting their interactions, looking for subtle signs of encroachment. When Eli offered a suggestion on how to streamline a particular process at the center, she'd initially felt a pang of defensiveness, a flicker of "He's trying to change how I do things." It was irrational, she knew. He was simply being helpful, his analytical mind naturally seeking efficiency. But the fear was there, a cold knot in her stomach, whispering that this was the beginning, the subtle erosion of her autonomy. She had to consciously remind herself that collaboration wasn't capitulation, that shared decision-making wasn't a loss of self.

The coastal setting, which had initially felt like a sanctuary, now seemed to amplify her internal struggle. The vastness of the ocean, its boundless horizon, mirrored the endless possibilities of a life with Eli. But it also mirrored the potential for her own identity to become lost in that immensity. She would stand on the shore, the waves crashing against the sand, and feel a strange echo of her past relationships, the ones where she had molded herself to fit the expectations of others, dimming her own light to reflect theirs. This wasn't Eli's fault, not in the slightest. He celebrated her strengths, encouraged her passions, and seemed genuinely interested in her perspective. But the ingrained conditioning ran deep, a persistent hum of anxiety that questioned whether this feeling of being wholly accepted was sustainable without eventually demanding a sacrifice of her core self.

She remembered a conversation they'd had a few weeks ago, late one evening after a particularly grueling rescue. They'd been sharing a quiet meal, the day's adrenaline slowly subsiding. Eli had been talking about his own dreams, the quiet aspirations he held for the future, and then he'd turned to her. "What about you, Mara?" he'd asked, his gaze steady and open. "What do you dream about when you're not saving lives?" For a moment, she'd faltered. Her immediate instinct was to deflect, to turn the conversation back to the practicalities of their work, to the immediate concerns of the rescue center. Her dreams felt too personal, too vulnerable, too... undefined. She'd always been more comfortable with tangible problems, with concrete solutions. Abstract desires, especially those that hinted at a future where her identity was intertwined with another's, felt like uncharted territory, fraught with the potential for getting lost.

When she finally, hesitantly, spoke about her desire to perhaps write a book, to capture some of the stories she'd witnessed, Eli had leaned forward, his interest palpable. "That's incredible, Mara," he'd said, his voice warm with genuine encouragement. "You have such a way with words, even when you're just explaining a rescue plan. I can see you doing that. I'd love to read it." His enthusiasm had been a balm, a validation she hadn't realized she was craving. Yet, even in that moment of shared excitement, a tiny voice of doubt had surfaced. Was this encouragement a genuine appreciation of her talent, or a subtle nudge towards a more domesticated, less demanding future? The fear wasn't about Eli's intentions; it was about her own deep-seated belief that to be loved, she had to be smaller, less individual.

She found herself withdrawing slightly, a subtle tightening of her emotional reins. It was a familiar defense mechanism, one she'd employed countless times before. When she felt overwhelmed by the prospect of intimacy, she would create a small, safe distance, a buffer zone where she could observe and analyze without fully immersing herself. She would become quieter, more reserved, her responses more measured. Eli, with his keen perception, noticed. He didn't press, didn't demand an explanation. Instead, he offered a quiet, reassuring presence. A gentle hand on her arm as they passed, a shared smile that spoke volumes, a steady gaze that conveyed his unwavering support.

One afternoon, while sorting through supplies, Mara found herself staring at a stack of old charts, their edges softened with time and salt. She remembered how she used to be, fiercely protective of her solitary pursuits, her small apartment a sanctuary from the demands of the outside world. She'd cultivated a life that was entirely her own, meticulously curated to reflect her preferences and her boundaries. The thought of integrating another person's life into that carefully constructed space felt overwhelming. It wasn't just about sharing a home; it was about sharing a life, a future, a tapestry of experiences. And the fear that this weaving together might unravel the original threads of her own identity was a constant, low-grade hum of anxiety beneath the surface of her growing happiness.

She realized that her fear of dissolution was tied to her perception of commitment itself. For so long, commitment had been a word associated with stagnation, with the loss of freedom, with the slow fading of individual spirit. She had seen it in the older couples in her hometown, their lives seemingly intertwined to the point of indistinguishability. They were a unit, yes, but where was the spark, the individual flame? Her own mother's complete absorption into her father's life had been a stark warning. It was a vision of love that Mara found terrifying. She craved a different kind of connection, one where two whole, independent individuals chose to build a life together, their individual strengths complementing rather than dissolving into one another.

But how to reconcile this desire with the deeply ingrained belief that deeper connection inevitably meant a loss of self? It was a paradox that gnawed at her. She would watch Eli interact with his colleagues, his easy camaraderie and genuine concern for their well-being, and admire his ability to connect without losing himself. He was steadfast, but he wasn't rigid. He was kind, but he wasn't a doormat. He was clearly capable of deep commitment, but his own identity seemed robust, unyielding. She yearned to understand how he managed it, this balance she so desperately struggled to find.

The rescue center, with its constant demands and its inherent reliance on teamwork, provided an unintentional training ground. Each rescue, each shared challenge, forced her to engage, to trust, to rely on others. And with Eli, it felt different. There was a safety in his presence, a quiet assurance that he wouldn't exploit her vulnerability. He saw her strength, not her weakness, and that perception, that belief in her, was slowly beginning to chip away at her defenses.

One evening, as they were cleaning up after a long shift, Eli found her staring out at the darkening sea, her expression pensive. He came up behind her, not touching, just standing close enough that she could feel the warmth radiating from him. "You're quiet tonight," he observed, his voice a low rumble.

Mara sighed, leaning her forehead against the cool glass of the window. "Just… thinking."

"About anything in particular?" he prompted gently.

She hesitated, the words catching in her throat. It felt like a precipice, a moment where she could either retreat or take a leap of faith. "About… how easy it is to get lost," she admitted, her voice barely a whisper. "In things. In people."

Eli was silent for a moment, and Mara braced herself for him to dismiss her fears or offer a platitude. Instead, he said, "It is. But it's also possible to find yourself, isn't it? To discover new parts of yourself when you're with someone who sees you clearly."

His words resonated, a gentle counterpoint to her internal anxieties. He wasn't denying the potential for loss, but he was offering an alternative narrative – one of discovery, of expansion. It was a subtle shift in perspective, but for Mara, it felt significant. She turned to face him, his silhouette framed against the fading light.

"I'm afraid of losing myself," she confessed, the words tumbling out, raw and honest. "Of becoming… someone else. Someone I don't recognize."

Eli's expression softened, his eyes filled with a quiet understanding that went deeper than words. He reached out, not to pull her into a hug, but to gently cup her cheek. His touch was warm, grounding. "You are you, Mara," he said, his voice steady and sure. "And I wouldn't want you any other way. My hope is that when you're with me, you feel even *more* like yourself, not less."

His sincerity was a potent force, a gentle tide washing over the rocks of her ingrained fear. He wasn't asking her to change, to adapt, to subsume herself. He was offering a space where her authentic self could not only survive but thrive. It was a radical concept, one that clashed with the narrative she had so carefully constructed for herself. But as she looked into his eyes, she saw a reflection not of her own potential diminishment, but of a shared future, built on mutual respect and a profound appreciation for who they each were, individually and together. The fear hadn't vanished entirely, but for the first time, it was accompanied by a burgeoning sense of hope, a quiet whisper that perhaps, just perhaps, this deep connection with Eli wasn't an erasure, but an amplification.

Eli's world, once as predictable as the ebb and flow of the tide he so often observed, was beginning to feel like a landscape in flux. The rescue center, a sanctuary of purpose and shared endeavor, had become more than just a workplace; it was a cornerstone of his identity, a place where his skills and his empathy found constant, meaningful application. He'd cultivated a life here, one rooted in the rhythm of the ocean, the camaraderie of his team, and, increasingly, in the quiet, steady presence of Mara. Yet, the currents of his own ambition, long held in gentle check, were beginning to stir, carrying with them whispers of possibilities that lay beyond the familiar horizon of their coastal town.

These opportunities weren't the result of a sudden, jarring upheaval, but rather a slow accumulation of recognition. His work with marine rescues, particularly his innovative approaches to specialized equipment and emergency response protocols, had garnered attention. Initially, it was quiet murmurs, then invitations to consult on minor projects, and now, more substantial proposals were landing on his desk. A research institution in the north was seeking expertise for a long-term marine conservation study, requiring a dedicated field coordinator. A maritime safety organization, impressed by his problem-solving skills during a particularly challenging past incident, was exploring the possibility of him leading a series of training workshops on advanced rescue techniques, which would involve significant travel. Each prospect was a testament to his dedication, a validation of years of hard work, and a potential stepping stone to a broader impact.

But with each enticing prospect came a familiar knot of internal conflict. These were not merely career advancements; they represented a fundamental re-evaluation of his current path, a divergence from the stability he'd so carefully built. He found himself drawn to the intellectual stimulation, the challenge of tackling new problems on a grander scale. The thought of contributing to significant conservation efforts or shaping the safety practices of a wider community sparked a deep-seated desire within him. However, these aspirations felt inextricably linked to a potential disruption of the life he was so content with, the life he shared with Mara.

He'd always considered himself a man of principle, of steady resolve. Stability, to him, had always been synonymous with reliability, with a grounded sense of purpose. He valued consistency, the comfort of knowing what tomorrow would likely bring, and the deep satisfaction of building something enduring. The rescue center, with its vital mission and its predictable cycle of challenges, embodied this ideal. And Mara, her fierce independence and her vibrant spirit, had become the equally vital cornerstone of his personal stability. She was his anchor, his calm in the storm, the person who brought a unique and vibrant color to his world. Their shared laughter, the quiet understanding that passed between them, the way their routines had woven together seamlessly – it was a tapestry of contentment he cherished.

The emerging opportunities, however, forced him to question the very definition of stability. Was it merely the absence of upheaval, the comfort of the familiar? Or could it be something more dynamic, something that encompassed growth and evolution while still maintaining its core strength? He recognized that true stability wasn't about remaining stagnant; it was about having a strong foundation upon which to build, adapt, and even expand. But how did one reconcile personal ambition, the drive to explore and achieve, with the commitment to a shared life, to a partnership built on mutual presence and shared experiences?

He found himself observing Mara with a renewed intensity, trying to discern how her own deeply ingrained need for independence coexisted with her burgeoning feelings for him. She had fought so hard to define herself, to carve out her own space in the world, and he admired that fiercely. He saw the vulnerability beneath her strength, the genuine fear of losing herself in the process of loving someone. He understood, perhaps more deeply than she realized, the echoes of past experiences that informed her caution. His own fear wasn't of her withdrawal, but of inadvertently causing her the very pain she so carefully guarded against.

He thought back to their conversations, to the tentative admissions of fear she'd shared. He remembered the evening she'd confessed her apprehension about getting lost, about becoming someone she didn't recognize. His response had been genuine, a heartfelt reassurance that he saw her, truly saw her, and valued her for exactly who she was. He had intended to convey that his love was a space for her to be *more* herself, not less. But now, as he contemplated these new professional paths, he wondered if his words were enough to counter the ingrained narrative she carried. Would these new ventures, these periods of travel and focused dedication, feel like a threat to her hard-won autonomy?

The research institution's offer, in particular, gnawed at him. It represented a chance to contribute to a significant, long-term ecological project, a cause that resonated deeply with his core values. It would involve extended periods away from the coast, immersed in a different environment, collaborating with a diverse team of scientists. The intellectual challenge was immense, the potential for impact substantial. But it also meant significant time away from Mara, from the predictable rhythm of their days, from the simple, profound comfort of their shared evenings.

He wrestled with the notion of what he truly wanted. He desired a life that was both meaningful and fulfilling, a life where he could contribute his skills and follow his passions. But he also craved the deep, abiding connection he had found with Mara. He realized that stability wasn't solely about the external circumstances of his life, but about an internal equilibrium. It was about aligning his actions with his values, about finding a way to pursue his ambitions without sacrificing the relationships that sustained him.

He began to articulate his thoughts, not to Mara, but to himself, in the quiet hours before dawn or during long stretches of solitary driving to remote coastal sites. He considered the essence of his connection with Mara. It wasn't about possession, or about one person subsuming the other. It was about partnership, about two individuals choosing to build a life together, their strengths complementing each other. Their relationship had already shown him that a deep connection didn't necessitate a diminishment of self; rather, it could foster growth and self-discovery. Mara's own journey, her cautious but persistent opening up, was a testament to this. He had witnessed her fears, and he had also witnessed her courage in facing them.

He thought about the training workshops. These offered a different kind of prospect – less time away, more focused on sharing his expertise. It was a way to expand his influence, to mentor others, without the same degree of geographical separation. He could still be present for Mara, still maintain the rhythm of their shared life. Yet, even this presented a subtle challenge. It would require him to step further into a leadership role, to become a public face of maritime safety, which was something he'd always shied away from, preferring the tangible, hands-on nature of rescue work.

The internal dialogue continued, a quiet hum beneath the surface of his days. He recognized that his reluctance wasn't just about the logistics of travel or the demands of a new role. It was about a subtle fear of disrupting the delicate balance he had found. He was afraid of what change, even positive change, might introduce. He valued the peace he had cultivated, and the prospect of upending it, even for potentially greater fulfillment, was daunting.

He found himself drawn to the quiet contemplation of the ocean. Standing on the shore, watching the waves crash against the rocks, he sought parallels to his own internal landscape. The ocean was vast, powerful, and ever-changing, yet it also possessed a profound and enduring stability. Its rhythms were constant, its depths immense. He realized that true stability wasn't about rigidity, but about resilience, about the capacity to adapt and endure while remaining true to one's fundamental nature.

He envisioned a future where his work in marine safety and conservation expanded, but where his connection with Mara remained the unwavering core. He imagined them navigating these new opportunities together, supporting each other's growth, their individual paths intertwining rather than diverging. It was a vision that required a conscious effort to reconcile ambition with commitment, to redefine what stability meant not just for himself, but for their relationship.

He understood that his own definition of stability had been too narrow, too focused on the external and the predictable. He began to grasp that true stability was an internal state, a sense of inner peace and purpose that could weather external changes. It was about building a life with Mara that was resilient, adaptable, and deeply rooted in mutual respect and understanding. The opportunities that were emerging weren't inherently disruptive; they were potential avenues for growth, for a richer, more impactful life, provided they were approached with intention and clear communication.

He knew he couldn't make these decisions in a vacuum. Mara was an integral part of his life, and any significant change would impact her as well. He needed to approach these prospects not as solitary pursuits, but as shared possibilities, or at least as elements that needed to be integrated into their shared life. The fear of causing her distress, of triggering her anxieties about self-erasure, was a significant consideration. He was committed to ensuring that his pursuit of fulfillment wouldn't come at the cost of her hard-won sense of self.

This internal deliberation was a process of refinement, of clarifying his own desires and understanding their implications. He wasn't running from commitment; he was seeking to understand how to embrace it fully, in all its complexity. He realized that his stability was not merely about a place or a person, but about a state of being, a congruence between his inner self and his outward actions. And increasingly, he saw that Mara was not an obstacle to this stability, but a vital component of it. Her presence had brought a depth and richness to his life that he hadn't known he was missing, and he was determined to protect and nurture that, even as he explored the expanding horizons of his own potential. The choices ahead were significant, but for the first time, he felt a quiet confidence that he could navigate them, not by choosing between his ambitions and his relationship, but by finding a way to weave them together into a more robust and meaningful future.

The salt spray kissed Mara's cheeks, a familiar comfort that usually settled her. Today, however, it seemed to carry an undertow of something restless, something akin to the churning in her own chest. She watched Eli across the small, sun-drenched deck of the research vessel, his brow furrowed in concentration as he checked the readings on a piece of equipment. He was so intrinsically part of this environment, as much a fixture as the gulls wheeling overhead or the ancient, weathered docks. It was a part of him she understood, a language spoken in the mechanics of the boat, the needs of the ocean, the well-being of the creatures they were here to study.

Their conversations, though more frequent now, often felt like navigating a minefield of unspoken assumptions. She'd found herself pausing before speaking, searching for the right words, the ones that wouldn't betray the deeper anxieties she carried. Eli, in turn, seemed to tread with equal care, his questions gentle, his observations insightful, but never probing too deeply into the shadowed corners of her heart. It was a dance of politeness and affection, underscored by the vast, silent ocean that stretched out before them, mirroring the unarticulated gulf that sometimes yawned between them.

She remembered the night before, the way the lamplight had softened the lines around his eyes as he'd talked about the upcoming conference. He'd outlined the responsibilities, the networking opportunities, the potential for collaboration with other institutions. He'd spoken with a quiet enthusiasm, the same steady passion that ignited when he discussed a particularly challenging rescue or a new conservation initiative. And she had listened, nodding, offering smiles that felt thinner than usual, her mind racing to keep pace with his words, trying to find the place where his expanding world intersected with the one they had so carefully built together.

"It's a good opportunity, isn't it?" he'd asked, his gaze lifting from the notes he was reviewing.

She'd felt a pang, a sharp, unexpected jab of something akin to dread. "It sounds... significant, Eli." The words felt inadequate, hollow. She wanted to say more, to express the fear that his horizons were expanding so rapidly that they might soon stretch beyond her reach. But the words caught in her throat, tangled with the fear of appearing possessive, of dimming his light. So she'd settled for the understated acknowledgment.

He'd reached across the table then, his fingers brushing hers, a small, grounding touch. "I'm glad you think so. I wouldn't want to pursue anything that felt... out of sync with us."

The sincerity in his voice was a balm, a reassurance that he *saw* her, that he valued their shared life. But the echo of her own hesitation lingered. Was it enough? Could his intention truly override the potential consequences of his ambition? She'd learned, over years of guarding her heart, that intentions, however pure, could sometimes pave the road to unintended distance.

Later that week, while walking along the shoreline, the vastness of the ocean had seemed to press in on her. The rhythmic crash of waves, usually a soothing symphony, now sounded like a relentless reminder of time passing, of opportunities missed, of paths not taken. She'd stopped, her toes sinking into the damp sand, and watched a lone seagull wheeling against the pale sky. It was free, unburdened, its flight a testament to its own inherent purpose. She envied that freedom, and then, shamefully, she envied Eli's apparent ease in embracing his.

He had caught up to her, his footsteps soft on the sand. He didn't speak immediately, simply walked beside her, his presence a quiet anchor. She appreciated the silence, the unspoken understanding that she needed a moment to herself. It was in these moments, these pockets of shared stillness, that she felt closest to him, where the space between their words seemed to hold more meaning than any conversation.

He finally broke the quiet, his voice low. "Thinking?"

She managed a small smile, kicking at a piece of driftwood. "Just... observing."

He picked up a smooth, grey stone, turning it over in his hand. "It's a beautiful day for it. Almost makes you want to just... be."

"Almost," she agreed, the unspoken qualifier hanging heavy in the air between them. 'Almost' was a dangerous word. It hinted at a desire for something more, something that wasn't being fully realized.

He looked at her then, a soft question in his eyes. "You've been quiet lately, Mara. Everything okay?"

This was it. The opening. The chance to articulate the knot of apprehension that had been tightening in her chest. But the words still wouldn't come. Instead, she offered a carefully constructed half-truth. "Just... tired. Long days at the gallery."

She gestured vaguely towards the town, a flimsy shield against the vulnerability she felt exposed to.

He accepted it, of course. He always did. His trust in her was unwavering, a testament to the foundation they had built. But she saw the flicker of something in his gaze, a subtle acknowledgment that he sensed there was more, a subtle redirection of his inquiry that suggested he understood her need for space, for the right moment. He didn't push. He never did. And in his gentle yielding, she saw both the strength of their connection and the quiet torment of her own reticence.

The silence that followed was different, charged with the weight of what had been left unsaid. It stretched between them, as vast and deep as the ocean, filled with the unspoken anxieties that Mara couldn't yet voice and the questions Eli wisely refrained from asking. She watched him skip the stone he held, its trajectory arcing gracefully before it disappeared into the waves. It was a small act, a moment of simple distraction, yet it spoke volumes about his capacity for finding peace in the present, for letting go of what couldn't be controlled.

That evening, as they sat on their small porch, the scent of honeysuckle heavy in the twilight air, Eli shared more about the research proposal. He spoke of the potential for groundbreaking discoveries, for contributing to a global understanding of marine ecosystems. His eyes lit up as he described the fieldwork, the challenges, the intellectual rigor. He was, she knew, speaking a language of passion, a language that defined him.

"It would mean quite a bit of travel," he admitted, his voice softening as he met her gaze. "Weeks, sometimes months, at a time. Different locations."

She felt a familiar tightness in her chest. Months. The word felt like a chasm opening between them. She forced a smile. "That sounds... intense."

He reached for her hand, his thumb tracing circles on her skin. "It would be. But I was thinking... we could make it work. You could come with me for some of it, perhaps? Or we could set up video calls, make sure we're still connecting every day."

His earnestness was disarming, his desire to include her palpable. He was trying, she knew, to bridge the potential distance with practical solutions, with a proactive effort to maintain their connection. And she appreciated it, truly she did. But it also highlighted the fundamental difference in their current perspectives. He saw the challenges as logistical hurdles to be overcome, while she saw them as potential erosions of the precious, fragile intimacy they had cultivated.

"It's a lot to think about," she said, her voice a low murmur. She didn't want to crush his enthusiasm, to be the voice of doubt that held him back from something that clearly meant so much to him. But she also couldn't offer the unreserved excitement he deserved, the unqualified support that would make him feel truly seen and understood.

He squeezed her hand gently. "I know. And we will. We'll figure it out. Together."

His words were a promise, a statement of intent. But the space between them, the quiet pause after his declaration, was filled with the unspoken acknowledgment that 'figuring it out' might require more than just logistics. It would require navigating the currents of fear, of unspoken anxieties, of deeply held beliefs about what it meant to be truly connected.

The next day, Mara found herself drawn to the old lighthouse at the edge of town. She climbed its spiraling stairs, the worn stone cool beneath her fingertips, until she reached the lantern room. The view was breathtaking, a panoramic sweep of the ocean stretching to the horizon, the town a small cluster of buildings nestled against the coastline. From this vantage point, the world seemed both immense and intimately connected. The currents, though unseen, were the invisible threads that guided the ships, that shaped the coastline, that dictated the very rhythm of life here.

She thought of Eli, his own internal currents pulling him towards new opportunities, towards a wider world. She understood his ambition, his need to explore and contribute. It was a part of the man she loved. But her own currents, shaped by past experiences, pulled her towards the safety of the shore, towards the steady, predictable rhythm of what was known. Her fear wasn't of him leaving, but of him leaving a part of himself behind, or worse, of her shrinking herself to fit into the space his expanding life might leave.

She remembered a conversation they'd had a few weeks prior, after a particularly difficult day at the gallery. She'd confessed, in a rush of vulnerability, her fear of losing herself, of becoming an appendage rather than an equal partner. His response had been immediate and heartfelt. He'd taken her face in his hands, his gaze earnest. "Mara, I see *you*. You are the most vibrant, independent soul I've ever known. My love for you isn't about possession; it's about wanting to share in that incredible light. If you ever feel yourself fading, you tell me. We'll shine a bigger spotlight."

The memory brought a fragile warmth to her chest. He had meant it. She knew he had. But the ingrained patterns of self-protection were hard to unlearn. The fear, a persistent whisper in the back of her mind, suggested that even the brightest spotlight could cast long shadows.

She looked out at the endless expanse of water, the sun glinting off its surface like scattered diamonds. The ocean was a place of both profound beauty and immense power, a force that demanded respect, that held its secrets close. And so, she realized, was their relationship. It was beautiful, powerful, and held its own depths, its own unspoken truths.

Eli joined her later, his presence a quiet comfort as he leaned against the railing beside her. He didn't need to ask what she was thinking. The shared silence was enough. He simply offered his shoulder, a silent invitation for her to lean into him, and she did, the solid warmth of his presence a grounding force.

"It's easy to get lost out here, isn't it?" he said softly, his gaze sweeping across the horizon. "To feel like you're the only thing that matters."

She nodded, her cheek resting against his arm. "But then you see the currents, the way everything is connected. The tide, the wind, the creatures... they all influence each other."

He turned his head, his eyes meeting hers. "Exactly. And we're no different, are we? Our lives are connected, even when they stretch in different directions." He paused, his thumb gently stroking her arm. "I don't want to lose you, Mara. And I don't want to lose myself. I just... I want to find a way for us to grow, together."

His words, spoken with such quiet sincerity, resonated deeply. They acknowledged the inherent tension, the delicate balance they were striving to achieve. He wasn't dismissing her fears; he was inviting her to explore them with him, to find a shared path forward.

"I'm afraid, Eli," she admitted, the words finally breaking free, raw and honest. "I'm afraid of you becoming someone I don't recognize, or of me becoming someone I don't want to be, just to keep up."

He pulled her closer, holding her tightly. "Oh, Mara," he whispered, his voice thick with emotion. "You are already someone I recognize. You are the most complete version of yourself. My ambition isn't about changing you, or changing us. It's about... expanding the canvas. And I want you to be right there with me, painting our masterpiece."

She let out a shaky breath, the tension in her shoulders easing slightly. His metaphor, his gentle reassurance, was a balm to her wounded anxieties. It wasn't about her having to change, but about them creating a bigger space together.

"But what if... what if the colors don't match?" she whispered, the lingering doubt surfacing.

He pulled back just enough to look her in the eye, his gaze steady and unwavering. "Then we'll find new colors. We'll blend them. We'll create something even more beautiful. But we'll do it together. You and me. Always."

In the quiet expanse of the lighthouse lantern room, surrounded by the vastness of the ocean, the space between their words began to feel less like a chasm and more like a promise. It was a space for growth, for exploration, for the quiet, profound evolution of two souls choosing to navigate the currents of life, hand in hand. The unspoken anxieties hadn't vanished entirely, but they had been acknowledged, met with a tenderness and a commitment that offered the first true flicker of hope.

The rhythmic whine of the winch, usually a comforting sound that signaled the successful retrieval of a marine animal, had taken on a sharp, almost frantic edge. It was a sound Mara had associated with purpose, with tangible good. But today, it felt like a drumbeat counting down to an unknown crisis. The rescue center, their shared sanctuary and the beating heart of their community, was under siege. Not by a single, dramatic event, but by a confluence of crises that seemed to have descended with the ferocity of a rogue wave.

It had started subtly, a trickle of increased calls that had soon become a torrent. A pod of dolphins, disoriented by unusually strong offshore currents, had stranded themselves on a shallow sandbar. The sheer number of animals, struggling and distressed, had stretched their small team to its absolute limit. Then, as if the ocean itself was testing their resolve, a late-season squall had blown in, not a full-blown hurricane, but a nasty, persistent storm that churned the seas and made any open-water rescues near impossible, trapping them with the animals they had already brought in. The deluge of rain had turned the access road to the center into a muddy quagmire, making it difficult for their limited staff to even get to work, let alone transport much-needed supplies.

Eli, usually so measured and calm in the face of adversity, was a whirlwind of focused energy. His usual quiet contemplation was replaced by a constant stream of directives, his voice carrying a new urgency as he coordinated with the veterinary team, the volunteer coordinators, and even the local Coast Guard for additional manpower. Mara watched him, a familiar pang of admiration mixed with a growing sense of unease. He was in his element, tackling a complex, multifaceted problem with an unwavering resolve that was breathtaking to witness. But this was more than just a challenging rescue; this was a full-blown operational emergency.

"We're running low on specialized feed for the sea turtles," Eli announced, his brow furrowed as he scanned a tablet displaying their dwindling inventory. "And the main filtration system for the rehabilitation tanks is showing critical pressure drops. If that goes, we're in serious trouble. We need a replacement part, and fast." His gaze swept over Mara, a hint of desperation in his usually steady eyes. "The supplier says it's backordered for at least two weeks. We can't wait that long."

Mara felt a familiar clench in her stomach, the one that always surfaced when the weight of their shared responsibility felt crushing. The rescue center wasn't just a job for them; it was a living, breathing entity that relied on their dedication, their resources, and their collective will. The financial strain of operating such a facility was a constant undercurrent, but this sudden surge in need, coupled with the logistical nightmares, threatened to capsize them entirely.

"Fundraising," she stated, the word feeling heavy and inadequate against the magnitude of their immediate needs. "We need to launch an emergency appeal. Immediately."

Eli nodded, running a hand through his already dishevelled hair. "I've already drafted a preliminary appeal, but we need more than just a plea for money. We need to show them the urgency, the scale of what we're dealing with. And we need people on the ground, volunteers, to help us manage the influx, to clean, to feed, to keep the facility running. It's a logistical nightmare, Mara."

The storm outside mirrored the tempest brewing within the rescue center. The wind howled, rattling the windows of the administrative office where they had retreated to strategize. The incessant drumming of rain on the roof was a stark contrast to the quiet, almost meditative conversations they had been having about their future, about the delicate balance between their individual dreams and their shared life. Now, those introspection-laden discussions felt like a distant luxury, replaced by the immediate, visceral demands of survival.

"I'll get the social media team on it," Mara said, her voice firming with a renewed sense of purpose. "We can blast out updates, videos of the animals, the conditions. We need to tug at heartstrings, Eli. And we need to be transparent about what's needed." She pulled out her laptop, her fingers already flying across the keyboard, composing messages that were both urgent and empathetic. She knew how to connect with people, how to translate the raw emotion of their work into compelling narratives that inspired action. It was a skill she had honed through years of managing the gallery, but here, at the rescue center, the stakes felt immeasurably higher. This wasn't about selling art; it was about saving lives.

Eli watched her, a flicker of relief crossing his face. "Thank you, Mara. I don't know what I'd do without you here, right now. It's... a lot." He paused, his gaze drifting towards the window, where the rain continued to lash down. "This is what we signed up for, isn't it? The unpredictable nature of it all. The moments when you think you can't possibly do anymore, and then you find a way."

She met his eyes, a shared understanding passing between them. The anxieties that had been swirling around their personal lives – the whispers of doubt about their diverging paths, the fear of growing apart – seemed to recede in the face of this tangible, external crisis. Here, in the trenches of a genuine emergency, their strengths complemented each other, their shared commitment to the cause forging an unbreakable bond. She could see the weariness etched on his face, the lines of strain around his eyes, but beneath it all, there was a resilience, a core of determination that she found endlessly inspiring.

"It's different when it's this real, isn't it?" Mara mused, her fingers pausing on the keyboard. "When it's not just a conversation about 'what ifs,' but about 'what now.' When the need is so immediate, so undeniable, it cuts through all the noise."

Eli walked over to the window, placing a hand on her shoulder. His touch was warm, grounding. "Exactly. The currents outside are chaotic, but they're also predictable in their own way. The tides, the storms... they are forces of nature. What we're facing here, it feels like that. Like a force of nature we have to navigate. And we're doing it together."

He spoke of the filtration system, the urgency of its repair. Mara knew that Eli was a gifted problem-solver, but this was beyond his immediate expertise. He could troubleshoot, he could direct, but he wasn't an engineer. "Have you contacted any of the other marine biologists, colleagues from the university? Someone might have a contact, a lead on that part, or even a temporary workaround."

Eli's face brightened slightly. "Good thought. I reached out to Dr. Albright this morning, but she was heading out of town for a conference. I'll try again. And perhaps we can put out an urgent call to our volunteer network. Someone might have mechanical expertise, or know someone who does." He looked at her, a hopeful glint in his eyes. "This is where the community comes in, isn't it? We can't do it all ourselves."

The mention of community, of shared reliance, resonated deeply with Mara. It was something she had always valued, the interconnectedness of people working towards a common goal. In their personal lives, she had sometimes felt a pull towards independence, a need to prove her own self-sufficiency. But here, in the heart of the storm, she understood that true strength often lay in embracing vulnerability, in acknowledging that they needed each other, and the wider world, to weather the toughest challenges.

"I'll start drafting the appeal," Mara said, turning back to her laptop with renewed vigour. "We'll need to outline the most critical needs: the filtration system, specialized medical supplies, extra food, maybe even temporary staffing if we can't get enough volunteers to cover all the shifts. We'll need a dedicated fundraising page, and I'll start making calls to our major donors. They need to know what's happening."

Eli leaned against the desk, watching her work. "You're a force, Mara. Truly. I know how much you've been wrestling with... with everything. But seeing you dive into this, so focused, so capable... it helps. It really does."

His words, spoken with such genuine sincerity, touched her. She had been so consumed by her internal anxieties, by the fear of their divergent paths, that she had almost forgotten the strength that lay within her, the ability to rise to the occasion, to contribute meaningfully. This crisis, while overwhelming, was also strangely clarifying. It stripped away the abstract worries and presented them with concrete problems that demanded concrete solutions. And in tackling those problems together, their connection, far from fraying, seemed to be deepening.

The next few days blurred into a relentless cycle of activity. The rescue center became a hive of controlled chaos. Volunteers poured in, a testament to the community's deep affection for the work they did. Local businesses donated supplies, food, and even manpower. Mara's emergency appeal went viral, generating an outpouring of support that stunned even Eli. Donations, both large and small, flooded in, providing the crucial financial lifeline they desperately needed.

Mara found herself coordinating communication efforts, fielding calls from the media, managing the constant stream of updates on social media, and working with the volunteer coordinator to ensure everyone was assigned to the tasks where they were most needed. She was on her feet for hours on end, her mind a constant whir of logistics and problem-solving. Eli, meanwhile, was deep in the operational heart of the crisis, working tirelessly with the veterinary team to care for the rescued animals and overseeing the complex repairs to the filtration system.

One afternoon, amidst the din of activity, Mara found Eli in the main rehabilitation hall, his face streaked with grime, his clothes damp with saltwater. He was supervising the installation of a temporary, makeshift filtration system that the engineering volunteers had managed to construct. It wasn't elegant, but it was functional, and it was keeping the precious water clean. He looked exhausted, bone-weary, but his eyes still held that familiar spark of determination.

"We did it," he said, his voice hoarse but triumphant, as he saw her approach. He gestured towards the jury-rigged system. "It's not ideal, but it's holding. And the part for the main system is expected to arrive tomorrow. Albright's team found a supplier who could expedite it."

Mara smiled, a genuine, heartfelt smile that reached her eyes. "That's incredible, Eli. I'm so proud of you. Of all of us." She gestured towards the hall, where volunteers were diligently cleaning tanks, feeding young seals, and tending to the recovering turtles. "Look at this. Look at what we've accomplished."

He nodded, his gaze sweeping over the scene. "It's... humbling. To see everyone pull together like this. It makes you believe in the good in people." He met her gaze, his eyes soft. "And it makes me appreciate you, Mara. More than ever. You are so much more than just the quiet observer. You're a force. You're the steady hand that guides the ship through the storm."

His words, spoken in the midst of such tangible accomplishment, were a balm to her soul. The anxieties that had been lurking at the edges of her mind, the fears about their future, seemed to dissipate in the shared glow of their success. They had faced a crisis, a genuine threat to the well-being of the rescue center, and they had not only survived, but thrived, by working together. The external pressures had, paradoxically, brought them closer.

Later that evening, as the storm finally began to subside, leaving behind a sky washed clean and a world refreshed, Mara and Eli sat on the deck of the rescue center, the scent of salt and damp earth filling the air. The urgent calls had dwindled to a manageable trickle, and a fragile sense of calm had settled over the facility. The rescued animals were stable, the critical repairs were underway, and the community's generosity had secured their immediate future.

Eli reached for her hand, his fingers intertwining with hers. "We weathered it," he murmured, his thumb tracing soothing circles on her skin. "We weathered the storm."

Mara leaned her head on his shoulder, a sense of profound peace settling over her. "We did. And it feels… good. To have faced something so difficult, and to have come through it together." The contrast between the external chaos and their internal anxieties was stark. The rescue center's crisis had demanded their full attention, their complete focus, leaving little room for the introspective doubts that had been plaguing her. In the face of tangible adversity, their shared responsibility had become a powerful anchor, grounding them in the present and reminding them of the strength of their partnership.

"I was so worried," she confessed, her voice barely a whisper. "About the center, about us. I thought this might be the thing that would… pull us apart. The pressure, the demands on your time, on mine."

Eli turned her to face him, his gaze steady and full of love. "Mara, this crisis has shown me, more clearly than anything else, how much we need each other. Your strength, your ability to connect with people, to inspire them… it's incredible. You kept our community engaged, you rallied the support that saved us.

And I... I don't think I could have managed the operational side without your constant reassurance, your calm presence amidst the storm."

He squeezed her hand. "We were always going to face challenges. It's the nature of life, and it's certainly the nature of running a place like this. But what I learned, this past week, is that we face them better, stronger, *together*. The external pressures, the demanding rescues, the operational hurdles... they tested us, yes. But they also forged us. They showed us what we're capable of, as a team."

Mara felt a profound sense of relief wash over her, a quiet joy that settled deep in her bones. The anxieties hadn't vanished, not entirely. The future, with its inherent uncertainties, still beckoned. But the fear that had once felt so overwhelming, so paralyzing, had been replaced by a quiet confidence. They had navigated the currents of doubt, and in doing so, they had discovered a deeper, more resilient love, one forged not in calm waters, but in the heart of the storm. The shared responsibility, the mutual reliance, the tangible proof of their combined strength – these were the new currents guiding them, carrying them forward, together, towards a future that, while still unwritten, felt infinitely more hopeful.

The salty tang of the air, a scent that usually soothed Mara's soul, felt heavy with the unspoken on this particular evening. The immediate crisis at the rescue center had receded, leaving behind a quiet hum of recovery and a residual exhaustion that permeated everything. But with the external storms quelled, the internal ones, the ones that had been a constant, low-grade thrum beneath the surface of their lives, began to resurface with a renewed, almost defiant, insistence. She sat on the weathered porch swing, its gentle creak a familiar rhythm against the backdrop of the gentle lapping waves. Eli was inside, likely reviewing the latest rehabilitation reports, his mind already racing ahead to the next challenge. And she, Mara, found herself paralyzed by a different kind of challenge, one that felt infinitely more daunting: the prospect of genuine, unvarnished vulnerability.

Her entire life, Mara had operated on the principle of self-sufficiency. It was a shield, meticulously crafted and rigorously maintained, against the perceived vulnerabilities of a world that felt both exhilarating and precarious. She excelled at problem-solving, at managing, at presenting a calm, capable front. These were the languages she knew, the dialects she spoke with fluency and ease. But the language of her own heart, the one that whispered of fears, of insecurities, of a longing for something more profound than mere competence – that language felt like a foreign tongue, its grammar incomprehensible, its pronunciation a struggle.

She watched Eli move through their shared life with an openness that both fascinated and unnerved her. He possessed an innate ability to articulate his thoughts and feelings, to dissect his anxieties and present them for examination, not as weaknesses, but as integral parts of his being. He spoke of his hopes, his frustrations, his moments of doubt, with a disarming sincerity that drew people in, creating a space where shared humanity felt not just possible, but inevitable. For Mara, however, admitting fragility to Eli felt akin to pulling down the very foundations of her carefully constructed world. It was an admission that the strong, capable woman he admired might, in fact, harbor a core of uncertainty, a deep-seated fear of not being enough.

The recent crisis had, paradoxically, highlighted this internal chasm. While they had functioned as an unbreakable unit, tackling the operational emergencies with seamless efficiency, their personal conversations had been relegated to the periphery, overshadowed by the immediate demands of survival. Now, as the dust settled, Mara found herself adrift in the quiet aftermath, the unspoken anxieties returning with a vengeance. She had relied on Eli's strength, his unwavering support, and in the process, she had unconsciously retreated further into her shell, her silence a passive-aggressive assertion of her independence.

She thought of their conversations in the quiet pre-crisis days, the tentative explorations of their future, the underlying currents of doubt that had threatened to pull them under. She had felt him reaching for her, not just as a partner in their work, but as a partner in their lives, seeking a deeper connection, a shared understanding of their evolving selves. And she had, in turn, pulled away, her own fears acting as an invisible barrier, a subtle yet impenetrable wall.

The rhythmic sigh of the waves against the shore seemed to whisper accusations, reminding her of missed opportunities, of words left unsaid. The coastal air, usually her solace, now carried the weight of her unspoken anxieties, making the simple act of opening up feel like navigating treacherous waters, the kind where hidden reefs could rip the hull of even the most sturdy vessel. She imagined the words forming on her tongue, the confession of her deepest fears, and they felt clumsy, ill-formed, like a child fumbling with a language they had yet to master.

She remembered Eli's confession, a few weeks prior, about his own lingering insecurities regarding their diverging professional paths. He had voiced his worry that his passion for the rescue center might overshadow her own ambitions, that he might inadvertently hold her back. His willingness to lay bare such a raw vulnerability had resonated deeply with her, a testament to the trust he placed in their connection. Yet, instead of reciprocating with a similar openness, Mara had offered platitudes, reassurances that masked her own internal turmoil. She had deflected, subtly shifting the conversation back to the tangible, the practical, the safe.

Her self-reliance, while a source of strength, had also become a gilded cage. It meant she rarely asked for help, rarely admitted when she was struggling, and rarely allowed herself to be truly seen. She had perfected the art of appearing composed, even in the face of immense pressure, a skill honed through years of managing the demanding world of art curation. But here, with Eli, the stakes were different. This wasn't about presenting a polished facade to the world; it was about revealing the imperfect, vulnerable human being beneath.

She picked up a smooth, sea-worn stone from the railing, turning it over and over in her palm. It was solid, unchanging, a testament to the relentless forces that had shaped it. She envied its simplicity, its lack of internal conflict. Her own internal landscape, however, was a tempestuous sea, a constant churn of conflicting emotions and anxieties. The very idea of admitting she needed something from Eli, beyond the practical support they so readily offered each other, felt like a concession, a capitulation.

Was it pride? Or was it a deeper, more ingrained fear of being found wanting? The thought that Eli might perceive her vulnerability as weakness, as a lack of the very qualities he admired in her, was a chilling one. She had always striven to be his equal, his partner, not someone he needed to protect or coddle. The thought of leaning on him, truly leaning, felt like an inversion of their dynamic, a potential disruption of the delicate balance they had struck.

She watched Eli emerge from the house, a thermos of tea in his hand. He walked towards her, his expression soft, his eyes crinkling at the corners as he offered her a smile. "Thinking too much again?" he asked, his voice gentle, laced with that familiar, knowing warmth.

Mara forced a smile, her heart giving a little lurch. "Just enjoying the quiet," she replied, her voice carefully modulated, betraying none of the turmoil within. She accepted the mug of tea, its warmth a welcome sensation against her chilled fingers.

Eli sat beside her on the swing, its gentle motion mirroring the ebb and flow of their unspoken conversation. He didn't press, didn't demand. He simply existed beside her, a quiet, steady presence. This was his gift, she realized – his ability to create space, to allow silence to speak, to wait patiently for words that might never come. But his patience, while comforting, also amplified her own internal struggle. The longer she remained silent, the more her anxieties seemed to solidify, becoming more entrenched, more difficult to dislodge.

"You know," Eli began, his gaze fixed on the darkening horizon, "after everything that happened with the center, I've been doing a lot of thinking." He paused, taking a slow sip of his tea. "About what really matters. About what we're fighting for, not just out there," he gestured vaguely towards the ocean, "but in here." He tapped his chest lightly. "And I realized that while I'm good at the big picture, at the operational stuff, I'm not always great at the small things. The everyday things. The connection."

Mara's breath hitched. This was it. This was the opening, the invitation. Her mind raced, cataloging every possible response, every safe deflection. But the words caught in her throat, a tangled mess of fear and longing. She felt the familiar urge to retreat, to offer a comforting, non-committal phrase, to steer the conversation back to the practicalities of the rescue center.

"It's easy to get lost in the urgency," she managed, her voice a little too tight. "To let the demands of the work eclipse everything else. We've been so focused on keeping everything afloat, on making sure everyone else is okay."

Eli turned to her then, his eyes searching hers. "And are *we* okay, Mara?" he asked, his voice soft but direct. "Beyond the center. Beyond the rescues. Are we okay, together?"

The question hung in the air between them, heavy with unspoken history and uncertain future. Mara's self-reliance, her carefully constructed shield, felt like a betrayal in this moment. It was a barrier not just between her and the world, but between her and the man she loved, the man who was offering her a safe harbor, a place to land with all her imperfections.

She wanted to tell him about the gnawing fear that her ambitions, her dreams of a life beyond the rescue center, were a betrayal of their shared life. She wanted to confess that she sometimes felt suffocated by the weight of expectation, by the unspoken assumption that their paths were irrevocably intertwined. She wanted to admit that the thought of him not needing her, of her own contributions becoming less essential, filled her with a profound, unsettling dread.

But the words remained trapped, a flock of startled birds unable to take flight. She looked at Eli, at the genuine concern etched on his face, and the chasm between her internal landscape and her outward presentation felt impossibly wide. Speaking her deepest fears felt like attempting to communicate in a language she had never learned, a language of raw, unfiltered emotion, a language where every misspoken word could lead to irreparable misunderstanding. The salty air, once a source of comfort, now seemed to amplify the distance between them, a constant reminder of the unspoken gulf that separated her carefully guarded heart from his open one. This was the treacherous water she had to navigate, and for the first time, Mara wasn't sure she had the right charts.

CHAPTER THREE

The Art of Active Listening

The rhythmic sigh of the waves against the shore, a sound that had always been a balm to Mara's soul, now seemed to underscore the quiet tension that had settled between her and Eli. She felt his gaze, not as an intrusion, but as a gentle, persistent inquiry, an unspoken question hanging in the salty air. He didn't pry, didn't press for answers she wasn't ready to give. Instead, he settled beside her on the porch swing, his presence a quiet anchor in the swirling currents of her uncertainty. The swing's familiar creak became a soft counterpoint to the ocean's steady pulse, a comforting backdrop against which their unspoken dialogue continued.

Eli took a slow sip of his tea, his gaze fixed on the horizon where the last vestiges of sunlight were bleeding into the dusky sea. He seemed to be absorbing the moment, much like he absorbed her silences. There was no impatience in his posture, no frustration radiating from him. He was simply there, a steadfast presence, allowing the stillness to work its own kind of magic. Mara found herself studying him, her eyes tracing the quiet strength in his profile, the way his shoulders relaxed as he breathed in the ocean air. He was a master of observation, and she knew, with a growing certainty, that he was observing her, not with judgment, but with a deep, abiding care.

He finally spoke, his voice a low murmur that seemed to blend seamlessly with the ocean's song. "You know," he began, his words unhurried, "I've been thinking a lot lately about communication. Not just the words we say, but... everything else." He gestured vaguely with his mug, encompassing the vast expanse of the ocean, the darkening sky, and the quiet space between them. "It's easy to get caught up in the 'doing,' isn't it? In the immediate tasks, the problems that need solving. And sometimes, in the process, we forget to truly listen."

Mara nodded, a small, almost imperceptible movement. She felt a prickle of moisture at the back of her eyes, a surprising emotional response to his simple statement. He wasn't accusing her; he was sharing a realization, a vulnerability of his own. This was his way of creating a bridge, of inviting her to cross it without demanding she do so.

"I've been guilty of it too," he continued, his gaze now meeting hers. "Thinking I understood, when really, I was just waiting for my turn to speak, or trying to fix things before I'd even fully grasped the problem." He offered a faint smile, a hint of self-deprecation in his eyes. "It's something I'm trying to be more mindful of. To really hear what's being said, and what isn't."

He shifted slightly on the swing, his knee brushing hers. The contact was fleeting, yet it sent a jolt of warmth through her. "So," he said, his tone shifting to one of gentle inquiry, "when you say you're 'just enjoying the quiet,' what does that feel like for you? What does the quiet hold?"

The question was so open-ended, so devoid of expectation, that it disarmed her. It wasn't a demand for an explanation, but an invitation to explore. Mara looked out at the waves, their white caps catching the last of the light. The quiet, for her, held a maelstrom. It was the absence of external chaos, yes, but it was also the deafening roar of her own internal monologue, a cacophony of anxieties she'd been expertly suppressing.

"It... it feels a little like the moment after a storm," she began, her voice softer than she intended. She hesitated, searching for the right words. "The air is still, but there's this lingering energy. A sense of something having shifted, but you're not quite sure what." She took a breath, the sea air filling her lungs. "And the quiet... sometimes it's a relief. But sometimes," she admitted, her gaze flickering back to Eli, "it feels... vast. Like there's so much space, and I'm not sure what to fill it with."

Eli listened intently, his head tilted slightly. He didn't interrupt, didn't offer premature solutions. He simply absorbed her words, his eyes reflecting a deep understanding. He saw the flicker of uncertainty in her expression, the slight tension in her shoulders, the way her fingers traced the worn wood of the swing. He recognized the subtle language of her unspoken emotions.

"Vast," he repeated softly, as if tasting the word. "I can see that. It's a lot of room to hold all that's left after the storm passes. And it sounds like for you, Mara, that room can sometimes feel... a little overwhelming?"

He had zeroed in on the core of her discomfort without her having to explicitly state it. He had taken her metaphor of the vastness and gently probed its emotional weight. It was a testament to his patience, his willingness to sit with her in the discomfort, rather than trying to rush her through it.

Mara let out a slow exhale. "Yes," she whispered. "Overwhelming. Because I'm used to filling my space. With work, with planning, with... keeping things moving." She gestured vaguely, a half-formed thought about her curation career, the meticulous organization it demanded. "When things are still, it's like I'm forced to confront the spaces I've been avoiding."

"Spaces you've been avoiding," Eli echoed, his voice a calm undercurrent. He didn't ask *what* those spaces were. He understood, with his keen intuition, that the answer lay not in a specific event or circumstance, but in the internal landscape of her own feelings. "And when you confront them," he continued, his gaze steady, "what do you find there?"

The question hung in the air, pregnant with possibility. This was the precipice, the edge of the vulnerability she had been so carefully guarding. The ocean, in its ceaseless rhythm, seemed to urge her forward. The sound of the waves crashing against the shore was a constant, reassuring reminder of nature's enduring power, its ability to both erode and replenish.

"Fear," Mara admitted, the word a soft exhalation. It felt strangely liberating to say it aloud, to name the elusive shadow that had been haunting her. "Fear of... not being enough. Fear that the things I've built, the control I've maintained, are... fragile. That if I stop being the one who's always 'keeping things moving,' then everything will fall apart."

She looked at Eli, her heart pounding a frantic rhythm against her ribs. His expression was unreadable for a moment, and a fresh wave of anxiety washed over her. Had she misread him? Had she finally revealed a weakness that would shatter his perception of her?

But then, his eyes softened, a profound understanding dawning within them. He reached out, not to touch her, but to place his mug on the swing beside him, creating a small, deliberate space of stillness. "Fragile," he repeated, his voice gentle. "That's a heavy burden to carry, Mara. To feel like you have to be the constant force, the one holding everything together."

He paused, and Mara felt a subtle shift in his posture. He was leaning in, not physically, but emotionally, drawing closer to her experience. "You've always been so capable," he said, his voice laced with admiration. "So strong. And I admire that more than you know. But what if," he ventured, his tone carefully considered, "what if your strength doesn't come from *never* feeling fragile, but from knowing how to navigate that fragility? What if it's in admitting those feelings, in sharing them, that your true strength lies?"

His words resonated deeply within her, striking a chord she hadn't realized was there. He wasn't dismissing her fears; he was reframing them, offering a new perspective that didn't require her to shed the parts of herself she valued. He was suggesting that vulnerability wasn't the antithesis of strength, but perhaps its most profound expression.

"I... I don't know," she confessed, her voice barely a whisper. "It feels like letting go of the reins. Like admitting I can't do it all on my own."

"And what if you don't have to?" Eli asked, his gaze unwavering. "What if you don't *have* to do it all on your own? What if there's someone beside you, ready and willing to share the load? Not to take it from you, necessarily, but to walk with you, to offer their own strength when yours feels depleted?"

He was offering her his hand, not in a gesture of rescue, but of partnership. He was inviting her to consider a different kind of dynamic, one where reliance wasn't a weakness, but a testament to a deeper connection. The rhythmic sound of the waves continued, a steady, calming presence that seemed to underscore the sincerity of his offer.

"It's hard," Mara admitted, the admission feeling like a tiny crack in the dam she had built around her emotions. "It's been my default for so long. To just... handle it."

"I know," Eli said softly. He finally reached out, his fingers gently brushing her arm. The touch was electric, a silent affirmation of his presence, his understanding. "And it's a powerful habit to break. But I want you to know, Mara, that I see you. I see the strength, yes, but I also see the vulnerability you try to hide. And I don't see it as a flaw. I see it as... a part of you. A part that deserves to be acknowledged, to be held."

He paused, and then asked a question that made her heart leap. "What would it look like, Mara, for you to... lean? Not to crumble, not to fall, but to lean? Just a little bit. What would you need from me to feel safe enough to do that?"

The question was a revelation. He wasn't asking her to divulge everything at once. He was asking for her input, her needs. He was empowering her to set the pace, to define the boundaries of her own comfort. He was demonstrating, in the most profound way, the art of active listening – not just hearing her words, but understanding the unspoken emotions behind them, and creating a space where she could articulate those needs without fear.

Mara looked at him, at the genuine love and patience shining in his eyes. The vastness she had described as overwhelming began to feel less like an empty void and more like an open invitation. The gentle rhythm of the waves seemed to whisper encouragement, urging her to take the leap. The fear was still there, a low hum beneath the surface, but it was no longer the dominant note. It was being overshadowed by a burgeoning sense of hope, of possibility.

"I think," she began, her voice a little steadier now, "I would need to know that you're not going to try and fix it. That you're just... here. Listening."

Eli nodded slowly, his thumb tracing small circles on her arm. "I can do that," he promised, his voice firm and reassuring. "I can be here. I can listen. And I won't try to fix it unless you ask me to. My goal isn't to change you, Mara. It's to understand you. And to be understood by you, in return."

He shifted on the swing, turning to face her more fully. "Tell me more about these spaces you've been avoiding," he invited, his voice soft, his eyes conveying a deep well of patience. "What do they feel like? What do you see there, when you let yourself look?"

Mara felt a wave of emotion wash over her – relief, gratitude, and a profound sense of being seen. The journey ahead was still long, the process of peeling back the layers of her self-imposed armor a daunting prospect. But for the first time, she felt like she wasn't embarking on it alone. With Eli by her side, listening, truly listening, the vastness no longer felt so overwhelming. It felt, instead, like the beginning of a new landscape, one she was ready to explore, hand in hand. The steady cadence of the waves crashing on the shore provided a gentle, unwavering soundtrack to this quiet, profound shift within her.

The salt-laced air seemed to carry a new lightness, a subtle shift that mirrored the tentative unfurling happening within Mara. Eli's steady presence, like the enduring lighthouse guiding ships through the fog, had begun to erode the calcified layers of her carefully constructed defenses. It wasn't a dramatic dismantling, but a gentle, persistent softening, like the tide gradually reshaping the shore. Each quiet conversation, each shared silence on the porch swing, chipped away at the fortress she had built around her heart.

She found herself offering more than just veiled metaphors and abstract feelings. Small, disarmingly simple observations about her day, or a fleeting memory unearthed by a familiar scent, began to trickle out. These were not grand confessions, but tiny seeds of truth, planted in the fertile ground of Eli's unwavering attention. She'd mention the unexpected satisfaction of a perfectly aligned shelf in her studio, or the pang of nostalgia a certain shade of cerulean evoked. These weren't profound revelations, but they were genuine, and in their quiet authenticity, they felt like a monumental step.

Eli absorbed these fragments with the same quiet intensity he'd shown when listening to her talk about the storm. He'd nod, his gaze steady, never interrupting, never trying to steer the conversation towards a more significant disclosure. Instead, he'd offer a simple, "That sounds... satisfying," or a thoughtful, "I can see how that color would bring back memories." His validation wasn't effusive; it was present, a silent acknowledgment that her experiences, no matter how small, held weight.

One afternoon, while watching a flock of gulls wheel and dive against the vast expanse of the sky, Mara found herself saying, "I used to draw them. For hours. I loved the way they moved, so effortless. Like they understood the wind." She trailed off, a familiar wave of self-consciousness washing over her. The ease she attributed to the gulls was something she rarely felt herself.

Eli, who had been sketching in his own notebook, looked up, his eyes reflecting the same calm she was trying to find. "Effortless," he echoed softly. "Is that something you're searching for, Mara? That sense of effortless movement?"

The question was a perfect mirror, reflecting her own unspoken desires without demanding an answer. She hadn't articulated that search, not even to herself. But he had seen it, sensed it in the subtle way she watched the world, in the careful control she exerted over her own life.

"Sometimes," she admitted, her voice barely a whisper, the vastness of the ocean offering a comforting anonymity. "It feels like I'm constantly fighting against the current. Like everything requires so much... effort. So much planning, so much force." She gestured vaguely towards the sea, a symbol of the boundless energy she often felt drained by.

"And what if," Eli suggested, his voice gentle, "you didn't have to fight so hard? What if there were moments, like those gulls, where you could just... glide?" He didn't offer solutions, didn't suggest ways to find this effortless state. He simply presented the possibility, a whispered invitation to imagine a different reality.

The word "glide" settled into her mind, a foreign but appealing concept. Her life had always been about propulsion, about pushing forward, about overcoming obstacles. The idea of gliding, of yielding to the currents and finding a natural path, felt both terrifying and incredibly liberating. It was a glimpse into a version of herself she had long suppressed, a version that prioritized flow over force.

These moments of shared vulnerability weren't confined to their conversations. They were woven into the fabric of their days. A quiet morning spent reading side-by-side in the sun-drenched living room, the only sounds the rustle of pages and the distant cry of seagulls. A walk along the beach, where Eli would point out interesting shells or unusual driftwood, and Mara would find herself responding with a genuine observation, a shared appreciation for the small wonders of nature. He never pushed for more, never probed deeper than she was willing to go. He simply created the space, and waited, with infinite patience, for her to fill it at her own pace.

One evening, after a particularly challenging day at her studio, Mara found herself staring at a half-finished canvas, the vibrant colors mocking her creative block. She'd been wrestling with a particular composition for weeks, feeling an insurmountable pressure to produce something extraordinary. The fear of failure, of not living up to her own lofty expectations, had paralyzed her.

She didn't articulate the full extent of her frustration to Eli, not directly. Instead, she spoke of the paint, the way it seemed to resist her touch, the colors refusing to blend as she envisioned. "It's like I'm trying to force something that doesn't want to be made," she confessed, her voice tight with an emotion she was still learning to name.

Eli listened, his brow furrowed slightly in concentration. He didn't offer advice on technique or composition. He simply absorbed her words, his gaze fixed on her with an empathy that was almost palpable. "Sometimes," he said, after a long pause, his voice a low rumble, "the most beautiful things emerge when we stop forcing them. When we allow them to take their own shape."

He then picked up a smooth, sea-worn stone from the small collection on the windowsill. He turned it over in his fingers, admiring its contours, its subtle variations in color. "Look at this," he said, holding it out to her. "It's not perfect. It's rough in places, smoothed in others. But it's exactly as it should be. It's been shaped by the ocean, by time, by its own journey. And it's beautiful because of it, not in spite of it."

Mara took the stone, its coolness seeping into her palm. She ran her thumb over its worn surface, feeling the history etched into its form. It was a simple object, yet it spoke volumes. It was a tangible reminder that perfection wasn't the goal, that imperfection was an integral part of beauty, of life itself.

"You think," she began, her voice hesitant, the fear of revealing too much still present, but now tinged with a glimmer of hope, "you think that... I could be like this stone?"

Eli's smile was gentle, genuine. "I think," he said, his gaze holding hers, "that you are already beautiful, Mara. Exactly as you are. And the journey of unfurling, of letting your own shape emerge, is where even more beauty will be found."

This conversation, like so many others, didn't end with a dramatic resolution. There was no sudden epiphany, no instant cure for her anxieties. But it left Mara with a profound sense of peace, a quiet understanding that she was not alone in her struggle. Eli's consistent presence, his patient listening, and his gentle reframing of her fears had created a safe harbor within her own heart. The vastness of the sea, once a symbol of her overwhelming isolation, now felt like a boundless canvas of possibility, a space where she could finally begin to explore the contours of her own unfurling self. The fear was still a whisper, but hope was beginning to sing.

The rhythm of the waves had become a constant, comforting soundtrack to Mara and Eli's deepening connection. Their days, once marked by the tentative dance of getting to know each other, were now flowing with a natural ease, punctuated by shared meals, quiet evenings, and the unspoken understanding that bloomed between them. It was in this fertile ground of shared moments that the conversation, almost organically, turned towards the concept of 'togetherness.'

Mara found herself articulating it first, not in a grand pronouncement, but during a walk along the shoreline, the setting sun painting the sky in hues of orange and amethyst. "You know," she began, her voice a little softer than usual against the whisper of the surf, "I used to think being 'together' meant... well, losing yourself a bit. Like two rivers merging, the individual streams disappearing into a larger body of water." She picked up a piece of smooth, grey driftwood, turning it over in her hands, its weathered surface a testament to its solitary journey. "I always held onto that part of myself, the distinct stream. I was so afraid of being swept away."

Eli walked beside her, his stride unhurried, his gaze sweeping across the horizon. He stopped and turned to her, his expression one of quiet contemplation. "That's an interesting image, Mara. The merging rivers. But what if togetherness isn't about losing your boundaries, but about building a bridge between them?" He gestured to the vast expanse of the ocean. "Look at the ocean. It's made up of countless individual drops of water, each distinct, yet they form this immense, unified entity. They coexist. They influence each other, certainly, but they don't cease to be themselves."

Mara considered his words, the metaphor resonating deeply. It was a far cry from her previous anxieties, from the fear of dissolution. "A bridge," she murmured, the idea taking root. "So, not merging, but connecting? Sharing the space, but respecting the separate shores?"

"Exactly," Eli confirmed, his eyes crinkling at the corners as he smiled. "It's about recognizing that we are two whole people, with our own histories, our own dreams, our own needs. And then, consciously choosing to build a life that accommodates both of those wholes, side-by-side. It's about creating a shared landscape, not a melted-down common one."

This conversation, initiated on the beach, became a recurring theme in their interactions over the following weeks. It wasn't a one-time discussion, but an ongoing exploration, a mutual charting of their shared territory. They discovered that 'togetherness,' for them, was not a destination, but a continuous process of negotiation and affirmation. They talked about their individual needs, those quiet hums of self-preservation and personal fulfillment that existed independent of their relationship.

Mara, for instance, spoke about her need for solitude, not as an act of rejection, but as a vital part of her creative process. "Sometimes," she admitted one rainy afternoon, curled up on the sofa with mugs of steaming tea, "I just need hours alone in my studio. It's not that I don't want to be with you, Eli. It's that I need that space to sort through my thoughts, to let the ideas breathe. If I'm constantly in company, I feel... stifled. My own inner voice gets drowned out."

Eli listened, his usual quiet attentiveness in full force. He didn't interrupt with reassurances or try to minimize her need. Instead, he acknowledged its validity. "I understand," he said, his voice steady and calm. "And I appreciate you telling me. I have my own versions of that. I need time to work on my boat, to feel the wood under my hands, to let the quiet of the workshop envelop me. It's where I recharge, where I find my balance." He paused, his gaze thoughtful. "So, our together time is important, but so are our separate spaces. We need to honor both, don't we?"

This exchange, so simple yet so profound, laid the groundwork for establishing boundaries – not as restrictive fences, but as clear pathways that ensured both individuals felt secure and respected. They began to articulate their expectations, not as demands, but as gentle requests, preferences that, when met, fostered a sense of harmony.

Mara found herself saying, "I'd love it if, on days when I'm really in the zone with my painting, you could just... let me be. Maybe leave a note instead of knocking. It sounds small, but it makes a huge difference to my concentration."

And Eli, in turn, might say, "When I'm out on the water, even if it's just for a short sail, I appreciate knowing you're not worried. A quick wave from the shore, or a text when I get back, lets me feel connected without feeling tethered."

These were not the dramatic pronouncements of romance novels, but the quiet, steady building blocks of a lasting partnership. They were conversations that fostered trust, the kind of trust that allowed them to be vulnerable without fear of judgment or overstepping.

The serene backdrop of their coastal town seemed to amplify the sincerity of these discussions. The timeless ebb and flow of the tides mirrored the natural rhythm they were seeking to establish in their relationship. The vast, open sky offered a sense of limitless possibility, a feeling that their combined aspirations, even when separate, could reach for the stars.

One evening, they were sitting on their porch swing, the air alive with the scent of jasmine. Mara had been particularly inspired that day, and her studio was filled with the vibrant chaos of her creative energy. She had been wrestling with a new series, one that explored the multifaceted nature of strength, and the dialogue with Eli had been a quiet undercurrent to her artistic exploration.

"You know," she began, tracing the grain of the wooden swing with her finger, "I think I've always associated 'strength' with being impenetrable, with being able to stand alone against any storm. It's that lone lighthouse, you know? Standing tall, unyielding, visible to all but untouchable."

Eli gently put his arm around her, drawing her closer. "That's a powerful image," he said, his voice a low murmur against her hair. "But what if strength can also be found in connection? In the way the roots of trees intertwine, supporting each other against the wind? Or the way a flock of birds moves as one, adapting to the currents together?"

Mara leaned her head against his shoulder, a sense of profound peace settling over her. "I think that's what I've been discovering," she whispered. "That 'togetherness' doesn't diminish strength; it amplifies it. It allows for a different kind of resilience. A resilience that comes from knowing you have someone to lean on, someone who sees your vulnerabilities and doesn't see them as weaknesses, but as part of your whole, beautiful self."

They discussed their individual aspirations, the dreams that had been nurtured in solitude and were now ready to be shared. Mara spoke of her ambition to have her work exhibited in a gallery beyond their small town, of her desire to connect with a wider artistic community. Eli, in turn, shared his quiet dream of one day sailing across the Atlantic, a lifelong yearning that had always seemed just out of reach.

Instead of seeing these individual dreams as potential points of conflict or separation, they began to explore how they could support and inspire each other. "When you're ready to show your work," Eli said, his voice filled with genuine enthusiasm, "I'll be there, cheering the loudest. And maybe," he added, a hint of a smile in his voice, "when I finally set sail, you can capture the journey in your art. We can create something beautiful together, even when we're apart."

This was the essence of their developing 'togetherness': a conscious, deliberate choice to build a shared life without sacrificing their individual identities. It was a partnership built on the foundation of mutual respect, where each person's journey was not only acknowledged but celebrated. They learned to communicate their needs with clarity and kindness, understanding that open dialogue was the most effective way to navigate the complexities of two lives intertwining.

They established rituals that reinforced their connection. A shared Sunday morning coffee, where they'd read the paper and discuss their plans for the week. An evening walk, regardless of the weather, that provided a quiet space for reflection and connection. These were not rigid rules, but flexible anchors that kept them grounded in their shared commitment.

Mara realized that her fear of being consumed had been replaced by a quiet confidence in their ability to grow together, as individuals and as a couple. The bridge Eli had spoken of was not just a connection between their shores; it was a shared space, strong and wide enough for both of them to walk freely, hand in hand, or side by side, towards whatever future lay ahead. Their togetherness was not about becoming one, but about becoming a stronger, more vibrant 'us,' each part valued, each part essential, each part free to shine. The art of listening had led them to the art of truly seeing each other, and in that seeing, they found the courage to build something beautiful, something lasting, something that was uniquely theirs. It was an understanding that went beyond words, a feeling woven into the very fabric of their days, as constant and as comforting as the ocean breeze.

The rescue center, a place usually humming with a hopeful urgency, had been gripped by a palpable tension for the past few weeks. It wasn't just the usual ebb and flow of rescues; this was a sustained period of intense demand, stretching the staff and resources thin. Mara, with her innate empathy, felt the collective strain acutely. She saw the tired lines around her colleagues' eyes, the hushed, worried conversations that punctuated the breaks, and the sheer physical exhaustion that clung to them like the salty air. It was a shared burden, and she found herself increasingly drawn into Eli's orbit as they navigated it together.

One blustery Tuesday, the call came in just as the sun began to dip below the horizon, painting the sky in bruised shades of purple and grey. A fishing trawler, caught in a sudden squall miles offshore, had reported engine failure and was taking on water. The waves, which had been playful mere hours before, had transformed into angry, churning mountains. The sea, usually a source of solace for Mara, now seemed a formidable adversary. Eli, ever the pragmatist, was already assessing the situation, his brow furrowed as he studied the marine charts.

"This is going to be a tough one," Eli stated, his voice calm despite the gravity of the situation. He pointed to a particularly treacherous section of the coastline, a notorious graveyard for ships. "The wind is picking up fast, and the tide is pulling them towards the reef."

Mara felt a familiar knot of anxiety tighten in her stomach. She had always admired Eli's unflinching competence in these high-stakes scenarios, but this time, the fear was amplified by a new, insistent whisper – a fear of failure, not just for the crew of the trawler, but for *them*, as a team. She had witnessed firsthand the pressure that fell on the lead rescuers, the immense responsibility that could weigh a person down.

"What's our window?" Mara asked, her voice steady, a testament to her own growing resolve. She met Eli's gaze, a silent question hanging between them:

Can we do this?

Eli's response was immediate, a flicker of understanding passing between them. "We have maybe an hour, hour and a half, before it's too dangerous to launch. We need to move fast." He turned to the rest of the team, his instructions crisp and clear. "Lena, get the heavy-duty tow line ready. Ben, check the fuel levels on the *Sea Serpent* twice. Mara, I'll need you on navigation and communications. We can't afford any slip-ups out there."

The words, "I'll need you on navigation and communications," resonated with Mara. It wasn't a suggestion; it was an assignment, a clear indication that Eli trusted her with a critical role. It was a small thing, perhaps, but it was a tangible acknowledgment of her capabilities, especially in the face of their shared challenges. As they moved with practiced efficiency, a silent understanding settled between them. The usual polite distance they maintained at the center, born of professionalism, had dissolved. Now, their interactions were charged with a different kind of energy – a focused, collaborative current.

The launch of the *Sea Serpent*, their most robust rescue vessel, was a testament to their combined efforts. The wind whipped spray into their faces, and the boat pitched and rolled with unnerving violence. Mara, strapped into the co-pilot's seat, felt the roar of the engines, the shudder of the hull, and the relentless assault of the waves. Her hands, usually steady when holding a brush, now gripped the console with a white-knuckled intensity, her eyes glued to the radar screen. She relayed wind speeds, wave heights, and the trawler's increasingly desperate calls for help. Each transmission was punctuated by static and the howl of the storm, making communication a delicate, nerve-wracking dance.

"He's reporting a significant breach in the hull, Eli," Mara shouted over the din, her voice strained. "They're losing buoyancy fast."

Eli, his knuckles white on the steering wheel, his gaze fixed on the turbulent expanse ahead, nodded grimly. "Understood. We're closing in. Lena, be ready with the winch. Ben, keep an eye on the port side. We don't want to get too close to their stern."

The rescue itself was a blur of adrenaline and precision. The trawler, listing precariously, was a ghost in the storm-lashed darkness. Maneuvering the *Sea Serpent* alongside it, in such treacherous conditions, was a feat of seamanship that Mara had only ever read about. Eli's skill was undeniable, his movements economical and assured, each turn of the wheel a calculated risk. He navigated the heaving swells with an uncanny grace, bringing the rescue vessel within inches of the floundering trawler.

Lena, with remarkable strength and coordination, managed to secure the heavy-duty tow line. The moment of connection was fraught with tension, the metal links groaning under the strain. Then came the winch, the steady, rhythmic whirring a counterpoint to the storm's fury, pulling the exhausted fishermen aboard, one by one. Mara watched, her breath catching in her throat, as each figure, huddled and shivering, was brought to safety.

Amidst the chaos, Mara noticed Eli's unwavering focus. He was a commander, a leader, but also a partner. He would glance at her, a quick, reassuring nod, a silent acknowledgment of her role. She, in turn, provided him with the critical data he needed, her voice a calm anchor in the storm. There were no grand pronouncements, no dramatic displays of emotion. It was simply a shared mission, executed with skill and a profound, unspoken trust.

One of the rescued fishermen, a man whose face was etched with the harsh realities of his profession, grasped Eli's arm as he was being helped below deck. "Thank you," he rasped, his voice hoarse. "We thought... we thought we were done for."

Eli's response was a simple, "Just glad we could get to you in time. Get yourselves warm." He then turned back to Mara, his eyes, illuminated by the console lights, held a mixture of relief and exhaustion.

The journey back to shore was a testament to their shared effort. The *Sea Serpent* battled the relentless waves, towing the crippled trawler. Mara and Eli worked in tandem, monitoring the tow line, the trawler's condition, and the ever-changing weather patterns. They spoke in clipped sentences, their communication efficient and necessary. There were moments when Mara felt the weight of their responsibility pressing down on her, the sheer scale of the undertaking. But then she would look at Eli, his jaw set with determination, and a quiet strength would flow through her. They were in this together.

As they finally docked, the harbor lights a welcome beacon after the darkness, a wave of collective relief washed over the rescue team. The fishermen were safely transferred to the care of the paramedics, their ordeal over. The *Sea Serpent* was secured, its engine sputtering to a halt, mirroring the exhaustion of its crew.

Later that night, long after the last of the official reports had been filed, Mara found herself sitting with Eli in the quiet of the center's break room. The adrenaline had long since subsided, leaving behind a profound sense of weariness, but also a deep, quiet satisfaction. They sat in comfortable silence for a while, the only sound the gentle hum of the refrigerator.

"That was... intense," Mara finally said, her voice soft, almost a whisper.

Eli reached over and gently took her hand, his thumb tracing circles on her skin. "It was. But we handled it.

You handled it, Mara. Your navigation was spot on, and your calm under pressure... I don't think we could have done it without you."

Mara felt a warmth spread through her chest, a feeling that had nothing to do with the residual adrenaline. It was the warmth of acknowledgment, of genuine appreciation. "And you, Eli. The way you handled the boat... it was incredible. I've never seen anything like it."

"We're a good team," Eli said, his gaze steady and earnest. "When it comes down to it, when everything is on the line, we can rely on each other."

This wasn't just about a successful rescue. It was about a shared experience that had forged a new layer of understanding between them. The demanding operation had stripped away any lingering hesitations, any unspoken doubts. They had faced a crisis, not as individuals working side-by-side, but as a unified force. The inherent risks, the split-second decisions, the sheer force of nature they had contended with – it had all served to highlight their capacity for working together, for trusting each other's judgment implicitly.

The following days at the rescue center continued to be demanding. The storm had left a trail of its fury, and the calls for assistance remained high. But something had shifted. The shared burden no longer felt like a crushing weight, but a challenge they were better equipped to face. The intensity of the rescue mission had, paradoxically, brought them closer, solidifying their bond not through shared leisure, but through shared adversity.

Mara found herself observing the dynamics at the center with a new perspective. She saw how the younger volunteers, witnessing the seamless collaboration during the trawler rescue, seemed to absorb the unspoken lessons of teamwork. They saw Eli and Mara, and others, communicating effectively, supporting each other, and achieving a common goal against daunting odds. This shared struggle, she realized, wasn't just about saving lives; it was about demonstrating, in the most tangible way possible, the power of unity.

One afternoon, while debriefing a minor rescue involving a disabled sailboat, Mara found herself articulating this newfound understanding. "It's like... when we're out there," she began, gesturing vaguely towards the sea, "all the individual worries, the personal hesitations... they just fall away. There's only the mission. And because we're doing it together, that mission feels achievable, even when it's incredibly difficult."

Eli listened intently, his usual quiet presence a comforting anchor. "That's the essence of it, isn't it?" he replied. "The shared responsibility. It doesn't dilute your own capacity, it amplifies it. It means you're not alone in carrying the weight, and that makes the burden not just lighter, but also more meaningful."

He continued, his gaze thoughtful, "Think about the trawler. It was a terrifying situation. If either of us had faltered, if there had been any doubt or hesitation in our actions, the outcome could have been drastically different. But because we were both fully present, fully committed to our roles, and trusting each other, we succeeded. That success wasn't just mine, or yours, or Lena's, or Ben's. It was ours. All of ours."

Mara nodded, a sense of profound understanding dawning on her. The rescue center, with its constant demands and inherent risks, had become an unexpected crucible for their relationship. It was in the heart of these shared struggles that their partnership was truly being tested and, more importantly, strengthened. The turbulent sea, which had once seemed an adversary, was now a testament to their ability to navigate not just the waves, but the deeper currents of commitment and collaboration. They had discovered that carrying a shared burden, when done with trust and respect, could be the most profound form of connection, proving that true strength often lay not in standing alone, but in standing together, united against the storm. The successful rescue was more than a testament to their skills; it was a powerful, undeniable affirmation of their capacity for unified action, a deep-seated understanding that together, they could weather any storm.

Mara found herself tracing the rim of her teacup, the ceramic cool against her fingertips. The quiet hum of the rescue center had settled into a comfortable rhythm after the recent flurry of activity, a stark contrast to the adrenaline-fueled nights and the constant gnawing of uncertainty. Yet, even in these moments of relative calm, she felt a subtle shift, a deepening in the unspoken language between herself and Eli. It wasn't born of effortless understanding, but of a conscious, deliberate effort. They were no longer simply colleagues who found themselves thrown together by circumstance; they were actively constructing something, brick by careful brick, a structure built not on the ease of shared routine, but on the sturdy foundation of intentionality.

It was the small things, she mused, the seemingly insignificant choices that spoke volumes. The way Eli would pause before entering a room, his gaze sweeping to find her, a silent query in his eyes before he spoke, as if assessing the best way to approach her. Or the way she, in turn, would hold back a dismissive thought, a familiar instinct to retreat into her own head when faced with a differing perspective, and instead, choose to listen, truly listen, to his reasoning. These weren't grand gestures, but they were the quiet, consistent acts of deliberate engagement that were solidifying their bond.

Take, for instance, the evening after the storm that had tested their limits. The world outside was still a symphony of wind and rain, but inside the rescue center, a fragile peace had begun to emerge. The fishermen were safe, the *Sea Serpent* was being meticulously checked for any lingering damage, and the immediate crisis had passed. Eli had found her in the dimly lit kitchen, staring out at the rain-lashed windows, the residual tension still coiling in her stomach. Her instinct was to withdraw, to cocoon herself in the solitude she often sought after intense situations. The easy path would have been to offer a perfunctory "Good job" and retreat to her quarters, to process the lingering echoes of the ordeal alone.

But Eli hadn't taken the easy path. He had walked over, not with a boisterous clap on the back or a relieved sigh, but with a quiet presence that felt like an offering. He hadn't demanded conversation, hadn't forced her to articulate the swirling emotions within her. Instead, he had simply poured himself a mug of the same lukewarm tea she was nursing, and stood beside her, looking out at the tempestuous sea. The silence between them was different then. It wasn't the silence of avoidance, but the silence of shared reflection, a tacit acknowledgment that they had navigated something significant together, and that processing it, even in silence, was a communal endeavor.

"You were incredible out there, Mara," he'd said eventually, his voice low, cutting through the drumming of the rain. It wasn't the casual praise of a coworker; it carried the weight of genuine observation, of witnessing her strength under immense pressure. He hadn't just seen her perform her duties; he had seen *her*.

And in that moment, Mara had felt a flicker of resistance, a ingrained habit of downplaying her own contributions, of deflecting compliments. The easy thing would have been to murmur a thank you and steer the conversation back to the practicalities of the rescue. But she recognized the intentionality in his words, the deliberate effort he was making to connect, to acknowledge her. So, she chose to lean into it. She met his gaze, a small smile touching her lips. "So were you, Eli. I've never seen anyone handle the boat like that."

It was a simple exchange, yet it felt monumental. It was a conscious choice to meet his effort with her own, to reciprocate the open acknowledgment, to extend the tendrils of connection rather than retract them. It was the deliberate act of choosing vulnerability, of allowing herself to be seen and appreciated, and in doing so, fostering a deeper sense of connection. This was the essence of intentionality – the active choice to engage, to communicate, to be present, even when the easier, more familiar path was to retreat.

Their days continued to be a dance between the unpredictable demands of their coastal lives and the quiet cultivation of their burgeoning relationship. There were days when the radio crackled with urgent calls, when the biting wind whipped across the docks, and when the sheer exhaustion threatened to consume them. On those days, the instinct to hunker down, to focus solely on the task at hand, was overwhelming. Yet, even in the midst of such urgency, moments of intentionality would surface.

Mara recalled a particularly harrowing call involving a kayaker caught in an unexpected rip current. The rescue was swift, efficient, and ultimately successful, but the kayaker had been visibly shaken, sputtering and disoriented on the shore. As the paramedics attended to him, Mara had found herself feeling a familiar pang of helplessness, a residue of the fear she'd experienced watching him struggle against the unforgiving sea. Eli, who had been steering the rescue boat, had returned to shore and, instead of immediately launching into the debriefing with the team, had approached her.

He hadn't asked if she was okay, a question that often felt hollow, a perfunctory check-in. Instead, he had simply said, "That was a close one. You kept a clear head on the comms." It was an observation, not a question, and it was specific. He had noticed her focus, her ability to relay critical information amidst the chaos. And Mara, instead of offering a dismissive "It was nothing," had allowed herself to acknowledge the truth of his words. "It felt like it," she'd replied, her voice still carrying a trace of the tension. "But seeing him come back... that's what matters."

Eli had nodded, his gaze steady. "It is. And you played a vital part in that. We all did. Together." The emphasis on "together" wasn't just a platitude; it was a statement of fact, reinforced by their shared experience. He was intentionally reinforcing the idea that their success was a collective achievement, a testament to their collaboration. And Mara, by accepting his acknowledgment, by engaging in that brief, honest exchange, was reinforcing her willingness to build something with him, something that went beyond the operational demands of the rescue center.

This intentionality extended to their communication, or rather, the conscious effort they made to refine it. Mara had always been a listener, but often, her listening was passive, a prelude to her own thoughts. With Eli, she found herself actively striving for deeper understanding. She would ask follow-up questions, not out of obligation, but out of genuine curiosity. She would pause before responding, ensuring she had fully processed his words, not just the surface meaning, but the underlying sentiment.

There was a particular instance when they were discussing the logistics of a planned training exercise. Eli, typically direct, had outlined a scenario that Mara, with her perspective on the psychological impact of rescues, felt might be overly aggressive, potentially causing undue stress on the trainees. Her initial reaction was to bristle, to fall back on the easy assertion of her own expertise. But she remembered the promise she was making to herself, to him, to the developing connection between them.

Instead of stating her disagreement as a fact, she had framed it as a concern, a question born of her experience. "Eli," she'd begun, her tone gentle, "I understand the need for a realistic challenge, but I'm wondering if we might consider a slightly less intense scenario for the first round. My concern is that pushing them too hard too soon might have the opposite effect, discouraging them rather than motivating them. What are your thoughts on maybe softening the approach initially?"

She watched his face, bracing herself for a potential defensiveness. But Eli hadn't reacted with annoyance or dismissal. He had paused, his brow furrowing in thought, and then he had actually *considered* her perspective. "That's a fair point, Mara," he'd said, his voice thoughtful. "I hadn't considered the psychological impact in quite that way. My focus was on the technical execution. Tell me more about what you envision."

That moment, that willingness on both their parts to engage with each other's perspectives, to move beyond their initial assumptions and actively seek common ground, was a powerful testament to their intentionality. They weren't just talking; they were collaborating, building a shared understanding, and making decisions together. It was the antithesis of the easy route, which would have been for Eli to simply proceed with his plan or for Mara to grudgingly accept it without voicing her concerns. Instead, they had chosen the harder, more rewarding path of open dialogue and mutual respect.

The ease of their coastal life, with its inherent unpredictability, often served as a backdrop against which their intentional choices shone even brighter. A sudden fog rolling in, demanding immediate attention and swift action, could easily have caused them to revert to a more functional, less personal form of interaction. Yet, even in the midst of such challenging conditions, Mara noticed Eli making an effort to check in with her, not just about the navigational details, but about her well-being.

"Deep breaths, Mara," he'd said during a particularly dense fog that had descended without warning, making visibility almost zero. He hadn't said it as a command, but as a gentle suggestion, an offering of calm amidst the rising anxiety. And Mara, instead of simply nodding and burying herself in her instruments, had met his gaze across the console and offered a small, reassuring smile. "I'm okay, Eli. Just focusing on the sonar." It was a simple exchange, but it was a deliberate act of acknowledging his concern and reaffirming her own composure, a quiet affirmation that they were in this together, and that their connection was a source of strength, not a distraction.

It wasn't always smooth sailing, of course. There were moments when old habits resurfaced, when a sharp word was spoken in haste, or a misunderstanding festered for a brief, uncomfortable period. But what set their evolving relationship apart was their commitment to addressing these moments, to not letting them slide into the comfortable oblivion of unaddressed issues. They had learned, through trial and error, that the ease of avoidance was a dangerous illusion. It might feel easier in the short term, but it eroded the foundation of trust and genuine connection.

Mara remembered a time when she had felt overlooked during a planning meeting for a new outreach program. Her ideas, meticulously prepared, had seemed to be brushed aside in favor of a more established colleague's less developed proposal. The easy response would have been to withdraw, to retreat into her own quiet resentment, to assume that her contributions wouldn't be valued. But the lessons of intentionality, learned in the crucible of shared rescues and quiet conversations, had taken root.

Later that day, she had approached Eli, not with an accusation, but with a clear, concise articulation of her feelings and her observations. "Eli," she'd begun, her voice steady, "I wanted to talk about the outreach program meeting earlier. I felt that my proposal wasn't fully considered, and I'm concerned that we might be missing an opportunity to engage the community in a more meaningful way. Could we discuss it?"

Eli, to his credit, hadn't become defensive. He had listened intently, his gaze steady, and he had asked clarifying questions. He had acknowledged her concern, not as a criticism of his leadership, but as a valid observation. And then, they had had a conversation, a genuine dialogue, where he explained his reasoning, and Mara had been able to articulate her vision more fully. The outcome wasn't necessarily a complete overhaul of the plan, but it was a compromise, a refinement that incorporated some of Mara's key suggestions. More importantly, it was a demonstration that their relationship was built on the willingness to navigate difficult conversations, to prioritize understanding over the ease of silence.

This commitment to intentionality was more than just a strategy; it was becoming an intrinsic part of their interaction. It was about actively choosing to see the best in each other, even when faced with challenges. It was about making a conscious effort to communicate their needs and desires, rather than expecting the other person to intuit them. It was about showing up, fully present, not just physically, but emotionally and mentally, even when exhaustion beckoned.

The unpredictable rhythm of their coastal life, with its ever-present threat of storms and its calls for rescue, had, ironically, provided the perfect environment for this kind of intentional growth. It stripped away the superficial, the non-essential, and left them with the core of their connection. In the face of genuine peril, the trivialities of everyday life fell away, and what remained was the fundamental need for trust, support, and understanding. And it was in actively cultivating these qualities, in choosing to engage with intention rather than ease, that Mara and Eli were forging a bond that was not only resilient but also deeply meaningful.

They were learning that the most profound connections weren't found in effortless harmony, but in the conscious, ongoing effort to understand, to support, and to grow together, even when the tide was against them.

CHAPTER FOUR

Bridging the Emotional Divide

Mara found herself returning to the water's edge with increasing frequency, the rhythmic ebb and flow of the tide mirroring the hesitant shifts within her own heart. The ocean, with its ancient, unwavering presence, had always been her confidante, a silent witness to her solitary thoughts. But now, its immensity seemed to hold a new dimension, a reflection of the burgeoning emotional landscape she was navigating with Eli. It was a space where the usual barriers she erected – the carefully constructed walls of self-reliance and guarded independence – felt less formidable, less necessary. The salt-laced air, carrying the cries of gulls and the distant roar of waves, seemed to whisper permission, a gentle invitation to shed the layers of her past.

She remembered one late afternoon, the sun a bruised orange sinking below the horizon, painting the sky in hues of rose and violet. Eli had found her sitting on the weathered planks of the old jetty, her gaze lost somewhere between the darkening sea and the scattering of stars beginning to prick the twilight.

He hadn't approached with the usual easy banter or a direct question. Instead, he had simply sat beside her, a comfortable distance between them, his presence a quiet anchor. The silence that settled was not the strained silence of awkwardness, but the companionable silence of shared observation.

"It's a different kind of quiet tonight, isn't it?" he'd murmured finally, his voice low, barely disturbing the gentle lapping of waves against the pilings.

Mara had nodded, her eyes still fixed on the vast expanse. "It feels... expectant. Like it's holding its breath for something."

"Maybe it is," Eli had replied, his gaze following hers. "Or maybe it's just letting go of the day, making space for the night." He had paused, then added, "Like us, sometimes."

That simple analogy, delivered with such understated grace, had struck a chord. It was a gentle acknowledgement of their shared journey, a recognition that they, too, were in a process of letting go, of creating space for something new to emerge between them. It wasn't a demand for revelation, but an offering of understanding. In that moment, Mara had felt a subtle tremor of her carefully guarded defenses begin to loosen. He wasn't trying to pry or to excavate her past; he was simply acknowledging the present, the shared moment, and their evolving connection within it.

Another time, a week later, a fierce storm had blown in with little warning, lashing the coast with relentless fury. The rescue center had been a hive of controlled chaos, the air thick with the scent of brine and the urgency of preparations. When the immediate crisis had passed, leaving behind a world scrubbed clean and glistening under a pale, watery sun, Mara found herself seeking the solace of the sea once more. She stood near the shoreline, watching the agitated waves churn, the residual tension from the ordeal still humming beneath her skin. She was accustomed to processing such events internally, to absorbing the fear and the adrenaline until it dissipated on its own.

Eli, his face etched with the weariness of the night's efforts, approached her. He carried two steaming mugs, the aroma of strong coffee a welcome contrast to the damp air. He offered one to her without a word, a gesture of quiet solidarity.

"That was a tough one," he said, his voice rough. He didn't ask how she was holding up, a question she often found herself deflecting with a curt "Fine." Instead, he simply shared his own experience, his own exhaustion. "Felt like the sea was trying to swallow us whole there for a while."

Mara accepted the coffee, its warmth seeping into her cold hands. She met his gaze, and for the first time, she didn't feel the need to present a facade of unflappable composure. "It was," she admitted, her voice barely above a whisper. "There was a moment... when the waves were coming over the bow... I thought..." She trailed off, the memory vivid, the fear a cold knot in her stomach. She hadn't intended to share that vulnerability, to give voice to the flicker of terror that had momentarily seized her.

Eli didn't flinch. He simply listened, his presence steady and unjudgmental. When she finished, he didn't offer platitudes or reassurances that the danger had passed. Instead, he said, "I saw it too. And I saw you, Mara. Keeping the boat steady. You were a rock out there."

His words weren't just a compliment; they were an observation of her strength in the face of her own admitted fear. He had seen her vulnerability, and he had seen her courage. He hadn't recoiled from the former; he had acknowledged and validated the latter. It was a subtle but profound difference. He was not just seeing her competence; he was seeing *her*, the woman who experienced fear and chose to act despite it. This was the beginning of a profound shift, a crack in the armor she had worn for so long.

The trust Mara was beginning to place in Eli wasn't a sudden, seismic event. It was more akin to the slow, steady erosion of a cliff face by the persistent kiss of the waves. It was built in the quiet moments, in the shared silences, in the unassuming gestures that spoke of genuine regard. He didn't seek to diminish her independence or to replace her self-sufficiency. Instead, his presence offered a different kind of strength, one that complemented her own, like two different instruments harmonizing to create a richer melody.

She started to notice how his strengths provided a counterpoint to hers. Where she was meticulous, he was adaptable. Where she often over-analyzed, he possessed an intuitive understanding. He saw the broader picture, the strategic advantage, while she honed in on the critical details, the nuanced implications. He didn't dismiss her thoroughness; he valued it. And she, in turn, found herself not resentful of his more decisive approach, but intrigued by it, learning to trust his instincts as she trusted her own meticulously gathered data.

There was a particular instance when they were planning the logistics for a new supply run to a remote fishing village. Mara had spent hours poring over charts, calculating fuel consumption, weather patterns, and potential hazards. She presented her findings with her usual precision, detailing every contingency. Eli listened patiently, nodding along, but then he introduced a variable she hadn't considered: the unwritten social calendar of the village elders.

"They're having their annual harvest festival in two weeks, Mara," he explained, pointing to a spot on the map. "If we time our arrival for just before then, they'll be more inclined to help us unload quickly, and we might even get invited to share in their festivities. It'll save us a day of sheer hard work."

Mara blinked, her mind still grappling with the hydrographic data. "A festival? I hadn't factored that in." Her initial thought was to dismiss it as a minor detail, a deviation from the optimal logistical plan. But then she remembered the countless times

Eli had navigated the intricate web of human relationships that underpinned their coastal community, often with an ease she envied.

"It's not just about the schedule, is it?" she mused aloud, more to herself than to him.

Eli offered a gentle smile. "It rarely is, out here. Sometimes the most efficient route isn't the one on the map, but the one that takes people into account."

In that moment, Mara felt a significant shift. She wasn't just acknowledging his practical insight; she was recognizing the wisdom in his approach, a wisdom born of empathy and an understanding of community dynamics that her purely analytical mind sometimes overlooked. She saw that his presence didn't dilute her own capabilities but amplified them, offering a broader perspective that enriched their joint efforts. She allowed herself to be seen not just as a competent professional, but as someone who was learning, growing, and open to different forms of knowledge.

The ocean continued to be a silent arena for these internal transformations. Mara would often find herself walking along the shore after a particularly meaningful conversation with Eli, the cool sand yielding beneath her feet, the vast, indifferent expanse of the sea a comforting presence. It was here, with the immensity of the ocean stretching before her, that she felt the weight of her own carefully constructed solitude begin to lift. The memories of past hurts, the ingrained habits of self-protection, felt less potent under the boundless sky.

She began to understand that her guardedness, while once a necessary shield, had also become a barrier to genuine connection. Eli, with his quiet persistence and his genuine interest, was slowly and steadily chipping away at that barrier, not through force, but through consistent, gentle pressure. He didn't demand access to her inner world; he created an environment where she felt safe enough to offer it, piece by piece.

One evening, as they sat on the deck of the rescue center, sharing a simple meal of freshly grilled fish, the conversation turned to their respective pasts. Mara had always been adept at deflecting personal questions, steering conversations back to work or to the immediate environment. But with Eli, something was different. He spoke of his own early days, of the challenges he'd faced, of the mentors who had shaped him, not with bravado, but with a quiet humility that invited reciprocity.

When he eventually turned the conversation back to her, his gaze steady and open, Mara found herself hesitating, her usual defenses rising. But then she looked at him, at the genuine curiosity in his eyes, and she made a conscious choice. She didn't offer a sanitized version of her life. Instead, she spoke about her early fascination with the sea, about the loss that had driven her towards a life of service, about the quiet fear that had always accompanied her independence. It wasn't a torrent of confessions, but a carefully chosen stream, a tentative offering of her inner self.

"I always felt like I had to be the one in control," she admitted, her voice barely audible above the murmur of the waves. "Like if I wasn't strong enough, if I wasn't always prepared, then... everything would fall apart."

Eli reached out, his hand hovering just above hers on the table, a gesture of support that didn't intrude. "But you are strong, Mara," he said, his voice soft. "And you are prepared. But strength isn't about never feeling fear. It's about facing it. And sometimes, it's about letting someone else face it with you."

That was the crux of it. Eli wasn't an intruder into her world; he was an invitation to share it. He offered a different kind of strength, not one that overshadowed her own, but one that stood beside it, a supportive presence that allowed her to breathe a little easier, to be a little less vigilant. Her trust in him wasn't a surrender of her autonomy; it was an expansion of her capacity for connection, a recognition that she didn't have to navigate every challenge alone. The vastness of the ocean, once a symbol of her solitude, was slowly transforming into a metaphor for the depth of feeling she was finally allowing herself to explore, a depth that Eli, with his steady gaze and his quiet understanding, was helping her to discover.

Eli's understanding of partnership wasn't born in a vacuum; it had been forged in the crucible of observation and experience, shaped by the unique rhythm of life in their small coastal community. He'd seen too many relationships buckle under the weight of unspoken expectations and the corrosive tide of resentment. His vision was a deliberate counterpoint to that, a conscious cultivation of a different kind of connection. He believed, with an unwavering conviction, that true partnership wasn't about two halves making a whole, but about two whole individuals choosing to walk alongside each other, their paths intersecting and weaving together, creating a richer, more vibrant tapestry.

He found a quiet moment to articulate this during a rare lull in their demanding work. The rescue center was quiet, the air still carrying the faint scent of salt and the distant, mournful cry of a gull. Mara was meticulously cataloging a new shipment of supplies, her brow furrowed in concentration, while Eli leaned against a sturdy wooden beam, watching her. He waited until she finished, her movements precise and economical, before speaking, his voice a low murmur that didn't startle her.

"You know, Mara," he began, his gaze steady as it met hers, "I've been thinking a lot about how we work together. Not just here, at the center, but... beyond." He paused, allowing the words to settle. "I've seen relationships where one person feels like they're always carrying the other, or where one person's dreams get put on hold indefinitely for the sake of the other. That's not a partnership, not to me."

Mara paused in her task, her pen hovering over the ledger. She met his gaze, a hint of curiosity in her eyes, but no alarm. She had come to trust that Eli's quiet moments of reflection often led to insights that were both profound and gently delivered.

"What is it, then?" she asked, her voice calm, receptive.

Eli pushed himself off the beam, taking a few slow steps towards her. He didn't crowd her space, but rather stood at a comfortable distance, his presence reassuring rather than imposing. "It's about seeing each other, truly seeing each other, and valuing what each person brings to the table. It's about acknowledging that we both have our own strengths, our own individual paths, and that those paths can intersect in a way that elevates both of us, without diminishing either."

He gestured vaguely towards the vast expanse of the sea visible through the open doorway. "Think about the ocean. It's immense, powerful, and it has its own currents, its own tides. But it also exists in relation to the land, to the sky. It shapes the coast, and the coast shapes it, in a constant, dynamic exchange. It's not one trying to conquer the other, but a continuous interaction."

He saw a flicker of understanding in her eyes. "So, you're saying a partnership is like that? Independent entities, but with a profound connection and influence on each other?"

"Exactly," Eli affirmed, a genuine smile touching his lips. "It's about mutual respect for autonomy. It means I don't expect you to be a second me, and I hope you don't expect me to be a second you. My vision is that we can build something together, a shared life, a shared future, but from a place of two complete individuals. It's about collaboration, not assimilation. It's about supporting each other's growth, even when that growth might take us in slightly different directions for a time."

He remembered his own father, a man of gruff practicality who had always viewed marriage as a business arrangement. There was love, yes, but it was often expressed through provision and protection, not through open emotional dialogue. Eli had watched him, and he'd seen the unspoken burdens his mother carried, the quiet compromises she made. It had left him with a deep-seated desire for something more reciprocal, a partnership where vulnerability was not a weakness to be hidden, but a bridge to deeper understanding.

"My parents," Eli continued, his voice softening with a touch of nostalgia, "they loved each other deeply, I know that. But they communicated mostly through action, through doing things for each other. There wasn't much... talking about feelings. My dad was a bit like you used to be, Mara, very self-contained. He believed a man's job was to provide and protect, and that sharing your worries made you less of a man. I saw how much that cost him, and perhaps it cost my mother too, in ways she never expressed."

He met Mara's gaze again, his expression open and earnest. "I learned from that. I learned that strength isn't about never showing cracks. It's about being able to show them, to admit when you're struggling, and to trust that the person standing beside you won't use it against you, but will instead offer a hand. For me, true strength is in that vulnerability, in the courage to be open. It's in recognizing that you don't have to carry every burden alone."

He was consciously sharing this, not to elicit sympathy, but to demonstrate the kind of openness he envisioned for them. He wanted Mara to see that his commitment wasn't about possession or control, but about a shared journey. He wanted to show her that he valued her independence, her capabilities, and that his desire was to build *with* her, not to build *over* her.

"I've always believed," Eli elaborated, choosing his words with care, "that in a partnership, you have to actively create space for the other person's dreams and aspirations. It's not enough to just not stand in their way. You have to be a willing participant, an active supporter. If one person's vision is the only one that gets pursued, then eventually, resentment will build, and the foundation will start to erode. It's like a shared garden; you can't just plant your favorite flowers and expect the other person to be happy with only seeing your choices bloom. You have to tend to both, nurture both, and sometimes, even plant seeds that neither of you anticipated, but that grow into something beautiful for both of you."

He looked down at his hands for a moment, a rare show of introspection. "I've made mistakes in the past, trying to be the provider, the fixer. I've sometimes assumed I knew what was best, or I've tried to shield people from difficult truths, thinking

I was protecting them. But I learned that often, people need the truth, and they need to face challenges themselves, with your support, not in place of it. It's about trusting their ability to navigate, just as you'd want them to trust yours."

Mara listened intently, her earlier task momentarily forgotten. Eli's words resonated with a quiet conviction that felt both profound and deeply personal. She recognized the underlying philosophy, the deliberate effort to build something different, something more equitable than what she had witnessed or experienced in the past. His vision wasn't about grand pronouncements or overwhelming gestures, but about the steady, consistent cultivation of mutual respect and shared endeavor.

"So, your commitment," Mara ventured, her voice thoughtful, "it's not about claiming ownership, but about offering a shared space, a mutual investment?"

Eli met her gaze, his eyes alight with understanding. "Precisely. It's about saying, 'I see you, I value you, and I want to walk this road with you, not as your guide or your follower, but as your partner.' It means celebrating your victories as if they were my own, and it means standing with you when things get tough, not to take over, but to help you find your footing. It means understanding that sometimes your needs will take precedence, and other times mine will, and that's not a sign of imbalance, but of the ebb and flow of life itself."

He thought of the many conversations he'd had with the older fishermen in town, men who had spent their lives navigating the capricious seas, and in doing so, had learned the fundamental principles of interdependence. They knew that no single boat could control the weather, but a fleet, working together, sharing information, and lending a hand, could weather almost any storm. He saw that same wisdom in the quiet way Mara approached her work, and in the growing ease between them.

"I've learned a lot from watching people here," Eli admitted, his gaze drifting towards the open door, where the afternoon sun cast long shadows across the weathered wooden floor. "I've seen couples who finish each other's sentences, not because they're telepathic, but because they've spent years truly listening to each other. I've seen people who have built businesses together, and the success wasn't just about one person's drive, but about how they complemented each other's skills. And I've seen relationships that faltered, and often, it was because one person felt unseen, unheard, or unappreciated. That's the kind of partnership I don't want. I want the kind that grows stronger with time, like a well-anchored vessel that becomes more resilient with every tide."

He turned back to Mara, his expression earnest. "What I want to build with you, Mara, is something that allows both of us to thrive, individually and together. It's about creating a shared vision, but not one that erases our individual perspectives. It's about shared responsibility, but not about a rigid division of labor. It's about recognizing that we're two different people, with different experiences and different ways of seeing the world, and that those differences are not obstacles, but the very things that can make our partnership richer, more dynamic, and more resilient. It's about making conscious choices, every day, to invest in each other, to communicate openly, and to approach any challenges as a team."

He saw a subtle shift in her posture, a softening around her eyes. He knew that for Mara, who had guarded her independence so fiercely, the concept of partnership might feel like a potential threat to her autonomy. He wanted to alleviate that fear, to show her that his vision was one of amplification, not absorption.

"I'm not looking to change who you are, Mara," Eli said, his voice low and sincere. "I admire your strength, your intelligence, your self-reliance. My hope is that my presence in your life, and our growing connection, can be a support, a complementary force, not a replacement for any of that. I envision a partnership where we can lean on each other, share our burdens and our joys, and grow together. It means being willing to be vulnerable, to share our fears as well as our triumphs, and to trust that we will be met with understanding and acceptance. It means being committed to the process, to the ongoing work of building and nurturing this connection, even when it's not easy."

He paused, letting the weight of his words settle. He wanted her to understand that this wasn't a passive wish, but an active intention. He was committed to demonstrating this ideal, not just in words, but in his actions. His focus wasn't solely on the grand gestures or the romantic moments, but on the foundational aspects of their relationship – the trust, the communication, the mutual respect that could weather any storm. The quiet, reflective nature of their coastal town, with its constant reminder of nature's power and the importance of community, had instilled in him a deep appreciation for these foundational elements.

"It's about building a life together, brick by brick," Eli concluded, his voice filled with a quiet conviction. "Not a life where one person dictates the design, but one where we both contribute, where we both have a say, and where we both feel proud of what we create. It's about choosing, every day, to invest in 'us,' while still honoring and nurturing the 'you' and the 'me.' That, to me, is the heart of a true partnership."

The hushed quiet of the rescue center, usually a place of urgent activity and the comforting scent of antiseptic and sea salt, had taken on a new quality. It was a stillness that wasn't empty, but filled with the unspoken, with a new kind of awareness that had begun to bloom between Eli and Mara. It was in the way their gazes lingered a moment longer, in the gentle exhalation of breath that signaled understanding without words, in the shared smiles that acknowledged a deeper, more intimate truth. This was the nascent stage of their shared vulnerability, a delicate unfolding that promised to reshape the very foundations of their connection.

Mara found herself sharing anxieties she hadn't voiced to anyone, not even her closest friends. The weight of responsibility, the constant pressure to perform, the fear of failure – these had been private battles she waged in the solitude of her own mind. But with Eli, they began to surface, not as complaints or demands, but as quiet confessions whispered into the soft evening air. One evening, as they were cleaning equipment after a particularly harrowing rescue, she confessed, "Sometimes, Eli, I feel like I'm just... treading water. Like I'm doing enough to stay afloat, but not enough to truly move forward. And I worry that if I admit that, if I show that I'm not always strong, that I'll... I'll disappoint everyone. Myself included."

Eli didn't immediately offer a solution or a platitude. Instead, he set down the syringe he was holding, his movements slow and deliberate. He simply walked over to her, not to touch, but to stand beside her, his presence a solid, reassuring anchor. He looked out the window at the darkening sea, the waves lapping gently against the shore, a familiar rhythm that had always been a source of solace. "I understand that feeling, Mara," he said, his voice low and steady. "The pressure to be capable, to be the one who has all the answers. It's a heavy burden to carry alone." He turned to her then, his eyes reflecting the dim light from the room. "But you're not alone in feeling that way. I've felt it too. Moments where the tide feels too strong, where you question if you have the strength to keep swimming."

His words weren't a dismissal of her feelings, but an affirmation of them. He didn't try to fix her worry; he simply acknowledged its validity and shared a similar experience. It was this mirroring, this quiet validation, that began to build the bridge. It wasn't about offering advice; it was about offering companionship in the face of doubt. He understood, perhaps more than she realized, the deeply ingrained instinct to project an image of unwavering competence, especially in their line of work. He'd seen it in his father, in his colleagues, and he'd wrestled with it himself.

"There are days," Eli continued, his gaze thoughtful, "when I look at the challenges we face here, the sheer scale of need, and I feel utterly overwhelmed. The sheer impossibility of it all can be paralyzing. I don't always admit that out loud, even to myself. It's easier to focus on the next task, the immediate problem. But knowing that there's someone else who understands that underlying fear, that undercurrent of 'what if I'm not enough?'... that makes it easier to face the dawn."

He spoke not as a leader offering reassurance, but as a fellow traveler admitting to his own navigation of difficult terrain. He was revealing a part of himself that was less polished, less certain, and in doing so, he was creating a safe harbor for Mara's own nascent vulnerability. It was a radical departure from the stoic self-reliance she had cultivated for so long. This wasn't about weakness; it was about a shared humanity, a recognition that perfection was an illusion and that true strength lay in the courage to be imperfect, together.

"It's like the sea itself," Mara murmured, her voice barely a whisper, finding an analogy in their shared environment. "We see its power, its vastness, and we respect it. But we also know it has its calms, its moments of terrifying storms, and its unpredictable currents. We don't pretend it's always serene, do we? We prepare for its moods. And perhaps... perhaps we can do the same with our own internal landscapes."

Eli nodded, a gentle smile playing on his lips. "Exactly. We don't deny the storms, Mara. We learn to navigate them. And when we can share the watch, when we can call out warnings to each other, or simply offer a steady hand on the tiller, the journey becomes not just survivable, but... bearable. Even, dare I say, meaningful." He paused, the silence stretching comfortably between them. "Admitting you're struggling isn't a sign of failure; it's an invitation for connection. It's saying, 'I'm human, and I need a fellow human to stand with me, not to fix me, but to simply be present.'"

He remembered a time in his early twenties, a period of intense self-doubt and a failed business venture. He'd felt adrift, ashamed, and utterly alone. He'd kept it bottled up, projecting an image of success he didn't feel, until a close friend, noticing his withdrawal, had gently confronted him. "Eli," he'd said, his voice full of concern, "you don't have to pretend with me. Whatever it is, we can face it." That simple act of being seen, of being allowed to be imperfect, had been a lifeline. He wanted to offer that same lifeline to Mara, to create a space where the masks could come off, where the carefully constructed facades could be set aside.

"It's about trusting each other with the parts of ourselves we're most afraid to show," Eli added, his gaze steady and earnest. "The doubts, the insecurities, the moments of absolute uncertainty. When you share those, it's not an act of weakness, but an act of profound courage. It says, 'I trust you with my vulnerability, and I believe you will honor it.'" He took a breath, his voice deepening slightly. "And when that trust is met with empathy, with understanding, rather than judgment or dismissal, it creates a bond that's incredibly strong. It's an intimacy that goes beyond shared experiences; it's an intimacy of the soul."

He saw a flicker of something akin to relief in Mara's eyes. It was a subtle shift, a slight softening of the tension she habitually carried in her shoulders. She had spent so much of her life in a posture of self-sufficiency, of guarding her inner world. The idea that vulnerability could be a strength, a pathway to deeper connection, was a revolutionary concept for her.

"I think," Mara said slowly, carefully choosing her words, "that for so long, I've equated emotional openness with being exposed, with being vulnerable to attack. I've seen it happen to others, seen how people can use perceived weaknesses against them. So, I built walls. High ones." She offered a small, self-deprecating smile. "But you're right. Treading water is exhausting. And sharing the burden... it feels less like a burden and more like a shared endeavor."

Eli reached out then, his hand hovering for a moment before gently covering hers on the counter. His touch was warm, firm, and reassuring. It wasn't a possessive gesture, but a simple, quiet affirmation of connection. "And we can build those walls together, Mara," he said softly. "Not to keep each other out, but to protect what we're building between us. A safe space where we can both be our truest selves, flaws and all. We can learn to lower them, strategically, when we feel safe, and raise them when we need to regroup. It's not about dismantling them entirely, but about learning to manage them, together."

He envisioned their relationship not as a perfect, polished facade, but as a sturdy, well-loved cottage, weathered by the elements but filled with warmth and light. The imperfections – the slightly creaky floorboards, the occasional draft – would be part of its charm, part of its history. They would be reminders of their resilience, of their ability to adapt and to find comfort within its walls, no matter what the weather outside.

"It's like when a ship is damaged at sea," Eli continued, his thoughts weaving a new metaphor. "The crew doesn't just abandon it. They work together. They patch the holes, they bail out the water, they conserve their resources. They might be scared, they might be exhausted, but they have each other. They share the fear, and they share the work. And in that shared struggle, a camaraderie is forged that can be stronger than any storm. They don't pretend the damage isn't there; they acknowledge it, and they work through it, side by side."

He saw Mara's gaze soften as she looked at their joined hands, a silent acknowledgment of the shift occurring between them. The language of shared vulnerability wasn't spoken in grand pronouncements, but in these quiet moments of shared presence, of mutual acknowledgment. It was in the simple act of admitting a fear, and having it met not with solutions, but with quiet understanding and a shared breath. It was in the realization that true intimacy wasn't about being flawless, but about being seen, fully and completely, and still being cherished.

"The hardest part, I think," Mara confessed, her voice a little shaky, "is accepting that I'm not responsible for fixing everyone else's problems, or even for being the one to always offer comfort. Sometimes, I just need to be comforted. And that feels... selfish, somehow. Like I'm not pulling my weight."

Eli squeezed her hand gently. "It's not selfish, Mara. It's human. And it's part of a partnership. You pour into me, and I pour into you. It's a reciprocal flow. If one person is always the giver, the reservoir eventually runs dry. My goal isn't to have you be a perpetual wellspring of strength. My goal is for us to be each other's shelter, each other's replenishment. When you're tired, I want to be able to offer you a place to rest. When I'm struggling, I want to know I can lean on you, not to have you solve my problems, but simply to be a steady presence."

He looked around the rescue center, the familiar equipment now seeming to hum with a new potential. This space, which had always been about saving lives, was becoming a space where their own emotional lives were being nurtured and strengthened. The challenges of their work, the inherent risks and uncertainties, were not being ignored, but were serving as fertile ground for a deeper, more resilient connection.

"Think about the stories we hear from the fishermen," Eli mused, drawing another parallel from their coastal existence. "They talk about the storms they've weathered, the close calls, the sheer terror. But they also talk about the bonds forged in those moments. The way they relied on each other, the unspoken understanding that passed between them. It's not just about surviving; it's about how those experiences shape them, how they become stronger, more connected through shared hardship."

He met Mara's gaze again, his expression open and sincere. "And that's what I see for us, Mara. Not a relationship devoid of challenges, but one where our challenges, our vulnerabilities, become the very things that bind us closer. Where admitting a fear doesn't weaken us, but allows us to access a deeper well of strength, together. Where the courage to be imperfect becomes our greatest asset." He held her gaze, his unspoken promise hanging in the air: that he was willing to walk this path with her, to embrace the messy, beautiful reality of shared vulnerability, and to build something enduring, something true, on the bedrock of their shared humanity. The gentle sound of the waves outside seemed to echo his sentiment, a constant, rhythmic reminder that even in its vastness and power, the ocean found its balance, its depth, in the ebb and flow, in the constant, intimate exchange with the shore.

The rhythmic sigh of the waves against the shore had been a constant soundtrack to Mara and Eli's developing connection. Yet, as the sanctuary of the rescue center hummed with the quiet urgency of their evolving relationship, the predictable cadence of the ocean was soon to be disrupted by a far more terrestrial turbulence. Internal friction, simmering beneath the surface like unseen currents, began to pull at the fabric of their collaborative efforts, demanding not just their attention, but their seasoned problem-solving skills.

It began with a subtle shift in the demeanor of the rescue center's seasoned veterinarian, Dr. Aris Thorne. A man who had dedicated decades to the welfare of marine life, Thorne possessed a gruff exterior that masked a fiercely protective heart. He was a creature of habit, his routines meticulously crafted over years of experience, and any deviation from them, however minor, was met with a sharp disapproval. The unspoken understanding that had begun to bloom between Mara and Eli, a silent acknowledgment of shared vulnerability and burgeoning affection, did not escape his notice, nor did it entirely earn his approval. He saw it as a potential distraction, a softening of the hard edges required for their vital work.

The first overt sign of this tension manifested during a routine morning briefing. A pod of dolphins had been sighted stranded on a less accessible stretch of coast, a situation requiring immediate, coordinated action. Eli, as always, was preparing to outline the logistical strategy, his focus sharp and his words concise. Mara, however, had a slightly different approach in mind, one that involved a more immediate, almost intuitive, deployment of specific rescue personnel based on their individual strengths and past successes with similar situations.

"Eli, with the currents in that cove, I think Anya would be best suited for the initial water retrieval. She's got that steady hand with the smaller juveniles, and her swimming speed is unparalleled when the tide's this high," Mara suggested, her voice calm but firm.

Eli paused, considering. "Anya's speed is a factor, yes, but Liam's experience with anchoring in rough surf is critical for the main retrieval net. We need him securing the lines first."

It was a difference in tactical approach, a minor disagreement in the grand scheme of things, but Dr. Thorne's voice cut through the air, sharp as a gulls cry. "Are we strategizing or reminiscing about past rescues? The dolphins aren't going to wait for us to hold hands and sing kumbaya. Eli's plan is sound. Stick to the established protocol, Mara. Efficiency, not sentiment, is what saves lives here."

The words landed like a cold spray, stinging and unexpected. Mara felt a familiar flush creep up her neck, a defensive warmth that she'd learned to control over years of navigating a male-dominated field. She glanced at Eli, who had stiffened slightly at Thorne's pronouncement. His jaw was tight, and his gaze, usually so open when he looked at her, had become guarded, almost wary. It was as if Thorne's blunt assessment had not only highlighted their professional differences but had also subtly cast their developing personal connection in a negative light, an accusation of undue emotional influence on their work.

"With all due respect, Doctor," Mara responded, her voice even, though the tremor of suppressed emotion was a subtle undercurrent, "my suggestion was based on Anya's proven success in precisely these types of swift-water rescues. Liam is an excellent anchor, but Anya's agility in those conditions can mean the difference between a successful retrieval and further distress for the animals. It's not sentiment; it's informed strategy."

Eli stepped in, his tone measured, though the underlying tension was palpable. "Perhaps we can incorporate both. Liam will secure the anchor lines as planned. Once the primary net is stable, Anya can take point on the juvenile retrieval, with a secondary team ready to assist if needed. Does that address both concerns?"

Thorne grunted, a sound that conveyed grudging acceptance rather than genuine agreement. "As long as the primary objective – securing the pod – remains paramount. Now, move out. Time is a luxury we don't have."

The mission itself was successful, a testament to the team's underlying competence and Eli and Mara's ability to find a working compromise even under duress. However, the seed of discord had been sown. In the days that followed, a palpable coolness settled between Mara and Eli, not an absence of feeling, but a forced professionalism that masked the subtle erosion of their newfound ease. Thorne's words had, perhaps unintentionally, created a wedge, making Mara hyper-aware of any interaction with Eli that could be misconstrued as unprofessional, and making Eli, in turn, more cautious, more guarded.

The internal conflict escalated when a critical piece of equipment, the specialized transport cradle used for larger stranded animals, malfunctioned spectacularly during a routine maintenance check. It was a vital piece of machinery, its smooth operation essential for safely moving the often-fragile rescued creatures from the beach to the rehabilitation pools. The cradle, a complex arrangement of hydraulics and padded supports, had been showing signs of wear, a fact that had been noted in the maintenance logs, but its failure was more sudden and severe than anticipated.

Eli, who had been overseeing the cradle's diagnostics, was the first to discover the extent of the damage. A crucial hydraulic line had ruptured, leaking fluid and rendering the entire mechanism immobile. The timing was disastrous; a young, injured whale calf had been brought ashore just hours before, its condition fragile and requiring immediate transfer.

"Damn it!" Eli's frustration boomed through the workshop, a stark contrast to his usual controlled demeanor. He kicked lightly at the base of the inert cradle, the metallic clang echoing his own internal shock. He knew Thorne would be furious; the cradle was his responsibility, and its failure reflected poorly on the entire operation, and by extension, on him.

Mara arrived moments later, drawn by the sound of Eli's outburst. She saw the scene immediately – the pools of hydraulic fluid on the floor, the disabled cradle, and Eli's rigid posture, his shoulders hunched with a familiar weight of responsibility that now seemed amplified by anger.

"What happened?" she asked, her voice soft, a stark contrast to the storm brewing around him.

Eli turned, his eyes dark with a mixture of anger and exhaustion. "The hydraulic line. It blew. Completely. Thorne's going to have my head. He warned us about pushing it too hard, about the wear and tear." He ran a hand through his already disheveled hair. "And I *told* him we needed to prioritize its replacement after the last seal rescue. But he insisted we focus on the sonar equipment. Now look. We're stuck. And that calf... he's not going to wait."

Mara's immediate instinct was to offer comfort, to soothe his frustration. But the memory of Thorne's earlier admonishment, and Eli's subsequent withdrawal, held her back. She recognized the familiar pattern of his self-reliance, his tendency to internalize blame, and she understood that Thorne's critique, however blunt, had resonated. She saw how it had reinforced his internal narrative of always being the one to solve problems, and how the pressure to do so was now manifesting as anger.

"It's not entirely your fault, Eli," she began, choosing her words carefully. "We all agreed on the sonar equipment's priority. It was a collective decision, based on the information we had at the time."

"But I'm the one in charge of the equipment maintenance," Eli countered, his voice strained. "I should have pushed harder. I should have foreseen this. Now, we have a distressed calf, and no way to move it safely. We'll have to improvise, and that's always a risk." He turned away from her, his gaze fixed on the immobile cradle as if it were a personal failing.

Mara felt a pang of disappointment, a subtle ache in her chest. He was shutting her out, retreating into his familiar fortress of self-blame. The emotional bridge they had been carefully constructing seemed to be buckling under the unexpected strain. This was precisely the kind of situation where their newfound understanding should have come into play – where she could offer him the space to express his frustration without judgment, and where he could accept that vulnerability, even in the face of professional setbacks, was not a sign of weakness.

"Eli," she said, her voice gaining a new firmness, a gentle but insistent tone that cut through his self-recrimination. "Look at me."

He hesitated for a moment, then slowly turned back to face her. His eyes were shadowed with fatigue, and a flicker of something akin to desperation lurked beneath the anger.

"We're not going to improvise with a distressed calf," Mara stated, her gaze unwavering. "That's not our way. We find solutions. And we do it together. You're not responsible for every single thing that goes wrong, Eli. You're one person. And I'm here. We are a team. Remember what we talked about? About sharing the burden?"

She took a tentative step towards him, her hand reaching out, not to touch, but to hover in the space between them, a silent offering of support. "You identified the problem. You know the extent of the damage. That's not a failure; that's the first step to finding a fix. Now, let's figure out how to get that calf to the pool without using the cradle. What do we have? Tarps? Stretchers? Extra hands from the shore patrol?"

Eli looked at her, truly looked at her, and saw not accusation or pity, but a steady, unwavering resolve. He saw the same determination that had inspired him from the moment he first met her, the quiet strength that underpinned her empathy.

He recognized that his instinct to blame himself was a deeply ingrained habit, but her presence was a reminder that he didn't have to carry that weight alone.

"The shore patrol," he murmured, his voice losing some of its harsh edge. "They have a reinforced cargo net we use for debris removal. It's... not ideal, but it's sturdy."

"And we can use the all-terrain vehicles to bring it closer," Mara added, her mind already racing through the possibilities. "We'll need to create a clear path, ensure the terrain is stable. We'll need to work quickly, but carefully. And Thorne will need to be informed. He needs to know we have a plan."

Eli took a deep breath, the tension in his shoulders easing slightly. He saw not just a colleague, but a partner, stepping up, not to fix him, but to stand with him. The external pressure from Thorne, the internal pressure of responsibility, and the immediate crisis with the calf – all of it was still there, but it felt less overwhelming when faced with Mara's unwavering support.

"Alright," Eli said, his voice regaining its steady rhythm, though it was now imbued with a renewed sense of collaboration. "Let's brief the shore patrol. And you're right, we need to inform Thorne. I'll handle that, but I want you there with me."

The decision to inform Thorne together was a significant one. It was an acknowledgment that their professional lives, and their personal connection, were intertwined, and that they would face challenges as a unit, not as isolated individuals. As they walked towards Thorne's office, the air between them still held a residual tension from the cradle incident, but it was now overlaid with a nascent sense of solidarity.

Thorne's reaction was, as Eli had predicted, gruff. He paced his small office, his weathered face set in a grim line as Eli explained the situation, Mara standing quietly beside him, her presence a subtle anchor.

"A ruptured hydraulic line?" Thorne's voice was a low growl. "I warned you about that cradle. It's been groaning for months. You should have pushed harder for that replacement, Eli. You know how critical that piece of equipment is."

Eli met Thorne's gaze, his own steady. "I understand, Doctor. We made a judgment call based on the immediate needs of the sonar upgrade. It was a calculated risk, and it didn't pay off. We're not going to let that jeopardize the calf's well-being. Mara and I have a plan to transfer it using the shore patrol's cargo net and the ATVs."

Mara stepped forward, her voice clear and confident. "We've assessed the terrain, Doctor. The ATV access is viable, and the net is strong enough. We'll ensure the calf is handled with the utmost care during the transfer. We've also notified the rehabilitation team to prepare the pool and have a vet on standby."

Thorne stopped pacing and looked from Eli to Mara, his expression unreadable for a moment. He saw not defiance, but competence. He saw not a romantic entanglement threatening to derail their work, but two individuals who, despite a significant setback, were collaborating effectively to mitigate the damage. The tension between them, which he had interpreted as a distraction, now appeared to him as a shared responsibility, a mutual reliance that was, in its own way, a form of strength.

"A cargo net," Thorne mused, stroking his chin. "Crude, but it might work. As long as you're both absolutely certain about the stability of the terrain. One wrong move with that calf, and it could be more harm than good. Ensure clear communication with the shore patrol. No room for error." He finally met Eli's eyes, then Mara's. "See that it's done. And Eli, you'll personally oversee the repairs to that cradle. I want a full report on my desk by Monday, detailing the failure and the proposed solution. And no more cutting corners on maintenance. Is that understood?"

"Yes, Doctor," Eli replied, a sense of relief washing over him. Thorne's acknowledgment, however curt, was a form of acceptance.

As they left Thorne's office, the immediate crisis averted, a different kind of understanding settled between Mara and Eli. The professional conflict, the equipment failure, and Thorne's gruff disapproval had served as an unexpected crucible, testing the strength of their burgeoning connection. They had navigated it not by retreating into their own spaces, but by actively choosing to face it together.

"He's still going to be a challenge," Mara said quietly, as they walked back towards the rehabilitation area.

Eli nodded, a faint smile touching his lips. "He is. But we handled it. We presented a united front, and we had a solution. That's what matters." He paused, his gaze meeting hers. "Thank you, Mara. For... not letting me get lost in the blame. For reminding me that we're a team."

The unspoken acknowledgment hung in the air between them, a silent testament to the growth they were experiencing. The rescue center, a place of healing and recovery for marine life, was also becoming a space where their own emotional resilience and their capacity for deep, abiding connection were being forged. The ceaseless motion of the ocean outside, with its unpredictable tides and powerful currents, seemed to mirror the complexities of their own lives, a constant reminder that even in the face of turbulence, finding an anchor in each other was the truest form of strength. The challenges they faced, both in their work and within themselves, were not obstacles to their relationship, but rather the very elements that were shaping it into something robust, something enduring, something profoundly real.

The rhythmic sigh of the waves against the shore had been a constant soundtrack to Mara and Eli's developing connection. Yet, as the sanctuary of the rescue center hummed with the quiet urgency of their evolving relationship, the predictable cadence of the ocean was soon to be disrupted by a far more terrestrial turbulence. Internal friction, simmering beneath the surface like unseen currents, began to pull at the fabric of their collaborative efforts, demanding not just their attention, but their seasoned problem-solving skills.

It began with a subtle shift in the demeanor of the rescue center's seasoned veterinarian, Dr. Aris Thorne. A man who had dedicated decades to the welfare of marine life, Thorne possessed a gruff exterior that masked a fiercely protective heart. He was a creature of habit, his routines meticulously crafted over years of experience, and any deviation from them, however minor, was met with a sharp disapproval. The unspoken understanding that had begun to bloom between Mara and Eli, a silent acknowledgment of shared vulnerability and burgeoning affection, did not escape his notice, nor did it entirely earn his approval. He saw it as a potential distraction, a softening of the hard edges required for their vital work.

The first overt sign of this tension manifested during a routine morning briefing. A pod of dolphins had been sighted stranded on a less accessible stretch of coast, a situation requiring immediate, coordinated action. Eli, as always, was preparing to outline the logistical strategy, his focus sharp and his words concise. Mara, however, had a slightly different approach in mind, one that involved a more immediate, almost intuitive, deployment of specific rescue personnel based on their individual strengths and past successes with similar situations.

"Eli, with the currents in that cove, I think Anya would be best suited for the initial water retrieval. She's got that steady hand with the smaller juveniles, and her swimming speed is unparalleled when the tide's this high," Mara suggested, her voice calm but firm.

Eli paused, considering. "Anya's speed is a factor, yes, but Liam's experience with anchoring in rough surf is critical for the main retrieval net. We need him securing the lines first."

It was a difference in tactical approach, a minor disagreement in the grand scheme of things, but Dr. Thorne's voice cut through the air, sharp as a gulls cry. "Are we strategizing or reminiscing about past rescues? The dolphins aren't going to wait for us to hold hands and sing kumbaya. Eli's plan is sound. Stick to the established protocol, Mara. Efficiency, not sentiment, is what saves lives here."

The words landed like a cold spray, stinging and unexpected. Mara felt a familiar flush creep up her neck, a defensive warmth that she'd learned to control over years of navigating a male-dominated field. She glanced at Eli, who had stiffened slightly at Thorne's pronouncement. His jaw was tight, and his gaze, usually so open when he looked at her, had become guarded, almost wary. It was as if Thorne's blunt assessment had not only highlighted their professional differences but had also subtly cast their developing personal connection in a negative light, an accusation of undue emotional influence on their work.

"With all due respect, Doctor," Mara responded, her voice even, though the tremor of suppressed emotion was a subtle undercurrent, "my suggestion was based on Anya's proven success in precisely these types of swift-water rescues. Liam is an excellent anchor, but Anya's agility in those conditions can mean the difference between a successful retrieval and further distress for the animals. It's not sentiment; it's informed strategy."

Eli stepped in, his tone measured, though the underlying tension was palpable. "Perhaps we can incorporate both. Liam will secure the anchor lines as planned. Once the primary net is stable, Anya can take point on the juvenile retrieval, with a secondary team ready to assist if needed. Does that address both concerns?"

Thorne grunted, a sound that conveyed grudging acceptance rather than genuine agreement. "As long as the primary objective – securing the pod – remains paramount. Now, move out. Time is a luxury we don't have."

The mission itself was successful, a testament to the team's underlying competence and Eli and Mara's ability to find a working compromise even under duress. However, the seed of discord had been sown. In the days that followed, a palpable coolness settled between Mara and Eli, not an absence of feeling, but a forced professionalism that masked the subtle erosion of their newfound ease. Thorne's words had, perhaps unintentionally, created a wedge, making Mara hyper-aware of any interaction with Eli that could be misconstrued as unprofessional, and making Eli, in turn, more cautious, more guarded.

The internal conflict escalated when a critical piece of equipment, the specialized transport cradle used for larger stranded animals, malfunctioned spectacularly during a routine maintenance check. It was a vital piece of machinery, its smooth operation essential for safely moving the often-fragile rescued creatures from the beach to the rehabilitation pools. The cradle, a complex arrangement of hydraulics and padded supports, had been showing signs of wear, a fact that had been noted in the maintenance logs, but its failure was more sudden and severe than anticipated.

Eli, who had been overseeing the cradle's diagnostics, was the first to discover the extent of the damage. A crucial hydraulic line had ruptured, leaking fluid and rendering the entire mechanism immobile. The timing was disastrous; a young, injured whale calf had been brought ashore just hours before, its condition fragile and requiring immediate transfer.

"Damn it!" Eli's frustration boomed through the workshop, a stark contrast to his usual controlled demeanor. He kicked lightly at the base of the inert cradle, the metallic clang echoing his own internal shock. He knew Thorne would be furious; the cradle was his responsibility, and its failure reflected poorly on the entire operation, and by extension, on him.

Mara arrived moments later, drawn by the sound of Eli's outburst. She saw the scene immediately – the pools of hydraulic fluid on the floor, the disabled cradle, and Eli's rigid posture, his shoulders hunched with a familiar weight of responsibility that now seemed amplified by anger.

"What happened?" she asked, her voice soft, a stark contrast to the storm brewing around him.

Eli turned, his eyes dark with a mixture of anger and exhaustion. "The hydraulic line. It blew. Completely. Thorne's going to have my head. He warned us about pushing it too hard, about the wear and tear." He ran a hand through his already disheveled hair. "And I *told* him we needed to prioritize its replacement after the last seal rescue. But he insisted we focus on the sonar equipment. Now look. We're stuck. And that calf... he's not going to wait."

Mara's immediate instinct was to offer comfort, to soothe his frustration. But the memory of Thorne's earlier admonishment, and Eli's subsequent withdrawal, held her back. She recognized the familiar pattern of his self-reliance, his tendency to internalize blame, and she understood that Thorne's critique, however blunt, had resonated. She saw how it had reinforced his internal narrative of always being the one to solve problems, and how the pressure to do so was now manifesting as anger.

"It's not entirely your fault, Eli," she began, choosing her words carefully. "We all agreed on the sonar equipment's priority. It was a collective decision, based on the information we had at the time.”

“But I’m the one in charge of the equipment maintenance,” Eli countered, his voice strained. “I should have pushed harder. I should have foreseen this. Now, we have a distressed calf, and no way to move it safely. We’ll have to improvise, and that’s always a risk.” He turned away from her, his gaze fixed on the immobile cradle as if it were a personal failing.

Mara felt a pang of disappointment, a subtle ache in her chest. He was shutting her out, retreating into his familiar fortress of self-blame. The emotional bridge they had been carefully constructing seemed to be buckling under the unexpected strain. This was precisely the kind of situation where their newfound understanding should have come into play – where she could offer him the space to express his frustration without judgment, and where he could accept that vulnerability, even in the face of professional setbacks, was not a sign of weakness.

“Eli,” she said, her voice gaining a new firmness, a gentle but insistent tone that cut through his self-recrimination. “Look at me.”

He hesitated for a moment, then slowly turned back to face her. His eyes were shadowed with fatigue, and a flicker of something akin to desperation lurked beneath the anger.

“We’re not going to improvise with a distressed calf,” Mara stated, her gaze unwavering. “That’s not our way. We find solutions. And we do it together. You're not responsible for every single thing that goes wrong, Eli. You're one person. And I'm here. We are a team. Remember what we talked about? About sharing the burden?"

She took a tentative step towards him, her hand reaching out, not to touch, but to hover in the space between them, a silent offering of support. "You identified the problem. You know the extent of the damage. That's not a failure; that's the first step to finding a fix. Now, let's figure out how to get that calf to the pool without using the cradle. What do we have? Tarps? Stretchers? Extra hands from the shore patrol?"

Eli looked at her, truly looked at her, and saw not accusation or pity, but a steady, unwavering resolve. He saw the same determination that had inspired him from the moment he first met her, the quiet strength that underpinned her empathy. He recognized that his instinct to blame himself was a deeply ingrained habit, but her presence was a reminder that he didn't have to carry that weight alone.

"The shore patrol," he murmured, his voice losing some of its harsh edge. "They have a reinforced cargo net we use for debris removal. It's... not ideal, but it's sturdy."

"And we can use the all-terrain vehicles to bring it closer," Mara added, her mind already racing through the possibilities. "We'll need to create a clear path, ensure the terrain is stable. We'll need to work quickly, but carefully. And Thorne will need to be informed. He needs to know we have a plan."

Eli took a deep breath, the tension in his shoulders easing slightly. He saw not just a colleague, but a partner, stepping up, not to fix him, but to stand with him. The external pressure from Thorne, the internal pressure of responsibility, and the immediate crisis with the calf – all of it was still there, but it felt less overwhelming when faced with Mara's unwavering support.

"Alright," Eli said, his voice regaining its steady rhythm, though it was now imbued with a renewed sense of collaboration. "Let's brief the shore patrol. And you're right, we need to inform Thorne. I'll handle that, but I want you there with me."

The decision to inform Thorne together was a significant one. It was an acknowledgment that their professional lives, and their personal connection, were intertwined, and that they would face challenges as a unit, not as isolated individuals. As they walked towards Thorne's office, the air between them still held a residual tension from the cradle incident, but it was now overlaid with a nascent sense of solidarity.

Thorne's reaction was, as Eli had predicted, gruff. He paced his small office, his weathered face set in a grim line as Eli explained the situation, Mara standing quietly beside him, her presence a subtle anchor.

"A ruptured hydraulic line?" Thorne's voice was a low growl. "I warned you about that cradle. It's been groaning for months. You should have pushed harder for that replacement, Eli. You know how critical that piece of equipment is."

Eli met Thorne's gaze, his own steady. "I understand, Doctor. We made a judgment call based on the immediate needs of the sonar upgrade. It was a calculated risk, and it didn't pay off. We're not going to let that jeopardize the calf's well-being. Mara and I have a plan to transfer it using the shore patrol's cargo net and the ATVs."

Mara stepped forward, her voice clear and confident. "We've assessed the terrain, Doctor. The ATV access is viable, and the net is strong enough. We'll ensure the calf is handled with the utmost care during the transfer. We've also notified the rehabilitation team to prepare the pool and have a vet on standby."

Thorne stopped pacing and looked from Eli to Mara, his expression unreadable for a moment. He saw not defiance, but competence. He saw not a romantic entanglement threatening to derail their work, but two individuals who, despite a significant setback, were collaborating effectively to mitigate the damage. The tension between them, which he had interpreted as a distraction, now appeared to him as a shared responsibility, a mutual reliance that was, in its own way, a form of strength.

"A cargo net," Thorne mused, stroking his chin. "Crude, but it might work. As long as you're both absolutely certain about the stability of the terrain. One wrong move with that calf, and it could be more harm than good. Ensure clear communication with the shore patrol. No room for error." He finally met Eli's eyes, then Mara's. "See that it's done. And Eli, you'll personally oversee the repairs to that cradle. I want a full report on my desk by Monday, detailing the failure and the proposed solution. And no more cutting corners on maintenance. Is that understood?"

"Yes, Doctor," Eli replied, a sense of relief washing over him. Thorne's acknowledgment, however curt, was a form of acceptance.

As they left Thorne's office, the immediate crisis averted, a different kind of understanding settled between Mara and Eli. The professional conflict, the equipment failure, and Thorne's gruff disapproval had served as an unexpected crucible, testing the strength of their burgeoning connection. They had navigated it not by retreating into their own spaces, but by actively choosing to face it together.

"He's still going to be a challenge," Mara said quietly, as they walked back towards the rehabilitation area.

Eli nodded, a faint smile touching his lips. "He is. But we handled it. We presented a united front, and we had a solution. That's what matters." He paused, his gaze meeting hers. "Thank you, Mara. For... not letting me get lost in the blame. For reminding me that we're a team."

The unspoken acknowledgment hung in the air between them, a silent testament to the growth they were experiencing. The rescue center, a place of healing and recovery for marine life, was also becoming a space where their own emotional resilience and their capacity for deep, abiding connection were being forged. The challenges they faced, both in their work and within themselves, were not obstacles to their relationship, but rather the very elements that were shaping it into something robust, something enduring, something profoundly real.

The ceaseless pull and release of the tide became, for Mara and Eli, more than just a natural phenomenon; it evolved into a profound metaphor for the rhythm of their own commitment. The ebb and flow, the constant motion, was a living testament to the fact that love, like the ocean, was not a static state but a dynamic force. It wasn't about reaching a final, unchanging destination of "happily ever after," but about the continuous, conscious decision to navigate the currents together, to adapt to the changing tides, and to find solace and strength in each other's presence.

They began to see that the grand, sweeping declarations of love, while beautiful, were only the introductory chapters of a much longer, more intricate narrative. The true substance of their bond lay not in grand gestures, but in the quiet consistency of their actions, in the small, everyday choices they made to prioritize each other, to understand, and to support. This understanding was not a sudden revelation, but a slow dawning, nurtured by shared experiences and illuminated by the very challenges that had threatened to pull them apart.

Mara found herself consciously appreciating Eli's quiet strength, not as an impenetrable wall, but as a bedrock of reliability she could lean on. She learned to recognize the subtle signs of his internal struggles, the fleeting shadows in his eyes, the almost imperceptible tension in his shoulders. And instead of waiting for him to articulate his burdens, she began to offer a silent presence, a hand lightly placed on his arm during a difficult conversation, a shared cup of coffee in the early morning quiet before the day's chaos descended. These were the subtle acts of presence that spoke louder than any dramatic pronouncement, building a sanctuary of understanding between them.

Eli, in turn, discovered a new dimension to his own emotional landscape. He had always prided himself on his self-sufficiency, on his ability to tackle problems head-on and solve them independently. Yet, Mara's unwavering support during the cradle incident had shown him that true strength wasn't about carrying every burden alone, but about the courage to share it. He began to actively seek her perspective, not just on operational matters, but on the more complex emotional currents that flowed through their lives. He learned to voice his anxieties, his frustrations, and his hopes, not as confessions of weakness, but as invitations for connection, for shared understanding. This openness, this willingness to be seen in his vulnerability, was a profound act of trust, a commitment to the depth of their relationship.

Their shared work at the rescue center became a microcosm of this evolving commitment. When faced with a particularly challenging rescue, one that required intricate planning and unwavering teamwork, they found themselves anticipating each other's needs, communicating with an almost telepathic synchronicity. It wasn't that disagreements vanished; they still occurred, small ripples on the surface of their shared purpose. But now, instead of allowing these differences to create fissures, they saw them as opportunities to refine their approach, to learn more about each other's perspectives, and to emerge with a stronger, more resilient strategy. The process of navigating these professional disagreements became a deliberate practice in empathetic communication, a daily reinforcement of their commitment to finding common ground.

One evening, after a particularly grueling day that involved the successful rescue of a young sea turtle entangled in discarded fishing gear, they sat on the weathered wooden deck of the rescue center, the salty breeze carrying the scent of the ocean. The sky was a canvas of deepening twilight, painted with hues of orange and purple.

"It's strange," Mara mused, her voice soft as she traced a pattern on the damp wood with her fingertip. "We always talk about the 'happily ever after,' like it's some kind of finish line. But it feels more like... this." She gestured vaguely towards the vast expanse of the sea. "Constant movement. Always something new to navigate."

Eli turned to her, his gaze steady and filled with a warmth that had deepened with time. "I used to think 'happily ever after' meant everything would be perfect, no more problems. But that's not realistic, is it? Life, and love, are about the journey. It's about choosing to face the storms, and celebrating the calm, *together*." He reached for her hand, his fingers lacing with hers, a familiar, comforting grip. "It's about the commitment to keep showing up, even when it's hard. Especially when it's hard."

He squeezed her hand gently. "Like with Dr. Thorne. I could have shut down, blamed myself, and pushed you away. But you didn't let me. You stood with me. You reminded me that we're a team. That's not a fairytale ending; that's the real, messy, beautiful work of building something that lasts."

Mara leaned her head against his shoulder, a sigh of contentment escaping her lips. "And you, Eli. You've learned to let me in. To trust that I'm not just a distraction, but a partner. That's a different kind of strength, and it's just as vital." She lifted her head to meet his eyes. "It's the conscious choice to invest, every single day. To keep choosing each other, even when the siren call of old habits or external pressures tries to pull us in different directions."

The analogy of the tide, ever-present in their coastal lives, resonated deeply. The ocean never remained the same; it ebbed and flowed, its moods shifting with the weather and the seasons. Yet, its presence was constant, a powerful force that shaped the very landscape around them. Similarly, their love was not meant to be a placid, unchanging lake, but a living, breathing ocean, capable of both gentle lapping waves and powerful, transformative tides.

The "happily ever after" they were building was not a static monument, but a dynamic ecosystem. It was a space where challenges were not threats to be avoided, but opportunities for growth. It was a testament to the fact that true commitment was an active verb, a continuous process of tending, nurturing, and rediscovering. It was a testament to the fact that love, in its most enduring form, was not about finding perfection, but about the shared, daily pursuit of growth, connection, and a love that deepened with every turning of the tide.

Their journey together was far from over; it was, in fact, just beginning to reveal its true, profound depths, a continuous unfolding of shared lives, built on a foundation of conscious choice and unwavering dedication.

CHAPTER FIVE

Seeds of Future Plans

Mara had always been a planner. Her life, much like the intricate ecosystems she studied, was a series of interconnected systems, each meticulously managed and accounted for. For years, her career had been the sun around which all other planets in her orbit revolved. The rescue center, with its demanding schedule and unpredictable emergencies, had initially felt like a deviation from that singular focus. But as Eli had woven himself into the fabric of her days, a new constellation began to form in her mind. It wasn't a replacement of her stars, but an expansion, a broadening of her celestial map.

The idea of a shared future with Eli had, at first, felt like a potential point of friction. Her ambitions had always been fiercely independent, forged in a world that often questioned a woman's capacity for serious scientific pursuit. She had learned to rely solely on her own ingenuity and determination. The thought of intertwining those deeply personal aspirations with another person's life felt akin to introducing a variable into a perfectly balanced equation. Would his presence dilute her focus? Would his needs eclipse her own? These were the anxieties that had whispered in the quiet hours, the ghost of past challenges echoing in her mind.

Yet, as the weeks turned into months, and the rhythm of their lives settled into a comfortable, though not always predictable, cadence, Mara found her perspective shifting. It wasn't a sudden epiphany, but a gentle, persistent unfolding, much like the slow bloom of a rare marine flower. She began to see that commitment wasn't about sacrifice, but about synergy. It wasn't about merging into a single entity, but about two distinct, vibrant lives finding a harmonious resonance. Eli's presence hadn't diminished her ambition; it had, in fact, begun to refract it, casting it in a new light, revealing possibilities she hadn't previously considered.

She found herself staring out at the vast expanse of the ocean, the same ocean that had always represented both her passion and her professional playground, and envisioning it not just as a space for her research, but as a shared horizon. The rescue center, once a temporary professional haven, was slowly transforming into something more foundational, a place where her work and her heart could coexist. This wasn't a concession; it was an evolution. Her ambition, once a solitary pursuit, was now seeking a collaborator, a confidante, someone with whom to share the triumphs and to weather the inevitable storms.

The concept of "happily ever after" had always felt somewhat ill-defined to Mara. In her scientific mind, it implied a static state of perfection, an endpoint that rarely existed in the natural world. The oceans themselves were in constant flux, their depths teeming with life that adapted and evolved. Her relationship with Eli, she realized, needed to mirror that dynamism. It wasn't about achieving a perfect, unchanging union, but about embracing the ongoing process of growth, adaptation, and mutual discovery. Her professional goals, which had once seemed so separate and so singularly hers, now felt like they could be enriched by the shared journey.

Consider the project she'd been nurturing for years: a comprehensive study on the migratory patterns of a specific endangered seabird species that frequented the coastline. It was a project that demanded extensive fieldwork, data analysis, and funding applications. In the past, she had envisioned undertaking it largely alone, a solitary endeavor that would mark her professional arrival. Now, she began to sketch out a different narrative. Could Eli, with his practical skills and his unwavering support, play a role? Not in the scientific execution, perhaps, but in the logistics, the resource management, the sheer emotional scaffolding that such a long-term, demanding project required.

She imagined evenings spent poring over maps, not just of the ocean, but of her proposed research sites. She pictured him offering practical advice on equipment, on travel arrangements, on the often-arduous process of securing grants. It wasn't about him taking over her work, but about him becoming an integral part of the ecosystem that allowed her work to flourish. This vision didn't diminish her personal achievement; it amplified it, infusing it with the richness of shared experience. Her ambition wasn't being compromised; it was being grounded, made more resilient, more real, by the steady presence of Eli and the constant, grounding rhythm of their coastal existence.

This re-evaluation extended to the very nature of her aspirations. For so long, her professional identity had been paramount, the bedrock upon which she had built her self-worth. She had often viewed any personal entanglement as a potential distraction, a vulnerability to be guarded against. But Eli had subtly challenged that narrative. His own quiet strength, his dedication to the rescue center, his deep connection to the natural world—all of these resonated with her own values, creating a profound sense of alignment.

She began to think about her long-term career trajectory. She had always seen herself advancing, climbing the academic or research ladder, her success measured by accolades and publications. But what if success could also be defined by impact, by contribution, by the creation of a sustainable sanctuary where both healing and research could thrive? The rescue center itself was a testament to that possibility. It was a place born from a passion for conservation, a practical application of scientific knowledge, and a deep-seated empathy for living creatures. Eli was as integral to its success as she was, his steady hand guiding its operational heart.

Mara found herself drawn to the idea of expanding the center's research capabilities, not as a means to personal aggrandizement, but as a way to deepen their collective impact. This wasn't a departure from her independent ambitions; it was a reorientation. She saw how her scientific expertise could complement the center's operational needs, how her research could inform their rescue efforts, and how Eli's operational acumen could provide the stable framework for her scientific endeavors. It was a dance of complementary strengths, each partner enhancing the other's movements.

The quiet coastal life they shared, once a temporary refuge from her more demanding professional life, was now becoming the very foundation upon which she was building her future. The predictable rhythm of the tides, the scent of salt in the air, the cries of the gulls—these elements, once mere background noise, were now woven into the fabric of her aspirations. They represented stability, constancy, and a profound connection to the natural world that fueled her passion. Eli, with his steady gaze and his quiet understanding, was becoming synonymous with that same sense of grounding.

She would often find herself watching him at work, his movements efficient and sure as he tended to the rescued animals or oversaw the maintenance of the center's facilities. There was a quiet competence about him that she admired deeply. He wasn't driven by ego or the pursuit of external validation; his motivation stemmed from a deep-seated desire to care for the vulnerable, to preserve the delicate balance of their coastal environment. This alignment of purpose was, for Mara, a far more powerful draw than any shared ambition for individual recognition.

One afternoon, while discussing the potential for a new, long-term research grant focused on marine mammal rehabilitation, Mara found herself articulating a vision that felt both deeply personal and inherently collaborative. "I've been thinking, Eli," she began, her voice thoughtful, "about how we could integrate my migratory bird research more directly with the center's outreach programs. Imagine, educating local communities not just about rescue, but about the broader ecological picture, the interconnectedness of it all. And for my part, I could use the center's existing infrastructure, its connections, to gather more real-time data, to observe patterns that I might otherwise miss."

Eli listened intently, his gaze never leaving her face. "That makes sense, Mara. We've always focused on immediate rescue, but you're right, the long-term health of the ecosystem is paramount. And if your research can contribute to that, it benefits us all. How would you see that working, logistically?"

His immediate engagement, his willingness to explore the practicalities rather than dismiss the idea as a tangential pursuit, was precisely what Mara had come to cherish. He didn't just listen; he processed, he considered, he contributed.

"Well," Mara continued, a spark igniting in her eyes, "we could establish a dedicated research wing, perhaps in that unused storage area. And I could train a few volunteers on basic data collection protocols. It wouldn't detract from the rescue operations; it would augment them, providing a more holistic understanding of the challenges we face." She paused, then added, with a touch of vulnerability, "It's a big undertaking. Years of work. I've always envisioned it as a solo journey, but… it would mean so much to have your support, not just as my partner, but as someone who understands the importance of this place, of what we're doing here."

Eli reached across the small table in their shared office, his hand covering hers. His touch was warm, reassuring. "Mara, this rescue center is as much my life's work as it is yours. If your research can help us protect this coastline, and these creatures, then it's something we build together. You're not embarking on a solo journey. You're expanding our journey."

His words settled over her like a warm blanket, dispelling the last vestiges of her solitary ambition. It wasn't about abandoning her dreams; it was about realizing that some dreams were best nurtured, and ultimately achieved, in the shared light of a committed relationship. Her ambitions, once sharp and narrowly focused, were now broadening, softening at the edges, becoming more resilient, more deeply rooted in the fertile ground of their shared life. The steady rhythm of the ocean, the constant presence of Eli, and the shared purpose of the rescue center had converged, creating a powerful, grounding force that allowed her own personal growth to flourish, not in isolation, but in vibrant, interconnected bloom. She was no longer just a scientist pursuing her own discoveries; she was a partner, a collaborator, building a future that was as expansive and as enduring as the sea itself.

The salty air, a familiar balm that had so often soothed Mara's restless spirit, now carried a new weight, a subtle shift in its fragrance that spoke of decisions made and futures being forged. Eli, always a man of quiet contemplation, had been wrestling with a significant crossroads. The opportunities laid out before him were tempting, shimmering with the promise of advancement and a departure from the predictable rhythms of their coastal existence. Yet, as he'd navigated these possibilities, his gaze had consistently returned to the same anchoring point: Mara, and the life they had painstakingly, lovingly, built together.

He remembered the late-night conversations, the hesitant whispers of his own ambitions, and the way Mara had listened, her brow furrowed in concentration, not with judgment, but with a deep, unwavering understanding. She had never pressured him, never steered him, but her own quiet dedication to her work, her passion for the delicate balance of the marine world, had provided him with a silent benchmark. He'd seen how she found fulfillment not just in the grand pronouncements of scientific discovery, but in the day-to-day, the small victories, the consistent nurturing of life that the rescue center embodied. And he realized, with a clarity that settled deep within his bones, that his own definition of success needed to echo that sentiment.

The offer to lead a new environmental initiative on the mainland was undeniably prestigious. It involved significant resources, a wider scope, and the potential for widespread impact. He could picture the polished conference rooms, the strategic meetings, the satisfaction of orchestrating large-scale change. For a time, it had felt like the logical next step, the natural progression of his career. He had imagined himself, perhaps, commuting back and forth, maintaining a presence, but the mental calculus had quickly become unsustainable. The more he'd envisioned the physical distance, the more he'd felt a hollow ache, a sense of disconnection from the very foundation he'd come to cherish.

His heart wasn't in the abstract strategies of distant boardrooms; it was here, on the wind-swept shores, in the comforting roar of the waves, and in the steady rhythm of Mara's presence beside him. He'd witnessed firsthand the profound impact of their work at the rescue center, the tangible difference they made in the lives of injured animals, the vital role they played in the health of the local ecosystem. He saw how Mara's scientific rigor, when applied to the operational needs of the center, created something far more powerful than either could achieve alone. Her research wasn't just an academic pursuit; it was an intrinsic part of the sanctuary they were building.

And then there was Mara herself. The initial apprehension he'd sometimes sensed in her, the ingrained habit of self-reliance, had softened and bloomed into a beautiful, deep trust. He saw how she had begun to integrate her ambitious research goals with the practical realities of the rescue center, envisioning a future where her work was amplified, not diminished, by their shared life. Her willingness to weave her professional aspirations into the fabric of their daily existence, to see him not as an interruption but as a vital partner, had solidified his own resolve.

He'd spent an entire evening walking the shoreline, the moon casting a silvery path across the water, his mind a whirlwind of pros and cons. He'd picked up smooth, sea-worn stones, turning them over and over in his hands, much like he was turning over the possibilities in his mind. The weight of the stones felt grounding, real. He thought about the long hours he'd already invested in the rescue center, the late nights spent repairing equipment, the early mornings coordinating volunteer efforts, the quiet satisfaction of seeing a rehabilitated animal return to the sea. These weren't just tasks; they were the building blocks of a life he genuinely loved.

The mainland offer, while impressive on paper, represented a departure from that lived reality. It was a promise of a different kind of fulfillment, one that felt... less tangible, less deeply rooted. He realized that stability, for him, wasn't solely about climbing a career ladder or accumulating professional accolades. It was about the quiet certainty of waking up beside Mara, about the shared purpose that permeated their days, about the deep satisfaction of contributing to something meaningful, right here, where their hearts resided.

He imagined explaining his decision to the proponents of the mainland initiative. It wouldn't be a grand speech, but a simple, honest statement of priorities. He would explain that his commitment lay with the tangible, with the immediate, with the nurturing of a sanctuary that was already blossoming. He wouldn't frame it as a sacrifice, but as a conscious choice, a redirection of his energy towards a path that offered a richer, more integrated form of fulfillment.

There was a profound beauty in the established routine they shared, a symphony of predictable rhythms that allowed for unexpected harmonies. The ebb and flow of the tides mirrored the ebb and flow of their days. The consistent need for care and attention at the rescue center provided a constant, grounding purpose. And Mara, with her brilliant mind and her growing willingness to share her world with him, was the most captivating melody in that symphony.

He understood that for Mara, her research had always been a solitary endeavor, a testament to her own resilience and intellect. The idea of integrating it more fully with the rescue center, of making it a shared endeavor, was a significant evolution for her. His decision to remain, to actively invest in that shared vision, was his way of affirming that evolution, of showing her that her courage in opening her heart and her ambitions to him was reciprocated with his own unwavering commitment.

He decided to tell Mara that evening. He wanted to see the relief, and perhaps the quiet joy, bloom in her eyes. He knew she wouldn't have openly expressed her anxieties, but he'd sensed them, those subtle hesitations that spoke of a woman who had learned to guard her heart fiercely. His choice was a testament to the trust they had built, a silent acknowledgment of the profound bond that had formed between them amidst the rustling sea grasses and the endless expanse of the ocean.

He found her in the small office, poring over charts, her brow furrowed in concentration, a faint smudge of ink on her cheek. The scent of old paper and sea salt filled the air, a fragrance that was, to him, the very essence of home. He watched her for a moment, admiring the fierce intelligence in her gaze, the quiet determination that had always drawn him in.

"Mara," he said softly, his voice a low rumble that cut through the quiet hum of the office.

She looked up, her eyes brightening as she saw him. "Eli. You're back earlier than I expected."

He walked over, leaning against her desk, his gaze meeting hers. "I've made a decision."

A flicker of anticipation crossed her face. "About the initiative?"

He nodded, a slow, deliberate movement. "I'm not taking it."

Her breath hitched, and then a smile, soft and genuine, spread across her lips. It was a smile that reached her eyes, chasing away the lingering shadows of professional worry. "Oh, Eli. Are you sure?"

He reached out, gently brushing the ink smudge from her cheek with his thumb. "Never been more sure of anything in my life." He paused, letting the weight of his words settle. "This place, Mara... you... this is where I want to be. This is where I'm building my life. The opportunities elsewhere... they're significant, yes, but they don't offer what I've found here. They don't offer the chance to build something real, something lasting, with you, in a place that matters so much to both of us."

He saw a tear well up in her eye, but it was a tear of happiness, of profound relief. "I was worried," she admitted, her voice a little thick. "I know how much you've poured into the center, and how important it is for you to feel like you're progressing. I didn't want you to feel... held back."

"Held back?" Eli chuckled, a warm, rich sound. "Mara, you've given me more than any promotion ever could. You've shown me that true fulfillment isn't about how far you go, but about the quality of the ground you stand on, and who you stand it with. My ambition isn't gone; it's just been... re-routed. It's about investing in what we have, in making this sanctuary, this work, even stronger, together."

He reached for her hand, lacing his fingers through hers. Her skin was warm, her grip firm. "I see now that stability isn't just about a career path. It's about commitment. It's about choosing to be present, to pour your energy into the people and the place you love. And that's what I'm choosing. I'm choosing us, Mara. I'm choosing this life."

He felt a profound sense of peace settle over him. The restless energy that had been churning within him for weeks had finally subsided, replaced by a quiet certainty. The path forward was clear, not because it was paved with external validation, but because it was rooted in the deep, unwavering soil of their shared life. He looked at Mara, her eyes shining with unshed tears, and knew, with absolute conviction, that he had made the right choice. The future, it turned out, was not about chasing distant horizons, but about cultivating the rich, fertile ground right beneath their feet, together. He was exactly where he was meant to be.

The salt-laced breeze, a constant companion to their lives, seemed to whisper encouragement as they settled onto their usual worn deck chairs, the setting sun painting the sky in hues of apricot and rose. The day's work at the sanctuary had been particularly demanding, a flurry of rescued seabirds and diligent care that left them both pleasantly weary. Yet, as they watched the last sliver of sun dip below the horizon, a comfortable quiet settled between them, a prelude to a deeper conversation that had been simmering beneath the surface. Eli's decision to remain, to anchor his future here, had been a monumental step, a powerful affirmation of their bond. Now, with that foundational piece firmly in place, the landscape of their shared dreams began to unfold with a newfound clarity.

"You know," Mara began, her voice soft as she traced the rim of her teacup, the ceramic warm against her fingers, "when you told me you were staying... it wasn't just about the rescue center, was it?"

Eli turned his gaze from the darkening sea to her, a gentle smile playing on his lips. "No, it wasn't. It was about... us. About building something more than just a successful sanctuary. It was about building a life." He reached out, his hand finding hers, his thumb stroking the back of her palm. "And I realized, more than ever, that I wanted that life with you."

A small, contented sigh escaped Mara. "I felt that too. It was like... like the world tilted back into place. I'd been so focused on my research, on making it work, on finding a way to integrate it all, that I hadn't quite let myself imagine what 'us' could truly be, beyond just working alongside each other." She looked out at the vast expanse of the ocean, its immensity mirroring the burgeoning possibilities in her mind. "It felt like a very solitary pursuit for so long, my work. And then, you... you made it feel like a shared endeavor."

"And it is," Eli stated with quiet conviction. "Your research, your passion for understanding the intricate web of marine life, it's not just something that happens *here*. It's something that's woven into the fabric of our lives. It's part of why this place is so special, and why I chose to stay. I see how your discoveries, the small breakthroughs, can directly impact the way we care for these animals. It's not just theoretical; it's tangible. And I want to be a part of that, to support it, to celebrate it with you."

He squeezed her hand. "I've been thinking a lot about what happens next. Not just about the rescue center's operational needs, but about *our* needs. Your needs, Mara. What do you envision for yourself, for your work, in the coming years? And how do we make that happen, together?"

Mara's heart swelled at the sincerity in his voice, at the genuine desire to understand and collaborate. This was the evolution she had only dared to hope for. "I've been thinking about that too," she admitted, her gaze dropping to their entwined hands. "For so long, my ambition felt like a burden, something I had to carry alone. The idea of a position on the mainland, while exciting on one level, also felt... isolating. It would have meant pulling myself away from the very environment that inspires me, and from... well, from you."

She met his eyes, her own shining with a newfound vulnerability. "What I dream of, Eli, is a future where my research isn't a separate entity, but a vital, integrated part of the sanctuary. I want to see us expand our research capabilities, perhaps even establish a small, dedicated lab space here, where we can analyze samples, develop more targeted conservation strategies, and educate others. I want to see us become a hub, not just for rescue, but for cutting-edge marine conservation research."

Eli listened intently, his expression one of deep engagement. He nodded slowly. "A hub. I like the sound of that. And how do we get there? What are the practical steps?"

"Well," Mara began, a spark of excitement igniting in her eyes, "we'll need to secure more funding, obviously. I've been looking into grants specifically for environmental research and conservation initiatives. Some of them are quite substantial, and with your expertise in project management and your growing network, I believe we could put together some very compelling proposals. And then there's the space... we could potentially convert that old boathouse into a functional lab. It would require renovation, of course, but it's a solid structure, and it's close enough to the water for easy sample collection."

"The boathouse," Eli mused, picturing the weathered building that had been largely disused for years. "It has potential. We'd need to consider power, water, ventilation... but it's certainly feasible. And you're right about the grants. I've been thinking about how to leverage my own skills to benefit the sanctuary beyond just the day-to-day operations. Applying for funding is something I can definitely take the lead on, working closely with you on the research proposals."

He paused, a thoughtful expression on his face. "And what about you, beyond the lab? What does your ideal day look like, a few years from now, when all of this is in motion?"

Mara leaned back, a dreamy smile gracing her lips. "My ideal day... I'd wake up here, with you. I'd spend the morning with the animals, ensuring they're all healthy and thriving. Then, I'd head to the lab, perhaps collaborate with a visiting researcher or student, analyze some data, write up my findings.

In the afternoon, I might lead a workshop for local students or community members, sharing what we're learning. And then, in the evening, we'd sit right here, just like this, watching the sunset, talking about our day, about the discoveries we've made, about the challenges we've overcome." She turned to him, her gaze earnest. "It's a vision that includes everything I'm passionate about, and it's a vision that includes you, every step of the way."

Eli reached out and gently brushed a strand of hair from her cheek. "It sounds beautiful, Mara. Truly beautiful. And it's a vision I wholeheartedly share. We'll build that lab. We'll apply for those grants. We'll make this sanctuary a beacon of research and conservation." He paused, his voice deepening with emotion. "And we'll do it together. This is our dream now, not just yours."

The acknowledgment, the unwavering partnership in her dream, meant more to Mara than words could express. She had spent so long protecting her ambitions, guarding them from the potential disappointment of not being understood, or worse, of being dismissed. Eli's complete embrace of her vision was a testament to the profound trust they had forged. "And what about you, Eli? What are your dreams for our future, beyond supporting mine?"

He chuckled softly, the sound a warm vibration in the twilight. "My dreams are intertwined with yours, Mara. I dream of seeing this place thrive, of knowing we've made a significant difference in the lives of these creatures and the health of this coastline. I dream of continuing to build our home, to make it a place of warmth and sanctuary for us and for those who come to us for help. And I dream of us, growing older together, still sharing these sunsets, still finding new wonders in the world, still supporting each other's passions."

He laced his fingers through hers again, a gesture of comfort and connection. "I see us creating a life that's rich and fulfilling, not just in terms of our professional achievements, but in the quiet moments, too. Family dinners, Sunday mornings, exploring the coastline, simply being present with each other. I don't need grand gestures or outward validation; I need the steady, unwavering presence of you, and the satisfaction of knowing we're building something meaningful, side by side."

"That sounds like... everything," Mara whispered, a profound sense of peace washing over her. "It's the stability I craved, but also the adventure I secretly yearned for. A life built on a solid foundation, but with endless horizons to explore, together."

The conversation flowed effortlessly, branching into the practicalities of their shared life. They discussed finances, the need to carefully manage their resources to fund the research expansion while maintaining the sanctuary's operations. Eli, with his background in project management, had already begun sketching out potential budget models in his mind, identifying areas where they could seek specific funding for infrastructure and equipment. Mara, in turn, detailed the scientific equipment they would require, the specialized software for data analysis, and the potential for collaborating with academic institutions for equipment sharing.

"We'll need to be smart about it," Eli said, his brow furrowed in concentration as he mentally navigated spreadsheets. "We can't do everything at once. Perhaps we start with the boathouse renovation and essential lab equipment, while simultaneously applying for the larger grants for ongoing research projects and staffing. We'll need to be methodical, prioritize needs versus wants."

"Absolutely," Mara agreed. "The crucial element will be securing a consistent stream of funding for the research itself, not just the infrastructure. We'll need to identify grants that cover personnel, supplies, and long-term project support. And perhaps we can also explore opportunities for educational outreach programs, charging a small fee for workshops or guided tours, to supplement our income."

The prospect of adding educational components to their work was something Mara had considered before, but had always filed away as a distant possibility. Now, with Eli's practical mind at the table, it felt tangible. "That's a good idea, Eli. We have so much to share. Teaching others about marine biology, conservation, and the importance of the sanctuary could be incredibly rewarding, both financially and intrinsically."

They talked late into the night, the moon rising higher, casting a silver sheen over the water. Their discussions weren't about compromises in the sense of giving something up, but about creative solutions, about finding the most effective and harmonious ways to weave their individual aspirations into a unified tapestry. They spoke of potential challenges – the occasional difficulty in securing grants, the demanding nature of both rescue and research, the inherent unpredictability of working with nature. But for every potential obstacle, they found a shared strength, a collaborative spirit that made even the daunting seem surmountable.

"I know this might mean more long hours for both of us, at least initially," Eli admitted, his hand resting lightly on Mara's knee. "Building something this ambitious takes dedication. But I also know that when we're working towards a shared goal, a goal that we both believe in so deeply, it doesn't feel like a burden. It feels... purposeful."

"It does," Mara echoed, her voice filled with gratitude. "And knowing that I have you by my side, that you're not just supporting my dream, but actively building it with me, makes all the difference. I used to think I had to be a lone wolf to achieve anything significant. But you've shown me the power of partnership, the beauty of shared endeavor."

He turned her towards him, his gaze steady and full of affection. "And you, Mara, have shown me that true success isn't measured by outward achievement alone, but by the depth of connection, the richness of shared purpose, and the love that anchors us. We're building more than a sanctuary, and more than a research facility. We're building a life, together. And I wouldn't trade that for anything."

As they sat there, the rhythmic lapping of the waves against the shore a gentle soundtrack to their conversation, Mara felt a profound sense of arrival. The vastness of the ocean, once a symbol of her own solitude and the immensity of her task, now represented the boundless possibilities of their shared future. The seeds of their plans, sown in honesty and nurtured by unwavering commitment, were beginning to sprout, promising a future as rich and deep as the sea itself. They were no longer just individuals pursuing separate paths; they were a unit, a team, charting a course together, their hearts set on a horizon they would navigate, hand in hand. The sea, ever present, seemed to approve, its vastness a silent promise of the depth and breadth of the life they were creating.

The rescue center, a place of constant activity and quiet dedication, was poised on the cusp of a new chapter, mirroring the evolution of Mara and Eli's own lives. The established rhythm of rescue, rehabilitation, and release, while still the heart of their mission, was beginning to pulse with a new ambition, a strategic reorientation that promised to amplify their impact. This wasn't a sudden shift, but a gradual blossoming, nurtured by years of dedicated work and a growing understanding of the broader ecological challenges facing their coastal haven.

Eli, his hands still bearing the faint scent of kelp and disinfectant from a morning spent tending to a rescued puffin with a damaged wing, surveyed the main rehabilitation area. The familiar rows of kennels and specialized enclosures were meticulously maintained, each occupied by an animal on its journey back to health. Yet, his gaze drifted beyond the immediate needs, to the administrative office where Mara was poring over spreadsheets, her brow furrowed in concentration. The administrative side, while essential, had always felt like a secondary layer to the hands-on care and the burgeoning research. Now, however, it was becoming a focal point for strategic planning, for charting the course of the sanctuary's future.

"You know," Eli began, leaning against the doorway, his voice a low rumble that didn't disturb Mara's focus, "I was talking with Captain Finn yesterday. He mentioned that the local fishing cooperative is starting to explore more sustainable practices. They're looking for resources, for guidance on how to reduce bycatch and minimize their impact on marine habitats."

Mara looked up, a flicker of interest in her eyes. "Really? That's fantastic news. We've been trying to engage with them for years, but the reception has always been... tepid, at best. They saw us as a nuisance, mostly."

"Things are changing," Eli confirmed, walking further into the room and perching on the edge of her desk. "The economic realities are shifting, and they're starting to see the value in what we do, or at least, the necessity of adapting. They're specifically asking about educational outreach programs, about workshops that can teach them best practices and introduce them to new, less impactful fishing gear."

A slow smile spread across Mara's face. "This is it, then. This is the shift I've been hoping for. It's not just about rescuing animals anymore; it's about influencing the systemic issues that cause them harm in the first place. It's about becoming educators, advocates, and partners in conservation."

Eli nodded, his gaze meeting hers, a shared excitement building between them. "Exactly. And it means the rescue center's role needs to evolve. We've always been reactive – picking up the pieces after the damage is done. But if we can proactively engage with the community, with industries like fishing, we can prevent some of that damage from happening in the first place. It's a much more sustainable model for conservation, and frankly, for the sanctuary's long-term viability."

"But how do we manage that?" Mara mused, tapping her pen against her chin. "Our resources are already stretched thin with the day-to-day operations and the nascent research projects. Adding a comprehensive outreach and education program... it's a significant undertaking."

"That's where our roles might need to adapt, and where we can leverage what we've built," Eli said, his mind already whirring with possibilities. "I've been thinking about how to streamline our operational management. We've got a solid team of volunteers, and I believe we can implement some more robust training protocols, perhaps even bring on a dedicated volunteer coordinator. That would free up more of my time to focus on strategic partnerships and community engagement."

He gestured towards the window, where the sun glinted off the water. "Imagine the sanctuary as not just a place of healing for animals, but as a center of learning for the community. We could host regular workshops on sustainable fishing, marine debris reduction, responsible tourism. We could develop educational materials for schools, maybe even create a small visitor center, something modest to start, where people can learn about our work and the challenges facing our marine ecosystems."

Mara's eyes lit up. "A visitor center... that's brilliant. It would not only generate much-needed revenue but also provide a platform to showcase the impact of our work. We could have interactive exhibits, information about the species we rescue, the threats they face, and the ways people can help. And the workshops... that could be where the real change happens. By educating the people who are directly interacting with the environment, we empower them to become part of the solution."

"And this is where your research becomes even more vital," Eli added, his voice resonating with pride. "Your findings on the impact of certain fishing practices, your data on pollution levels, your understanding of migratory patterns – that's the scientific backbone of our educational initiatives. We can translate your complex research into accessible, actionable information for everyone from local fishermen to school children."

"So, my role would expand beyond just conducting research and analyzing data," Mara said, a thoughtful expression settling on her features. "It would involve translating that research into practical applications and educational content. I could work on developing curriculum for the workshops, designing the exhibits for the visitor center, and perhaps even collaborating with local schools on marine science programs."

"Precisely," Eli confirmed. "Your expertise is the foundation. My strength lies in logistics, in building relationships, and in project management. Together, we can build this new facet of the sanctuary. I can focus on securing partnerships, managing the implementation of new programs, and overseeing the operational aspects of the visitor center and outreach initiatives. You can focus on the scientific integrity of our message, the development of educational content, and ensuring that our outreach efforts are grounded in accurate, up-to-date research."

He paused, a gentle smile gracing his lips. "It means a shift for both of us. Less time hands-on with every single rescued animal, perhaps, and more time in meetings, developing proposals, and strategizing. But it's a necessary evolution if we want to have a truly lasting impact."

Mara met his gaze, her heart full. This was precisely the kind of shared vision she had longed for. It wasn't about sacrificing their passions, but about finding ways to amplify them, to integrate them into a larger, more impactful whole. "I'm ready for that shift, Eli. I've seen firsthand how much our work means to the animals we save, but I've also seen the bigger picture, the systemic problems that are overwhelming our efforts. To be able to actively address those problems, to be a part of changing the narrative from one of rescue and recovery to one of prevention and protection... that's incredibly exciting."

"And it's a path that requires a strong foundation," Eli added, his hand finding hers on the desk, their fingers intertwining. "The rescue center itself is that foundation. It's our history, it's our shared purpose, and it's the tangible proof of our commitment. Expanding its role doesn't diminish its core mission; it enhances it. It means we can save more lives, not just by rescuing them from immediate danger, but by creating a healthier environment for them in the long run."

"We'll need to think about the practicalities," Mara said, her mind already cataloging the requirements. "For the outreach programs, we'll need dedicated staff or highly trained volunteers to lead the workshops and manage the logistics. For the visitor center, we'll need to consider design, construction, and ongoing maintenance. And the funding... this will require a significant investment."

"I've already started looking into grant opportunities," Eli said, a glint in his eye. "There are several foundations that focus on marine conservation, community engagement, and environmental education. Your research will be key in making our proposals compelling. We can highlight how our expanded role will directly contribute to the health of the local marine ecosystem and the sustainability of the coastal community."

"And we can explore partnerships with local businesses," Mara suggested. "Perhaps tourism operators who want to offer eco-friendly experiences, or restaurants committed to sustainable seafood. They could sponsor specific programs or contribute to the visitor center. It becomes a collaborative effort, a shared investment in the future of our coastline."

"That's a great idea," Eli agreed. "The more stakeholders we can bring on board, the stronger our impact will be. And importantly, this evolution will also allow us to be more strategic about our rescue efforts. If we can reduce the number of animals injured due to preventable causes, our resources can be directed towards more critical cases or towards specialized rehabilitation for animals with unique needs."

He leaned back, a contented sigh escaping him. "It's like everything is falling into place. Your passion for research, my skills in management, the sanctuary's established reputation, and now, the community's growing openness to change. It's a perfect storm of opportunity."

Mara smiled, her heart swelling with affection and a deep sense of partnership. "It's more than just opportunity, Eli. It's about us, building something meaningful together, something that extends beyond our personal lives and leaves a positive legacy. The rescue center has always been a special place for us, the crucible where our connection was forged. Now, it's becoming the very framework for our shared future, a place where our personal commitments and professional ambitions can flourish in tandem."

"And we'll have to be mindful of our own balance," Eli added, his tone shifting to one of gentle concern. "This expansion will undoubtedly demand more of our time and energy. We'll need to consciously carve out moments for ourselves, for our relationship, amidst the whirlwind of new initiatives."

"I know," Mara said, her gaze soft as she looked at him. "But knowing that we're working towards this together, that we're a team in every sense of the word, makes even the most demanding challenges feel manageable. I can't imagine facing this growth without you by my side. Your unwavering support, your practical insights, your belief in me and in our shared vision... it's everything."

"And your brilliance, your dedication, your deep understanding of the natural world... it inspires me every day," Eli reciprocated, his thumb gently stroking the back of her hand. "This isn't just about saving animals or educating the community; it's about building a life together, a life rooted in purpose and shared passion. The rescue center is our anchor, and this evolution is like unfurling new sails, charting a course towards a horizon we've only just begun to imagine."

The conversation continued, the practicalities of grant writing, curriculum development, and partnership building weaving seamlessly with their personal reflections on their evolving roles. They discussed the potential for creating volunteer opportunities specifically for the new outreach programs, allowing for greater community involvement and providing valuable experience for aspiring marine biologists and conservationists. They talked about the possibility of attracting visiting researchers who could contribute to both the sanctuary's understanding of local marine life and the development of its educational materials, further solidifying its position as a hub for marine conservation.

Eli envisioned a robust communication strategy, utilizing social media and local media channels to highlight the sanctuary's new initiatives and successes, drawing in both support and participants. Mara, in turn, was already mentally outlining potential research projects that could be directly informed by the community engagement, creating a feedback loop where practical challenges identified by fishermen could become the focus of scientific inquiry, leading to more effective and tailored solutions.

The shift in the rescue center's role was more than just an operational adjustment; it was a profound statement of intent. It signified a move from being a reactive emergency service to becoming a proactive force for change, a catalyst for a healthier relationship between the community and its precious marine environment. And at the heart of this transformation were Mara and Eli, their personal commitment to each other blossoming into a shared professional endeavor, their love story intertwined with the future of the coast they called home. The rescue center, once a symbol of their individual passions, was now a testament to their collective strength, a beacon of hope for both the creatures it protected and the community it served. It was a testament to their evolving roles, not just as individuals, but as partners, as a force for good, their future as bright and as vast as the ocean that stretched before them.

The salty air, usually a comforting balm, carried a different kind of energy today – one of anticipation, of a shared future being meticulously pieced together. Mara and Eli had spent hours poring over plans, their initial excitement about expanding the rescue center's educational outreach now grounded in the tangible steps required to make it a reality. The conversations had shifted from grand visions to the nitty-gritty of budgeting, curriculum development, and volunteer training. It was in these moments, amidst the rustle of paper and the soft glow of lamplight in Mara's office, that the true architecture of their partnership was being built, brick by careful brick.

Eli, ever the pragmatist, had laid out a comprehensive timeline for the visitor center's development, complete with phased construction and potential funding sources. He had already drafted preliminary grant proposals, his executive summary painting a vivid picture of the sanctuary's vital role and its ambitious plans for community engagement. Mara, meanwhile, had begun sketching out the core modules for the sustainable fishing workshop, drawing from her extensive research on marine ecosystems and the direct impact of human activity. Her expertise, once confined to the scientific journals and the quiet solitude of her lab, was now being translated into accessible language, designed to resonate with the very people whose practices had often put marine life at risk.

"I've identified a few promising grant opportunities," Eli said, tapping a highlighted section of a document. "One specifically focuses on conservation education, and another on fostering community resilience in coastal areas. They both seem like strong fits for our expanded mission." He slid the papers across the desk. "I've roughed out the initial application narratives, emphasizing the synergistic relationship between our rescue efforts and our proactive outreach. It highlights how preventing harm is just as crucial as healing it."

Mara picked up the documents, her brow furrowed in concentration as she absorbed the details. "This is excellent, Eli. You've captured the essence of what we're trying to achieve. I can take these and weave in more specific examples from our rescue data – details about the types of injuries we see most often, the species most affected, and how our educational programs will directly address those causes." She pointed to a line in his proposal. "And this mention of 'legacy impact'... that's a crucial point. It's not just about short-term fixes; it's about creating lasting change."

"Exactly," Eli affirmed, leaning back in his chair, a comfortable silence settling between them as Mara absorbed his work. This was the rhythm they had found, a seamless blend of his practical execution and her deep-seated knowledge. It wasn't about one person dictating the terms, but about a constant, fluid exchange of ideas, each building upon the other. He watched her, the way her eyes lit up when she grasped a complex point, the way her hand moved expressively as she spoke, and he felt a profound sense of gratitude for the foundation they had already laid – a foundation of mutual respect and an unwavering belief in each other's capabilities.

"For the workshops," Mara continued, her voice gaining momentum, "I'm thinking we need to start with a pilot program. Perhaps focus on knot-tying techniques that reduce snagging, or demonstrate the use of biodegradable fishing lines. We could invite a few key figures from the fishing cooperative to attend a small, informal session, make it less intimidating, more collaborative."

"A pilot program is a smart move," Eli agreed. "It allows us to refine the content and gauge the reception before a wider rollout. I can reach out to Captain Finn and see who he recommends for that initial group. He's been instrumental in opening those doors, and his endorsement carries a lot of weight." He paused, then added, "It's also about building trust, Mara. Not just with the fishermen, but between us. Showing them that we're not here to lecture, but to partner. That we understand their livelihoods, and we're offering solutions that work for them, too."

The mention of trust resonated deeply with Mara. It was the silent, yet most significant, component of their shared endeavor.

She knew that trust wasn't a declaration; it was a daily practice, a series of small, consistent actions that, over time, solidified into an unshakeable bond. She thought back to the countless times Eli had stepped in to support her when she was overwhelmed by the research, or when she'd offered her perspective on operational matters that he was wrestling with. Each instance, no matter how minor, had been a quiet reaffirmation of their commitment to each other and to their shared purpose.

"It is," she said softly, meeting his gaze. "And it's something we're building not just with the community, but between ourselves, too. Every time we have a disagreement and work through it respectfully, every time we're honest about our limitations or our concerns, we're strengthening that foundation. It's not always easy, especially when we're both so passionate about our work, but the fact that we can have these conversations... it's everything."

Eli reached across the desk, his hand covering hers. His touch was warm, steady. "It is everything," he echoed. "And it's about being there for each other, even when the plans go awry. Remember that time we had that massive storm roll in, and the power went out for two days? We were scrambling to keep the incubators running, the oxygen levels stable. I was exhausted, ready to throw in the towel. But you... you just quietly went and got the old hand-crank generator from storage, and we worked through the night together, one of us feeding the generator while the other monitored the animals. That's trust. Knowing that no matter how bad it gets, we're in it together."

Mara squeezed his hand, a fond smile playing on her lips. "And you were the one who stayed up all night meticulously documenting every fluctuation, every intervention, even though you were running on fumes. That's trust, too. Knowing that your commitment to accuracy, to the integrity of our work, is unwavering, even when the pressure is immense." She shifted in her chair, drawing closer. "This expansion, it's going to test us, Eli. There will be more late nights, more unexpected challenges, more moments where we'll have to rely on each other more than ever."

"And we'll rise to them," Eli stated with quiet confidence. "Because we've already proven we can. This isn't just about creating a new program; it's about deepening our partnership. Your dedication to the scientific rigor of our outreach, ensuring we're providing accurate, evidence-based information, that's your trust in the integrity of our mission. My commitment to managing the logistics, securing the funding, and building the relationships, that's my trust in our ability to execute this vision effectively." He interlaced their fingers. "It's a constant cycle, isn't it? We trust each other to do our parts, and by doing our parts well, we earn each other's trust even more."

He looked around the office, at the charts, the research papers, the photographs of rescued animals that adorned the walls – a testament to years of tireless work and shared dreams. "This place, the sanctuary, it's a physical manifestation of that trust. We built it together, not just the buildings and the enclosures, but the reputation, the community's faith in what we do. Now, we're extending that trust outwards, to the wider community, and inwards, by entrusting each other with the future of this vital work."

Mara nodded, her gaze sweeping over the familiar space. The steady rhythm of the rescue center, the quiet hum of life-support systems, the occasional chirping of a recovering bird – it was all a constant reminder of the deep-seated trust that had been forged here. It was the trust in their shared purpose, the trust in their ability to heal, and now, the trust in their capacity to educate and inspire. "It's like the tides," she mused. "They're predictable, reliable. You know they'll come in, and you know they'll go out. There's a certainty to it, a comfort in that constancy. That's what our trust feels like, Eli. A steady, unwavering force that we can always count on."

"And we have to keep nurturing it," Eli added, his voice softening. "It's not something we can take for granted, even now. We need to continue to be open with each other about our stresses, our triumphs, our fears. When I'm feeling overwhelmed by the financial projections, I need to be able to tell you, and know that you'll listen and offer support, not judgment. And when you're exhausted from a difficult research analysis, I need to be there to take some of the operational load off your shoulders."

"And I'll always be there to remind you of the 'why'," Mara promised, her thumb tracing small circles on the back of his hand. "When the paperwork and the meetings start to feel all-consuming, I can share stories of the individual animals whose lives are directly impacted by the funding we secure, or by the knowledge we impart. It's easy to get lost in the details, but remembering the core mission, the lives we're touching, that's what fuels us."

He leaned in, his forehead resting against hers. The scent of salt and sea, so intrinsic to their lives, was also the scent of their shared commitment. "This is more than a sanctuary, Mara. It's our legacy. And building that legacy requires a foundation of trust that is as solid and as enduring as the coastline itself." He pulled back slightly, his eyes searching hers. "Are you ready to lay those next bricks with me?"

A radiant smile spread across Mara's face, a smile that held the depth of their shared history and the boundless promise of their future. "Always, Eli. Always." The plans for the visitor center, the curriculum for the workshops, the grant proposals – they were more than just documents. They were blueprints for a future built on unwavering trust, a testament to a love that had grown and strengthened, mirroring the enduring rhythm of the tides that whispered their constant, reassuring promise.

CHAPTER SIX

Facing Impermanence

Mara traced the condensation ring left by her water glass on the polished wood of her desk. The cool dampness was a stark contrast to the warmth that had settled between her and Eli just moments before, a warmth that now seemed to recede, leaving behind a faint chill. It wasn't a physical cold, but a tremor that ran through her, a familiar sensation that had become an unwelcome companion in recent weeks. The plans for the expanded outreach, the grant proposals, the detailed timelines – they were all tangible, measurable, and reassuringly concrete. But beneath the surface of their shared ambition, a different kind of reality was beginning to assert itself, one that felt as vast and as daunting as the ocean stretching out beyond her window.

The ocean. It had always been her sanctuary, a place of profound solace and endless fascination. But lately, as she gazed out at its shifting moods, its boundless expanse, it felt less like a balm and more like a mirror. The relentless ebb and flow of the tides, the way the waves crashed and receded, erasing the delicate etchings left on the sand – it was a constant, visceral reminder of impermanence. And as her feelings for Eli deepened, so too did her awareness of this universal truth, a truth that had begun to manifest as a gnawing fear.

It was the fear of loss. Not a sudden, dramatic event, but the slow, inevitable unraveling of things, the gradual fading of joy, the quiet departure of connection. The intensity of her love for Eli, a love that had blossomed unexpectedly and taken root with astonishing tenacity, had brought with it an equally profound capacity for pain. The thought of losing him, of losing the easy camaraderie, the shared laughter, the quiet understanding that now permeated their days, was an ache so deep it threatened to steal her breath.

She'd always been good at compartmentalizing, at building walls around her heart. Years spent immersed in the solitary world of scientific research had honed her ability to focus, to shut out distractions, to maintain an almost detached objectivity. It was a skill that had served her well in her professional life, allowing her to navigate the demanding realities of marine conservation without succumbing to the emotional toll of witnessing so much destruction and suffering. But Eli... Eli had a way of chipping away at those carefully constructed defenses, his unwavering warmth and genuine affection making it increasingly difficult to maintain her emotional distance.

He encouraged her to embrace vulnerability, to allow herself to feel the full spectrum of emotion, and in his presence, it often felt safe to do so. But as soon as he stepped away, or even as the weight of their shared future pressed in, the old anxieties would resurface, whispering their insidious warnings.

What if this, too, is temporary? What if it all slips away?

She tried to rationalize it. It was human nature to fear loss, especially when something was deeply cherished. But this felt different, more pervasive. It wasn't just a fleeting worry; it was a persistent undercurrent that threatened to destabilize the solid ground she and Eli were building together. She found herself consciously holding back, not in their shared work – that was sacred ground, a place where their collaboration was pure and uninhibited – but in the quieter moments, in the intimacy that was beginning to bloom between them.

There were times when Eli would reach for her, a simple gesture of affection, and she would find herself stiffening, a fraction of a second too slow to reciprocate, a subtle hesitation that he might or might not notice. She hated herself for it. It felt like a betrayal of the trust he had so readily extended to her, a betrayal of the future they were so diligently planning. But the fear was a formidable adversary, a shadow that clung to her, whispering that if she didn't hold onto a part of herself, if she didn't maintain a certain level of emotional reserve, the eventual pain of loss would be even more unbearable.

The vast, unpredictable ocean outside her window seemed to embody this unsettling feeling perfectly. One moment, it would be a calm, azure expanse, reflecting the clear blue sky. The next, it could be whipped into a frenzy by an unseen storm, its power and fury a stark reminder of its inherent wildness, its refusal to be tamed. It was beautiful, awe-inspiring, and utterly untamable. And so, she feared, was the potential for loss.

She remembered a conversation they'd had weeks ago, when the idea of expanding the rescue center's educational outreach had first taken concrete shape. Eli had been talking about the long-term vision, the impact they hoped to create, and he'd said, "This is more than just a project, Mara. This is a legacy. We're building something that will outlast us, something that will continue to make a difference long after we're gone."

At the time, his words had filled her with a sense of profound purpose and shared destiny. Now, they echoed with a different resonance.

Outlast us. The phrase, which had once felt like a testament to enduring impact, now carried a sting. It implied an end, a time when their collective presence would be no more. And the thought of that future, a future where Eli wasn't by her side, was a chasm she was terrified to look into.

She had always been independent, self-reliant. Her childhood had taught her the harsh lessons of unpredictability, of how quickly circumstances could change, leaving one adrift. Her parents, while loving, had been consumed by their own struggles, leaving Mara to navigate much of her emotional landscape alone. She'd learned to find solace in books, in nature, in the quiet pursuit of knowledge. Love, in its most profound and vulnerable form, had always felt like a luxury she could not afford to fully embrace, a risk she was not sure she was equipped to take.

But Eli. He had a way of making that risk feel not just acceptable, but essential. He was her anchor, her safe harbor, the one person who saw her, truly saw her, and loved her not in spite of her vulnerabilities, but because of them. And that, paradoxically, was the very source of her deepest fear. The more she allowed herself to be seen, the more she opened herself up to his love, the more she exposed herself to the potential for unimaginable pain.

She found herself scrutinizing his every word, his every gesture, searching for subtle clues that might indicate a wavering of his affections, a hint of disillusionment. It was an unfair and exhausting internal monologue, a self-sabotaging dance she had performed many times before in past relationships, always with the same predictable, painful outcome. But with Eli, the stakes felt immeasurably higher. This wasn't just about a romantic connection; it was about a shared purpose, a profound alignment of values and dreams. Losing him would mean not just the end of a love story, but the unraveling of a future she had only recently begun to truly believe in.

She would retreat into her work, burying herself in data, in research, in the comforting certainty of scientific inquiry. The complex equations, the intricate ecosystems, the observable, measurable phenomena of the natural world – these were places where she felt in control, where uncertainty could be systematically analyzed and, often, mitigated. The messy, unpredictable realm of human emotion, however, was a territory she was still struggling to navigate.

Sometimes, in the quiet of the evening, when Eli was engrossed in his own work, or when he was out tending to the sanctuary, she would find herself staring at him, a silent plea in her eyes.

Please don't leave. Please don't change. Please, whatever happens, stay. It was a silent prayer, whispered into the space between them, a desperate attempt to imbue their shared present with a permanence she knew, intellectually, did not exist.

She knew that her fear was not entirely rational. Eli had shown her nothing but steadfast devotion, unwavering support, and a love that felt as solid and as dependable as the earth beneath her feet. He was patient with her silences, understanding of her occasional withdrawal, and always, always, he found his way back to her, his warmth and affection a gentle, persistent invitation to let down her guard.

But the ocean was a constant, powerful reminder. Its immense power, its unpredictable nature, its relentless cycle of creation and destruction – it was a force of nature that demanded respect, a force that could not be controlled. And her fear, she realized with a sinking heart, was her own internal storm, a tempest brewing within the seemingly calm waters of her present happiness.

She picked up a smooth, grey stone from her desk, a memento from a beach walk with Eli. She ran her thumb over its cool, worn surface. It had been shaped by the relentless action of the waves, smoothed and perfected by forces beyond its control. Was she, too, being shaped by the currents of her fear? Was she allowing it to smooth away the rough edges of her true feelings, to erode the very foundation of the connection she so desperately wanted to preserve?

The plans for the visitor center, the workshops, the grant proposals – they were all moving forward, a testament to their shared vision and their unwavering commitment to the sanctuary. Eli's enthusiasm was infectious, his practicality a grounding force. He spoke of community engagement, of sustainable practices, of educating the next generation, and his words painted a vivid picture of a future brimming with hope and purpose.

But in the quiet moments, when the excitement of their shared endeavors subsided, the old anxieties would creep back in. The vastness of the ocean, the unpredictable nature of the tides, the inevitable passage of time – these were the constant, unspoken reminders of impermanence. And her love for Eli, as deep and as precious as it was, had amplified her awareness of this universal truth. The thought of losing him, or of losing the precious connection they had forged, was a fear that Mara fought to suppress, even as Eli's steady presence encouraged her to embrace a deeper, more vulnerable form of intimacy. The ocean, her lifelong sanctuary, now seemed to mirror the unsettling feeling of vulnerability that lay beneath the surface of her happiness.

The rhythmic whisper of the waves against the shore had always been a source of solace for Eli. Today, however, it felt like a gentle, insistent reminder of a truth he had long embraced: change was not an enemy to be feared, but an intrinsic part of existence, as natural and as unavoidable as the tides. He watched Mara, her brow furrowed in concentration as she reviewed grant proposals, her usual bright eyes shadowed by a flicker of apprehension he had come to recognize. He understood the source of that shadow. The very depth of their connection, the profound joy he found in her presence, had, for Mara, become intertwined with a nascent fear of loss. He knew she wrestled with the concept of impermanence, a concept he had learned to navigate not by resisting it, but by deepening his appreciation for the present.

He caught her eye, offering a soft, encouraging smile. He knew she saw the ocean, and through it, the vastness of what lay beyond their immediate grasp. He, too, saw the ocean, but for him, it was a symbol of enduring strength, of a power that ebbed and flowed but never truly ceased. The sheer immensity of it, the constant motion, the way it reshaped the coastline with a patient, relentless force – it was a testament to life's enduring capacity for transformation. He didn't see it as a harbinger of what might be lost, but as a beautiful, powerful entity that simply *was*. And in that understanding, there was a profound peace.

He walked over to her, his footsteps soft on the worn wooden floorboards of the office. He placed a hand on her shoulder, his touch a silent offering of comfort and reassurance. "Hey," he murmured, his voice a low rumble. "You're doing great work here. These proposals are thorough, and the vision is... inspiring." He squeezed gently, feeling the slight tension in her muscles. He knew that while she focused on the tangible aspects of their shared mission – the rescue center, the outreach programs, the intricate details of conservation – her mind often drifted to the more nebulous, and for her, more unsettling, aspects of their lives together.

"It's just... all of it," she finally said, her voice barely above a whisper, gesturing vaguely towards the papers spread before her. "The plans, the expansion, the future we're building. It feels so solid, so real. And then I look out there," she nodded towards the window, where the vast expanse of the ocean stretched to the horizon, "and I'm reminded how quickly everything can shift. How nothing truly stays the same."

Eli knelt beside her chair, his gaze meeting hers. He saw the vulnerability in her eyes, a raw honesty that always tugged at his heart. He reached out, gently tucking a strand of hair behind her ear. "I know," he said softly. "The ocean can be a powerful reminder, can't it? Of how much is beyond our control." He paused, letting his words sink in. "But it's also a reminder of what endures. The tides always return, Mara. The waves keep coming. And even when the shore is reshaped, life finds a way to adapt, to thrive."

He wanted her to understand that his own perspective on change wasn't born of a lack of feeling, but of a deep-seated understanding. He had seen enough of life to know that clinging too tightly to any one moment, any one state of being, was a recipe for heartache. His parents, though loving, had been nomadic, constantly chasing new opportunities, new horizons. While it had instilled in him a certain adaptability, it had also taught him that home wasn't a place, but a feeling, a connection. And that connection, he had discovered, was something one actively built and nurtured, not something one passively received and then feared losing.

"It's not about denying the possibility of change, Mara," he continued, his voice laced with a quiet earnestness. "It's about choosing what we focus on. I could spend my days worrying about when the next storm will hit, when the tide will go out and leave us stranded. Or I can choose to appreciate the beauty of the waves as they crash today, to build a stronger foundation on the shore, to ensure we have the resources to weather whatever comes." He traced the line of her jaw with his thumb, his touch feather-light. "And most importantly, I can focus on *us*. On the strength we find in each other, right now."

He understood that Mara's experiences had taught her to be cautious, to protect herself from the potential sting of disappointment. Her dedication to her work, her meticulous nature, were all defenses, honed by years of self-reliance. He admired that strength, but he also yearned for her to see that in their relationship, she didn't need to build those walls. He wanted to be her safe harbor, not a place she had to guard.

"Remember when we were planning the initial expansion of the center?" Eli asked, shifting slightly to sit on the floor beside her chair, his back resting against the cool wood. "You were so worried about the unforeseen costs, the potential delays. And we worked through every single one. We adapted. We found solutions. And the center is thriving because of it." He smiled at the memory. "That's what we do, Mara. We face challenges, we adapt, we grow. It's not about being fearless; it's about being resilient. It's about knowing that even if things change, we have the capacity to face it, together."

He believed that their love, their partnership, was a testament to this resilience. It wasn't built on a fragile promise of permanence, but on a robust commitment to navigate whatever came their way. He thought of the countless hours they had already spent working side-by-side, the debates, the laughter, the shared moments of quiet understanding. Each experience, each challenge overcome, had woven them closer together, creating a tapestry of shared history that was their true strength.

"I think about the future, of course," Eli admitted, his gaze drifting out to the sea. "I envision the outreach programs flourishing, the animals thriving, the sanctuary becoming a beacon of hope. But my vision isn't about a static, unchanging paradise. It's about a dynamic, living entity, one that will evolve, that will face new challenges and find new solutions. And the same goes for us." He turned back to Mara, his expression earnest. "Our relationship isn't a finished sculpture, Mara. It's a living, breathing thing. It's meant to grow, to change, to adapt. And that's what makes it so beautiful, so precious."

He saw the flicker of understanding in her eyes, a subtle softening of the tension in her shoulders. He knew this was a process, a journey they were on together. He couldn't simply erase her fears, but he could offer a different perspective, a steady hand, and an unwavering belief in their ability to face whatever came next. He wanted her to feel as secure in their love as he did, to understand that his commitment wasn't dependent on the absence of change, but on their shared strength to embrace it.

"Think of it this way," Eli proposed, his voice gentle. "If you're so focused on the possibility of the tide going out, you miss the wonder of the waves themselves. You miss the feel of the water, the warmth of the sun, the joy of swimming in the present. And if you're always braced for the storm, you might not notice the beauty of the rainbow that follows." He smiled, a warm, genuine smile that reached his eyes. "I don't want you to miss the beauty of what we have, Mara, because you're too busy worrying about what might happen. I want us to savor every moment, to build something so strong, so deeply rooted, that whatever the future holds, we can face it with our heads held high, together."

He knew that the plans they were meticulously crafting for the outreach programs and the visitor center were more than just professional endeavors. They were a tangible manifestation of their shared values, their mutual respect, and their profound affection for each other. He saw in those plans a blueprint for a future they were actively building, brick by brick, with intention and with love. And that, he felt, was the most powerful antidote to the fear of impermanence.

"This work we're doing," Eli continued, his voice filled with quiet conviction, "it's not just about saving animals. It's about building something lasting, something that contributes to the world. And in doing that, we're building a legacy, not just for the sanctuary, but for us. For our future. And that future, Mara, is something I'm not afraid of. Because I have you. And with you, I know we can handle anything."

He reached out and took her hand, his fingers interlacing with hers. He felt the slight tremor that ran through her, but also the answering warmth, the subtle tightening of her grip. It was a small gesture, but it spoke volumes. It was an acknowledgment, a silent agreement to face the present, and whatever came after, together. He looked out at the ocean again, its vastness no longer a source of dread, but a testament to the endless possibilities that lay before them. The rhythmic ebb and flow, the constant movement, was not a sign of instability, but of life's enduring, beautiful, and ever-present force. And in its timeless presence, Eli found a profound sense of peace, a quiet confidence that, with Mara by his side, they could navigate any tide, weather any storm, and continue to build something beautiful, something real, something that would endure. He squeezed her hand, a silent promise echoing the sentiment in his heart: they would cherish the present, build a strong foundation, and face the future, whatever it held, as a united force, their love a constant, unwavering anchor against the ever-shifting currents of life.

Mara's gaze lingered on the horizon, her fingers tracing the condensation rings left by her mug on the wooden desk. The rhythmic sigh of the waves, once a comforting lullaby, now seemed to echo the unsettled currents within her. She had listened to Eli, absorbing his words like a thirsty plant soaking up rain. His perspective on change, so grounded and serene, was a balm to her soul, yet it also highlighted the chasm of her own anxieties. For so long, she had navigated life by anticipating the worst, by building fortresses around her heart, a habit ingrained by past hurts and a keen awareness of life's inherent fragility. Eli's steady presence had begun to dismantle those defenses, but the foundation of her fear remained, a persistent hum beneath the surface of their growing intimacy.

She looked at him then, truly looked at him, seeing not just the man who loved her, but the man who was patiently teaching her to love herself, to trust in the present. His hand rested lightly on her knee, a silent anchor. The urge to speak, to finally unburden herself of the specter that haunted her quiet moments, became almost overwhelming. It was a terrifying prospect, laying bare the deepest, most vulnerable parts of herself, especially to someone she cherished so profoundly. What if her fears seemed irrational, a burden he couldn't possibly carry? What if her honesty pushed him away, leaving her exposed and alone?

The silence stretched, punctuated only by the distant cry of a gull and the ceaseless murmur of the sea. Eli's thumb moved in slow, reassuring circles on her skin. He didn't press, didn't demand. He simply waited, his gaze soft, his presence a testament to his unwavering support. It was this quiet patience, this deep well of understanding, that finally gave her the courage she needed. She took a deep, shaky breath, the scent of salt and pine filling her lungs.

"Eli," she began, her voice barely a whisper, rough with disuse and emotion. She swallowed, trying to find her footing. "There's something... something I need to say." Her eyes met his, and she saw no judgment, only a gentle invitation to continue. "You talk about change, about embracing it, and I... I understand it, intellectually. I see the beauty in it, in the resilience of nature, in the way you face things. But for me..." Her voice faltered again. "It's still so hard. The idea that things can just... disappear."

She looked away, out towards the vast expanse of blue, her gaze unfocused. "It's not just about the sanctuary, or our work. It's about... us. About this." She gestured vaguely between them. "This feeling of being so... solid. So safe. It's wonderful, Eli, more wonderful than I ever thought possible. But the thought of it not lasting... it's terrifying. It's a constant knot in my stomach." Tears pricked at the corners of her eyes, blurring the distant shoreline. She had never spoken these words aloud, not to anyone. They had festered in the quiet corners of her mind, a secret shame.

"I see how you are," she continued, her voice gaining a little strength, though it trembled with the weight of her confession. "You're so present, so focused on building and appreciating what we have *now*. And I try, I really do. But there are times, especially at night, or when I'm alone with my thoughts, when a wave of dread washes over me. What if something happens? What if one of us changes, or the circumstances change, or… or something just breaks us apart? It feels like this beautiful, fragile thing we've built, and I'm so afraid of the wind that might knock it down."

She finally turned back to him, her eyes glistening, her heart laid bare. "I'm so afraid of losing this, Eli. Losing you. It's a fear that feels so deep, so primal, that it sometimes paralyzes me. And I hate myself for it, because I feel like I should be stronger, more like you. I should be able to just enjoy this, without this constant whisper of 'what if'." The confession hung in the air between them, heavy and raw. She braced herself for his reaction, for the possibility of her fears being too much, of her vulnerability being a burden.

Eli listened with an attentiveness that was both profound and humbling. He didn't interrupt, didn't offer platitudes. He simply absorbed her words, his expression a mixture of empathy and a deep, unwavering love. When she finished, he didn't pull away. Instead, he moved closer, his arms encircling her as she sat slumped in her chair. He held her gently, allowing her the space to cry, to release the pent-up anxiety that had been weighing her down.

"Oh, Mara," he murmured into her hair, his voice thick with emotion. "Thank you. Thank you for telling me." He pulled back just enough to look into her eyes, his thumbs wiping away the tears that had begun to stream down her face. "Do you think I don't understand fear? Do you think this serenity you see is something I was just born with?" He chuckled, a soft, warm sound. "My fear just looks different. It's the fear of *not* being present, of missing the moments, of letting life pass me by because I was too busy worrying about the next thing. We all have our ghosts, Mara. Yours just wear a different costume."

He shifted so he was kneeling in front of her, his hands resting on her shoulders. "What you're feeling isn't a weakness. It's a testament to how much you value what we have. It's a sign of how deeply you love, and how much you're willing to protect that love. That's not something to be ashamed of. It's something to be honored." He looked out at the ocean again, his gaze steady. "You see the waves, and you see the potential for them to pull away, to leave you exposed. I see the waves, and I see the strength of the ocean, its constant renewal, its ability to shape and reshape, to bring life even to the harshest shores. Both perspectives are valid, Mara. Both are part of the truth."

"The fear you feel," he continued, his voice earnest, "it's valid. It's real. And it's okay to feel it. My only hope is that it doesn't eclipse the joy. My hope is that we can acknowledge the fear, but not let it define our present. You don't have to be fearless to build something beautiful, Mara. You just have to be brave enough to build it anyway. And you *are* brave. You're braver than you know."

He leaned in, pressing his forehead against hers, their breaths mingling. "This connection we have," he whispered, his voice a comforting caress, "it's not fragile. It's resilient. It's like the coastline itself. The storms come, the tides shift, but the core of it remains. We are building something with intention, with love, with a shared vision. And that foundation, Mara, is stronger than any fear."

He pulled back slightly, his eyes searching hers. "And if the worst were to happen, if change, in its most devastating form, were to come between us... would we break? Or would we find a way to carry the love, the lessons, the memories, and continue to grow, even in the face of that loss? I believe we would. I believe in

us that much." He gently touched her cheek. "Your fear of impermanence is a part of you, and I accept all of you, Mara. The parts that are bright and vibrant, and the parts that are shadowed and anxious. They are all what make you, you. And I love every single piece."

He stood up, offering her a hand. "Come," he said, his voice gentle. "Let's walk on the beach. The tide is going out, and the sand is usually firmest then. We can walk together, and you can tell me more about these fears, or we can just walk in silence. Whatever feels right. But know this, my love: you are not alone in this. Not ever."

As they walked hand in hand down to the shore, the cool, damp sand yielding beneath their feet, Mara felt a lightness she hadn't experienced in years. The raw vulnerability of her confession hadn't shattered their connection; it had deepened it. Eli's unwavering acceptance, his willingness to meet her fear with empathy and strength, had created a space where her anxieties, though still present, no longer felt like a solitary burden. The vast, indifferent ocean still stretched before them, a constant reminder of life's ever-changing nature, but now, walking beside Eli, with his hand warm in hers, she felt a quiet confidence settle within her. The future was still an unknown, a landscape of shifting tides, but she no longer felt like she had to face it alone, braced for the worst. She had found a partner, a confidant, a steadfast love, and in that, she had found a new kind of strength. The whisper of impermanence was still there, but now, it was joined by the stronger, more resonant melody of shared resilience, of a love that was not afraid to acknowledge its own vulnerabilities, and in doing so, found an even deeper, more enduring beauty.

The rhythmic lullaby of the waves, which had once soothed Mara's soul, now seemed to underscore a growing unease that had nothing to do with the personal anxieties Eli had so gently helped her unpack. As they walked along the shore, the retreating tide revealing a tapestry of glistening shells and intricate seaweed, a different kind of impermanence began to cast its shadow. It wasn't the abstract fear of losing a cherished relationship, but a tangible threat that loomed over the very place that had become their shared sanctuary: the marine rescue center.

It had started subtly, a ripple in the usual administrative currents. Whispers among the volunteers, hushed conversations in the break room, a certain tension in the air that Mara, in her newfound emotional openness, was now acutely attuned to. Eli, ever the pragmatist, had noticed it too. He'd seen the furrow in the brow of their most dedicated grant writer, the clipped responses from the local council liaison, the way the usually bustling donation box seemed to gather dust with unsettling regularity.

"Have you noticed anything... off, lately?" Eli had asked one evening, his voice deliberately casual as he helped Mara clean salvaged fishing nets. He didn't want to alarm her, but he also knew the value of shared awareness.

Mara nodded, her movements slowing. "I have. It's like... the energy has shifted. People are still committed, but there's an undercurrent of worry. What is it, Eli? Is it about the funding renewal for the specialized rehabilitation tanks?"

He sighed, running a hand through his hair. "That's part of it, yes. The Oceanic Conservation Grant. It's been our lifeline for the past three years, especially for the more intensive care cases. Their review meeting is next month, and the word from our contact is that the landscape has changed. There's a new directive from the board, a greater emphasis on immediate, tangible conservation efforts, like beach cleanups and policy advocacy, rather than, as they put it, 'long-term patient care.'"

Mara's stomach clenched, a familiar echo of her personal fears, but now directed outwards. "But... that's absurd! Our long-term patient care *is* tangible conservation. Each animal we rehabilitate and release is a success story, a vital part of the ecosystem."

"I know, darling," Eli said, his voice firm but gentle. "And we'll fight it. But it means we need to be prepared for the possibility that it might not be renewed. And that's not the only storm brewing on the horizon." He paused, his gaze sweeping across the darkened harbor, where the lights of distant boats bobbed like uncertain promises. "The regional council is also considering a new zoning proposal for the coastal areas. They're talking about 'managed development,' which, in plain English, usually means more tourism infrastructure, more development, and potentially, more environmental impact. Our permit to operate within this specific stretch of coastline is tied to the current environmental protections. If those change..."

The implication hung heavy in the air, as tangible as the salty mist that kissed their faces. The rescue center, their shared passion, their haven, the place where they had found so much meaning and connection, was facing a future shrouded in uncertainty. It felt like a cruel irony, that as they learned to navigate the shifting tides of their own hearts, the very ground beneath their shared purpose was beginning to feel less solid.

"So, what does this mean, practically?" Mara asked, her voice small.

Eli pulled her closer, his arm a warm, steady presence around her shoulders. "It means we need to diversify. We need to strengthen our local fundraising efforts, appeal to individual donors more aggressively, and explore partnerships with other organizations that align with our mission. It means re-evaluating our current operational costs, looking for efficiencies without compromising the quality of care. It means engaging with the council, presenting a united front, and making a very strong case for why the rescue center is not just a sanctuary for animals, but a vital community asset. And it means, Mara, that we might have to face some difficult decisions."

The word 'decisions' hung in the air, freighted with unspoken possibilities. Mara thought of the dedicated volunteers, the injured seals who depended on their care, the delicate ecosystems they worked to protect. The idea of the center's future being threatened felt like a personal attack, a brutal reminder of the impermanence she had been trying so hard to accept.

"I... I don't know how we're going to manage," she admitted, the weight of it pressing down on her. "It feels like too much, all at once."

"We'll manage because we have to," Eli said, his voice imbued with a quiet conviction. "And we'll manage because we have each other. Remember what we talked about? About facing fears, about not letting them paralyze us? This is that, on a larger scale. These are external storms, and they are significant, but we are not without our resources. We have our knowledge, our passion, our community support, and most importantly, we have our commitment to each other. If we can weather the storms that come between us, we can certainly weather these."

He led her to a weathered bench overlooking the dark, restless sea. The moon, a sliver of silver, cast a faint luminescence on the water, making the waves appear like a series of unfolding anxieties. "Think about it," Eli continued, his voice thoughtful. "The ocean itself is a constant cycle of change. Tides go in, tides go out. Storms rage, and then the waters calm. The coastline is reshaped, but it endures. We are like that, Mara. We adapt, we rebuild, we find new ways to navigate the currents."

He reached for her hand, his fingers interlacing with hers. "This grant, this zoning proposal – they are external forces. They are beyond our immediate control, but our reaction to them is not. We can choose to be overwhelmed, or we can choose to be resolute. We can choose to see only the threat, or we can see the opportunity to strengthen our foundations, to innovate, to prove just how vital this work is."

Mara looked at him, his face illuminated by the faint moonlight, his eyes filled with a steady determination. His calmness wasn't a denial of the difficulties, but a testament to his belief in their ability to overcome them. It was the same quiet strength he had shown when she had confessed her deepest fears about their relationship. He wasn't ignoring the potential for loss; he was acknowledging it, and then choosing to focus on what they could build, what they could protect, what they could nurture.

"It feels different when it's the center," she confessed, her voice laced with a new layer of vulnerability. "It's not just us. It's... all of them. The animals, the volunteers, the mission itself. It feels like so many lives are tied to this. If it fails..." She couldn't finish the sentence. The thought of the sanctuary being dismantled, of the animals being displaced, was almost unbearable.

"I understand," Eli said softly, squeezing her hand. "And that shared responsibility, that collective purpose, is precisely what will give us the strength. Think of the community that has rallied around us. We can tap into that. We can organize fundraising events, volunteer drives, awareness campaigns. We can educate the public about the importance of marine conservation and the specific needs of our center. We can show the grant committee and the council that this is not just a project, but a living, breathing entity that is deeply embedded in the fabric of this community."

He stood up, pulling her gently to her feet. "Let's go back. We have a lot to discuss, a lot to plan. And tonight, we'll start by sketching out a preliminary proposal for diversifying our funding streams. We'll brainstorm new donor outreach strategies. And tomorrow, I'll start drafting a letter to the council, outlining our concerns and requesting a meeting to discuss the zoning implications."

As they walked back towards the warm glow of the rescue center, Mara felt a subtle shift within her. The fear was still present, a low hum beneath the surface, but it was no longer the dominant note. Eli's steady presence, his pragmatic approach, and his unwavering belief in their ability to navigate this challenge, were building a new kind of resilience within her. The external uncertainties mirrored her internal ones, but now, facing them together, they felt less like an insurmountable threat and more like a call to action.

The next few weeks became a whirlwind of activity. Eli, with his knack for organization and his calm leadership, spearheaded the strategic planning. Mara, drawing on her newfound confidence and her deep empathy for the center's mission, poured her energy into communication and community engagement. They worked late into the nights, poring over spreadsheets, drafting grant proposals, and crafting compelling appeals to potential donors. The familiar scent of disinfectant and sea salt in the air, which had once been a source of comfort, was now also a constant reminder of the stakes involved.

They organized a "Save Our Sanctuary" fundraising gala, a massive undertaking that involved the entire community. Local businesses donated auction items, musicians volunteered their time, and chefs offered their services. Mara, usually reserved, found herself on stage, her voice clear and strong as she spoke about the vital work of the rescue center, her passion for the injured animals palpable. She spoke of a rescued pelican, its wing mended and its flight restored, a symbol of hope against the odds. She spoke of the collaborative spirit that had brought them all together, a testament to the power of shared purpose. Eli stood at the back of the room, his gaze fixed on her, a look of profound pride on his face. He saw not just a woman fighting for a cause, but a woman who had faced her deepest fears and emerged stronger, more capable, and more radiant than he could have ever imagined.

Simultaneously, Eli, with the help of a retired environmental lawyer who was a staunch supporter of the center, began meticulously dissecting the proposed zoning changes. They attended public hearings, armed with data and expert testimony, their arguments grounded in ecological impact assessments and the proven benefits of the rescue center's work. Mara often accompanied him, her presence a quiet anchor, her own growing understanding of the complexities of environmental policy impressing those who witnessed their unified front. They learned to anticipate objections, to reframe arguments, and to speak with a unified voice that resonated with conviction.

The grant committee's decision loomed large. The letters of support they had gathered poured in – from marine biologists, from local fishermen who had witnessed firsthand the center's impact, from families whose children had been inspired by the rescued animals. They even received a heartfelt letter from a former patient, a young woman whose own recovery from a serious illness had been profoundly aided by her volunteer work at the center. Mara and Eli had strategically highlighted the center's role not just as an animal hospital, but as a place of healing and connection for humans as well.

One blustery afternoon, as the tide began its relentless march back up the shore, the email arrived. Mara's heart pounded in her chest as she opened it, Eli's hand resting reassuringly on her shoulder. The subject line was stark: "Oceanic Conservation Grant Decision." She scrolled down, her breath catching in her throat. The verdict was not a complete rejection, but a partial renewal. They would receive a significant reduction in funding, enough to maintain basic operations and continue treating less complex cases, but not enough to sustain the specialized rehabilitation tanks. It was a blow, a stark reminder that their victory was not absolute.

"It's... not what we hoped for," Mara said, her voice barely above a whisper. Tears welled in her eyes, not of despair, but of frustration.

Eli pulled her into a hug. "It's not a rejection, Mara. It's a challenge. And we are up to the challenge." He held her close, the rhythmic crashing of the waves outside a stark counterpoint to the quiet determination settling within them. "This means we accelerate our local fundraising. It means we become even more efficient. It means we might have to scale back on some of the most intensive, long-term cases for a while, focusing our reduced resources on those with the best prognosis. It's not ideal, but it's not the end."

As if on cue, the council announced a delay in their zoning proposal decision, citing the need for further environmental impact studies and community consultations. It was a reprieve, a temporary pause in the storm, but the underlying threat remained. The future of the rescue center, once a beacon of certainty in their lives, now felt as unpredictable as the ocean itself.

They sat together that evening, watching the waves surge and recede, a constant, visual metaphor for the ebb and flow of their current struggle. Mara traced the condensation rings left by her mug on the wooden table, a familiar gesture that now seemed to carry a deeper meaning. The uncertainties surrounding the rescue center mirrored the personal anxieties she had once wrestled with in solitude. But now, facing these external challenges, she felt a different kind of strength. It was the strength of partnership, the quiet confidence that came from knowing that no matter what storms arose, she and Eli would face them, not with dread, but with a shared resolve, their love and commitment serving as their unshakeable anchor. The rescue center's future was uncertain, but their ability to face that uncertainty, together, felt more solid than ever before.

The news of the grant reduction and the looming zoning changes had settled over Mara and Eli like a persistent coastal fog, obscuring the clear path they thought they were on. The rescue center, their shared passion and a tangible representation of their shared values, was suddenly a landscape of potential loss. Yet, as they navigated these turbulent waters, a deeper understanding of their own bond began to surface, as solid and enduring as the ancient cliffs that guarded their coastline.

"It's not about promising 'forever' in a way that denies life's inherent changes," Eli said one evening, his arm around Mara as they watched the moonlight shimmer on the restless water. They had learned to find solace in these quiet moments, the rhythmic sigh of the waves a constant reminder of nature's ceaseless cycles, both beautiful and formidable. "It's about committing to the *now*, to the *us*, with the full knowledge that 'now' will inevitably evolve. It's about choosing, every single day, to turn towards each other, even when the horizon looks uncertain."

Mara leaned into his warmth, the steady beat of his heart a reassuring rhythm against her own. She had spent so long fearing impermanence, viewing it as a personal failing, a weakness to be overcome. But the challenges facing the rescue center, and by extension, their shared life, were forcing a shift in perspective. The grant reduction wasn't a sign of their inadequacy, nor was the zoning proposal a personal affront. They were simply external forces, the unpredictable swells and currents of life, much like the storms that battered their coastline.

"I used to think commitment meant building a fortress against all outside threats," Mara mused, her gaze fixed on the distant, twinkling lights of the harbor. "A place where nothing could ever touch us, where change was banished. But that's not sustainable, is it? Life *is* change. The coastline is always being reshaped by the tides, the weather. And we are too."

Eli nodded, his thumb stroking the delicate skin of her arm. "Exactly. Commitment isn't about achieving a static state of 'happily ever after' where nothing ever shakes the foundation. It's about the ongoing, intentional work of reinforcing that foundation. It's about honesty, vulnerability, and the willingness to adapt *together*. It's about looking at the storm on the horizon and saying, 'We might not be able to stop it, but we can face it side-by-side. We can learn to dance in the rain.'"

Their relationship, much like the rescue center itself, had been built on a bedrock of shared purpose and open communication. They had learned to articulate their fears, their hopes, and their needs, not as demands, but as invitations for deeper understanding and connection. This practice, honed through countless conversations and quiet moments of reflection, had equipped them with a powerful tool for navigating the current uncertainties. When the news of the grant reduction hit, their first instinct wasn't to blame or retreat, but to share their feelings, to acknowledge the disappointment and the worry, and then, to strategize.

"Remember when you told me about your fears of not being enough?" Mara asked, her voice soft. "I remember feeling that same fear, that if I wasn't perfect, if I didn't have all the answers, you would eventually find me wanting. But we talked through it. We acknowledged that neither of us is perfect, and that perfection isn't the goal. The goal is growth, and supporting each other's growth."

Eli turned to her, his eyes alight with a familiar warmth. "And we're doing that now, aren't we? The center is facing significant challenges, and it's forcing us to be more resourceful, more creative, and more unified than ever before. We're learning to be more efficient with our resources, to be more persuasive in our advocacy, to be more deeply connected to the community that supports us. These aren't things we would have necessarily learned if everything had remained smooth sailing. The challenges are, in a way, strengthening the very fabric of our commitment."

He stood and pulled her to her feet, his gaze steady and full of affection. "Our commitment to each other isn't just about our feelings for one another, Mara. It's about the active choices we make. It's about showing up, day after day, for the things we believe in, and for the people we love. It's about building something that can withstand the natural forces of change, not by trying to be impervious, but by being flexible and resilient."

The analogy to the coastline felt increasingly apt. The relentless waves, the shifting sands, the occasional fierce storms – they were all part of the coastline's enduring beauty. The coastline didn't disappear; it adapted. It found new formations, new strengths. Similarly, their commitment wasn't a rigid structure, but a living, evolving force. It was the conscious decision to remain entwined, to learn from the challenges, and to find new ways to navigate the inevitable changes life presented.

"So, the grant reduction means we have to work harder on local fundraising, and be even more strategic about our expenses," Mara said, her mind already sifting through the practical implications. "And the zoning proposal means we need to keep advocating for the center's value, demonstrating its vital role in the community and its minimal environmental impact. It feels overwhelming, but also... clarifying."

"Clarifying, yes," Eli agreed. "Because it strips away any pretense of a guarantee. It forces us to focus on what we *can* control: our effort, our dedication, our ability to work together. Our commitment to the center is a reflection of our commitment to each other. We pour our energy into it because it's a shared endeavor, a tangible manifestation of our values. And our commitment to each other is what allows us to pour that energy, to face these external pressures without fracturing internally."

He took her hands, his grip firm and reassuring. "Think about the volunteers, Mara. Their dedication doesn't waver because the grant is reduced. They continue to show up, to clean the tanks, to feed the seals, to educate visitors. Their commitment is rooted in their belief in the mission, and in the community that surrounds it. Our commitment to each other is similar, but it's the core. It's the anchor that allows us to engage with the wider world, to take on these external challenges, and to keep our center, and our relationship, strong."

The concept of commitment as an anchor wasn't about immobility; it was about stability. An anchor doesn't prevent a ship from sailing or from facing choppy seas; it prevents it from being swept away by the currents. It provides a fixed point from which to navigate, a place of return. In their relationship, their shared commitment was that anchor. It allowed them to sail into uncertain waters, to face the inevitable storms, knowing they had a solid, reliable point of connection, a place where they could always find shared purpose and unwavering support.

"It's about actively choosing to stay moored, even when the waves are high," Mara said, a newfound clarity dawning in her eyes. "It's not about the absence of challenge, but about the presence of a steadfast core. We are choosing to be that steadfast core for each other, and that allows us to tackle the external challenges, like the center's funding, with more resilience."

Eli smiled, a deep, loving smile that reached his eyes. "Precisely. We are not guaranteeing that the rescue center will always be funded at its current level, or that the zoning laws will never change. Those are external factors. But we *are* guaranteeing that we will face those uncertainties together, with honesty, with support, and with a shared determination to do our best. That's the power of commitment. It doesn't eliminate impermanence; it provides the strength and security to navigate it."

The weight of the future still felt present, the financial realities and the policy shifts were not to be dismissed lightly. But now, instead of feeling like a crushing burden, it felt like a shared responsibility, a call to action that they were uniquely equipped to answer. Their love for each other, tested and deepened by past challenges, had become an unshakeable anchor, grounding them amidst the shifting tides of life. They understood that true commitment wasn't a passive state of being, but an active, ongoing choice to stand together, to adapt, and to build a future, not in denial of change, but with the quiet strength that came from facing it, hand in hand, as an unyielding team. The coastline, in its perpetual state of becoming, was a constant reminder that enduring strength often lay not in rigidity, but in adaptability, and that their commitment, much like the land itself, would continue to find its form and its resilience in the face of every tide.

CHAPTER SEVEN

Redefining 'Forever

The familiar cadence of waves meeting the shore had always been Mara and Eli's lullaby, a constant, soothing presence in their coastal lives. But lately, that rhythm had taken on a new significance, mirroring the subtle yet profound shift in their understanding of commitment. The grand pronouncements of forever, once the cornerstone of their shared dreams, now felt like echoes from a different era, replaced by the quiet power of daily presence and the steadfastness of consistent effort. They were learning that love, much like the sea they lived beside, was not a placid, unchanging entity, but a dynamic force, forever in motion, demanding constant attention and gentle, unwavering nurture.

"It's not about the vow itself, is it?" Mara mused one afternoon, her fingers tracing the condensation on her iced tea glass as they sat on their porch, the salty breeze ruffling her hair. The rescue center, though facing its challenges, was alive with the hum of activity – volunteers tending to recovering seabirds, the gentle clatter of equipment, the distant cries of gulls. It was a testament to their collective effort, a living, breathing entity that demanded their constant attention, their *presence*. "It's about showing up. Every single day. Not with grand gestures, necessarily, but with the willingness to simply *be* there. To listen, to support, to share the load, even when it's mundane."

Eli nodded, his gaze fixed on the horizon, where the endless blue of the sky met the equally vast expanse of the ocean. He had learned to see their love not as a destination, but as a journey, a continuous unfolding. "Exactly. Forever isn't a finished product; it's an ongoing creation. It's in the early mornings, making coffee for each other before the world wakes up. It's in the quiet evenings, simply sitting in comfortable silence, knowing that the other person is there. It's in the shared grocery lists, the remembered appointments, the small acts of service that weave the tapestry of our days together." He turned to her, a gentle smile gracing his lips. "It's in the conscious choice to prioritize each other, not just in the big moments, but in the ordinary ones too. The grant reduction, the zoning proposal – these are big moments, yes, and they test us. But our ability to navigate them is rooted in the strength of our everyday connection. It's in the thousand tiny moments that have built this foundation, this deep well of trust and shared history."

Mara reached out, her hand finding his. His skin was warm, familiar. "I used to think commitment meant guaranteeing an outcome. That if I promised forever, I had to ensure a certain kind of future, free from doubt or hardship. But life doesn't work that way. The sea doesn't promise a calm surface every day.

It roars, it crashes, it recedes. Yet, it always returns. Its essence remains, even as its form changes." She squeezed his hand. "Our love is like that, isn't it? It's not about guaranteeing a storm-free existence, but about being the constant, the anchor, that holds firm *through* the storms. It's about the choice to remain present, to engage, to care, even when things are difficult."

Their days had become a testament to this evolving understanding. The challenges at the rescue center, once a source of significant anxiety, had inadvertently become a catalyst for deeper connection. They found themselves instinctively turning to each other, not for solutions, but for shared strength. Eli would arrive at the center, his brow furrowed with concern over a new lead on potential funding cuts, and Mara would meet him with a quiet reassurance, a cup of his favorite tea already waiting, her presence a silent affirmation of their shared purpose. She, in turn, would confide her worries about a particular animal's slow recovery, and he would be there, not to dismiss her concerns, but to listen, to offer a different perspective, or simply to hold her hand as she poured out her heart. These weren't grand pronouncements of love; they were the steady, reliable beats of a shared heart.

"Remember when we first bought this house?" Eli asked, his gaze sweeping across the familiar coastline visible from their porch. "We talked about renovations, about painting the living room blue, about the future we would build within these walls. It was all about the *plan*, the *vision*." He chuckled softly. "And we have done so much of that. But the real joy, the real depth, came from the living *in* it. From the scraped knees, the spilled wine, the laughter that echoed through these rooms. It was in the messy, beautiful, everyday life we created, not just in the blueprint."

Mara's smile widened. "And now, the center is like that too. It's not just about the mission statement or the strategic plan anymore. It's about the dedicated volunteer who stays late to finish a report, the veterinarian who works tirelessly to save a stranded dolphin, the child who visits with a handmade card. It's about the collective spirit, the shared dedication that manifests in countless small, vital actions. And our role in that – our *presence* – is what nourishes it. It's not enough to have a good idea; it requires ongoing, committed effort."

This shift in perspective had allowed them to approach the challenges with a renewed sense of purpose, rather than despair. The grant reduction meant a tightening of belts, yes, but it also meant a greater reliance on their community, a deeper engagement with the very people they served. It was an opportunity to showcase their resilience, their resourcefulness, and, most importantly, their unwavering commitment to their cause. The zoning changes, while potentially disruptive, became an impetus to articulate even more clearly the center's irreplaceable value, its integration into the fabric of their coastal town.

"I used to feel like if I wasn't actively *doing* something, if I wasn't fixing the problem, then I wasn't contributing," Mara admitted, her voice laced with a vulnerability that Eli had come to cherish. "I equated presence with productivity. But now, I understand that sometimes, the most profound contribution is simply being a stable, loving presence for the other person, or for the community, even when the path forward isn't clear. It's about radiating a steady calm, a belief that we can weather this together."

Eli reached over and gently brushed a strand of hair from her cheek. "And that belief is so powerful, Mara. It's contagious. When you are present, truly present, with your heart open, it creates a space for others to do the same. It allows them to feel seen, to feel supported. It's not about having all the answers; it's about offering your unwavering belief in the possibility of a solution, and in the strength of the people working towards it."

He stood, stretching his long limbs, and walked to the edge of the porch, breathing in the sea air. "Think about the migrating birds that pass through here. They don't stop every night to ponder the vastness of their journey. They simply fly, guided by instinct, by the pull of the seasons. They rely on the winds, the currents, but also on their own internal compass, their innate drive to reach their destination. Our commitment is like that internal compass. It doesn't eliminate the need for navigation, for adaptation, but it provides the unerring direction."

The coastline, with its ancient cliffs and ever-shifting sands, was a constant reminder of this delicate balance between permanence and change. The cliffs, seemingly immutable, were slowly being eroded by the relentless caress of the waves. The sands, constantly reshaped by the tides, were nevertheless a stable foundation for the dunes and the life that thrived there. Their love, too, was finding this new equilibrium. It was solid, grounded in shared values and deep affection, yet flexible enough to adapt to the evolving landscape of their lives.

"It's about showing up with our whole selves, isn't it?" Mara said, joining him at the railing, their shoulders brushing. "Not just the parts that are strong and capable, but the parts that are uncertain, the parts that are weary. It's about offering that vulnerability as an invitation for connection, for shared resilience. The 'forever' we're building isn't a fortress against the world; it's a home within it, a place where we can retreat, recharge, and then step back out, stronger, together."

Eli wrapped an arm around her, pulling her close. The rhythmic crash of the waves below seemed to underscore his words. "And the presence, Mara. That's the key. It's not just a promise whispered in the dark; it's the light left on, the meal prepared, the listening ear offered without judgment. It's the quiet affirmation, 'I am here.' And in that simple, consistent presence, we find our true 'forever.' It's not a destination we reach, but a continuous act of choosing each other, over and over again, in the grand and the small moments. It is the steady, unwavering heartbeat of our shared life, resonating with the timeless rhythm of the sea."

He tilted her chin up, his eyes holding hers, full of a love that had deepened and matured, much like the ancient landscape around them. "We are not promising a life devoid of challenge. We are promising that whatever challenges arise, we will face them together, with our presence, our commitment, and our unwavering belief in each other. That is the true meaning of forever, for us. It is in the steadfastness of our presence, the quiet, enduring strength of our day-to-day love."

The news of the grant reduction and the impending zoning changes, which had once threatened to cast a long shadow over their future, now felt like the natural ebb and flow of the tide. They were not a sign of impending doom, but simply the current reality that their shared commitment was designed to navigate. Their relationship had evolved from a series of promises about a distant, idealized future to a deeply ingrained practice of present-day connection. The abstract concept of 'forever' had solidified into the tangible reality of Eli's hand in Mara's, the shared glance across a crowded room, the comforting weight of a familiar presence beside them each night. They understood that their love, like the enduring coastline, was not defined by its stillness, but by its capacity to adapt, to withstand, and to continuously find strength in its deepest, most constant form: their unwavering, daily presence for one another. The sea's endless motion became their symbol, a testament to a love that was not static, but vibrantly, beautifully, eternally alive.

The shift Mara and Eli had undergone wasn't a single, dramatic epiphany, but rather a series of quiet, deliberate decisions, each one a brick laid in the foundation of their evolving understanding of "forever." They were learning that love, at its most enduring, wasn't a passive state of being, but an active, ongoing process of creation. It was in the conscious choice to lean in, rather than pull away, when faced with the inevitable friction of two lives intertwined.

Consider the everyday moments, the seemingly insignificant choices that, in retrospect, formed the bedrock of their commitment. There were times, of course, when weariness would settle in, when the demands of the rescue center, or the pressures of their personal lives, would leave them feeling drained. In those moments, the instinct might be to retreat, to seek solace in solitude, to nurse their own exhaustion. But Mara and Eli were learning to override that impulse. Instead of shutting down, Mara would find herself deliberately seeking Eli out. It might be a simple question about his day, offered with a soft tone, an invitation for him to share, even if he felt too tired to elaborate. Or it might be the quiet act of making his favorite cup of tea, a small gesture of care that said, "I see you. I'm here." Eli, in turn, had cultivated a similar intentionality. When he sensed Mara withdrawing, perhaps lost in thought about a particularly challenging case at the center, he wouldn't pry or push. Instead, he would offer a quiet presence, a hand gently placed on her arm, a silent acknowledgment that he was a safe harbor. He understood that sometimes, the most profound connection came not from words, but from the silent reassurance of being truly seen and understood. These weren't grand declarations; they were the steady, persistent whispers of a love that chose to show up, day after day.

One evening, after a particularly taxing day at the center, the air in their small cottage felt heavy with unspoken stress. A promising rehabilitation had taken an unexpected turn for the worse, and Mara carried the weight of that disappointment home. Eli, sensing her quiet struggle, didn't immediately try to solve the problem or offer platitudes. Instead, he put on some soft music, the kind that always soothed her, and began preparing a simple, comforting meal. He didn't demand an explanation, didn't press her to talk. He simply created an atmosphere of peace and ease, a silent offering of respite. When Mara finally felt ready to speak, her voice thick with unshed tears, he listened without interruption, his gaze steady and compassionate. He didn't offer easy answers, for he knew there were none. Instead, he offered his presence, his unwavering support. He validated her feelings, not by agreeing that the situation was dire, but by acknowledging the depth of her empathy and the validity of her distress. "It's okay to feel this way, Mara," he said softly, his hand reaching for hers across the dinner table. "You poured so much of yourself into that little one, and it's natural to feel this pain when things don't go as hoped. Your dedication is what makes you extraordinary, even when the outcome isn't what we wished for." That simple act of validation, that conscious choice to be present with her grief rather than trying to erase it, was more potent than any grand gesture. It was a testament to the deliberate cultivation of understanding over judgment, patience over frustration.

Eli, too, found himself making conscious choices that reinforced their bond. There were times when he felt the urge to disengage, particularly when faced with Mara's occasional bouts of idealism or her passionate, sometimes overwhelming, advocacy for a cause. His natural inclination might be to offer a pragmatic counterpoint, to ground her in reality. But he was learning that this wasn't always what she needed. More often, she needed to feel heard, to have her passion acknowledged, even if he couldn't fully share her perspective at that exact moment. He began to practice active listening, not just hearing her words, but seeking to understand the emotional currents beneath them. He would ask clarifying questions, not to challenge her, but to deepen his comprehension. "So, if I'm understanding correctly, what concerns you most is the long-term impact on the nesting grounds, not just the immediate disruption?" he might ask, his tone genuinely curious. This deliberate effort to bridge their perspectives, to choose connection over the easy path of disagreement or dismissal, created a space where Mara felt truly seen. It fostered an environment where vulnerability was met not with criticism, but with curiosity and acceptance.

The zoning proposal, a looming administrative hurdle that threatened to complicate their operations at the rescue center, had initially sparked a wave of anxiety for both of them. Mara, ever the optimist, was quick to rally the community, to organize petitions and attend public meetings. Eli, while supportive of her efforts, found himself wrestling with the practical implications, the potential bureaucratic quagmire. He could have easily allowed his own concerns to manifest as doubt, to subtly or overtly express reservations about the feasibility of their opposition. But he consciously chose a different path. He recognized that Mara's energy and passion were vital to their cause, and that his role was to support and complement, not to undermine. He made it a point to be present at those meetings, even when he had a long day at the office. He would sit beside her, a quiet, steady presence, his hand often resting on her knee, a silent anchor. He would offer his analytical skills, helping her to research zoning laws or draft persuasive arguments, but he did so with an attitude of collaboration, not correction. He was choosing to invest his energy in bolstering her strengths, rather than focusing on potential weaknesses. This conscious decision to align their efforts, to choose shared purpose over individual apprehension, transformed a potentially divisive issue into an opportunity for them to work more closely than ever.

Their communication, too, had undergone a significant metamorphosis. Gone were the days of assuming the other knew what they were thinking or feeling. They had learned the hard way that assumptions were fertile ground for misunderstanding and resentment. Now, they made a deliberate effort to articulate their needs and their emotions, even when it felt awkward or vulnerable. Mara might say, "I'm feeling overwhelmed by the upcoming fundraising event. I need a few quiet evenings to myself this week to recharge, if that's okay." Eli, in turn, might confess, "I'm finding it hard to concentrate at work today. I'm worried about the new permit application, and I could really use a distraction this evening, maybe we could go for a walk?" These were not complaints; they were honest, vulnerable declarations that invited their partner to participate in their well-being. This commitment to open and honest communication, this conscious choice to speak their truth with kindness and respect, was a vital safeguard against the erosion of intimacy. It allowed them to navigate the inevitable rough patches not by ignoring them, but by addressing them head-on, with a shared commitment to finding a resolution that honored both of their needs.

The value of these conscious choices extended beyond the interpersonal realm and permeated their shared aspirations. The rescue center, a project born from their shared passion, now demanded their constant, engaged participation. It wasn't enough to have envisioned its creation; they had to actively nurture it, to make deliberate decisions about its direction and its needs. When a new conservation initiative required significant financial investment, they didn't immediately retreat into personal savings. Instead, they sat down together, not to debate whether they *could* afford it, but to strategize *how* they could make it happen. They chose to explore grant opportunities, to organize community fundraising events, to re-evaluate their personal spending habits. This was a collective decision, born from a shared commitment to the center's mission, and it required a willingness to sacrifice immediate personal gratification for a larger, shared goal. Eli might have opted for a new piece of equipment for his workshop, or Mara might have dreamt of a new piece of art for their home. But in that moment, their conscious choice was to prioritize the needs of the center, and in doing so, they reinforced the strength of their partnership. They were not individuals with separate desires, but a unified front, making deliberate choices together.

This principle extended even to their leisure time. They had learned that "quality time" wasn't something that just happened; it had to be intentionally scheduled and protected. In their busy lives, it was easy for days to slip by without any dedicated time for just the two of them. So, they made a conscious choice to carve out those moments. It might be a standing Saturday morning breakfast date, or a weekly movie night, or simply an agreement to put away their phones and truly connect for an hour each evening. These weren't obligations; they were deliberate acts of prioritizing their relationship amidst the chaos of their lives. Eli understood that Mara craved his undivided attention, and he made it a point to give it to her during those designated times, putting aside work emails and silencing his notifications. Mara, in turn, made sure that their time together was truly restorative, not a continuation of stressful conversations or problem-solving. She chose to focus on shared joy, on lighthearted conversation, on simply enjoying each other's company. This deliberate cultivation of shared experiences, this commitment to nurturing their connection, ensured that their relationship didn't become a casualty of their busy schedules.

The evolution of their understanding of "forever" was inextricably linked to the value they placed on conscious choice. It was the understanding that commitment wasn't a passive inheritance, but an active creation. It was the deliberate decision to choose empathy over indifference, patience over impatience, and connection over isolation. Each day presented them with opportunities to make these choices, and with each conscious decision to invest in their relationship, they were not only strengthening their bond, but also redefining the very meaning of a lasting love. It was a love built not on grand pronouncements, but on the quiet, consistent power of choosing each other, again and again, in the tapestry of their everyday lives. This was the essence of their new "forever," a vibrant, living testament to the enduring power of intentionality.

Eli found himself staring out at the expanse of the ocean, a familiar ritual that often brought a profound sense of calm and perspective. The rhythmic crash of waves against the shore, the endless horizon where the sapphire blue of the sea met the pale cerulean of the sky – it was a constant, a reassuring presence in a world that often felt fleeting. He'd spent years chasing horizons, restless and unanchored, always seeking something just beyond his grasp. But now, watching the tide ebb and flow with an ancient, unwavering rhythm, he saw not an escape, but a foundation. He saw a reflection of the future he was building, brick by deliberate brick, with Mara.

He remembered a time when "forever" felt like a cage, a suffocating promise that would inevitably stifle his spirit. His youthful wanderlust, a seemingly insatiable hunger for new experiences, had always warred with any notion of settling down. The idea of putting down roots, of committing to a single place, a single person, had felt like an admission of defeat, a surrender of his freedom. He'd romanticized the nomadic life, the thrill of the unknown, the allure of a life lived on the edge of possibility. But that restlessness, once a driving force, had slowly begun to feel like an emptiness, a constant ache for something he couldn't quite define. He'd been running, he realized now, not towards something exciting, but away from the quiet fear of commitment, away from the vulnerability it demanded.

The shift hadn't been instantaneous, but rather a gradual dawning, illuminated by the steady glow of Mara's presence. Her quiet strength, her unwavering dedication to the creatures they cared for, her ability to find beauty and purpose in the everyday – it had all seeped into his consciousness, reshaping his perceptions. He'd watched her pour her heart and soul into the rescue center, not for recognition or reward, but because it was her calling, her way of contributing to the world. And in her dedication, he'd found a new kind of passion, one that was grounded, purposeful, and deeply satisfying.

Standing there, the salt-laced wind whipping through his hair, Eli finally felt a profound clarity about his long-term vision. It wasn't about grand adventures or fleeting thrills anymore. It was about building something solid, something lasting, with Mara by his side. His vision was rooted in this very place, this rugged coastline that had, against all odds, become home. It was about the rescue center, not just as a project, but as a shared legacy, a testament to their combined efforts and their deep love for the natural world. He saw himself continuing to work alongside her, their partnership evolving, their understanding deepening with each passing season.

He envisioned a life where the sanctuary expanded, where they could offer refuge to even more creatures in need. He saw opportunities for educational outreach, for inspiring the next generation to care for the environment. This wasn't a passive dream; it was a blueprint, meticulously crafted in the quiet hours, fueled by a love that had become his anchor. He saw himself continuing to hone his skills, perhaps even mentoring younger veterinarians who shared their passion, creating a ripple effect of care that extended far beyond their immediate reach. He imagined the rescue center becoming a beacon of hope, a symbol of what could be achieved when passion met purpose.

His desire for a partnership with Mara was multifaceted. He craved the intensity of their connection, the spark that ignited whenever they were together, the deep intellectual and emotional resonance that had become so integral to his life. But he also yearned for the quiet comfort of shared routines, the simple joy of knowing she was there, a constant in the ebb and flow of their lives. He wanted a love that was both a thrilling adventure and a peaceful harbor. He had always equated stability with stagnation, but now he understood that true stability was born from a shared commitment, from the conscious choice to build a life together, weathering storms and celebrating sunshine side-by-side.

He found a particular solace in the ocean's immensity. It was a constant reminder that while life could be turbulent, there was an underlying power, an enduring strength that prevailed. The ocean wasn't static; it was a dynamic entity, constantly in motion, yet always fundamentally itself. This mirrored the kind of partnership he envisioned with Mara – one that was vibrant and evolving, yet grounded in an unshakeable core of love and respect. He saw the way the waves shaped the coastline over centuries, not through force, but through persistent, gentle persistence. That, he realized, was the essence of a lasting relationship.

His restlessness hadn't vanished entirely, but it had been transmatured. It was no longer a desperate urge to escape, but a quiet drive to contribute, to create, to build something meaningful. He looked forward to the challenges that lay ahead, not with apprehension, but with a sense of purpose. He envisioned them navigating the complexities of running their sanctuary, facing financial hurdles and the emotional toll of their work, but doing so as a united front. He saw them learning, growing, and adapting together, their bond strengthening with each shared experience.

He thought about the small cottage they shared, its walls filled with the echoes of their laughter and their quiet conversations. He saw it expanding, perhaps, to accommodate their growing dreams, or simply remaining as it was, a cozy testament to the life they had already built. The key, he knew, was not the physical structure, but the shared foundation within. He saw the garden Mara was so proud of, flourishing under her care, and he envisioned their shared life mirroring that growth, a vibrant tapestry woven with shared experiences and mutual respect.

He imagined their future holidays, not spent in exotic locales, but here, by the sea, perhaps with a small group of close friends, or simply reveling in each other's company. The notion of "getting away" had lost its appeal; their greatest escape was often found in simply being present with each other, in the familiar comfort of their shared home. He saw their lives becoming richer, deeper, not through accumulation of possessions or experiences, but through the deepening of their connection.

Eli traced the outline of a distant sailboat with his eyes. It was a solitary vessel, navigating the vastness, and he understood its journey. But he knew, with a certainty that settled deep in his bones, that his greatest journey was not one of solitary exploration, but of shared passage. He no longer sought to be the captain of his own isolated ship, but a willing, dedicated crewmate on a vessel built for two, charting a course toward a horizon that promised not just adventure, but enduring love and a life well-lived, side-by-side with Mara. His vision was clear, solid, and as vast and profound as the ocean before him. It was a vision of a shared future, built on passion, stability, and an unwavering commitment to the woman who had shown him the true meaning of forever. He was ready to embrace it, not as an obligation, but as the greatest adventure of his life.

The salt-laced breeze, once a solitary companion to her contemplative strolls along the shoreline, now carried the comforting echo of Eli's footsteps beside her. Mara had always found solace in the quiet solitude of the coast, in the vastness of the ocean that mirrored the untamed parts of her own spirit. For years, she had navigated her life with a fierce independence, a quiet strength honed by necessity and a deep-seated belief that she was most effective when shouldering her burdens alone. The rescue center, a testament to her unwavering dedication, had been her sanctuary and her sole focus. It was a place she had built with her own hands, her heart poured into every brick, every carefully tended enclosure, every late night spent coaxing a frightened animal back to health. She had viewed shared responsibility not as an invitation, but as a potential dilution of her purpose, a risk of compromising the integrity of her vision.

Yet, the subtle shift had begun long before she consciously acknowledged it. It was in the quiet understanding that passed between her and Eli as they worked side-by-side, mending a broken fence, or the shared sigh of relief when a difficult surgery was successful. It was in the way he anticipated her needs before she voiced them, the unspoken agreement that settled over them during late-night feeding rounds, the effortless rhythm they fell into when tending to a new arrival, a frightened creature in need of their collective care. Eli's presence had become not an intrusion, but an augmentation. He didn't just offer help; he offered a partnership, a shared vision that expanded the possibilities of what they could achieve together.

This new understanding of shared responsibility wasn't a sudden revelation, but a gentle unfolding, much like the tide itself, gradually reshaping the familiar contours of her life. She found herself actively seeking his input, not out of necessity, but out of a genuine desire to weave his perspective into the fabric of the rescue center. It began with small things: asking his opinion on the best location for a new aviary, discussing the financial projections for the coming year, or even just sharing the anxieties that sometimes gnawed at her in the quiet hours before dawn. Each shared decision, each collaborative effort, felt like a strengthening of an invisible cord, binding them closer.

She remembered a particularly challenging week, when a severe storm had wreaked havoc on the coast, bringing with it a surge of injured wildlife. The days had blurred into a relentless cycle of rescue, rehabilitation, and round-the-clock care. Before Eli, she would have submerged herself in the chaos, fueled by adrenaline and sheer willpower, emerging exhausted and depleted. But this time was different. Eli had been a constant, steady presence. He had seamlessly taken over tasks she would have normally handled herself, managing the intake of new animals, coordinating with volunteers, even stepping in to assist with the more physically demanding aspects of care. He hadn't just been helping; he had been sharing the weight, allowing her to focus her energy where it was most critical, without the gnawing worry of what else was being neglected.

The relief, she realized, wasn't just in the alleviation of her workload, but in the profound emotional support she received. Eli's calm demeanor, his reassuring words, his unwavering belief in their ability to overcome the challenges, had been a balm to her frayed nerves. He saw her exhaustion not as a weakness, but as a testament to her dedication, and he responded not with pity, but with a quiet, capable partnership. In those moments, surrounded by the scent of damp fur and antiseptic, the steady hum of generators, and the soft cries of injured animals, Mara felt a new depth of connection, a sense of 'us' that was more powerful than anything she had experienced before.

This evolving perspective extended beyond the practicalities of the rescue center. It permeated their personal lives, infusing their shared moments with a richer understanding of mutual reliance. She found herself willingly taking on tasks that had once felt like impositions, like preparing a hearty meal after a long day, or organizing their shared living space. These were not sacrifices, but offerings, small gestures of love and commitment that reinforced their bond. She saw these acts of domestic partnership not as a step backward from her independent stride, but as a natural progression of a love that was meant to be shared in all its facets.

Mara had always believed that true strength lay in self-sufficiency. It was a mantra she had lived by, a shield she had carefully constructed around her heart. Vulnerability, she had assumed, was the antithesis of strength. But Eli had shown her a different truth. He had, with gentle persistence, chipped away at her defenses, not by force, but by consistently demonstrating his own vulnerability, his own willingness to lean on her. He shared his worries about the center, his moments of self-doubt, his hopes for their future, and in doing so, he had created a safe space for her own insecurities to surface.

The first time she had truly allowed herself to be vulnerable with him, to confess a deep-seated fear about the center's financial stability, she had braced herself for judgment or, worse, pity. Instead, Eli had listened with an attentiveness that settled her racing heart. He had held her hand, his thumb tracing soothing patterns on her skin, and then he had met her gaze with unwavering resolve. "We'll figure it out, Mara," he had said, his voice a low rumble of reassurance. "Together." That simple promise, spoken with such conviction, had dissolved years of ingrained anxiety. It wasn't just about finding a solution; it was about the shared endeavor, the implicit trust that they would face any challenge as a united front.

Her embrace of shared responsibility was also a conscious effort to honor Eli's unwavering belief in her. He saw her not just as a capable rescuer, but as a partner, someone whose thoughts and feelings mattered deeply. He never dismissed her ideas, even when they were ambitious or unconventional. Instead, he would engage with them, dissect them, and often, find ways to integrate them into their shared vision. This validation was a powerful force, encouraging her to step further out of her shell, to trust her own instincts in a new light, and to believe that her contributions, when combined with his, were more than the sum of their parts.

She began to actively delegate more tasks to the volunteers, something she had previously resisted, fearing that others wouldn't uphold the same meticulous standards. But Eli encouraged her, offering to train new recruits alongside her, providing a buffer of support that eased her apprehension. He helped her develop clear protocols and training modules, making the process more efficient and less draining for her. This shared effort in building their team was a subtle yet significant shift, acknowledging that the success of the rescue center was not solely her responsibility, but a collective endeavor they were both invested in.

The quiet satisfaction she felt when they successfully navigated a complex situation together, whether it was a large-scale animal rescue or a difficult conversation with a potential donor, was a reward in itself. It wasn't the adrenaline rush of solitary triumph, but a deep, resonant sense of accomplishment, a shared victory that solidified their partnership. She found herself looking forward to these moments, to the collaborative problem-solving, the shared laughter that often punctuated even the most stressful days, the quiet moments of reflection where they could acknowledge their combined efforts.

Her perspective on 'forever' had also undergone a profound metamorphosis. Once, the word had conjured images of a static existence, a predictable path that stifled growth. Now, she saw it as a dynamic unfolding, a lifelong journey of shared discovery and mutual evolution. The responsibility they shared wasn't a cage; it was the very scaffolding upon which they were building a life, a sturdy framework that allowed them to reach higher, to dream bigger, and to weather any storm.

She found herself confiding in Eli about her dreams for the rescue center's future, not just as an administrator, but as a visionary. She spoke of expanding their rehabilitation programs, developing community outreach initiatives, perhaps even establishing a small veterinary clinic on-site. These were aspirations she had once kept carefully guarded, fearing they were too grand, too unattainable. But Eli listened with an open heart, his own eyes alight with the possibilities. He didn't just offer encouragement; he offered concrete suggestions, helping her to break down these ambitious goals into manageable steps. He would research potential grants, explore partnership opportunities with local organizations, and patiently discuss the logistical challenges.

This shared dreaming, this collaborative planning, was perhaps the most profound aspect of her embrace of shared responsibility. It was an acknowledgment that her individual aspirations were amplified and strengthened when intertwined with Eli's. She was no longer just building her dream; she was building *their* dream, a shared future that was richer, more robust, and infinitely more rewarding because it was a collaborative masterpiece. The vulnerability that came with sharing these deep-seated hopes was met not with hesitation, but with an enthusiastic affirmation, a powerful testament to the security she had found in their partnership.

The weight of the world, which she had so often carried alone, now felt considerably lighter. It was still present, the challenges of running a rescue center were ever-present, but it was a shared burden, distributed and therefore, more manageable. She discovered a newfound energy, a renewed passion for her work, fueled by the knowledge that she was not alone in her endeavors. The quiet satisfaction of her solitary achievements had been replaced by a more profound joy, a sense of profound belonging that came from building something meaningful, not just for herself, but with the person she loved. Mara was no longer just the heart of the rescue center; she was a vital, contributing part of a larger, stronger whole, and in that shared space, she found a deeper, more resilient sense of purpose, and a love that felt as vast and enduring as the ocean itself.

The first real test of this newfound openness arrived on a Tuesday, indistinguishable from any other day at the rescue center in its outward appearance. The air was filled with the usual symphony of barks, chirps, and the comforting hum of activity. But within Mara and Eli, a quiet tension had been brewing for days, a subtle undercurrent that had begun to ripple beneath the surface of their easy companionship. It centered, as so many things did these days, around the future of the center, specifically a proposal for a significant expansion that Eli had brought to her.

Mara had been wrestling with it privately, her mind a tempest of conflicting thoughts. The expansion represented growth, a leap forward that aligned with the vision they had so often discussed. Yet, it also meant a substantial financial commitment, a risk that felt particularly daunting given the recent unexpected expenses with the old generator and the ongoing need for specialized veterinary equipment. She had spent sleepless nights poring over projections, her gut churning with a mixture of excitement and gnawing apprehension. She knew, with absolute certainty, that she couldn't navigate this decision alone. The old instinct to shoulder it all, to present a confident, unburdened front, warred with the newer, stronger impulse to share, to trust, to lean.

Eli found her that afternoon in her small office, the late afternoon sun casting long shadows across her desk, illuminating dust motes dancing in the air. She was staring at the blueprints, her brow furrowed, a half-eaten apple beside her, forgotten. He entered quietly, his presence a gentle ripple in the stillness. He didn't immediately speak, sensing the internal storm she was weathering. Instead, he simply sat on the edge of her desk, his gaze steady and warm, a silent offer of support.

"You've been quiet today," he finally said, his voice soft, devoid of accusation. "More than usual."

Mara's shoulders sagged slightly, the tension releasing in a slow exhale. She looked up at him, her eyes filled with a vulnerability she no longer felt compelled to hide. "I have," she admitted, her voice barely above a whisper. "It's... it's this expansion. It's a lot, Eli."

She gestured vaguely at the papers spread before her. "On paper, it's brilliant. It's everything we've talked about. More space for the animals, better facilities, the potential to take on more complex cases. But the numbers... they're daunting. And I'm scared. Scared of what happens if we overextend ourselves, if something unexpected comes up again. Scared of failing, of letting everyone down, the animals, you..." Her voice caught, the confession tumbling out in a rush. The words, once trapped behind a dam of pride and self-reliance, now flowed freely, a torrent of her deepest anxieties.

Eli reached out, his hand covering hers on the desk. His touch was firm, grounding. He didn't flinch at her words, didn't offer platitudes or quick reassurances that felt hollow. He simply listened, his thumb stroking the back of her hand, a steady, comforting rhythm.

"Mara," he said, his voice resonating with a sincerity that bypassed all her defenses. "Thank you for telling me. Truly. I've been wondering if something was on your mind, but I didn't want to pry. I'm not expecting you to have all the answers, or to be fearless. That's not what partnership means."

He paused, gathering his thoughts. "This expansion is a big step, I know. And yes, there are risks. There are always risks when you're trying to build something significant. But we're not going into this blind. We've been working through the financial projections, haven't we? We've identified potential funding sources. We've talked about contingency plans. And even if something unforeseen happens," he met her gaze directly, his eyes earnest, "we'll face it. Together. That's the strength in it, Mara. It's not about avoiding the challenges; it's about knowing you don't have to carry the weight of them alone."

His words were a balm to her soul, a gentle but firm dismantling of the fears she had been amplifying in her own head. She realized, with a clarity that surprised her, that her fear wasn't just about the financial implications of the expansion; it was about her own perceived inadequacy, her ingrained belief that she had to be the sole guarantor of success. Eli's unwavering belief in their shared capacity, his refusal to let her retreat into her solitary worries, was a powerful antidote to her ingrained self-doubt.

"But what if... what if my fear is justified?" she asked, the question hanging heavy in the air. "What if I'm seeing potential pitfalls you're not, because I'm too close to it? Or what if I'm just being... overly cautious, and I'm holding us back?"

Eli gently squeezed her hand. "Then we talk about it," he said, his tone even and reassuring. "We dissect it. You tell me every single 'what if,' and I'll tell you what I see. We'll look at it from every angle. If your caution is justified, we'll adjust the plan. We'll scale back, we'll find a different approach. If I'm being overly optimistic, you'll be the one to pull me back. That's how we make good decisions, Mara. Not by one person carrying the burden of foresight, but by sharing the load of analysis, of dreaming, and yes, of worrying too."

He leaned closer, his gaze intent. "And it's not about holding us back. It's about ensuring we move forward responsibly. Your insight, your meticulous nature, is what has made this place what it is. Don't ever doubt that. My role isn't to override that, it's to complement it, to offer a different perspective, to be your sounding board, and your partner in navigating the complexities."

They spent the next hour like that, her office transforming from a space of solitary struggle to one of collaborative exploration. Mara laid out her detailed financial spreadsheets, her voice gaining confidence as she explained each line item, each projected expense. Eli listened intently, asking clarifying questions, not to challenge her, but to understand. He shared his own research on grant opportunities, his enthusiasm for potential partnerships with local businesses that could sponsor specific wings of the new facility.

He spoke of how the expanded facilities would allow them to implement a more robust foster program, reducing the strain on the center and increasing the number of animals they could help. He painted a picture of a dedicated space for behavioral rehabilitation, a dream Mara had harbored for years but had deemed too ambitious to pursue. He didn't dismiss her concerns about unforeseen expenses; instead, he proposed the idea of setting aside a larger contingency fund, a dedicated savings pot specifically for emergencies, something they hadn't prioritized before.

"It's like building a seawall," Eli explained, drawing a parallel to their coastal surroundings. "You don't just build it to withstand the average tide. You build it to withstand the storm. We need that buffer, that extra layer of protection for the unexpected waves."

As they spoke, the initial anxiety that had coiled in Mara's stomach began to loosen its grip. The process of articulating her fears, of seeing them dissected and addressed with such calm logic and unwavering support, was incredibly liberating. It wasn't just about finding solutions to the expansion's challenges; it was about the profound relief of not having to carry the burden of doubt alone. She realized that Eli's honesty, his willingness to be vulnerable about his own hopes and even his occasional uncertainties, created a safe harbor for her own.

There was a moment when Mara confessed a deeper, more personal fear, one that had been lurking beneath the surface of her professional anxieties. "Sometimes," she admitted, her voice quieter, more introspective, "I worry that if this place grows too much, if it becomes too 'big,' I'll lose that... that personal connection. The one-on-one care, the feeling of being intimately involved in every animal's journey. That's what drives me. And I'm scared that with more staff, more volunteers, more animals, I'll just become a manager, and I'll lose the heart of it all."

Eli reached across the desk and took both her hands this time. His gaze was steady, full of understanding. "Mara, that heart is *you*. It's your compassion, your dedication, your unwavering commitment to their well-being. No amount of growth, no number of people, can ever replace that. What we're building isn't about replacing you; it's about creating a larger vessel for your compassion to flow through. And the more hands we have helping, the more animals we can reach, the more lives we can save. You'll still have those intimate moments. They'll just be alongside many, many more."

He tilted her chin up gently. "And when you feel that connection slipping, when you feel overwhelmed, you tell me. We'll carve out time. We'll make sure you still have those quiet moments with the animals that matter most to you. This isn't about diluting your role, it's about expanding our capacity to do good. And if that means you need to step back from some administrative tasks to spend an extra hour with a traumatized kitten, then that's what we'll arrange. Your well-being, and your connection to this work, is just as important as any blueprint or budget."

The honesty between them that afternoon was a powerful force. It wasn't always easy; admitting fears and doubts never is. There were moments when Mara's voice wavered, when Eli had to pause to choose his words carefully, ensuring his honesty was delivered with tenderness, not bluntness. But the effect was transformative. The tension that had settled over them dissipated, replaced by a quiet hum of shared purpose. The blueprints on the desk no longer represented a daunting solo challenge, but a tangible promise of a future they were building, brick by collaborative brick.

Later that evening, as they walked along the beach, the sun dipping below the horizon, painting the sky in hues of orange and lavender, a sense of profound peace settled between them. The rhythmic crash of the waves, once a solitary echo of her own thoughts, now felt like a harmonious accompaniment to their shared journey. The vastness of the ocean, which had once represented her own independent spirit, now mirrored the boundless potential of their partnership.

"You know," Mara said, her voice soft, carried on the gentle breeze, "I used to think that being strong meant being completely self-sufficient. That admitting I needed help, or that I was afraid, was a sign of weakness." She kicked a piece of driftwood, sending it skittering across the sand. "But today... today you showed me that the real strength lies in being honest. In being willing to lay it all out, the good and the scary, and trusting that the other person will meet you there."

Eli slipped his arm around her shoulders, pulling her close. "And you showed me that honesty isn't just about confessing fears," he replied, his voice warm against her ear. "It's about sharing dreams, too. It's about believing that your vision, when brought into the light and shared, has the power to become even bigger, even more vibrant."

He stopped walking and turned her to face him, his hands resting gently on her waist. The last vestiges of sunlight illuminated the earnestness in his eyes. "Mara, I love you. And I love this place, this work, this life we're building. But it's the 'we' that makes it all truly strong. The willingness to be open, to be truthful, even when it's uncomfortable. That's the bedrock. That's our forever."

Mara leaned her forehead against his, breathing in the salty air and the comforting scent of him. The word 'forever,' which had once felt like a distant, abstract concept, now felt tangible, solid, and deeply rooted in the honest, open space they had created between them. It wasn't about the absence of challenges, but the unwavering certainty that whatever came their way, they would face it, together, with open hearts and honest words, their connection as clear and pure as the calm sea on a perfect day. The decision about the expansion was still to be finalized, but the fear had been replaced by a quiet confidence, a shared resolve that was far more valuable than any financial projection. They had, in essence, built their own seawall, not of concrete and stone, but of trust and unwavering honesty, a foundation strong enough to weather any storm.

CHAPTER EIGHT

The Weight of External Voices

The quiet strength Mara and Eli had found in their shared honesty began to be tested not by internal doubts, but by the gentle, persistent currents of external opinion. It started subtly, almost imperceptibly, like the shifting tides that shaped their coastline. Over cups of tea with her Aunt Carol, a woman whose love for Mara was as boundless as her concern, or during casual encounters with colleagues at the rescue center, the questions, tinged with well-meaning curiosity, began to surface.

"So, Mara," Aunt Carol would begin, her voice laced with a warmth that always made Mara feel cherished, "Eli seems like such a good man. Are you two thinking about... you know... the future? Marriage, perhaps?" The unspoken implication hung in the air, a familiar, familial anticipation that Mara had grown up with. Aunt Carol's advice, always delivered with a comforting smile and a plate of freshly baked cookies, was never critical, but it carried the weight of generations, of societal expectations that whispered of timelines and milestones. Mara found herself offering vague, reassuring smiles, grateful for the love behind the questions, but also a little weary of the constant, albeit gentle, pressure to define their relationship in conventional terms.

Then there were Eli's friends. Liam, his oldest friend, a pragmatic accountant with a sharp mind and an even sharper wit, would corner Eli after a Friday night gathering. "Mate, you two are great together, really. But are you sure you're on the same page about, you know, *long-term*? She's all about the animals, which is amazing, but is there room for a wife, kids, the whole shebang in that life? You've got to be practical, you know. Don't want to get caught on the back foot later." Liam's counsel, though framed in friendly banter, mirrored Aunt Carol's in its underlying assumption that their relationship, as it stood, might be lacking a certain future-proofing. Eli would nod, his usual easygoing demeanor tightening just a fraction, appreciating Liam's loyalty and concern for his well-being, but feeling a quiet frustration that their current happiness wasn't enough of a testament to their future.

These well-intentioned observations, these whispers of advice from those who loved them, began to create a subtle dissonance. It wasn't that they disagreed with the advice itself; rather, it was the implication that their current path, the one they were meticulously carving out together, might need to be steered towards a pre-approved destination. The expansion of the rescue center, a project that had brought them closer through shared deliberation, now became another focal point for external input.

"You know, Mara," Sarah, a fellow volunteer with a knack for organizing fundraising events, said one afternoon, her brow furrowed with earnest concern as she helped sort donations, "I heard you and Eli are thinking of expanding. That's wonderful! But have you thought about the impact on your personal lives? It sounds like a huge commitment, and you two are still so... new, in a way. Are you sure you can handle that kind of pressure together right now? Maybe focus on the center first, then solidify your relationship?" Sarah's words, though delivered with a sympathetic nod, planted a tiny seed of doubt. Was their relationship being tested too soon? Were they pushing too hard, too fast, by taking on such a significant project together?

Mara found herself replaying these conversations in her mind, the words echoing long after they were spoken. She would catch herself scrutinizing Eli, looking for signs that he might be feeling the same pressure, or worse, that he might be swayed by these external voices. It was a silent battle she waged within herself, a struggle to hold onto the certainty she felt when she was with him, away from the cacophony of opinions.

One evening, as they walked along the shoreline, the usual comfortable silence between them was punctuated by Mara's restless pacing. The waves crashed against the sand, a rhythmic counterpoint to the turmoil brewing within her.

"Everything alright?" Eli asked, his voice a calm anchor in her rising anxiety. He didn't need her to articulate her worries;

he could sense the shift in her energy, the familiar shadow of self-doubt that occasionally flickered across her face.

Mara stopped, turning to face him. The moonlight cast a soft glow on his features, and she saw not a hint of doubt, but the steady reassurance that had become her bedrock. "It's just... everyone seems to have an opinion, doesn't it?" she began, choosing her words carefully. "About the expansion, about us. Aunt Carol asked again about marriage, and Liam cornered you the other day, didn't he? And Sarah seemed to think we're moving too fast with the expansion." She sighed, the sound lost in the wind. "It makes me wonder if we're missing something, if we're not seeing the bigger picture they seem to perceive."

Eli listened patiently, his gaze never leaving hers. He didn't dismiss her feelings, didn't try to placate her with platitudes. Instead, he reached out, his hands finding hers. "Mara," he said, his voice firm and gentle, "their advice comes from a place of love and concern. And it's natural for people who care about us to have hopes and expectations. But their picture of our future isn't necessarily the one we're building."

He squeezed her hands, his thumb tracing soothing circles. "Aunt Carol wants to see me happy, and she associates happiness with marriage. Liam wants to make sure I'm not making a foolish mistake. Sarah's concerned about the stress of the expansion. All valid points, from their perspectives. But their perspectives aren't ours. They're not living our journey. They don't feel what we feel when we're working side-by-side, or the quiet understanding that passes between us without words."

He drew her closer, his arm wrapping around her waist. "Remember what we talked about? About building our own seawall, not just for the storms outside, but for the tides of opinion that try to pull us off course? This is one of those tides. It's important to listen, to consider, but it's more important to discern what truly resonates with *us*."

Mara leaned into his embrace, the familiar scent of salt and sea air mingled with his own comforting presence. "But what if they're right?" she whispered, the old insecurity surfacing. "What if we're being naive? What if all this... us, the expansion... is too much, too soon?"

Eli tilted her chin up, his eyes reflecting the starlight. "Naive about what, Mara? About loving each other? About wanting to build something significant together? About the fact that challenges are inevitable, but so is our ability to face them? We are not moving too fast; we are moving at *our* pace. And this expansion, as daunting as it is, is a reflection of our shared vision, a testament to our dedication. It's not a test of our relationship; it's an opportunity to strengthen it."

He paused, letting his words sink in. "Think about it. Liam's advice is practical, yes, but it's also based on a certain narrow definition of success. He's focused on ticking boxes. We're focused on building a life. And yes, that life will eventually include a partnership, and perhaps a family, but it will be on our terms, built on the foundation of what we already have: trust, respect, and a shared purpose. Sarah's worry about pressure is understandable, but she doesn't see the strength we've already found in navigating difficulties together. We've learned to communicate, to support each other, to find solutions. That's not something you rush; it's something you build, and we've been building it, steadily and surely."

"It's easy for others to offer advice based on their own experiences and expectations," Eli continued, his voice laced with a gentle conviction. "But we are the ones living this. We are the ones who have to feel the weight of the decisions, and the joy of the accomplishments. We have to be honest with ourselves, first and foremost. Their opinions are like whispers on the wind, Mara. Some carry messages we need to hear, but most are just noise. We need to learn to distinguish between the two."

They continued their walk, the conversation flowing more easily now, the initial anxiety dissipating with each shared thought. Mara realized that the external voices, while well-meaning, were designed to fit her and Eli into pre-existing molds. Her own ingrained tendency to be self-reliant, to shield others from her worries, had made her particularly susceptible to these external pressures, as if she were seeking validation from the outside world for the choices she and Eli were making.

"It's like they're trying to steer us towards a safe harbor they've already charted," Mara mused, kicking a stray piece of seaweed.

"But what if our 'safe harbor' looks completely different? What if it's not a conventional port at all?"

"Exactly," Eli agreed, pulling her into a warm hug. "And we're not just aiming for a safe harbor; we're building our own ship, charting our own course. The expansion is part of that journey, not a detour. And our relationship is the compass that guides us. It's already proven its worth, hasn't it? It's navigated the unexpected expenses, the late nights, the moments of doubt. It's stronger for it."

He stopped again, his eyes searching hers. "And when people offer advice that feels... off, or intrusive, we don't have to engage with it deeply. We can acknowledge it, thank them for their concern, and then gently redirect. 'Thank you for your thoughts, Aunt Carol. We're very happy and taking things one step at a time.' Or, to Liam, 'We appreciate your concern, mate. We're on the same page and have a plan.' It's not about being dismissive; it's about protecting our space, our autonomy."

Mara felt a sense of relief wash over her. It wasn't about shutting people out, but about setting healthy boundaries. It was about trusting her own intuition, and more importantly, trusting the partnership she had built with Eli. They had already demonstrated their ability to make sound, collaborative decisions, to weather storms, and to find strength in their vulnerability. Why should they suddenly doubt that foundation because of the well-intentioned, but ultimately external, opinions of others?

The following week, the subtle pressure continued. Eli's parents, visiting for the weekend, expressed their own hopeful anxieties. His mother, a woman of quiet grace and immense love, brought it up over Sunday dinner. "Eli, darling, your father and I were just discussing. This expansion sounds wonderful, but it's a big undertaking. Have you two talked about... setting timelines? For yourselves, I mean. Marriage, perhaps a family down the line? We just want to see you both settled and happy."

Eli handled it with the same gentle grace he'd shown with everyone else. "Mom, Dad, we're incredibly happy right now, building this dream together. The expansion is our priority, and we're taking things one step at a time. We'll figure out all the personal milestones in due time, when it feels right for us. What's most important is that we're strong as a couple, and we're making decisions together."

Later, Mara confided in Eli, "It's exhausting, isn't it? This constant undercurrent of 'shoulds' and 'whens.' It makes me want to retreat, to build higher walls."

Eli, however, saw it differently. "It's not about them, Mara. It's about us learning to navigate these waters. Every time someone asks, every time we have to gently redirect, we're reinforcing our own understanding of what matters to us. We're not just building a rescue center; we're building a life, and a relationship, and that requires intentionality. It requires us to be clear about our own values and our own timeline, independent of what others might expect."

He took her hand, his gaze earnest. "Think of it as sharpening our discernment. We're learning to listen to the love and concern, but to filter out the noise that doesn't align with our path. It's about honoring their good intentions while fiercely protecting our own narrative."

Their conversations about these external voices became less about anxiety and more about strategy. They developed a shared language, a knowing glance when a particular topic arose, a subtle nod that communicated, "We've heard this before, and we've got this." They realized that the true strength of their connection lay not in its isolation from the world, but in its ability to absorb external influences without compromising its core. They could be open to advice, to perspective, without relinquishing their right to make their own choices, to define their own future. The well-meaning advice, rather than dividing them, served to solidify their partnership, reminding them that their most important counsel would always come from within, from the quiet, honest space they had created between themselves. They were a team, learning to distinguish the gentle advice of trusted allies from the clamor of a world that often mistook expectation for wisdom. And in that discernment, they found a deeper, more resilient strength, as enduring as the coastal cliffs that stood against the constant tide.

The scent of antiseptic and damp fur had become as familiar to Mara as the briny air of the coast. The rescue center, once a sanctuary, was now a hub of amplified activity, a reflection of the burgeoning challenges they faced. The expansion, a project born of hope and necessity, had indeed brought a new wave of demands, a relentless tide of responsibilities that threatened to engulf their personal lives. The carefully constructed seawall they had envisioned was being battered not just by external opinions, but by the sheer, unyielding force of their commitment.

The initial surge of excitement surrounding the planned expansion had quickly been tempered by the stark realities of funding. Grant applications, once a hopeful trickle, now became a torrent of meticulously crafted proposals, each one requiring hours of research, careful budgeting, and persuasive prose. Mara found herself poring over spreadsheets long after the last injured seabird had been tended to, her mind a labyrinth of figures and projected costs. The grants they applied for were highly competitive, often demanding detailed plans for sustainability and community engagement, which meant dedicating precious hours to writing reports and presentations.

"Another rejection," Mara sighed, dropping a thick envelope onto Eli's desk, the crisp paper a stark contrast to the worn surfaces of their shared workspace. The disheartening thud echoed the dull ache in her chest. "They said the proposal was strong, but that other projects had a higher immediate impact. Immediate impact. As if saving a life isn't immediate enough."

Eli, who had been meticulously cleaning a splint for a stray cat, looked up, his brow furrowed with concern. He didn't need a lengthy explanation. He saw the slump of her shoulders, the faint lines of exhaustion etched around her eyes. He put down the splint and walked over, gently taking the envelope from her. "Let me see." He scanned the polite, yet firm, rejection letter. "It's a shame, Mara, but it's not a reflection of our work. We knew this wouldn't be easy. We'll regroup. There are other avenues."

But the "other avenues" were proving to be just as arduous. They initiated a crowdfunding campaign, hoping the community's affection for the center would translate into financial support. This meant a constant stream of social media updates, compelling stories of rescued animals, and public appeals for donations. Mara, who had always preferred the quiet satisfaction of hands-on work, found herself thrust into the role of digital marketer, crafting heartfelt captions and editing short videos of their success stories. Eli, with his innate ability to connect with people, spent his evenings at local community events, speaking passionately about their vision and gently nudging attendees towards their donation page.

The fundraising efforts, while occasionally yielding heartwarming successes, were a constant drain on their energy. Days blurred into a relentless cycle of caring for the animals, managing volunteers, and drumming up support. The pressure to perform, to constantly demonstrate the center's worth and potential, became a palpable weight. There were moments when Mara felt like a beggar, perpetually asking for help, for sustenance, for the means to continue their vital work.

Beyond the financial strain, a new layer of bureaucratic complexity had emerged. The expansion, involving structural changes and increased capacity, required extensive permits and approvals from local authorities. This meant navigating a maze of regulations, attending planning meetings, and dealing with inspectors who often seemed more interested in minutiae than in the overarching mission.

One particularly frustrating afternoon, Mara found herself in a sterile town hall office, arguing with a building inspector named Mr. Henderson. He was a man who seemed to relish pointing out code violations, his voice dry and unyielding.

"The proposed drainage system does not meet current environmental regulations, Ms. Davies," he stated, tapping a thick document with a manicured finger. "And the materials you've selected for the new enclosure are not rated for coastal exposure, despite the fact that you are located directly on the coast. It's... perplexing."

Mara's jaw tightened. "Mr. Henderson, we've consulted with engineers. The system is designed to handle runoff effectively, and these materials are specifically chosen for their durability and sustainability. We are a rescue center, not a luxury development. We're trying to do the best we can with limited resources, while also adhering to best practices for animal welfare and environmental responsibility."

He merely offered a thin-lipped smile. "Regulations are regulations, Ms. Davies. My job is to ensure compliance.

Perhaps if you had… planned more thoroughly from the outset, these issues wouldn't have arisen."

Mara bit back a sharp retort, forcing herself to breathe deeply. She knew arguing with him was futile. She would have to rework plans, potentially incur additional costs, all while the animals waiting for beds and specialized care continued to arrive. She left the town hall feeling deflated, the weight of systemic inertia pressing down on her.

Eli found her slumped in her car, staring blankly at the steering wheel. He opened the passenger door and slid in beside her. "Rough meeting?" he asked gently.

She nodded, a single tear escaping and tracing a path down her cheek. "He's… he's making it impossible, Eli. Every step feels like a battle. We're trying to build something good, and it feels like the system is designed to break us."

Eli reached over and took her hand. His touch was a steady anchor in her rising tide of despair. "I know it's hard, love. But we're not going to let him break us. We'll find a way around it. We always do." He squeezed her hand. "We'll find an engineer who can re-certify the drainage, or a more affordable coastal-grade material. This is just another hurdle. We've faced tougher ones."

His unwavering belief in their ability to overcome challenges was a balm to her weary spirit. Yet, even with his support, the constant pressure was taking its toll. The late nights spent poring over paperwork, the early mornings dealing with emergent rescues, the emotional toll of witnessing suffering and loss – it all began to seep into their personal time, creating a subtle but persistent friction.

One evening, after a particularly grueling day that had involved rescuing a pod of stranded dolphins, Mara found herself snapping at Eli over something trivial, like the placement of a coffee mug. The outburst, so unlike her usual calm demeanor, hung in the air, heavy with unspoken exhaustion and frustration.

Eli paused, his expression one of gentle surprise rather than anger. "Mara? Is everything okay?"

Mara's shoulders sagged. She immediately regretted her sharp tone. "I'm sorry, Eli. I... I didn't mean to snap. I'm just... so tired. And worried. We're so behind on the funding for the new veterinary suite, and that injured goshawk is still critical, and then there's that paperwork for the animal welfare licensing that's due next week..." The words tumbled out, a dam of pent-up stress finally breaking.

Eli pulled her into his arms, his embrace firm and comforting. "Shh, it's okay. I understand. We're both running on fumes." He held her for a moment, letting her feel his steady presence. "This isn't just about work, is it? It's about the weight of it all. The constant demand. The feeling that no matter how hard we try, it's never quite enough."

He pulled back slightly, so he could look into her eyes. "We have to remember why we're doing this. We're not just saving animals; we're building a refuge, a place of healing, for them and for the people who care about them. And we're building a future, together."

He gestured vaguely towards the blueprints spread across the dining table, a constant reminder of their ambitious project. "This expansion… it's a huge undertaking. It's testing us, yes, but it's also forcing us to be more resourceful, more resilient, more united than ever before. We're learning to delegate better, to prioritize, to lean on each other even more heavily."

He sat them both down, pulling a few stray papers away to make space. "We can't let the professional pressures consume us. We have to consciously carve out moments of respite. Even ten minutes, sitting by the water, watching the waves, without talking about grants or permits. Or a quiet dinner, just us, where the only thing on the agenda is enjoying each other's company."

He met her gaze, his eyes full of an unwavering affection. "Remember our promise to each other? To face challenges together? This is one of those challenges. It's about more than just the rescue center; it's about protecting *us*."

The relentless demands of the rescue center were a testament to the growing need for their services, a stark reminder that their efforts were not in vain. But the sheer volume of work, the constant flux of animal emergencies, and the intricate demands of expansion presented a unique kind of pressure. It was a pressure that didn't announce itself with loud pronouncements, but rather seeped into their lives like a persistent dampness, threatening to erode their foundations.

One week, a rare storm rolled in, far more severe than predicted. The coastal winds howled, lashing rain against the windows of the center, and the tides rose with alarming speed. They had to work through the night, securing loose structures, moving vulnerable animals to higher ground, and tending to those injured by the storm's fury. A section of their existing roof sprung a leak, threatening a critical ward of recovering patients, and the generator, their lifeline during power outages, sputtered ominously.

The storm was an intense, albeit temporary, surge of crisis. It required immediate, decisive action, and Mara and Eli moved in seamless sync. They directed volunteers, made difficult decisions about resource allocation, and offered words of comfort to anxious staff. The shared adrenaline, the common purpose, was a powerful bonding agent. They were a well-oiled machine, each anticipating the other's needs, their communication reduced to brief nods and knowing glances.

But the aftermath of the storm was just as taxing. Assessing the damage, filing insurance claims, and dealing with the influx of animals displaced or injured by the weather stretched their resources thin. The fundraising efforts, which had been gaining momentum, had to pivot to focus on storm recovery, diverting funds that were earmarked for the expansion. The bureaucratic hurdles seemed to multiply, with new safety inspections required and permits delayed due to storm-related disruptions.

"It's like one step forward, two steps back," Mara confided to Eli one evening, collapsing onto the sofa after a long day of sorting through sodden supplies. "We finally secured that grant for the new kennels, and then the storm hits, and now we need to re-roof half the existing building. It feels like we're constantly treading water, just trying to keep our heads above the surface."

Eli sat beside her, gently rubbing her back. "It does, doesn't it? But remember those dolphins we rescued? They were battered by the storm, disoriented, exhausted. But they kept swimming. They found their way back to deeper water, to safety. That's what we're doing, Mara. We're battered, but we're not broken. And we're swimming towards our goal."

He paused, his gaze soft. "This constant push and pull, the crises and the recovery, it's a part of building something significant. The rescue center itself is a testament to overcoming adversity. And our relationship... it's being forged in the same fire. It's easy to be strong when things are smooth sailing. But it's in these storms, when the pressure is immense, that we truly learn what we're made of, as individuals and as a couple."

He understood that their dedication to the center, while noble, was also a relentless taskmaster. It demanded their time, their energy, and their emotional reserves. The lines between work and life had blurred to an almost indistinguishable smudge.

There were no more clear-cut divisions, no distinct boundaries. The weight of external voices had been a challenge to their clarity of purpose; these professional pressures, however, were testing their very capacity to endure.

The resilience they had cultivated was being put to its ultimate test. Each rescued animal, each successful fundraising event, each bureaucratic hurdle overcome, was a victory. But these victories were hard-won, often at the expense of precious downtime, of simple moments of peace. Mara found herself constantly mentally cataloging tasks, her mind a swirling vortex of to-do lists, urgent appeals, and animal care protocols. Sleep offered little true respite, often filled with vivid dreams of distressed animals and overflowing kennels.

Eli, ever the pragmatist with a deep well of empathy, recognized the toll this was taking. He began to implement small, deliberate changes. He started ensuring they had at least one meal a day together, away from the hubbub of the center, even if it was just a simple sandwich on the porch overlooking the sea. He insisted on short walks along the beach each evening, even for fifteen minutes, a conscious act of reclaiming their shared space. He encouraged Mara to delegate tasks she had previously insisted on doing herself, trusting her team of volunteers more implicitly.

"You can't pour from an empty cup, Mara," he'd said one afternoon, gently taking a wilting plant from her desk and placing it by a sunny window. "And we, as a couple, are that cup.

We need to refill it, to give ourselves what we need, so we can continue to give to this center, to these animals."

The expansion, while a symbol of their hope and progress, had also become a focal point of their exhaustion. The sheer scale of the undertaking, combined with the daily demands of running a busy rescue, created a pressure cooker environment. It was a relentless cycle, much like the constant rhythm of the tides, that demanded unwavering focus and a profound wellspring of resilience. They were learning that building their dream required not only passion and dedication, but also a conscious, continuous effort to protect their own well-being, and the integrity of the relationship that fueled their every endeavor. The professional pressures were not just about the center's future; they were a crucible, testing the strength and endurance of their shared commitment to each other.

The salt-laced air, once a balm to Mara's soul, now carried a subtle undercurrent of anxiety. Eli's recent conversations, often hushed and laced with a restless energy, had begun to hint at a shift. It started with articles bookmarked on his laptop, then progressed to late-night research sessions where the glow of the screen illuminated a furrowed brow. He'd always possessed a restless intellect, a yearning to explore and understand, but this felt different. This felt like a current pulling him away.

"I've been looking into some postgraduate programs," he'd admitted one evening, his voice a little too casual, as they sat on the porch swing, the rhythmic creak of the chains a familiar counterpoint to the chirping crickets. The rescue center hummed with quiet activity in the background, a constant, comforting presence that had once felt like their entire universe.

Mara turned to him, her heart giving a small, uncertain lurch. "Programs? For what, exactly?" She tried to keep her tone light, but the question felt heavy, loaded with unspoken fears. She knew Eli's passion for marine biology extended far beyond their current scope, a deep-seated curiosity that had drawn him to the coast in the first place.

He hesitated, running a hand through his already tousled hair. "There's a fellowship. A really prestigious one, actually. Focused on deep-sea ecosystems. It's based... well, it's not exactly local." He paused, waiting for her reaction.

The words hung in the air between them. "Not local" was a polite euphemism. She already knew, with a prickle of dread, that he was likely talking about a place far removed from the familiar rhythm of their coastal town, far from the rescue center that had become so intrinsically woven into the fabric of their lives. "Where?" she finally managed, her voice softer than she intended.

"University of California," he said, his gaze fixed on the distant glimmer of the lighthouse. "They have some incredible research facilities. And the work they're doing... it's groundbreaking, Mara. It's exactly the kind of cutting-edge research I've always dreamed of being a part of." His eyes lit up with an almost childlike wonder, a spark she hadn't seen in months, overshadowed as they had been by the daily grind of fundraising and repairs.

Mara listened, a complicated mix of pride and apprehension swirling within her. She understood, instinctively, the magnetic pull of such an opportunity. Eli's brilliance deserved to be nurtured, his potential unleashed. But the thought of him leaving, even for a period, felt like a seismic shift. Their lives had become so deeply intertwined, so rooted in this place, this shared mission. The rescue center, with its ever-present needs, was more than just a job; it was a testament to their commitment, a tangible manifestation of their shared future.

"California," she repeated, the word tasting foreign on her tongue. "That's... a long way."

He nodded, his earlier enthusiasm dimming slightly under the weight of her unspoken concern. "I know. It's a significant commitment. And it would mean being away for... at least a year, maybe longer. But the research is so crucial, Mara. It could really make a difference." He reached for her hand, his fingers interlacing with hers. "I wouldn't even consider it if I didn't think it was important. And," he added, his gaze earnest, "I wouldn't do it without us being on the same page."

That was the crux of it, wasn't it? The "us." Their shared life, meticulously built, brick by emotional brick, on this very coastline. Mara's own roots ran deep here. The rescue center was her calling, a place where she felt her purpose most acutely. She'd poured her heart and soul into its expansion, her identity becoming inextricably linked with its survival and growth. The thought of separating their paths, even temporarily, felt like an unraveling.

"I... I need to think about this, Eli," she said, her voice barely a whisper. The easy intimacy of their shared life suddenly felt fragile, susceptible to the winds of individual ambition. She looked out at the dark, churning ocean, its vastness mirroring the uncertainty that had suddenly descended upon her.

Over the next few days, the conversation hung between them, an unspoken tension weaving through their shared meals and quiet evenings. Mara watched Eli, trying to decipher the unspoken thoughts behind his often-pensive silences. She saw the conflict in his eyes – the lure of groundbreaking research against the anchor of their shared life. She knew he wouldn't make this decision lightly, that the fellowship represented a pinnacle of his academic aspirations. And she, in turn, wrestled with her own conflicting emotions.

Her initial reaction of fear and apprehension began to temper, giving way to a more measured consideration. She loved Eli. She believed in his dreams. And a part of her recognized that his leaving, while daunting, wasn't a rejection of their life together, but rather an expression of his individual growth. The rescue center, while a shared passion, was not his sole defining purpose in the way it was hers. He had a broader intellectual curiosity that extended beyond the immediate needs of their coastal community.

One afternoon, while sorting through a mountain of donated blankets, Mara found herself replaying Eli's words.

"It's exactly the kind of cutting-edge research I've always dreamed of being a part of." She pictured him, hunched over a microscope, unraveling the mysteries of the deep sea, his mind alight with discovery. It was a compelling image, one that stirred a pang of bittersweet admiration.

Later that week, she found him meticulously cleaning a series of delicate instruments, his brow furrowed in concentration. She sat beside him, the familiar scent of disinfectant and saline filling the air. "Eli," she began, her voice steady, "I've been thinking. About the fellowship."

He looked up, his eyes questioning, a flicker of apprehension in their depths. He likely braced himself for an argument, for a plea to stay, for a lament of their diverging paths.

"I understand what this means to you," she continued, choosing her words carefully. "And I want you to be happy. Truly happy. Your work here, with the animals, it's vital. It's what we built together. But... I also know that your passion for discovery runs so deep. You need to explore that, Eli. You need to pursue those dreams, too."

A slow smile spread across his face, softening the lines of concern. He put down the instrument he was holding and turned to face her fully. "Mara, I... I didn't know what to expect. I was so worried about how you'd feel."

"I'm worried too," she admitted, her honesty a vital counterpoint to her resolve. "I'm worried about being apart. About the distance. About how much I'll miss you. And about how much the center will miss your steady hand." She gestured around the busy room, the quiet hum of activity a constant reminder of their shared responsibilities. "This is our life, Eli. The rescue center, this town, us. It's... it's everything I've built. And the thought of that changing, even temporarily, is... unsettling."

He reached out and gently cupped her cheek, his thumb tracing the curve of her jawline. "I know. And I wouldn't ask you to compromise on what you've built, on what you love. This isn't about abandoning anything. It's about... expanding our horizons. For both of us."

"Expanding horizons," Mara echoed softly. "That sounds... very academic." A small smile played on her lips. "What does that mean for us, Eli? If you go to California, what does that mean for 'us'?"

He leaned in, his forehead touching hers. "It means trust, Mara. It means faith. It means knowing that even when we're miles apart, our foundation is solid. It means knowing that this connection, this love we have, is strong enough to bridge any distance. We've already weathered so much together – the storms, the financial worries, the endless paperwork. This is just another challenge, a different kind of storm, perhaps. But we'll navigate it. Together."

He pulled back, his gaze searching hers. "I envision a future where our paths might diverge for a time, but ultimately converge. I see myself bringing back new knowledge, new perspectives, that could even benefit the center, benefit our work here. And I see you continuing to lead, to grow, here, stronger than ever. We can support each other's individual journeys while remaining deeply committed to our shared one."

His words were a balm, a reassurance that eased the knot of anxiety in her chest. But the practicalities remained. The rescue center was a demanding entity, requiring constant attention, hands-on care, and a stable leadership. The expansion, still very much in its crucial stages, couldn't afford to have its driving force absent for an extended period.

"But the expansion, Eli," Mara said, her brow furrowing again. "We're still in the thick of it. Permits, construction, fundraising... it's all so... immediate. How can I possibly manage all of this on my own, even with the team?"

Eli squeezed her hand. "You won't be entirely on your own. The team is incredible, and you've empowered them. And I'll be here, whenever I can, for as long as I can, before I leave. We'll strategize. We'll make a plan. Maybe I can postpone my departure slightly, ensure a smoother handover of responsibilities. Perhaps we can even explore options for you to visit, for extended periods, if the fellowship allows." He paused, his expression thoughtful. "And we'll be talking. Constantly.

Video calls, emails, late-night chats. We'll create new rituals to bridge the gap."

He pulled out his phone and began scrolling through something. "Actually," he said, a new urgency in his tone, "this fellowship has different start dates. I could potentially defer it by a few months. That would give us more time to solidify the expansion, to ensure everything is in place before I go. And it would give us more time to... prepare. For both of us."

Mara watched him, a profound sense of love and respect swelling within her. This was Eli. Always thinking, always planning, always seeking solutions that honored both his aspirations and their shared life. He wasn't just pursuing his own ambition; he was actively trying to minimize the disruption to their world.

"That would help," she admitted, a wave of relief washing over her. "A few extra months would make a significant difference. It would allow us to transition more smoothly." She knew the expansion wouldn't be finished in a few months, not by a long shot. But it would bring them to a more stable, manageable phase.

"And when I'm gone," Eli continued, his voice firm, "I want you to promise me something. Promise me you'll lean on the team. That you won't try to shoulder everything yourself. That you'll ask for help when you need it. And promise me you'll take time for yourself. To rest. To breathe. To remember that the rescue center needs you, yes, but it also needs a Mara who isn't completely depleted."

Mara nodded, her throat tight with emotion. "I promise. And you promise me... promise me you'll throw yourself into it. That you'll learn everything you can. And that you'll call, and you'll write, and you'll let me know you're okay. That you're thriving."

"I promise," he said, his voice laced with a sincerity that echoed her own. "We'll make this work, Mara. We'll prove that different life paths don't have to mean separate lives." He reached for her again, pulling her into a firm embrace. The scent of antiseptic, usually a comforting aroma, now felt tinged with the bittersweet knowledge of impending separation. But within that embrace, a new strength bloomed. It was the strength of understanding, of compromise, and of an unwavering commitment that transcended physical distance. They were different individuals with unique dreams, but their shared journey, forged in the heart of their coastal sanctuary, had created a bond that was as resilient as the tides themselves, capable of weathering any storm, or any distance. The path ahead might be less predictable, marked by the quiet hum of a long-distance connection rather than the shared rhythm of their days, but it was a path they would walk, side-by-side, even when separated by miles.

The rhythmic whisper of the waves against the shore had always been Mara's lullaby, a constant, soothing presence in her life. Tonight, however, as she stood on the weathered planks of the deck, the familiar sound seemed to carry a deeper resonance, a testament to the quiet strength she was actively cultivating within herself. The anxieties that had initially churned within her – the fear of Eli's departure, the vastness of the unknown, the quiet hum of skepticism from well-meaning acquaintances – were beginning to recede, replaced by a burgeoning sense of self-assurance. She acknowledged the validity of those initial fears; they were natural responses to the seismic shift that Eli's fellowship represented. But she also recognized that allowing them to dictate her future would be a disservice to herself, to Eli, and to the profound connection they had so carefully nurtured.

She closed her eyes, inhaling the briny air, and let her mind drift back to the early days of their relationship. She remembered the hesitant steps, the careful unveiling of her vulnerabilities, the quiet, almost fearful, anticipation of Eli's reaction each time she dared to share a deeper layer of herself. There had been moments, early on, when she'd felt an almost overwhelming urge to retreat, to shield her heart from potential hurt, to maintain a safe, measured distance. She recalled the stifling weight of that self-imposed caution, the way it had acted as a subtle barrier, preventing the full bloom of their intimacy. Eli's patience, his unwavering gentle persistence, had been the key that had unlocked those guarded chambers. He hadn't rushed her, hadn't pushed, but had instead created a safe harbor where she felt seen, understood, and cherished.

Now, standing on the precipice of another significant change, Mara found that those hard-won lessons were her anchor. The trust she had painstakingly built, not just in Eli, but in her own capacity to navigate complex emotional landscapes, felt solid beneath her. She had learned that vulnerability, when met with genuine love and respect, was not a weakness, but a profound strength. It was the bedrock upon which true intimacy was built. The very act of opening her heart, of sharing her fears and aspirations with Eli, had empowered her. It had shown her that she possessed an inner resilience she hadn't fully recognized before.

She thought of the countless conversations they had shared, the late-night talks that had stretched into the pre-dawn hours, the quiet moments of shared silence that spoke volumes. They had navigated disagreements, celebrated triumphs, and weathered the mundane challenges of everyday life together. Each shared experience, each act of understanding and compromise, had woven a stronger thread into the fabric of their relationship. Eli's dream of pursuing groundbreaking research in deep-sea ecosystems was not a betrayal of their shared life; it was an evolution of his individual journey, a journey that, she now understood with growing certainty, did not have to negate their shared one.

The voices of others, the subtle undertones of doubt that had occasionally surfaced, no longer held the same sway. She had heard the well-intentioned concerns from friends and family, the practical assessments of the difficulties of a long-distance relationship, the gentle questioning of how the rescue center would fare without Eli's constant presence. While she acknowledged the wisdom in their observations, she also recognized that these were external perspectives, filtered through their own experiences and anxieties. Her own conviction, born from the deep well of her love for Eli and her faith in their connection, was far more potent.

She remembered a particular conversation with her aunt, a woman who had always valued stability and predictability above all else. Her aunt had expressed concern, a soft worry in her voice, about "putting all her eggs in one basket" with Eli, especially given his newfound ambition that would take him so far away. "It's just that, Mara," her aunt had said, her brow furrowed with genuine care, "life has a way of throwing curveballs. And when you're so tied to someone else's path, it can be hard to find your own footing if things don't go as planned." At the time, those words had pricked at Mara's insecurities, planting a seed of doubt. But now, standing on the deck, the sea breeze ruffling her hair, she understood that her strength wasn't derived solely from the stability of her circumstances, but from her own inner fortitude, a fortitude that Eli had helped her discover and nurture.

She had, after all, poured her heart and soul into the rescue center. It was her calling, her passion, her life's work. And that passion was an intrinsic part of her identity, separate from, yet complementary to, her relationship with Eli. She was not defined solely by her role as Eli's partner; she was Mara, the dedicated rescuer, the compassionate caregiver, the unwavering advocate for the ocean's creatures. This foundation, built on her own passion and hard work, was unshakeable. Eli's pursuit of his dreams would not diminish her own; it would, she hoped, enrich it.

She recalled the hesitant way she had broached the subject of her own evolving role within the rescue center with Eli, the fear that he might perceive her dedication as an unwillingness to accommodate his aspirations. But Eli had met her confidences with nothing but encouragement. He had praised her vision, her tireless efforts, and had always reassured her that her commitment to the center was a source of inspiration to him. He had never made her feel as though her work was secondary to his or that her dedication to their shared coastal haven was a burden. This mutual respect, this celebration of each other's individual passions, was the true testament to the strength of their bond.

The practicalities of Eli's absence remained, of course. The expansion of the rescue center was still in a critical phase, demanding meticulous planning and constant oversight. There would be logistical challenges, moments of loneliness, and undoubtedly times when she would question her own ability to manage everything on her own. But within those challenges, she saw opportunities for growth. She would have to delegate more, trust her team more deeply, and perhaps discover new strengths within herself she hadn't yet tapped into. Eli's deferred start date offered a valuable buffer, a chance to solidify the current operational phase and ensure a smoother transition. It was a testament to his commitment, his desire to mitigate the impact of his departure on their shared life and the vital work they did.

She thought about the late-night research Eli had been doing, the earnest discussions about his fellowship, and the way he had consistently brought her into the conversation, valuing her perspective and her feelings. He hadn't presented his opportunity as a fait accompli, but as a shared exploration of possibilities. His commitment to ensuring they were "on the same page" was not just lip service; it was woven into the very fabric of how they approached decisions. This was the reassurance she needed: that their partnership was built on open communication, mutual respect, and a shared understanding that individual growth could coexist with a committed, shared future.

The vast expanse of the ocean before her, stretching out into the inky darkness of the night, no longer felt like a symbol of daunting separation, but of boundless possibility. It was a reminder that their world was larger than their immediate surroundings, that dreams could take them to distant shores, and that love, when rooted in genuine connection and trust, could transcend any geographical boundary. She had always been drawn to the sea, to its power, its mystery, and its enduring rhythm. And now, she saw that same enduring rhythm reflected in the strength of her own heart, in the resilience of her spirit, and in the unwavering commitment she shared with Eli. The external voices might continue to whisper their doubts, but they would fade into the background, drowned out by the more powerful, more resonant, and infinitely more true, melody of her own inner reassurance. She was ready to face what lay ahead, not with apprehension, but with a quiet confidence, knowing that she had built a foundation of self-trust and an unshakeable belief in the enduring strength of their love. The sea, in its magnificent and unending expanse, mirrored the depth of her own burgeoning strength and the promise of a future, however it unfolded, that they would navigate together.

Eli stood on the familiar stretch of coastline, the same coastline that had witnessed the blossoming of his love for Mara. The salty air, usually a balm to his soul, now carried a subtle tang of indecision. The fellowship in the deep-sea ecosystems, a dream meticulously nurtured over years of late nights and relentless study, was no longer a distant aspiration but a tangible offer, a golden ticket to a world of unparalleled scientific discovery. Yet, its arrival also illuminated a stark truth: the path it laid out was one that, for a significant period, would lead him away from the woman who had become the very anchor of his existence.

He traced the intricate patterns left by the receding tide on the damp sand, each swirl and ripple a metaphor for the complexities swirling within him. His work was his passion, an intrinsic part of his identity. The opportunity to delve into the mysteries of abyssal plains, to witness firsthand the bioluminescent wonders of the Hadal zone, was an unparalleled intellectual and professional calling. He had spoken of it to Mara, not with the bravado of someone announcing a singular conquest, but with the quiet hope of a shared adventure, a future where their individual pursuits could intricately intertwine. And Mara, with her characteristic grace and unwavering support, had listened, her eyes reflecting not doubt, but a profound understanding of his aspirations.

But understanding, he was discovering, did not always erase the practicalities, the quiet anxieties that lay beneath the surface of even the most secure love. The whispers of the world, the subtle but insistent voices of well-meaning mentors and colleagues, echoed in his mind. "This is a once-in-a-lifetime opportunity, Eli," Professor Armitage had said, his voice laced with an almost paternal encouragement. "The kind that can define a career. You can't let anything hold you back." And for a fleeting, disquieting moment, Eli had wondered if Mara, if their life together here, was becoming that 'anything.'

He picked up a smooth, grey pebble, its surface worn by countless tides, and turned it over and over in his palm. It felt substantial, grounded, much like the life he had built with Mara. Their rescue center, a testament to their shared dedication and passion for marine life, was more than just a project; it was their sanctuary, their purpose. He remembered the early days, the sheer grit and determination it had taken to establish it, the countless hours spent patching up injured seals and rehabilitating stranded dolphins. Mara's tireless energy and unwavering compassion had been the driving force, and he had reveled in being her partner, her steadfast support. He had believed, with every fiber of his being, that their life together would be one of shared endeavors, of building a future brick by brick, wave by wave.

The fellowship, however, presented a different kind of building, a solitary ascent into a realm of scientific prestige. He envisioned the laboratories, the research vessels, the hushed reverence of academic conferences. It was a world he had dreamed of, a world that promised recognition and the satisfaction of pushing the boundaries of human knowledge. But in his mind's eye, the image of Mara was always there, a silent, poignant counterpoint. Would she truly thrive amidst the transient nature of his research life? Could the deep roots she had planted here, in the very soil of their shared home, withstand the uprooting that his ambition might demand?

He walked further down the beach, the wind whipping strands of hair across his forehead. The waves crashed with a powerful, rhythmic insistence, a constant reminder of nature's immutable forces. He thought of Mara's quiet strength, the resilience she demonstrated daily at the rescue center. She possessed a capacity for empathy and dedication that he often found humbling. She wasn't someone who passively accepted circumstance; she actively shaped her world with kindness and an unshakeable sense of purpose. This was not a woman who would easily find fulfillment in the periphery of someone else's grand adventure, especially one that demanded extended absences and constant upheaval.

He recalled a conversation they had had just last week, after he'd received the official fellowship offer. Mara had been meticulously bandaging the wing of a young gull, her brow furrowed in concentration. He had shown her the email, his voice a mixture of elation and apprehension. She had read it, her expression unreadable for a moment, before offering a soft, "Eli, this is incredible. Truly remarkable." Then, she had looked up, her eyes meeting his, a gentle question in their depths. "What does this mean for us, for the center?"

He had seen the unspoken questions in her gaze: the logistical challenges, the potential strain on their relationship, the disruption to the rhythm of their lives. And in that moment, he had felt a prick of guilt, a realization that his pursuit of his individual dream might inadvertently cast a shadow on their shared life. He had reassured her, speaking of his commitment to finding solutions, to ensuring their connection remained a priority, to exploring ways to minimize the impact of his absence. He had promised to involve her in every decision, to make it a collaborative journey. But the echo of her unspoken question lingered, a quiet challenge to his own convictions.

He stopped, the water lapping at his ankles. The vastness of the ocean stretched before him, an infinite canvas of possibility and, he now understood, of personal sacrifice. He had always seen his ambition as separate from his commitment to Mara, a parallel pursuit that would eventually converge. But the fellowship demand a more active integration, a conscious decision about which path held greater weight in the grand scheme of his life. Was the pursuit of his scientific dreams worth the potential strain on the most precious relationship he had ever known?

He thought of the quiet evenings they spent together, the comfortable silence punctuated by the gentle murmur of the sea, the shared laughter over a simple meal, the profound intimacy that transcended words. These were the moments that grounded him, that reminded him of what truly mattered. The accolades and discoveries of the academic world paled in comparison to the warmth of Mara's hand in his, the quiet understanding in her eyes, the feeling of coming home.

He knew, with a certainty that settled deep within his bones, that his professional aspirations, however grand, could not come at the expense of this profound connection. He had built his life on a foundation of integrity and genuine affection, and to compromise that now would be a betrayal not only of Mara, but of himself. The desire for professional advancement was strong, a deeply ingrained ambition, but it was not the sole architect of his happiness. True fulfillment, he realized, lay in the careful balance of personal growth and unwavering commitment to the people and values that sustained him.

He turned back towards the shore, his steps more purposeful now. The wind still blew, the waves still crashed, but the internal storm had begun to subside. He would have to have a serious conversation with Mara, not just about the fellowship, but about the future they envisioned together. He needed to articulate his realization, to reaffirm his unwavering commitment to their shared life. The external voices, with their alluring promises of singular achievement, would always exist. But the truest voice, the one that mattered most, was the one that spoke of love, partnership, and the enduring strength of a shared journey. He would make a decision, not based on the fleeting glory of scientific discovery, but on the solid, unwavering foundation of his love for Mara and the life they were building, together. He would find a way to pursue his dreams without sacrificing the heart of his world. His commitment to Mara was not an obstacle to his ambition; it was, he now understood, the very compass that would guide him, ensuring that his pursuits would ultimately lead him back to her, always.

—

CHAPTER NINE

Moments of Quiet Understanding

The sun, a benevolent orb painting the western sky in hues of apricot and rose, cast long, ethereal shadows across the sand. Eli and Mara walked hand-in-hand, their footsteps a soft symphony against the gentle sigh of the waves. The familiar rhythm of the tide, a constant companion to their lives, seemed to echo the steady beat of their shared heart. It was a silence not born of awkwardness or avoidance, but of a profound, earned contentment. In the vast expanse of the darkening coastline, they found a pocket of profound peace, a sanctuary woven from unspoken understanding and the quiet comfort of each other's presence.

Mara's fingers were laced with Eli's, her thumb occasionally tracing the faint lines on his palm, a silent gesture of affection that spoke volumes. Eli, in turn, would tighten his grip, a subtle acknowledgment of her presence, a grounding anchor in the quiet immensity around them. The salty air, usually invigorating, now carried a sense of mellow tranquility, a balm to the day's lingering concerns. It was in these moments, stripped of the day's demands and the noise of the outside world, that their bond felt most palpable, most real. They weren't seeking conversation; they were simply *being*, together, a silent testament to the depth of their connection.

They paused at the edge of the water, the cool spray kissing their bare ankles. Eli turned to Mara, his gaze soft, mirroring the gentle swell of the ocean. He saw not just the woman he loved, but the quiet strength, the unwavering kindness, the inherent grace that defined her. And in her eyes, he saw a reflection of himself, a sense of belonging that no amount of professional acclaim could ever replicate. Mara leaned her head against his shoulder, a sigh of pure contentment escaping her lips. "It's perfect," she murmured, her voice barely a whisper against the wind.

Eli knew what she meant. It wasn't just the beauty of the sunset, or the soothing sound of the sea. It was the perfection of this shared moment, this uncomplicated, unadulterated peace. He wrapped an arm around her, pulling her closer. The rescue center, the demands of their work, the uncertainties of the future – all of it faded into the background, rendered insignificant by the simple, profound reality of their shared solitude. Here, on this stretch of familiar sand, their world was reduced to the two of them, a universe contained within the warmth of their embrace.

Later, back at their small cottage overlooking the sea, the scene shifted, yet the essence remained. The storm had passed, leaving behind a sky awash with a million stars, each one a tiny beacon in the velvet darkness. They sat by the window, a single lamp casting a warm glow, illuminating the pages of two books. Mara was immersed in a worn volume of poetry, her brow occasionally furrowing in contemplation, while Eli was engrossed in a scientific journal, a silent companion to his lifelong passion. Yet, even with their individual worlds held within their hands, their awareness of each other was a constant, gentle hum.

Mara would occasionally look up, her gaze finding Eli across the small space. He'd be lost in his reading, his lips slightly parted in concentration, and a soft smile would bloom on her face. Then, he'd feel her gaze, his head would lift, and their eyes would meet. A silent question, a shared smile, a reaffirmation of their bond – all passed between them in that fleeting exchange. It was a language of understanding that transcended words, a testament to the comfortable familiarity they had cultivated. He would return to his journal, and she to her poems, but the thread of their connection remained unbroken, a constant, reassuring presence.

The crackling of the fireplace, the gentle rustle of pages, the distant lullaby of the waves – these were the sounds that filled their shared solitude. There was no pressure to speak, no need for forced conversation. Their presence was enough. It was a mutual understanding that allowed them to exist in their own worlds while remaining deeply connected to each other. This wasn't a void waiting to be filled; it was a richness, a depth that allowed for individual pursuits without sacrificing the intimacy of their partnership.

Eli would sometimes pause in his reading, the complex equations and theories momentarily receding. He would watch Mara, the way her hair fell across her cheek, the gentle rise and fall of her chest as she breathed. In those moments, he felt a profound sense of gratitude. He had found not just a partner, but a kindred spirit, someone who understood his quiet nature, who found solace in the same simple pleasures. He recalled countless other evenings, before the fellowship had introduced its layer of complexity, when they had simply sat like this, content in their shared quiet. These memories were not just recollections; they were living, breathing testaments to the enduring strength of their bond.

He remembered one particular evening, shortly after they had officially opened the rescue center. It had been a grueling day, filled with emergency rescues and the constant, demanding needs of injured animals. They had arrived home exhausted, the scent of antiseptic and salt clinging to their clothes. Instead of collapsing into separate exhaustion, they had found themselves drawn to each other. They had sat on the old wooden steps of their porch, the cool night air a welcome relief. They hadn't spoken for a long time, just listened to the chirping of crickets and the distant murmur of the ocean. Then, Mara had leaned her head on his shoulder, and he had felt a profound sense of peace wash over him. "We did good today, Eli," she had whispered, her voice thick with fatigue but brimming with a quiet satisfaction. He had squeezed her hand, the gesture a silent acknowledgment of their shared accomplishment, their shared exhaustion, their shared purpose. That was the essence of their shared solitude – a silent understanding, a mutual affirmation that sustained them through both the triumphs and the trials.

The silence between them wasn't an absence of noise; it was a presence of understanding. It was in the shared glances, the gentle touches, the way they intuitively knew when the other needed a quiet presence. Eli found that in these moments, his thoughts became clearer, his anxieties less potent. Mara's quiet strength was a constant source of reassurance, a reminder of the stability they had built together. He didn't need her to solve his problems or to offer grand pronouncements; he just needed her to be there, a steady, unwavering presence in the sometimes-turbulent sea of his life.

He recalled a recent afternoon, a rare lull in the usual frantic pace of the rescue center. They had found themselves with a few free hours, and instead of succumbing to the urge to "catch up" on chores, they had simply gone for a walk along the shoreline. The tide was out, revealing a vast expanse of rippled sand and tide pools teeming with miniature worlds. They had walked in companionable silence, pointing out interesting shells or the fleeting dart of a sandpiper. Mara had bent down to examine a delicate piece of sea glass, her face alight with a child-like wonder. Eli had watched her, a deep warmth spreading through his chest. It was in these unscripted, unforced moments that their love felt most pure, most authentic. They didn't need grand gestures or elaborate plans; they simply needed each other's quiet company to feel complete.

He would often find himself reflecting on the nature of their connection. It wasn't the fiery passion of youthful infatuation, but something deeper, more enduring. It was a quiet flame, stoked by shared experiences, mutual respect, and an unwavering commitment to each other's well-being. These moments of shared solitude were the fuel that kept that flame burning bright. They allowed them to recharge, to reconnect, to remember why they had chosen each other in the first place.

The fellowship, with its inherent demands and potential for separation, had cast a long shadow over his thoughts. But in these quiet moments with Mara, the anxiety would recede, replaced by a renewed sense of clarity and purpose. He realized that his ambition, while important, was not the sole defining aspect of his life. His relationship with Mara, their shared life, their sanctuary at the rescue center – these were the cornerstones of his happiness. And these quiet moments, these pockets of shared solitude, were the reminders of what truly mattered. They were the affirmations that his deepest desires were not just about scientific discovery, but about building a life of meaning and connection, a life he shared with her. He knew, with an unshakeable certainty, that whatever path his career took, these moments of quiet understanding, of shared solitude, would always be the bedrock of their love. They were not just pauses in their busy lives; they were the very essence of their shared journey.

The language of touch had, for Eli and Mara, always been a nuanced dialect, spoken fluently in the quiet corners of their shared life. It was a language that had evolved organically, shedding the tentative grammar of their early days for the confident, intuitive phrasing of profound intimacy. Now, as they walked along the shoreline, the sun a warm caress on their skin, and the sea breeze whispering secrets against their faces, their hands intertwined became a vibrant conversation. Eli's thumb traced the delicate curve of Mara's knuckles, a silent reassurance, a gentle question about her day, her thoughts, her heart. He felt the subtle shift in her grip, a slight tightening that conveyed a contentment he understood without needing words. It was a reaffirmation, a silent echo of "I'm here, and I'm with you."

Mara, in turn, would angle her head towards Eli, her shoulder brushing his as they walked. The contact, seemingly accidental, was a deliberate anchor, a grounding force. It spoke of shared vulnerability, of a willingness to lean into each other's presence, to share the weight of their existence. When Eli's fingers tightened around hers, a fleeting squeeze that spoke of unspoken gratitude, she felt a warmth bloom in her chest, a silent acknowledgment that their connection was more than just a physical clasp; it was a tether to each other's souls. The salty air, usually invigorating, seemed to carry a deeper resonance today, a tangible manifestation of the profound peace that settled between them. It was a peace born from the understanding that their most important conversations often happened without a single word being uttered, in the gentle pressure of a palm, the soft brush of skin against skin.

The significance of these silent exchanges had become more apparent than ever in the wake of recent discussions and the looming complexities of Eli's fellowship. The external pressures, the potential for physical distance, had inadvertently amplified the importance of their immediate, tangible connection. It was in the simple act of holding hands that Mara found a tangible representation of their unwavering commitment. Her fingers, intertwined with his, were not just seeking comfort; they were weaving a silent promise of steadfastness. Each subtle shift in pressure, each gentle squeeze, conveyed a depth of emotion that no spoken declaration could fully capture. It was a silent vow, spoken in the language of touch, affirming their enduring bond.

Eli found himself constantly seeking out these small gestures of physical affirmation. A lingering touch on her arm as they passed in the kitchen, a hand placed on her back as she reached for something on a high shelf, these were not mere social courtesies; they were declarations of presence, of affection, of a deep-seated need to be physically connected. He noticed how Mara's eyes would soften, her lips curve into a gentle smile, in response to these seemingly insignificant touches. It was a silent validation, a mutual acknowledgment of the unspoken current that flowed between them. The warmth of the sun on their skin, the gentle sea breeze caressing their faces, seemed to amplify these sensations, making them feel even more profoundly present, more intimately connected. The world outside their immediate sphere, with its myriad demands and distractions, faded into insignificance when they were bathed in the golden light, their hands clasped, their bodies close.

The tactile communication between them had developed a rich vocabulary all its own. A light, lingering touch on the shoulder from Mara could convey anything from gentle encouragement to a silent plea for attention, depending on the subtle pressure and the duration. Eli understood it implicitly. He knew when her touch was a whisper of "I'm proud of you" after a challenging day at the center, or a subtle nudge towards a moment of shared quiet. He'd often find himself instinctively reaching for her hand, his fingers finding hers as if guided by an unseen force, a simple gesture that said, "I'm here for you, no matter what." The warmth of that touch was a reassurance, a tangible reminder that they were a unit, a team, navigating the complexities of life together.

He would sometimes trace the line of her jaw with his thumb, a gesture born from a deep well of affection and admiration. In those moments, the subtle tremor in his hand, the way his gaze softened, spoke of a profound tenderness that transcended mere physical attraction. It was an acknowledgment of her strength, her resilience, and the quiet beauty that resided within her. Mara's response was often a contented sigh, a slight lean into his touch, a silent testament to the emotional resonance of his gesture. It was a conversation of the soul, spoken through the delicate language of touch, weaving a tapestry of shared emotions, unspoken understandings, and a love that was as deep and vast as the ocean stretching out before them.

Their evening routines had also become imbued with this silent, tactile communication. As they sat by the window, the lamp casting a warm glow, Mara might reach out and rest her hand on Eli's knee. It was a simple act, but for Eli, it was a universe of meaning. It spoke of shared comfort, of a desire for proximity, and a quiet acknowledgment of their shared life. He would often respond by covering her hand with his, his fingers intertwining with hers, a silent agreement to simply be together, in comfortable silence. The crackling of the fireplace and the distant lullaby of the waves provided a gentle soundtrack to these moments, a natural harmony that underscored the serenity they found in each other's presence.

Eli recalled one particular afternoon, shortly after a particularly draining rescue operation. They had both returned to their cottage, the exhaustion clinging to them like the salt spray from the ocean. Instead of collapsing into separate silences, they had found themselves drawn to the worn armchair by the window. Mara had curled up against him, her head resting on his chest, her breath mingling with his. He had simply held her, his arm wrapped around her, his fingers absently stroking her hair. There were no words exchanged, no need for them. The gentle rhythm of their breathing, the steady beat of his heart against her ear, the subtle pressure of her body against his – these were the only communication necessary. It was a profound, silent affirmation of their shared experience, their shared burden, and their shared strength.

Mara, too, found herself relying more and more on these non-verbal expressions of affection. When Eli was deep in thought, wrestling with complex scientific theories or the anxieties surrounding his fellowship, she would often place a hand on his arm, a light, reassuring pressure that conveyed a silent "I'm here for you, I understand." Sometimes, she would simply rest her head on his shoulder, a silent gesture of solidarity and unwavering support. He would feel the tension in his shoulders ease, a subtle relaxation spreading through him, a silent acknowledgment of her comforting presence. It was a language of empathy, of shared burdens, spoken without a single syllable.

The warmth of the sun on their skin, as they walked hand-in-hand along the beach, was more than just a physical sensation; it was a shared experience that amplified their connection. The gentle breeze that ruffled their hair seemed to carry whispers of their unspoken thoughts, their shared dreams, their unwavering affection. When Mara's fingers tightened around Eli's, a subtle squeeze that spoke volumes, he understood it as a moment of deep contentment, a silent expression of gratitude for their shared journey. He would respond with a gentle pressure of his own, a silent affirmation of his reciprocal feelings, a reaffirmation of the profound bond that had grown between them.

He remembered a particular evening, not long after they had moved into their coastal home. A storm had raged outside, the wind howling and the waves crashing against the shore with relentless fury. Inside, they had been huddled together on the sofa, the flickering firelight casting dancing shadows on the walls. Mara had been quietly reading, but her hand had found its way to his, her fingers lacing with his. He had felt the familiar warmth spread through him, a sense of calm in the midst of the external chaos. He had squeezed her hand, a silent acknowledgment of their shared sanctuary, their shared peace amidst the storm. It was a testament to the power of touch, a silent anchor in a turbulent world, a constant reminder of the deep and abiding love that held them together.

The subtle shifts in their physical proximity also spoke volumes. When Eli found himself pacing the floor, his mind caught in a loop of anxious thoughts, Mara would often subtly shift closer, her knee brushing his as she sat. It was an invitation, a silent offering of comfort and companionship. He would often turn, meeting her gaze, and find a quiet understanding reflected there, an unspoken message of support that eased his racing mind. Sometimes, he would simply reach out and gently cup her cheek, his thumb stroking her skin, a gesture that conveyed a depth of love and gratitude that no words could ever fully articulate.

The tenderness with which they touched each other had become a hallmark of their relationship. It was in the way Eli would gently brush a stray strand of hair from Mara's face, the way he would tuck her in at night, his hand lingering for a moment on her arm, conveying a silent wish for peaceful slumber. It was in the way Mara would rest her head on his shoulder during quiet evenings, her presence a comforting weight that anchored him. These were not grand gestures, but small, intimate acts that spoke of deep affection, unwavering support, and a profound commitment to each other's well-being. They were the silent poetry of their love, written in the language of touch, a language they spoke fluently, with every shared glance, every gentle embrace, every lingering touch. The warmth of the sun on their skin, the salty breeze on their faces, were not just elements of the environment; they were silent witnesses to the deepening intimacy, the growing bond, the profound and unspoken love that permeated every aspect of their shared lives. They understood that in the quiet language of touch, they found a connection that was as essential and life-giving as the air they breathed, a testament to the enduring power of a love that was as deep and vast as the ocean beside them.

Eli's observational wisdom, much like the discerning eye of a seasoned sailor who could read the subtle shifts in the wind and the currents of the sea, often provided Mara with a quiet clarity she hadn't realized she was missing. He possessed an innate ability to perceive the unspoken, to understand the nuances of her internal landscape before she herself had fully mapped it. It wasn't a prying curiosity, but a gentle, almost intuitive awareness, born from a deep well of affection and a genuine desire for her well-being. He'd watch her, his gaze often thoughtful, as she navigated the daily currents of their lives, and more often than not, his quiet observations would emerge at precisely the right moment, like a beacon cutting through the fog.

One crisp afternoon, as they sat on their porch, the scent of salt and pine mingling in the air, Mara found herself unusually preoccupied. The impending fellowship was a growing presence, a nebulous concern that she hadn't quite articulated, even to herself. Eli, sensing the subtle tension in her shoulders, the slight faraway look in her eyes, didn't press with direct questions. Instead, he picked up a fallen pinecone from the porch floor, turning it over in his hands. "You know," he began, his voice soft, "sometimes, when the tide goes out, it reveals things we didn't even know were there. Shells, perhaps, or smooth, sea-worn glass. Things hidden beneath the surface." He paused, his eyes meeting hers, a gentle inquiry within their depths. "It doesn't mean the water wasn't there before, or that it's gone forever. Just... revealed in a new light."

Mara considered his words, the simple analogy resonating deeply. She realized she'd been so focused on the 'tide' of the fellowship, the potential upheaval it represented, that she hadn't considered what might be revealed in its ebb and flow. It was a subtle reframing, a gentle nudge towards possibility rather than just apprehension. "I suppose," she murmured, a small smile playing on her lips, "we're just waiting for the tide to go out, then." Eli's smile was warm, a silent acknowledgment of her understanding. He didn't offer solutions or pronouncements, just a shared perspective that eased the weight on her chest. He knew that often, Mara didn't need answers as much as she needed to feel seen and understood, and his quiet observations provided that space.

Another time, after a particularly challenging week at the marine center where a delicate rescue operation had consumed much of their energy, Mara had retreated into a quiet exhaustion. She'd felt a subtle frustration simmering beneath the surface, a sense of being overwhelmed by the sheer scale of the responsibility. Eli found her staring out at the restless ocean, her expression a mixture of weariness and something akin to defeat. He walked up behind her and gently placed his hands on her shoulders, his touch a soft anchor. "The ocean," he said, his voice a low rumble against her ear, "doesn't always give us what we expect. Sometimes it's calm and generous, other times it's… demanding. But it's always the ocean. Always itself." He kneaded her shoulders gently. "You can't control the storm, Mara, but you can guide the boat through it. And you're an exceptional navigator."

His words, so simple yet so profound, washed over her like a soothing wave. She had been so caught up in the difficulty of the recent events, feeling the weight of their unpredictability, that she'd lost sight of her own capabilities. Eli's observation wasn't a dismissal of her feelings, but a gentle reminder of her inherent strength, her resilience, her skill. He saw her not just as someone affected by the challenges, but as someone capable of facing them. He often spoke in metaphors drawn from his own world, the sea and the sky, but they always seemed to land with perfect precision in Mara's heart, offering a different lens through which to view her own experiences. He understood that sometimes, the most profound wisdom wasn't in grand pronouncements, but in the quiet recognition of a shared reality, and the gentle affirmation of one's own agency within it.

Eli's observational wisdom extended beyond just emotional states; it encompassed the smaller, everyday interactions as well. He noticed, for instance, how Mara's hands would often flutter to her throat when she was trying to articulate something difficult, a subconscious gesture of self-protection. He saw the way her gaze would dart towards the windows when a car pulled into their driveway, a lingering trace of her past anxieties. He didn't point these out in a way that made her feel exposed, but he would often respond to them with a quiet attentiveness that spoke volumes. If she fiddled with her necklace, he might reach out and gently cover her hand for a moment, his touch a silent reassurance, a subtle cue that he was there, ready to listen, ready to support.

One evening, as they were discussing potential renovations for their cottage, Mara became visibly flustered when a particular design element was brought up, something that touched upon a past insecurity. Her breath hitched, and her usual articulate demeanor faltered. Eli, without missing a beat, steered the conversation in a different direction, suggesting they focus on the more practical aspects first, the structural elements. Later, as they were clearing the dinner dishes, he casually remarked, "You know, that old lighthouse keeper used to say the most important part of building a strong structure isn't the decorative flourishes, but the foundation. If the foundation is solid, everything else can be built upon it, piece by piece." He met her eyes, a knowing softness in his gaze. "We'll get to the flourishes, Mara. But let's make sure the foundation is as strong as can be."

It was a subtle redirection, a gentle acknowledgement of her discomfort without forcing her to confront it head-on. He understood that for Mara, whose life had been marked by periods of instability, the idea of a solid foundation was paramount. By focusing on that, he was offering her a sense of control and security, allowing her to feel confident in their progress. He saw her strength, her resilience, and he knew that her past experiences, while shaping her, did not define her limitations. His observations were like the steady hand of a craftsman, carefully assessing the material, understanding its potential, and working with it patiently to create something beautiful and enduring. He didn't just see the surface; he understood the underlying structure, the history, and the potential for growth.

Eli's keen perception often manifested in his quiet acts of service, born from his observations of Mara's needs. He noticed how, after a long day of research and data analysis, her shoulders would sag, and her movements would become slower, more deliberate. He'd often find himself making her a cup of her favorite herbal tea, not as a grand gesture, but as a simple, intuitive act of care. He'd place it beside her, his hand briefly resting on her arm, a silent communication of "I see you. I understand. Rest." He learned to anticipate her unspoken desires, like the way she'd sometimes absentmindedly run her fingers over the smooth wood of their kitchen counter when she was lost in thought. He'd quietly place a small, polished stone, a piece of sea glass he'd found, in that exact spot, a tactile anchor that seemed to bring her back to the present with a gentle smile.

He also observed the subtle tells in her body language when she was feeling overwhelmed by social interactions, a tendency to retreat into herself, her gaze becoming more inward. During gatherings with friends, he wouldn't draw attention to it, but he'd create opportunities for her to step away, suggesting a quiet walk along the beach or a moment of respite on the porch, often with a murmured, "Let's get some air, just the two of us." These weren't attempts to control her interactions, but rather gentle provisions for her comfort, allowing her to recharge without feeling scrutinized or judged. He understood that her introverted nature wasn't a flaw, but a facet of her personality, and his role was to create an environment where she felt secure and understood, allowing her to engage on her own terms.

His wisdom wasn't always about anticipating needs; sometimes it was about offering a different perspective, a gentle recalibration of her focus. Mara, with her passionate dedication to conservation, often felt the weight of the world's environmental challenges acutely. She could become despondent when faced with setbacks or the sheer magnitude of the problems. Eli, with his scientific mind, approached these issues with a balanced perspective. He wouldn't dismiss her concerns, but he would often remind her of the progress being made, the dedicated individuals working tirelessly, and the ripple effect of individual actions.

One evening, after reading a particularly disheartening report about ocean pollution, Mara was unusually quiet and somber. Eli found her sitting by the window, the fading light casting long shadows. He sat beside her, not immediately speaking, but simply sharing the silence. Then, he began to speak about a specific, small-scale project he'd learned about – a community initiative to clean up a local bay. "It might seem like a drop in the ocean, Mara," he said, his voice gentle but firm, "but those drops, taken together, can fill a lake. And that community, they're not just cleaning the bay; they're inspiring others. They're creating a ripple. You create ripples every single day with your work at the center. Don't ever forget the power of that."

He wasn't offering platitudes; he was grounding her in tangible examples of hope and action. He helped her to see that despair was a luxury they couldn't afford, and that sustained effort, even in the face of overwhelming challenges, was where true change began. He understood that her passion, while a driving force, could sometimes lead her to feel the burden of the entire world. His wisdom lay in his ability to help her compartmentalize, to focus on the actionable, the achievable, and the hopeful, without diminishing the importance of the larger struggle.

He was a steady hand on the tiller, guiding her through the emotional storms, reminding her of the strength she possessed and the impact she was already making.

Eli's understanding of Mara's inner world was also reflected in how he responded to her moments of joy and accomplishment. He wouldn't just offer a perfunctory "well done." Instead, he'd observe the specific spark in her eyes, the almost imperceptible lift in her chin, and tailor his response to acknowledge the nuanced feeling behind it. When a particularly stubborn research question she'd been grappling with finally yielded a breakthrough, he noticed the quiet, almost shy smile that touched her lips, a smile that spoke of immense relief and deep satisfaction, far more than outward exuberance.

He might then simply walk over and place a hand on her back, his touch light and warm, and say, "I saw that look. That's the look of a problem solved. And you, Mara, you're a magnificent problem-solver." It wasn't just about the intellectual achievement; it was about recognizing the personal journey, the dedication, and the quiet triumph that had led to that moment. He understood that for Mara, her victories were often hard-won and deeply personal, and his validation of those private moments was more meaningful than any public acclaim. He knew that her greatest strengths lay not just in her intellect, but in her quiet tenacity, her unwavering commitment, and the profound depth of her character. His observations allowed him to celebrate not just the outcome, but the essence of who she was. He was, in essence, a gentle cartographer of her soul, charting its landscapes with an unwavering affection and a profound understanding.

The salty air, a constant companion in their coastal haven, had always been a source of solace for Mara. It carried with it the rhythm of the tides, the secrets of the deep, and a certain undeniable truth that resonated with her own evolving understanding of herself. In the quiet moments, often shared with Eli on their porch or during their meandering walks along the shore, she found herself listening not just to the external world, but to the subtle murmurs within. It was a growing awareness, a gentle unfolding of trust in a voice she had, for so long, silenced or ignored. This inner compass, once a hesitant whisper, was beginning to speak with a steady, unwavering tone, guiding her through the complexities of her own heart and the unfolding narrative of her life with Eli.

Her intuition, once a fluttering butterfly of fleeting impressions, was morphing into something more substantial, a reliable current beneath the surface of her thoughts. It had been a slow process, a gradual recalibration of her internal landscape. For years, she had relied on logic, on tangible evidence, on the well-trodden paths of reason. But Eli, with his quiet wisdom and his uncanny ability to see beyond the obvious, had inadvertently shown her the value of this other, more visceral form of knowing. He didn't preach about intuition; he embodied it, and in doing so, he created a space where Mara felt safe to explore her own. He saw her not just as a creature of intellect, but as a being of feeling, of instinct, and he nurtured that aspect of her with the same care he would tend to a delicate marine specimen.

She found herself noticing these shifts most keenly when she considered Eli. There were moments, fleeting but potent, when a particular look in his eyes, a subtle shift in his posture, or even the way he held his mug of tea, would convey a depth of understanding or a silent reassurance that bypassed words entirely. Before, she might have overanalyzed, sought confirmation, or questioned the validity of her own perception. Now, she simply allowed it to settle. She felt the truth of his commitment not in grand declarations, but in the consistent, quiet ways he showed up for her, day after day. It was in the way he remembered her preference for a specific blend of tea when she was stressed, or the way he'd instinctively reach for her hand during a particularly poignant moment in a film, his touch a silent anchor. These weren't actions that required elaborate justification; they were simply *him*, and her intuition told her, with growing certainty, that this was genuine, this was profound, and this was something she could build upon.

The impending fellowship, which had initially loomed as a dark cloud of uncertainty, was now being viewed through a different lens. Her intuition whispered not of impending separation or insurmountable challenges, but of opportunity, of growth, and of a shared resilience that could weather any storm. She recalled Eli's analogy of the tide, how it revealed what was hidden. She was beginning to understand that the ebb and flow of their lives, including the potential disruption of the fellowship, wouldn't diminish their connection but rather, might illuminate its strength. Her inner voice, once hesitant, now affirmed that their bond was not fragile, but resilient, like the ancient, weather-beaten rocks along their coastline, shaped by the elements but unyielding.

This growing trust in her intuition wasn't just about Eli; it was also about her own sense of self. The predictable rhythm of the ocean, the dependable cycle of the moon pulling the tides, had become a metaphor for her own inner workings. She was learning to trust that just as the ocean returned to shore, so too would she find her own stable ground. The anxieties that had once plagued her, the self-doubt that had often clouded her judgment, were beginning to recede, like the tide going out, revealing a stronger, more confident shoreline within. She started to recognize her own instincts not as impulses to be feared, but as valuable insights, honed by years of observation, both of the natural world and of her own experiences.

One blustery afternoon, as they watched the waves crash against the rocky shore, Mara found herself unusually pensive. The fellowship felt closer now, more tangible, and with it, a familiar tremor of apprehension. She had always been adept at analyzing data, at dissecting complex scientific problems, but when it came to her own emotional landscape, she often felt adrift. Yet, as she watched Eli, his gaze steady and focused on the horizon, a sense of calm settled over her. It wasn't a forced calm, but a deep, intuitive knowing that whatever lay ahead, they would face it together.

"It's like the storm that's gathering," she mused aloud, the wind whipping strands of hair around her face. "You can see it coming, feel the change in the air, the shift in the light. But you also know that storms pass. The sea always finds its balance again."

Eli turned to her, a gentle smile gracing his lips. "And you, my love," he said, his voice carrying easily over the roar of the waves, "you have the strength of the lighthouse. You can weather any storm, and you guide me through mine."

His words weren't just a compliment; they were an affirmation of what she was beginning to feel within herself. She was not a passive observer in her own life, nor was she at the mercy of external forces. She had an inner resilience, a capacity for navigating uncertainty that was as innate as the tides themselves. This realization, this dawning trust in her own intuition, was a profound shift. It allowed her to embrace the future not with trepidation, but with a quiet confidence, knowing that her inner compass was true, and that the connection she shared with Eli was a steadfast anchor in the ever-changing currents of life.

She began to notice the subtle ways her intuition guided her decisions, even in seemingly small matters. A decision about which research project to prioritize at the center, a choice about how to spend a rare afternoon of leisure – these were no longer purely analytical exercises. There was an added layer, a quiet nudge from within, that often pointed her towards the path that felt most authentic, most aligned with her deeper values. This wasn't about avoiding difficult choices, but about approaching them with a greater sense of inner certainty, a quiet assurance that she was capable of making the right ones for herself.

Her connection with Eli deepened as she allowed herself to trust these inner signals. When he spoke of his work, of the challenges he faced at the observatory, her intuition would often offer a silent understanding, a sensing of his unspoken weariness or his quiet pride in a scientific breakthrough. She learned to respond not just with logic, but with empathy, with a gentle reassurance that stemmed from a place of deep, intuitive connection. She no longer felt the need to dissect his every word or gesture, but rather to feel the resonance of his emotions, to understand him on a level that transcended mere communication.

One evening, as they sat by the fireplace, the flames casting dancing shadows on the walls, Mara found herself reflecting on their journey. She remembered the early days, the hesitations, the carefully guarded emotions. Now, the thought of their shared future felt not daunting, but comforting. Her intuition whispered of a deep, enduring love, a partnership built on mutual respect and unwavering support. It was a quiet assurance, a feeling of rightness that settled deep within her soul.

"You know," she began, her voice soft, "I used to overthink everything. I'd analyze every possibility, every potential pitfall. But lately..." she trailed off, looking at Eli, his gaze warm and attentive. "Lately, I just... know. It's a feeling, a certainty that's hard to explain, but it's there."

Eli reached across the small space between them, his hand finding hers, his thumb gently stroking her skin. "That's a beautiful thing, Mara," he said, his voice a low, comforting rumble. "To trust that inner knowing. It's like learning to read the stars. At first, they're just distant lights, but with time and observation, you learn their patterns, their stories. You learn to navigate by them."

His words resonated deeply. She was learning to navigate by the stars of her own inner landscape, guided by a wisdom that was both ancient and new. The predictable rhythms of nature, the steadfastness of the ocean, had taught her patience, resilience, and the quiet power of observation. And in Eli, she had found a mirror, a partner who not only understood and encouraged this burgeoning trust in herself, but who also amplified it, making it a cornerstone of their shared life. The future, once a nebulous entity shrouded in uncertainty, now felt like a clear, open horizon, and she, with her growing intuition as her guide, was ready to sail towards it, hand in hand with the man who had shown her the way.

The rescue center, a sprawling collection of weathered buildings perched precariously close to the ever-present spray of the Atlantic, had, almost imperceptibly, woven itself into the fabric of Mara and Eli's relationship. It wasn't merely the site of their professional lives, their shared dedication to the rehabilitation of injured marine life; it had become, in a profound and unspoken way, a sanctuary. Within its walls, amidst the briny tang of salt and iodine, the gentle murmur of the waves a constant backdrop, they had built not just a life together, but a foundation of shared purpose and mutual reliance. Each success, each small victory in coaxing a struggling seal back to health or ensuring a rehabilitated dolphin's safe release, was a testament to their combined efforts, a silent affirmation of their partnership.

Mara often found herself observing Eli within the organized chaos of the center. His movements, usually precise and deliberate, took on a different quality here. There was an economy of motion, a quiet confidence that radiated from him as he worked, whether he was meticulously cleaning a seabird's wing or calmly reassuring a distressed loggerhead turtle. It was in these moments, surrounded by the tangible needs of the creatures in their care, that Mara felt their connection solidify. The world outside, with its myriad complexities and potential anxieties, seemed to recede, replaced by the immediate, grounding reality of their shared mission. The center, in essence, was a crucible, testing and tempering their bond with every passing day.

She remembered the early days, a blur of unfamiliar routines and overwhelming responsibility. The initial awe of being part of such a dedicated team had quickly been tempered by the sheer volume of work, the constant vigilance required, and the emotional toll of witnessing so much suffering. Eli, in his quiet, unobtrusive way, had been her constant. He hadn't offered platitudes or grand pronouncements; instead, he'd simply been present. He'd been the steady hand that offered a scalpel at the precise moment she needed it, the reassuring presence beside her during a lengthy, delicate procedure, the one who brewed the strong, bitter coffee that fueled their late-night vigils. These were not gestures that demanded recognition, but acts of quiet solidarity that spoke volumes.

Now, as they navigated the demands of the upcoming breeding season, the center hummed with a renewed energy. The air, thick with the scent of antiseptic and fish, was also alive with the hopeful promise of new life. Mara found herself drawn to the enclosures where the younger animals were being nursed, the clumsy movements of seal pups, the tentative explorations of young gulls. It was a microcosm of their own journey, she realized – a process of nurturing, of patient guidance, of creating an environment where vulnerability could be met with strength and resilience.

One particularly humid afternoon, as a storm brewed offshore, the usual clamor of the center was amplified by the restless energy of the animals sensing the change in the weather. A young otter, rescued days earlier with a deep gash on its hind leg, was exhibiting signs of distress. Its usual playful exuberance had been replaced by a nervous, almost frantic energy, and Mara, despite her best efforts, was struggling to calm it. She felt a familiar knot of anxiety tighten in her chest, the weight of responsibility pressing down.

Eli, sensing her unease, appeared at her side, not with words, but with a shared look of concern. He knelt beside the enclosure, his presence a silent offering of support. He didn't try to take over, didn't offer unsolicited advice. Instead, he simply began to speak, his voice a low, steady rumble, narrating the weather, the rhythmic pulse of the sea, the steady breath of the shore. He spoke of the resilience of nature, of how even the fiercest storms eventually yielded to calm, of how the ocean, in its vastness, held both turbulence and peace.

Mara found herself listening, not just to his words, but to the calm cadence of his voice, the steady rhythm that seemed to weave itself into the frantic beat of the otter's heart. Slowly, almost imperceptibly, the otter began to settle. Its frantic movements subsided, its breaths deepened, and it eventually curled into a tight ball, its soft chirps replaced by a contented sigh. Mara looked at Eli, a wave of gratitude washing over her. In that simple act of shared presence, of quiet reassurance, he had reminded her of the strength that lay not in grand gestures, but in the profound power of unwavering support.

The rescue center was, for them, more than just a workplace; it was a shared narrative. It was where they had witnessed each other's compassion, resilience, and unwavering dedication. It was where the initial sparks of attraction had been fanned into the steady flame of a deep, abiding love. The challenges they faced there, the moments of intense pressure and the quiet triumphs, had forged a bond that was as strong and enduring as the ancient rocks that lined their coast.

Mara often found herself reflecting on the contrast between her life before Eli and her life now, within the embrace of the rescue center. Before, her days had been structured by the cold logic of scientific inquiry, her emotional landscape a territory she often avoided. Now, surrounded by the raw, unfiltered needs of these wild creatures, her own capacity for empathy and connection had been awakened and nurtured. The rescue center had become the unlikely setting for her own personal renaissance, and Eli, her steadfast partner, had been the gentle catalyst.

One evening, as the last of the staff departed and the center settled into its nocturnal quiet, Mara and Eli found themselves walking through the deserted grounds. The moon, a sliver of silver against the darkening sky, cast long, ethereal shadows. The air was heavy with the scent of salt and the distant cry of gulls. It was a moment of profound peace, a quiet interlude between the demands of their work and the promise of the night.

"You know," Mara began, her voice soft, the words carried on the gentle breeze, "sometimes I feel like this place... it's breathing with us."

Eli's hand found hers, his fingers lacing through hers with an easy familiarity. "It is," he agreed, his voice a low murmur. "It's where we found each other, in a way. Amongst all this... life. And healing."

They continued their walk in comfortable silence, the weight of the day lifting with each step. The rescue center, with its myriad inhabitants, its dedicated staff, and its constant hum of activity, was their shared world. It was a world that demanded their full attention, their unwavering commitment, and in return, it offered them a profound sense of purpose, a deep connection, and a sanctuary where their love could continue to grow, as steady and as resilient as the tides themselves. The rhythmic crash of waves against the shore, the distant call of a nocturnal bird – these were the sounds of their shared life, a symphony of purpose and quiet understanding, played out against the backdrop of the vast, untamed ocean. The challenges that lay ahead, whether personal or professional, felt less daunting within the protective embrace of this sanctuary they had built together, a testament to their shared strength and the enduring power of their love.

CHAPTER TEN

Answering the Tides' Call

Mara's journey toward fully embracing active participation in her relationship with Eli was not a sudden revelation, but a gradual, profound shift, akin to the slow erosion of a cliff face by the persistent kiss of the ocean waves. She had spent so much of her life guarding her heart, building intricate defenses against vulnerability, that the idea of truly *engaging* felt both exhilarating and terrifying. Her past had taught her that independence was strength, that self-reliance was the ultimate shield. Yet, watching Eli, witnessing his unwavering commitment to the rescue center, to the creatures they cared for, and, in his quiet way, to her, had begun to chip away at those ingrained defenses.

She started small, almost imperceptibly. It began with the simple act of truly listening, not just to the words Eli spoke, but to the unspoken anxieties and joys that lay beneath them. When he spoke of a difficult rescue, a creature too far gone to save, she learned to sit with him in his sorrow, offering not forced optimism, but a quiet, shared space for grief. She began to anticipate his needs, not out of obligation, but out of a growing understanding of his rhythm, his quiet cues. A steaming mug of tea placed beside him during a late-night examination, a shared glance across a crowded room that conveyed unspoken understanding, a gentle touch on his arm as he navigated a particularly stressful situation – these were her nascent offerings, the first tentative ripples of her active participation.

Her internal monologue, once a constant stream of self-assessment and caution, began to shift. The question was no longer "How can I protect myself?" but "How can I contribute? How can I nurture this?" The rescue center, with its constant ebb and flow of life and death, healing and loss, became her most potent teacher. She saw how the smallest of efforts could yield profound results. A carefully cleaned wound, a meticulously prepared meal, a patient observation of a recovering animal – these were not grand gestures, but essential components of healing. And wasn't love, she mused, a form of healing? A process that required constant tending, dedicated effort, and an unwavering belief in the possibility of a better outcome?

She began to challenge her own ingrained habits. The urge to retreat when faced with emotional complexity, the tendency to intellectualize rather than feel – these were old companions. But now, with Eli as her anchor, she found the courage to lean into the discomfort. When a disagreement arose, instead of withdrawing, she consciously chose to stay, to articulate her feelings, to seek understanding rather than resolution. It was like learning a new language, the language of vulnerability and honest communication, and with each fumbled sentence, each awkward silence, she felt herself growing stronger, her connection to Eli deepening.

One blustery afternoon, a storm was rolling in, the kind that churned the sea into a frothy chaos and sent the gulls in frantic arcs against the bruised sky. A young harbor seal pup, barely weaned and exhibiting signs of severe dehydration, had been brought in. Its labored breathing was a tiny, heartbreaking sound in the otherwise bustling ward. Mara had been working with it for hours, trying to coax fluids into its delicate system, her own anxiety mirroring the pup's distress. Eli found her in the dim light of the recovery room, her shoulders hunched, her brow furrowed.

Instead of his usual quiet presence, he knelt beside her, his gaze steady and full of empathy. "He's fighting," Eli said, his voice a low rumble that seemed to cut through the rising wind outside. "And you're fighting with him. That's everything, Mara."

His words, simple yet profound, struck a chord deep within her. It wasn't about having all the answers, or being perfectly competent in every situation. It was about being present, about aligning herself with the struggle, about choosing to be an active participant in the fight for life, for love. She met his gaze, a silent acknowledgment passing between them. "I know," she whispered, a tear tracing a path down her cheek. "I'm here."

From that moment, something shifted. The internal resistance, the subtle hesitancy that had always lurked at the edges of her emotions, began to dissipate. She started to initiate conversations, not about the day's rescues or the center's logistics, but about their dreams, their fears, their evolving understanding of each other. She asked Eli about his childhood, about the moments that had shaped him, not with the detached curiosity of a researcher, but with the genuine desire to know the man she loved more deeply. She shared her own vulnerabilities, the lingering shadows of past hurts, the quiet aspirations she had long kept locked away.

Her participation extended beyond words. She began to actively support Eli in his endeavors, not just by being a competent colleague at the center, but by understanding the deeper needs that fueled his dedication. She noticed how much he cherished the quiet solitude of the early mornings, the moments before the world fully awoke. So, she made a conscious effort to protect that time for him, ensuring he had his coffee brewed and his quiet space undisturbed. She learned to anticipate the physical toll his work took, offering gentle massages after long hours, ensuring he took time to rest, even when he resisted. These were not grand romantic gestures, but the steady, consistent acts of a woman who was choosing to be fully present, fully invested.

She found herself actively seeking opportunities to connect, to deepen their shared experiences. When Eli expressed an interest in a particular marine biology conference, she didn't just encourage him; she offered to help prepare his presentation, to research alongside him, to become a partner in his professional growth. When he spoke of wanting to learn to sail, she didn't dismiss it as a fleeting whim; she researched local sailing schools, signed them both up for introductory classes, and approached the challenge with an eagerness that surprised even herself.

The analogy of the tide became a constant touchstone in her mind. The tide didn't just passively arrive at the shore; it surged, it receded, it shaped the landscape, and it always, always returned. It was an active force, a constant, undeniable presence. And that, she realized, was what she wanted her love to be. Not a stagnant pool, but a living, breathing, dynamic force.

She started to actively cultivate their shared life beyond the rescue center. While the center was their sanctuary, their shared purpose, she recognized the importance of carving out spaces that were solely theirs, spaces where their relationship could breathe and evolve independent of the demands of their work. They began to plan weekend getaways, simple excursions that allowed them to disconnect from the immediate pressures of their lives and reconnect with each other. These trips were not about grand adventures, but about shared silences, shared laughter, and the quiet reaffirmation of their bond. They explored hidden coves, shared picnic lunches on windswept bluffs, and simply enjoyed each other's company, their hands entwined, their hearts open.

Mara began to understand that active participation wasn't just about doing things for Eli, or being present for him. It was also about allowing herself to be truly seen, to be vulnerable, and to trust him with the most fragile parts of herself. It meant letting go of the need to always be strong, to always be in control. It meant admitting when she was scared, when she was hurting, when she felt lost.

One evening, after a particularly emotionally draining day at the center, Mara found herself sitting by the ocean, the waves lapping gently at the shore. Eli joined her, not with words, but with a comforting silence. She felt the familiar urge to pull back, to compartmentalize her feelings, to present a composed exterior. But then she looked at Eli, at the genuine concern etched on his face, and she made a choice.

"I'm afraid, Eli," she confessed, her voice barely a whisper against the roar of the surf. "Sometimes I'm afraid I'm not enough. That I'll let you down."

The admission hung in the air, raw and vulnerable. She braced herself for his reaction, for a dismissal, a reassurance that felt hollow. But instead, Eli turned to her, his eyes reflecting the starlight. He didn't offer platitudes. He simply reached out and took her hand, his grip firm and reassuring.

"Mara," he said, his voice steady and calm. "You are more than enough. You are everything. And if you ever stumble, I'll be right here to catch you. That's not a promise, it's a fact." He squeezed her hand. "We stumble together, remember? That's how we learn. That's how we grow."

In that moment, Mara felt a profound sense of liberation. His acceptance, his unwavering belief in her, allowed her to shed the last vestiges of her self-imposed isolation. She leaned her head against his shoulder, breathing in the scent of salt and him, feeling the steady beat of his heart against her cheek. This was active participation – not just in the grand gestures of life, but in the quiet, intimate moments of shared vulnerability. It was about choosing to show up, fully and authentically, not just for Eli, but for herself, for the blossoming love that had found its footing on the wild, untamed shores of their shared lives. Her commitment was no longer a passive state of being, but a deliberate, ongoing act, as essential and as inevitable as the turning of the tide. She was no longer just present; she was actively engaged, a willing participant in the beautiful, evolving narrative of their love. The constant return of the ocean to the shore was a gentle, persistent reminder that love, like the sea, required constant engagement, a continuous surge of effort and intention. She was ready to answer that call, wholeheartedly.

Eli's devotion was not a fleeting storm, but a deep, unwavering current that ran beneath the surface of their lives, a constant source of reassurance for Mara. He didn't just speak of love; he embodied it in every quiet gesture, every steadfast action. His commitment was a tapestry woven with threads of passion and reliability, a masterpiece of enduring affection that Mara found herself increasingly reliant upon, and deeply grateful for. It was in the small, consistent acts that his devotion shone brightest, like the sun breaking through a morning mist, illuminating the world with its gentle warmth.

He had a way of anticipating her needs before she even recognized them herself. If Mara was lost in thought, her brow furrowed in concern over a rescued animal, Eli would appear with a cup of her favorite herbal tea, the steam rising like a silent question: "Are you alright?" He wouldn't pry, wouldn't demand an explanation, but his presence, his simple offering, was a profound statement of care. It was his way of saying, "I see you. I'm here with you." These were not grand pronouncements, but the quiet affirmations that built the foundation of their shared life. The steady rhythm of his presence became the heartbeat of her own peace, a silent symphony that soothed her anxieties.

His reliability was like the steady tide, predictable and essential. When Mara felt overwhelmed by the relentless demands of the rescue center, the weight of so many lives hanging in the balance, Eli was her unwavering anchor. He never faltered. He was the calm in the storm, the quiet strength that allowed her to gather her own. There were nights, after particularly difficult rescues or heart-wrenching losses, when Mara would lie awake, the echoes of despair still resonating within her. Eli, sensing her turmoil without a word being spoken, would simply reach for her hand, his touch a silent promise of solace. He would hold her, his presence a bulwark against the darkness, until the first rays of dawn painted the sky, a new day infused with his quiet strength.

This steadfastness wasn't born of obligation, but of a deep, intrinsic love that recognized the preciousness of their connection. Eli understood that love wasn't just about grand declarations or passionate embraces; it was also about the daily, meticulous tending of a relationship, the quiet commitment to showing up, time and time again. He invested in their future with the same dedication he poured into rehabilitating an injured sea turtle. He saw their shared life not as something to be passively enjoyed, but as a garden to be carefully cultivated, each day bringing new opportunities for growth and nourishment.

Mara often found herself observing him, marveling at the depth of his commitment. He would spend hours meticulously repairing the aging fence around the sanctuary, his hands calloused but his movements precise. He would dedicate evenings to meticulously researching new rehabilitation techniques, his brow furrowed in concentration. These weren't tasks that directly involved her, yet they were all part of the larger ecosystem of their life together, an ecosystem he nurtured with tireless devotion. He understood that the strength of their bond was built not just on shared moments, but on the individual efforts each of them made to support their collective well-being.

His passion for the rescue center was a mirror to his passion for her. He approached both with the same unwavering focus, the same deep-seated care. When he spoke of a particularly challenging rescue, his voice would carry a note of urgency, of deep concern for the creature's well-being. Mara recognized that same intensity in his eyes when he looked at her, a quiet fire that spoke of a love that was both fierce and tender. He was a man who gave his all, who poured his heart into everything he did, and Mara felt herself basking in the warmth of that all-encompassing devotion.

There was a tangible sense of security that Eli's presence provided. It was the kind of security that allowed Mara to shed her own protective layers, to breathe freely and to be her truest self. She knew, without a shadow of a doubt, that he would be there, a constant in a world that often felt chaotic. His love was like the unchanging horizon over the vast ocean, a steady, reliable line that promised continuity and hope. No matter how turbulent the waters, that horizon remained, a testament to the enduring nature of his commitment.

He celebrated her small victories with the same enthusiasm he showed for the major ones. If Mara managed to coax a shy bird to eat from her hand, Eli would smile, a genuine, heart-warming smile that conveyed his pride. He understood that true partnership wasn't about individual achievements, but about sharing in each other's joys and sorrows, about building a life where both felt seen, valued, and cherished. He actively fostered her growth, encouraging her to pursue her own interests, even when they didn't directly align with his. He would listen patiently as she described her latest project, his gaze steady, his attention undivided, making her feel as though her endeavors were as important as any of his own.

Eli's steadfastness wasn't about possession or control; it was about unwavering support and a profound respect for Mara's individuality. He never tried to mold her into something she wasn't. Instead, he embraced all facets of her being, the strong and the vulnerable, the confident and the hesitant. He offered her a safe harbor, a place where she could always return, where she would always be loved, unconditionally. This consistent affirmation allowed Mara to explore the edges of her own capabilities, to push beyond perceived limitations, knowing that Eli's belief in her was a constant, steady force at her back.

The way he handled conflict was another testament to his devotion. He never shied away from difficult conversations. Instead, he approached them with a calm rationality, a genuine desire to understand and to be understood. He saw disagreements not as threats to their relationship, but as opportunities for deeper connection, for refining their understanding of each other. He would listen intently, his gaze unwavering, and then respond with thoughtful consideration, his words always chosen to build bridges, not walls. This mature approach to conflict resolution fostered a sense of trust and safety, allowing Mara to navigate the inevitable challenges of a long-term relationship with confidence, knowing that they would face them together, as a united front.

He was her silent champion, her most ardent supporter. When Mara took on a new responsibility at the center, one that pushed her beyond her comfort zone, Eli was there. He didn't hover or offer unsolicited advice. Instead, he provided a quiet presence, a steady encouragement that spoke volumes. He would bring her coffee during late-night work sessions, offer a reassuring hand on her shoulder before a challenging meeting, or simply give her that knowing, supportive smile that communicated his faith in her abilities. These were the small, consistent acts that built an unshakeable foundation of trust and mutual respect.

Eli's devotion was a constant, gentle reminder of the enduring power of love. It was in the way he'd trace the lines of her palm when they sat in comfortable silence, in the way he'd remember the smallest details of conversations they'd had weeks ago, in the way he'd always make sure she got the last bite of her favorite dessert. These were not grand gestures, but the intricate, beautiful patterns of a life built together, a life where love was not just a feeling, but a deliberate, daily practice. His unwavering presence was a comforting constant, a deep well of affection that Mara knew she could draw from, day after day, year after year. He was the steady beat of her heart, the quiet promise of forever, etched not in grand pronouncements, but in the enduring, unwavering cadence of his devoted life.

The word 'us' had never felt so vast, so resonant, as it did when Mara looked at Eli. It wasn't a concept they'd arrived at through grand pronouncements or contractual agreements; it was a quiet unfolding, a gentle weaving of two individual threads into a single, vibrant tapestry. Their coastal home, with its salt-kissed air and the perpetual lullaby of the waves, was more than just a dwelling; it was the physical manifestation of this 'us,' a sanctuary built not just with wood and stone, but with shared dreams and unspoken understandings. Each sunrise that painted the sky in hues of rose and gold, each storm that raged against their windows only to retreat and leave behind a sky washed clean, mirrored the ebb and flow of their relationship. They had learned, through the quiet currents of their shared life, that 'us' was a living thing, constantly shaped and refined by the tides of experience.

For Mara, 'us' meant a profound sense of belonging, a feeling that permeated the very marrow of her bones. It was in the way Eli's hand instinctively found hers as they walked along the shore, his fingers interlacing with hers as if they were made to fit. It was in the shared glances that spoke volumes – a flicker of understanding when a particular bird song carried on the breeze, a shared amusement at a seal pup's antics, a silent acknowledgment of a worry that had crossed one of their minds. This wasn't a forced togetherness, a melding of identities where one lost themselves in the other. Instead, it was an expansion, a comfortable widening of their individual worlds to encompass each other. Mara's passions, her fierce dedication to the sanctuary, were not just tolerated or supported; they were woven into the fabric of their shared life. Eli would often be found at the edge of the conservation grounds, not interfering, but simply being present, a quiet sentinel who understood the importance of her work, his presence a steady anchor in the often-turbulent waters of animal rescue. He celebrated her victories, the successful release of a rehabilitated dolphin or the birth of a healthy seal pup, with a genuine, unadulterated joy that amplified her own. And in her quiet moments of doubt, when the weight of responsibility felt crushing, his belief in her was a gentle, unwavering force that lifted her spirits. 'Us,' for Mara, was the knowledge that she was seen, truly seen, not just for her strengths, but for her vulnerabilities as well, and loved all the more for it.

Eli, in his own quiet way, had defined 'us' as a sanctuary of shared strength and unwavering trust. He saw their union as a haven where both could shed their armor, where the pressures of the outside world couldn't penetrate. The coastal cottage, with its weathered charm and the rhythmic pulse of the ocean, was the embodiment of this. He cherished the way Mara's eyes would soften when she spoke of a new rescue, the passion that ignited her voice. He understood that her dedication to the natural world was an intrinsic part of who she was, and his love for her extended to a deep respect for all that she held dear. 'Us' for Eli meant partnership in its purest form – not just sharing a life, but actively building it together, brick by deliberate brick. He found immense satisfaction in the shared projects, the hours spent tending to their small garden, the evenings lost in conversation, the simple act of preparing meals together. These were the quiet rituals that solidified their bond, the mundane moments elevated by the presence of the one person who made them meaningful. He saw their love as a constant process of discovery, a journey of deepening understanding and appreciation. Mara's unwavering support of his own pursuits, her genuine interest in his research into marine conservation, was a testament to the mutuality of their respect. He knew that in Mara, he had found not just a partner, but a confidante, a fellow traveler who navigated life's complexities with grace and resilience, and he cherished the feeling of being her safe harbor as much as he cherished the feeling of her being his.

The essence of their 'us' was also found in their shared vulnerability. It wasn't about baring their souls in dramatic confessions, but in the quiet, unguarded moments. It was Mara, exhausted after a long day at the sanctuary, falling asleep on Eli's shoulder while he read, his arm a steady weight around her. It was Eli, admitting a rare moment of uncertainty about a particularly complex ecological problem, and finding Mara listening with an open heart and offering gentle, insightful questions that helped him untangle his thoughts. They had learned that true intimacy wasn't about perfection, but about the courage to be imperfect, to be human, and to know that in those moments of fragility, they would find not judgment, but unwavering acceptance. This openness extended to their shared future, the unspoken understanding that they were charting a course together. They didn't shy away from discussions about the years ahead, the potential challenges and joys they might face. Instead, they approached these conversations with a sense of collaborative exploration, acknowledging that their individual dreams would continue to evolve, and that their 'us' would adapt and grow alongside them.

Their coastal home became a tangible symbol of this evolving 'us.' The way the light filtered through the windows in the morning, illuminating dust motes dancing in the air, was a reminder of the beauty that could be found in the ordinary. The worn armchair by the fireplace, where countless conversations had unfolded, held the echoes of their shared history. Even the salt spray that seemed to find its way into every nook and cranny was a reminder of their environment, the natural world that had drawn them together and continued to shape their lives. They had meticulously curated this space, not just for aesthetics, but for function and comfort, each choice a reflection of their shared preferences and needs. Mara had her dedicated corner for sketching injured birds, her pencils and notebooks neatly arranged, while Eli's small study was filled with marine biology texts and charting equipment. These individual spaces, integrated seamlessly within the larger home, were a testament to their ability to honor both their individual pursuits and their collective life.

The rhythm of their days was a testament to their definition of 'us.' It was the quiet mornings, where coffee was shared in comfortable silence, the only sound the distant cry of gulls. It was the afternoons, filled with the demands of Mara's work and Eli's research, but always with the underlying awareness of each other's presence. And it was the evenings, when they would reconvene, sharing the day's events, often over a simple, home-cooked meal, their conversation flowing effortlessly, punctuated by laughter and shared reflections. There were no elaborate rituals or grand gestures demanded by their definition of togetherness. Instead, it was in the consistent, the predictable, the unwavering presence of one another that their bond was most profoundly felt. They had learned that the grandest declarations of love were often found in the quietest of moments, in the steady hand offered, the listening ear, the shared smile.

The tides, ever-present in their lives, served as a constant metaphor for their relationship. Just as the sea shaped the coastline, carving out coves and smoothing pebbles, their shared experiences had sculpted their 'us.' There were times of powerful surge, when their passion and shared purpose felt overwhelming, and times of gentle ebb, when the pace of life slowed, allowing for quiet reflection and deepening connection. They embraced both, understanding that the fullness of their bond lay in its ability to navigate all of nature's moods. The storms that battered their home were met with a shared resilience, a quiet determination to weather them together. They found strength in their unity, each leaning on the other when the winds blew fiercer, their shared purpose a beacon in the tempest. And when the calm returned, the air clear and the ocean serene, they savored the peace, a deeper appreciation for their sanctuary born from having faced adversity side-by-side.

Mara often found herself contemplating the evolution of their 'us.' It wasn't a static entity, a finished masterpiece. It was a living, breathing thing, constantly being painted with new experiences, new insights, new layers of understanding. The shared laughter over a silly mistake, the quiet comfort offered during a moment of personal grief, the collective joy found in a small, shared success – each of these moments added another hue to their shared canvas. They had learned to speak not just with words, but with actions, with gestures, with the silent language of shared presence. Eli's consistent habit of leaving her favorite blanket draped over her reading chair, or Mara's knack for knowing exactly when Eli needed a moment of quiet solitude, were small, yet profound, expressions of their deep understanding of each other. These acts of consideration, born from a place of genuine love and attentiveness, were the building blocks of their enduring connection.

Their coastal home was the heart of this evolving 'us.' It was where the dreams were nurtured, where the challenges were faced, and where the quiet moments of shared joy unfolded. The walls seemed to hold the echoes of their shared laughter, the lingering scent of sea salt and home. It was a space that reflected both their individual personalities and their harmonious union, a testament to their conscious effort to create a life that was uniquely theirs. The worn wooden floors bore the scuff marks of countless footsteps, each one a reminder of their shared journey. The mismatched furniture, collected over time, spoke of their shared aesthetic and their willingness to embrace imperfection.

Eli's perspective on their 'us' was rooted in a deep sense of partnership and mutual growth. He saw their relationship not as a destination, but as a continuous journey of discovery. He cherished Mara's independent spirit, her unwavering commitment to her work, and her ability to find beauty in the smallest of details. He understood that their individual strengths complemented each other, creating a more robust and dynamic whole. 'Us' for Eli was a space where both could thrive, where their unique qualities were not only accepted but celebrated. He found immense satisfaction in watching Mara grow, in witnessing her courage and resilience in the face of adversity. He knew that his role was not to 'fix' or 'guide' in a paternalistic way, but to be a steadfast source of support, a confidante, and a fellow traveler who appreciated the richness of her journey. He found that their shared life had a way of expanding his own horizons, introducing him to perspectives and experiences he might never have encountered otherwise. This mutual broadening of their individual worlds was, for him, one of the most profound aspects of their 'us.'

The coastal landscape itself had become an integral part of their 'us.' The ever-present sound of the waves was a constant reminder of nature's power and constancy, a soothing balm to their souls. They found solace in watching the sun dip below the horizon, casting fiery hues across the water, a shared ritual that brought a sense of peace and wonder. The rugged coastline, with its hidden coves and dramatic cliffs, mirrored the complexities and beauty of their own relationship. They had explored every inch of it together, each discovery becoming a shared memory, a new thread woven into the fabric of their 'us.' The winding paths along the bluffs, the secluded stretches of beach where they often walked hand-in-hand, had become their personal sanctuary, a place where the outside world faded away, leaving only the two of them and the vast expanse of the ocean.

Their shared commitment to the sanctuary was another cornerstone of their 'us.' It was a place where their individual passions converged, creating a unified purpose. They poured their energy and dedication into its mission, working side-by-side, their efforts amplified by their shared vision. The rescued animals became an extension of their collective care, each one a testament to their love and dedication. Mara's deep empathy for the creatures and Eli's methodical approach to their rehabilitation created a powerful synergy, a balance that benefited every animal that crossed their threshold. They understood that their work at the sanctuary was not just a profession, but a calling, and that sharing this calling deepened their bond in ways that mere words could never fully express. It was in the late nights spent tending to a sick animal, the early mornings spent cleaning enclosures, the shared triumphs of successful releases, that they truly solidified their 'us' as a force for good in the world.

The definition of 'us' for Mara and Eli was a continuous, evolving narrative, written in the language of shared experiences, mutual respect, and unwavering love. It was a testament to the fact that true partnership wasn't about finding someone to complete you, but about finding someone with whom you could build a more beautiful, more profound whole. Their coastal home, their shared work, their quiet routines – all of it was a living, breathing embodiment of their unique 'us,' a testament to the enduring power of connection, shaped by the ceaseless, graceful rhythm of the tides.

The low hum of the refrigerator was the only sound that punctuated the quiet of their kitchen, a domestic counterpoint to the ever-present murmur of the ocean outside. Dawn was beginning to paint the sky in soft pastels, and Mara traced the rim of her mug, the warmth seeping into her fingers. Eli sat opposite her, his gaze thoughtful as he watched the light catch the motes of dust dancing in the nascent sunlight. The conversation had, as it often did, drifted towards the sanctuary, towards the myriad possibilities and challenges that lay ahead.

"I was thinking about the proposal for the expansion," Mara began, her voice soft but clear. "We need to be ambitious, Eli. Not just for the sake of growth, but for the sake of the animals who will need us. The sea turtle population, in particular, is showing more strain. We need more dedicated rehabilitation space, maybe even a small, controlled breeding program if we can secure the funding and expertise."

Eli nodded, his expression mirroring her earnestness. "I agree. And I've been doing some preliminary research into sustainable funding models. Grants are a given, of course, but we also need to cultivate stronger community ties. Perhaps a 'sponsor an animal' program, more educational outreach events. Imagine the impact if we could involve local schools more directly, fostering that same sense of stewardship in the next generation."

"That's precisely it," Mara enthused, her eyes alight with the vision. "It's not just about rescuing and rehabilitating; it's about instilling a deep respect for the ocean and its inhabitants. We can be more than just a haven for injured wildlife; we can be a beacon of conservation. I've been sketching designs for a new observation deck, one that would allow visitors to see some of the non-critical care areas without disrupting the animals. Imagine families, children, seeing firsthand the work we do, the fragility of these ecosystems."

Eli reached across the table, his hand covering hers. His touch was grounding, a familiar comfort that always settled her restless energy. "It's a powerful vision, Mara. And one that feels... right. It aligns with everything we've built here. This isn't just your sanctuary, or my research lab; it's *our* sanctuary, *our* shared commitment. The expansion, the community programs, it's all an extension of that. It's about investing in a future we both believe in, not just for ourselves, but for the world around us."

"Sometimes," Mara confessed, her gaze softening as she met his, "I worry if it's too much. The responsibility feels immense, and then adding expansion, new initiatives... it's a lot."

Eli's thumb gently stroked the back of her hand. "We've faced challenges before, my love. Remember the winter of '19? The unprecedented storm surge that threatened to flood the entire lower level? We worked around the clock, side-by-side, securing every enclosure, moving animals to higher ground. We were exhausted, soaked, but we did it. Because we had each other.

This is no different. We approach it with the same strategy: break it down, tackle it together, and never lose sight of why we're doing it."

He continued, his voice a low, steady cadence. "And think about the synergy, Mara. Your innate understanding of the animals' needs, your intuition, coupled with my methodical approach to resource management and research. We're a force multiplier. I can analyze the data on migratory patterns to predict influxes of certain species, allowing us to prepare. You can design the most effective rehabilitation protocols based on your hands-on experience. It's a perfect... confluence."

"A confluence," Mara echoed, savoring the word. "Like the tides meeting. It makes sense. And the personal side of it... building our life here, it's intertwined with the sanctuary's future. When we talk about expanding, I'm not just thinking about more pens or better equipment. I'm thinking about our home, how we can create a sustainable living for ourselves here, dedicated to this work. Maybe even hiring a small, dedicated team in the coming years, freeing us up to focus on the most critical cases and the long-term strategic planning."

Eli's eyes crinkled at the corners. "The dream of a full-time veterinary technician or two? I can see it. And a resident marine biologist, perhaps, to assist with the more complex research aspects. It means we're not just running a rescue; we're establishing a hub. A place where knowledge is shared, where best practices are developed and disseminated. We can mentor others, pass on what we've learned."

"And what about our own research?" Mara asked, her gaze drifting to the window, to the endless expanse of the ocean. "You've been making such significant progress with your studies on the impact of microplastics on coastal ecosystems. If we have a more robust facility, more resources, imagine what we could achieve. We could collaborate with other research institutions, maybe even host visiting scientists."

"That's an exciting prospect," Eli admitted, a rare spark of ambition igniting his usually placid demeanor. "The data I've collected has been compelling, but limited by our current capacity. With a dedicated lab space, more advanced analytical tools... we could publish groundbreaking findings. It would elevate our work, and by extension, the importance of the sanctuary itself. It would give us a stronger voice in advocating for policy changes."

Mara leaned forward, a renewed energy infusing her. "Exactly! It's a feedback loop. A stronger sanctuary attracts better funding and more dedicated staff, which allows for more in-depth research, which in turn strengthens the sanctuary's reputation and impact. It's about creating a self-sustaining ecosystem of conservation and discovery, right here."

"And it's about us, too," Eli said, his voice dropping, a deep sincerity coloring his tone. "This work is demanding, often emotionally taxing. Having this shared purpose, this unified vision, makes it all the more profound. We're not just partners in life; we're partners in a mission. It's a different kind of commitment, a deeper one, forged in the shared responsibility for these vulnerable lives, and for the health of the ocean itself. It imbues every decision we make, every sacrifice we undertake, with a profound sense of meaning."

"I feel that," Mara breathed, her heart swelling with a familiar warmth. "There are days when the sheer volume of need can feel overwhelming. A sick dolphin calf, a colony of distressed seabirds... it's easy to get lost in the day-to-day crisis. But then I look at you, at how we navigate it together, and I remember the larger picture. We are building something lasting. Something that will continue to make a difference long after we're gone."

"And that's the beauty of it, isn't it?" Eli mused, his gaze distant for a moment, as if contemplating the vastness of time. "We're not just building a sanctuary; we're cultivating a legacy. A testament to the idea that two people, united by love and a shared purpose, can indeed make a tangible impact on the world. Our personal growth, our individual evolution, has led us to this point. We've learned to communicate, to compromise, to lean on each other. All of those skills, honed in our relationship, are now directly applicable to the success of this endeavor."

Mara smiled, a genuine, radiant smile that reached her eyes. "It feels less like a job, and more like... a calling we answer together. Every morning, the ocean calls, and we answer. Every injured creature that washes ashore, or gets tangled in discarded fishing gear, it's another tide pulling us towards action, and we embrace it. Our life here, our home, the sanctuary – it's all part of the same ebb and flow. It's a beautiful, chaotic, deeply fulfilling dance."

"And we're leading it," Eli added, his hand tightening around hers. "We're not just responding to the tides; we're learning to navigate them, to anticipate them, even to influence them in small but significant ways. The expansion plans, the research initiatives, the community engagement – these are all deliberate actions to steer our corner of the world towards a healthier, more sustainable future. It's the culmination of our journey, Mara. Everything we've learned, everything we are, it's all being poured into this. Into us, and into this place."

Mara squeezed his hand, a silent acknowledgment of the profound truth in his words. The early morning light had deepened, casting a warm glow across the room. Outside, the waves continued their ceaseless rhythm, a constant reminder of the powerful forces that shaped their lives, and the equally powerful forces that, together, they were capable of unleashing. The future of the rescue center, once a hazy dream, was now a tangible plan, intricately woven with the fabric of their shared life, a testament to the strength found not just in individual dedication, but in the unwavering unity of two hearts beating as one. The vision was clear, the path ahead illuminated by the dawn, and they were ready to walk it, hand in hand, their shared commitment a beacon against the horizon. The potential for growth was immense, but so too was their capacity to meet it, fueled by a love that was as deep and as constant as the ocean itself. They were not just building a sanctuary for animals; they were building a sanctuary for their shared future, a testament to the enduring power of connection and collective purpose. The planning wasn't just about logistics; it was an act of faith, a declaration of their commitment to each other and to the world they aspired to protect. Each step forward, each decision made, was a reaffirmation of their bond, a quiet promise whispered on the sea breeze, to face whatever the tides may bring, together. The synergy of their individual strengths, combined with their shared vision, created a potent force, capable of weathering any storm and charting a course towards a brighter tomorrow. This was more than just a rescue center; it was a living, breathing embodiment of their love, their dedication, and their unshakeable belief in a better future.

The title of the book, 'What the Tides Ask of Us,' no longer felt like a question hanging precariously in the air, but a profound statement that had guided their every step. Mara and Eli had discovered that the persistent currents of love and commitment were not demands to be feared, but invitations to be embraced. The 'tides' had asked for honesty, for the vulnerability that peeled back layers of self-protection, for the unwavering effort required to build a life not just beside each other, but truly *with* each other. They had learned to listen to the whispers of doubt, to the storms of disagreement, and to the gentle lapping of contentment, recognizing them all as the ocean's way of communicating its needs. And in the quiet dawn of their shared future, they had found the courage to answer. It wasn't a resounding shout, but a steady, confident affirmation, a deep-seated knowing that resonated in the salty air and the rhythm of the waves. This active participation in their own love story, this conscious choice to invest in its unfolding, was their most profound answer, an echo that stretched across the vast expanse of their coastal world, a testament to the powerful forces that had shaped them, both individually and as a united front.

Their journey had been a series of tides pulling them in different directions, testing the strength of their anchors, and sometimes threatening to carry them out to sea. But with each challenge, they had learned to adjust their sails, to trust the compass of their shared values, and to find solace in the knowledge that even in the roughest waters, they had each other. The sea turtles, with their ancient, instinctual journeys, had become their silent teachers, embodying resilience and a deep, inherent understanding of the call of their environment. They, too, answered the call of the ocean, embarking on arduous migrations, driven by an inner imperative that Mara and Eli had come to recognize within themselves. The sanctuary, once a symbol of their individual passions, had transformed into a crucible where those passions were forged into a shared destiny. It was a place where their deepest desires for healing and preservation intersected with their burgeoning understanding of what it meant to build a life rooted in love and mutual respect.

The expansion plans, once a daunting prospect filled with logistical nightmares and financial anxieties, now represented a tangible manifestation of their answered call. It was more than just bricks and mortar, more than just increased capacity for rescued animals; it was a physical embodiment of their commitment to a future where conservation and compassion were not just ideals, but integral components of their daily lives. Eli's meticulous research into sustainable funding models, Mara's visionary designs for educational spaces – these were not merely professional endeavors, but acts of love, meticulously crafted to ensure the sanctuary's longevity and its ability to serve a growing need. They were pouring their hopes, their expertise, and their very beings into this project, driven by the understanding that a thriving sanctuary was intrinsically linked to the health of their relationship and their shared life.

The decision to actively engage in the community, to invite schools and families into their world, was another powerful answer. It was a recognition that the ocean's health, and the well-being of its inhabitants, was a collective responsibility. They were no longer content to be isolated guardians; they were actively choosing to become educators, advocates, and inspirers. This outreach was not just about fostering a new generation of environmental stewards, but about strengthening the bonds that held their own community together, creating a shared sense of purpose that extended far beyond the sandy shores of their sanctuary. Mara's sketches for the observation deck, Eli's ideas for a 'sponsor an animal' program, these were not just practical strategies; they were expressions of their desire to share the profound connection they felt with the natural world, to open hearts and minds to the wonders and vulnerabilities of marine life.

The 'sponsor an animal' program, in particular, resonated deeply with Mara. It was a way to connect individuals to the tangible impact of their support, to give a face and a story to the often-abstract concept of conservation. She pictured a child, their eyes wide with wonder, carefully coloring a picture of a rehabilitated sea turtle, knowing that their small contribution had helped that creature find its way back to the vast blue. This was the kind of emotional resonance they aimed to cultivate, a gentle but firm reminder that every action, no matter how small, had the potential to ripple outwards, just like the tides. Eli's methodical approach to resource management ensured that these initiatives were not just idealistic dreams, but sustainable realities. He saw the interconnectedness of their efforts, the way a successful sponsorship program could directly fund specialized veterinary care, or how increased community engagement could lead to crucial donations for research equipment.

Their personal growth, once a quiet, internal process, had become inextricably linked to the sanctuary's evolution. The resilience they had cultivated through past storms, both literal and metaphorical, had equipped them to face the ambitious challenges ahead. Mara's innate empathy and intuition, which had always drawn her to the vulnerable creatures in need, now complemented Eli's analytical mind and strategic planning. They had learned to speak each other's language, to anticipate each other's needs, and to find strength in their differences. The sanctuary was not just a workplace; it was the living testament to their relationship, a space where their love was not only nurtured but actively expressed through their shared dedication to a cause greater than themselves.

Eli's research into microplastics, once a solitary pursuit confined to lab hours and quiet contemplation, was now poised for a significant leap forward. The planned expansion included dedicated, state-of-the-art laboratory facilities, a dream that had once seemed impossibly distant. This would not only allow him to delve deeper into the complexities of oceanic pollution but also to collaborate with a wider network of scientists, sharing their findings and contributing to global conservation efforts. Mara felt a surge of pride every time she thought about the impact his work would have, not just on their immediate environment, but on the broader scientific community. It was a testament to their shared belief that knowledge and action must go hand in hand, that understanding the problems was the first crucial step towards finding solutions.

The vision of a thriving, multi-faceted sanctuary – a hub for rescue, rehabilitation, research, and education – was no longer a distant aspiration but a tangible reality taking shape. The idea of hiring a small, dedicated team, of having veterinary technicians and marine biologists on staff, represented a new phase of growth, one that would allow Mara and Eli to focus on the strategic direction and the most critical cases. It spoke of a maturity in their endeavor, a recognition that true leadership often meant empowering others and building a sustainable infrastructure that could endure and expand. This was not about relinquishing control, but about entrusting their shared vision to a wider network of dedicated individuals, united by the same passion that had ignited their own journey.

As they stood on the cusp of this new chapter, looking out at the vast, shimmering expanse of the ocean, the title of their book, 'What the Tides Ask of Us,' settled upon them like a warm, familiar cloak. The tides had asked for presence, for dedication, for a willingness to learn and to grow. They had asked for sacrifice, for unwavering hope, and for the courage to believe in something bigger than themselves. And Mara and Eli, through their shared journey, their unwavering commitment, and their deep, abiding love, had answered. Their answer was not a singular event, but an ongoing, evolving response, a daily recommitment to the principles that guided them. It was in the early morning visits to the recovering seal pups, in the late-night data analysis sessions, in the shared laughter over a simple meal, and in the quiet understanding that passed between them without a single word. It was in the way they held each other during moments of doubt, and the way they celebrated each small victory, knowing that each one was a testament to the power of their collective spirit.

The ocean, with its relentless cycles of ebb and flow, had taught them the profound lesson of surrender and resilience. They had learned that sometimes, the greatest strength lay not in fighting against the currents, but in understanding them, in learning to navigate their power with grace and wisdom. Their decision to embrace the challenges, to actively participate in their love story and in the future of the sanctuary, was their ultimate answer. It was a quiet but powerful declaration that they were not simply observers of life's grand narrative, but active authors, weaving their own tale of love, commitment, and unwavering dedication. The vastness of their coastal world seemed to hold its breath, listening to the silent symphony of their shared purpose, a testament to the profound courage found in answering the call of the heart, and in building a future, tide by tide, together. Their commitment was not a static vow, but a living, breathing entity, constantly replenished by the rhythm of the ocean and the enduring strength of their bond. The decisions they made, the sacrifices they willingly embraced, were all woven into the intricate tapestry of their shared life, a beautiful, complex pattern of love, purpose, and profound understanding.

They had found their voice, not in shouting defiance, but in the steady, unwavering cadence of their hearts, answering the tides with a resounding, "We are here. We are ready. We are yours."

Chapter Eleven

The Horizon of Shared Tomorrows

Mara found herself standing at the edge of a vista that, not so long ago, would have sent tremors of apprehension through her. The vast expanse of the ocean, stretching out before her like an infinite canvas, no longer represented the daunting unknown but a promise of boundless possibilities. The salt-laced air, once a whisper of her anxieties, now carried the invigorating scent of growth and a future she was not just ready for, but actively shaping. This was not a passive observation of life's unfolding, but a conscious stepping into its current, a deliberate act of co-creation with Eli. The fear that had once clung to her like the damp mist of a coastal morning had receded, replaced by a quiet strength, a deep-seated confidence that resonated from the soles of her feet, firmly planted on the sand, to the very core of her being. She understood, with a clarity that settled like warm sunlight, that love wasn't a destination to be reached, but a journey to be embarked upon, a continuous dance with the ebb and flow of life, a constant, willing response to its gentle, persistent calls. And she was ready to answer, with every beat of her heart, with every breath she took.

Her personal evolution felt as tangible as the smooth, sea-worn stones she sometimes gathered along the shore. The woman who had once shied away from vulnerability, who had built walls to protect a tender, wounded self, was now finding liberation in openness. She could meet Eli's gaze, not with the flicker of uncertainty she'd once harbored, but with a steady, unwavering affection that spoke of a love that had been tested and found true. This newfound groundedness wasn't an absence of emotion, but a deeper, more robust understanding of it. She could acknowledge the fleeting shadows of doubt or the occasional ripples of disagreement, not as insurmountable obstacles, but as natural aspects of a relationship that was alive and dynamic. The sanctuary, her sanctuary, had become more than a refuge; it was the fertile ground where this personal metamorphosis had taken root and blossomed. Every rescued creature, every successful rehabilitation, every shared victory with Eli had contributed to the tapestry of her confidence, weaving in threads of resilience and self-acceptance.

The coastal landscape, so integral to her identity, had transformed from a symbol of her internal struggles into a vibrant representation of their shared aspirations. The rhythmic crash of waves against the shore, once a soundtrack to her anxieties about the future, now echoed the steady cadence of their commitment. The undulating dunes, with their ability to shift and reform yet remain steadfast, mirrored the adaptability and strength they had cultivated together. Even the migratory patterns of the sea birds, their unerring return to familiar shores, served as a poignant reminder of the deep, instinctual pull that bound her and Eli together. She saw their future not as a static point on a map, but as a dynamic, ever-evolving horizon, much like the one that stretched endlessly before her eyes, a panorama of possibilities waiting to be explored. This embrace of the unknown, this willingness to step beyond the comforting familiarity of the past, was her most profound act of courage, a testament to the transformative power of love and shared purpose.

Mara understood that the tides, in their ceaseless motion, were not simply a force of nature, but a metaphor for the active engagement required in their life together. They weren't passive recipients of love's bounty, but active participants in its creation. This realization had seeped into her very being, transforming her approach to everything from the expansion plans of the sanctuary to the quiet moments of intimacy she shared with Eli. She no longer waited for inspiration to strike or for perfect conditions to arise; she sought them out, actively nurturing the sparks that ignited their shared dreams. The sanctuary's expansion, once a source of logistical anxieties, now represented a tangible manifestation of this engaged approach. Her sketches for new research facilities, the vibrant educational spaces she envisioned, were not just architectural plans; they were declarations of intent, meticulously crafted to ensure the sanctuary's ability to serve, to heal, and to inspire for generations to come. Each line drawn, each material chosen, was imbued with her commitment, her foresight, and her unwavering belief in the vital work they were doing.

This active participation extended beyond the physical structures of the sanctuary and into the very fabric of their community. The decision to open their doors wider, to invite schools and families to share in the wonders of the marine world, was another deliberate step towards fulfilling the deeper calling she felt. It was a recognition that the health of the ocean, and the creatures within it, was a responsibility that extended far beyond the sanctuary's gates. She saw their outreach programs as ripples, spreading outwards, fostering a sense of shared stewardship, and nurturing a new generation of advocates for the ocean. The thought of children's faces lighting up as they learned about the plight of a rehabilitated sea turtle, or the quiet contemplation of families observing the grace of a rescued dolphin, filled her with a profound sense of purpose. This was the essence of her embraced future: a future where compassion, education, and a deep respect for nature were woven into the everyday lives of their community, a future they were actively building, one shared experience at a time.

Her artistic sensibilities, once channeled into solitary creative pursuits, now found a powerful outlet in articulating the sanctuary's vision. Her sketches were no longer mere artistic expressions but potent tools for communication, for inspiring support, and for translating complex ideas into accessible visuals. She envisioned the observation deck not just as a platform for viewing, but as a space for quiet reflection, for the silent communion between humans and the natural world. The "sponsor an animal" program, which Eli had so thoughtfully conceived, resonated deeply with her desire to create tangible connections. She saw it as a bridge, linking the abstract concept of conservation to the individual, personal experience of making a difference. The idea of a child carefully nurturing a bond with a specific animal, understanding its story and its needs, was a powerful testament to the kind of emotional engagement they aimed to foster. This wasn't just about raising funds; it was about cultivating empathy, about reminding people that every life, no matter how small or seemingly insignificant, held intrinsic value and deserved protection.

Eli's meticulous approach to the practicalities of such programs only deepened Mara's confidence. His ability to translate visionary ideas into sustainable realities, to meticulously manage resources and ensure that every donation had maximum impact, was a testament to their complementary strengths. He was the anchor that kept their shared dreams grounded, the strategist who ensured their aspirations were not mere flights of fancy but achievable goals. She saw the synergy in their partnership, the way her intuitive understanding of connection and her creative vision blended seamlessly with his analytical mind and pragmatic execution. This wasn't about one person leading and the other following; it was a harmonious dance, a constant exchange of support and inspiration, each recognizing and valuing the unique contributions of the other. The sanctuary was the embodiment of this partnership, a living, breathing testament to what could be achieved when two hearts and minds were aligned with a shared purpose and a profound love.

The expansion of the research facilities, a project close to Eli's heart, was another area where Mara felt a profound sense of shared commitment. She knew how deeply he cared about understanding the intricate threats facing the marine environment, and the prospect of providing him with the tools and resources to delve deeper into his groundbreaking work filled her with a quiet pride. The idea of him collaborating with other scientists, of their sanctuary becoming a hub for cutting-edge research, was a vision that ignited her own passion for discovery and advocacy. She saw how his dedication to unraveling the complexities of issues like microplastic pollution was not just an academic pursuit but an act of profound love for the ocean and its inhabitants. This shared belief in the power of knowledge, in the necessity of informed action, was a cornerstone of their relationship, a driving force behind their collective efforts.

As the plans for hiring a dedicated team began to solidify, Mara recognized this as a sign of their maturity and their commitment to the long-term sustainability of their vision. It wasn't about relinquishing control, but about empowering others, about building a robust infrastructure that would allow their work to grow and flourish beyond their individual capacities. This

was a testament to their shared understanding of leadership –
one that involved collaboration, delegation, and the nurturing
of talent within their team. It spoke of a confidence in their
ability to articulate their vision clearly, to inspire others to join
their cause, and to trust in the collective power of dedicated
individuals working towards a common goal. The sanctuary was
evolving, growing not just in size and scope, but in its capacity
to impact, to educate, and to heal, all under the umbrella of their
shared commitment.

Standing on the shore, the vastness of the sea before her,
Mara felt a profound sense of peace. The title of their book,
'What the Tides Ask of Us,' no longer posed a question, but
affirmed a truth. The tides had asked for their presence, their
dedication, their willingness to learn and to evolve. They had
asked for sacrifice, for unwavering hope, and for the courage to
believe in a future that was larger than themselves. And Mara,
with Eli by her side, had answered. Her answer wasn't a single
declaration, but a continuous unfolding, a daily recommitment
to the principles that guided their lives. It was in the gentle
touch of her hand on Eli's arm during a challenging moment,
in the shared laughter that punctuated a long day, in the quiet
understanding that passed between them without the need
for words. It was in the way she met the challenges of their
expanding world not with fear, but with a quiet strength, a
steady resolve, and an unshakeable belief in the power of their
shared love. The horizon ahead, once a source of apprehension,
was now a beacon of promise, a testament to a future they

were embracing, tide by tide, together, with open hearts and unwavering spirits. She was no longer afraid of what the tides might ask, for she knew, with absolute certainty, that she was ready to give.

Eli's gaze swept across the tranquil expanse of the ocean, a familiar tableau that had once been a source of his most profound internal turmoil. Now, it was the very embodiment of his peace, a gentle, unwavering testament to the life he and Mara were building. The ebb and flow of the tide, a constant rhythm that had always underscored the passage of time, no longer spoke of his own restless search for purpose, but of a profound sense of belonging. He had sailed through a tempest of uncertainty, navigating the turbulent waters of his own expectations and the perceived limitations of his past. There had been a time when the horizon felt less like a promise and more like an insurmountable barrier, a distant yearning that seemed perpetually out of reach. He had grappled with the fear of stagnation, the gnawing worry that his life's trajectory might be one of perpetual drifting, lacking a true north. But those days felt like a distant, half-forgotten dream.

Mara was his harbor. She was the lighthouse that guided him, the steady beacon that cut through the fog of doubt and illuminated the path forward. Her presence was a grounding force, an anchor that held him firm against any potential storm. It wasn't just about the grand gestures or the shared dreams for the sanctuary, though those were deeply cherished. It was in the quiet intimacy of their everyday lives, in the way she instinctively knew when he needed a moment of silent companionship, or when a gentle touch could speak volumes more than any words. The sanctuary itself, once a symbol of his solitary dedication, had transformed into a vibrant testament to their shared vision, a living, breathing manifestation of their combined strengths. He found immense satisfaction in witnessing Mara's artistic spirit breathe life into the sanctuary's expansion plans, her sketches and visions translating into tangible progress that resonated with a deeper purpose.

The sound of the waves, a constant serenade just beyond their doorstep, was no longer the murmur of his own unfulfilled desires but the soothing lullaby of a life he had chosen, a life he actively cultivated. He remembered the earlier days, the nights spent staring at the ceiling, wrestling with the question of what truly mattered. He had sought external validation, chased fleeting ambitions, and tried to fit himself into molds that were never quite the right shape. But Mara had shown him that true fulfillment wasn't found in distant shores or the accumulation of achievements, but in the depth of connection, in the unwavering commitment to another soul. Her resilience, her compassion, and her unyielding dedication to the creatures under their care had not only inspired him but had also mirrored the very qualities he now embraced within himself.

He often found himself simply observing her, struck by the grace with which she moved through their shared life. Whether she was tending to a newly arrived seabird, her touch infinitely gentle, or sketching out designs for a new educational program, her focus was absolute. It was this unwavering presence, this capacity for deep engagement, that had drawn him in and continued to hold him captive, in the most beautiful sense of the word. His earlier anxieties about his own direction had dissolved, replaced by a quiet certainty that his path was inextricably linked with hers. He no longer felt the pressure to be the sole architect of his destiny; he was content to be a co-creator, building a future alongside Mara, brick by brick, wave by wave.

He recalled a conversation they'd had not long ago, about the future of the sanctuary and the ambitious plans for its expansion. He had presented the data, the logistical challenges, the financial projections, his usual pragmatic approach. Mara had listened intently, her eyes alight with a vision that transcended mere numbers. She had spoken of the emotional impact, the stories that would be woven into the fabric of their work, the lives that would be touched, not just the animals they rescued, but the humans they inspired. It was in moments like those that he understood the true depth of their partnership. His analytical mind provided the structure, the framework, while her intuitive understanding of connection and her boundless creativity breathed soul into their endeavors. He felt a profound sense of gratitude for this synergy, for the way their different perspectives converged to create something far greater than either of them could achieve alone.

His own past struggles with finding a sense of stability, of a place to truly call home, had made Mara's presence even more precious. He had felt like a ship without a port, always ready to set sail at the first sign of discomfort or routine. But Mara offered a different kind of journey, one that was deeply rooted, one that celebrated the quiet joys of shared existence. The sanctuary, their home, had become that port, a place of unwavering calm. He found himself deliberately seeking out these moments of quietude, savoring the simple act of sitting beside her as the sun dipped below the horizon, casting a golden glow across the water. These were the moments that solidified his commitment, that reaffirmed his choice to anchor his life to hers.

The familiar aroma of salt and sea, once a reminder of his own rootlessness, now smelled of home, of permanence. He had finally understood that stability wasn't about avoiding change, but about building a strong foundation that could withstand its inevitable currents. And that foundation was Mara. Her unwavering belief in him, in their shared future, had given him the courage to shed the layers of self-doubt that had clung to him for so long. He no longer felt the need to prove himself, to constantly chase after some undefined ideal. He was enough, and their life together was enough. This realization was a quiet revolution, a profound shift that had brought an immeasurable sense of peace.

He watched a seagull soar overhead, its wings catching the late afternoon sun, and a faint smile touched his lips. It was a simple sight, yet it resonated with a deep sense of contentment. His life was no longer a series of unanswered questions, but a symphony of shared experiences, a quiet melody played out against the backdrop of the ever-present ocean. He was present, truly present, in each moment, appreciating the depth of their connection and the beauty of the life they had so carefully, so lovingly, built together. The horizon ahead was no longer a subject of apprehension, but a gentle invitation, a promise of more sunrises, more shared laughter, more quiet moments of profound understanding. He had found his stable harbor, and in Mara's arms, he knew he would always be home.

The sheer magnitude of the transformation within him was something he often revisited in quiet contemplation. There had been a time when he believed that purpose was a grand, external quest, a distant peak to be summited. He had chased after what he perceived as significant achievements, often at the expense of his own well-being and his capacity for genuine connection. The pursuit of external validation had been a relentless, draining endeavor. He had convinced himself that success lay in conquering, in achieving, in leaving an indelible mark on the world. But the truth, as it so often does, had arrived not with a thunderclap but with a gentle whisper, carried on the salt-laden breeze that swept across their coastal home.

Mara had been the conduit for that whisper, the one who had shown him the profound significance of the small, the quiet, the deeply personal. Her dedication to the sanctuary wasn't driven by a need for recognition, but by a pure, unadulterated love for the creatures she cared for, and for the environment that sustained them. He had watched, mesmerized, as she poured her heart and soul into every rehabilitation, every educational initiative, every carefully considered plan for expansion. Her passion was infectious, and it had begun to seep into him, transforming his own understanding of what it meant to live a meaningful life. He had once viewed his work as a solitary endeavor, a personal mission. Now, it was a shared journey, a collaborative effort that amplified their impact and deepened their bond.

He found himself looking forward to their evenings together with an anticipation that bordered on eagerness. The simple act of sharing a meal, of discussing the day's events, of simply being in each other's presence, had become the most precious part of his day. The rhythmic sound of the waves outside, which had once served as a backdrop to his internal anxieties, now provided a soothing counterpoint to their conversations, a constant reminder of the natural world they were striving to protect. It was a sound that spoke of continuity, of resilience, of a timeless rhythm that transcended the fleeting concerns of human endeavor. He had learned to appreciate this rhythm, to find solace in its unwavering presence.

His earlier restlessness, the constant urge to be elsewhere, to be doing more, had abated. He no longer felt the need to escape, to seek out new challenges simply for the sake of motion. He had found his challenge, his adventure, in the depths of his relationship with Mara and in the shared purpose of the sanctuary. He realized that true growth didn't always necessitate dramatic upheaval; it could also be found in the steady, consistent cultivation of love, commitment, and shared purpose. His presence, once characterized by a subtle undercurrent of unease, had become one of quiet strength and unwavering reassurance. He was no longer searching for his place in the world; he had found it, here, with Mara, in the sanctuary they had built, and in the life they were continuously shaping together.

The expansion plans for the sanctuary, once a topic that might have triggered his ingrained anxieties about resource management and potential pitfalls, now filled him with a sense of calm excitement. He saw how Mara's vision, coupled with his own practical expertise, created a powerful synergy. He was no longer just the one who ensured things ran smoothly; he was an integral part of bringing her dreams to life, and that felt profoundly fulfilling. He had learned to trust not only his own capabilities but also the power of their combined efforts. This trust extended to the growing team they were assembling, a testament to their shared belief in collaboration and the strength of collective endeavor. He was content to be a steady, supportive force, a reliable presence in the unfolding narrative of their lives.

He often reflected on the contrast between his former self and the man he had become. The driven, often solitary individual who had struggled to articulate his deepest desires had given way to a man who found profound joy in shared intimacy and a deep sense of purpose. The ocean, in its boundless beauty and its untamed power, no longer represented a metaphor for his own unmoored existence but for the vast, uncharted territory of their shared future, a future he faced not with apprehension, but with a quiet confidence and an abiding love. He had found his stable harbor, and it was more beautiful and more profound than he had ever dared to imagine.

Their connection, once a vibrant flame ignited by shared purpose and a serendipitous rescue, had settled into a steady, comforting glow. It was a love that had weathered its initial storms and emerged not just intact, but stronger, more resilient. The whirlwind of their early days, characterized by adrenaline and the urgent need to save, had given way to a different kind of intensity – the quiet, profound dedication of building a life together. This wasn't a love that rested on laurels, but one that actively, consciously, chose to bloom anew each day. It was in the mindful way they navigated their shared responsibilities, in the deliberate effort to understand each other's evolving needs, and in the unwavering commitment to nurture the unique ecosystem of their relationship. The spark hadn't died; it had simply transformed into a deep, enduring warmth, a testament to the intentionality that had become the bedrock of their partnership.

The early days of their life together at the sanctuary had been a period of exhilarating discovery, both of the wild creatures they cared for and of each other. Eli, with his innate understanding of systems and his quiet strength, and Mara, with her boundless compassion and her intuitive artistry, had found a remarkable synergy. But as the initial urgency of establishing their shared life had subsided, a new, more subtle phase began: the art of sustained companionship. This wasn't a passive drifting, but an active, conscious crafting of their future, brick by deliberate brick. They understood that love, like the delicate balance of the marine life they protected, required constant attention, gentle adjustments, and a deep respect for its intricate workings. Their days were no longer punctuated by dramatic rescues, but by the quiet rhythm of shared tasks, of deep conversations under starry skies, and of the mutual understanding that bloomed in the spaces between their words.

Eli often found himself reflecting on how much their relationship had evolved. It had been easy, in the initial stages, to be swept up in the sheer exhilaration of their shared mission. The sanctuary provided a tangible, pressing purpose that bound them together. But as the sanctuary flourished under their combined stewardship, and as their lives settled into a more predictable, yet no less fulfilling, cadence, they had to confront the question of how to sustain their connection beyond the immediate demands of their work. It was Mara, in her characteristic way, who had articulated it most beautifully during one of their quiet evenings overlooking the sea. "Our love isn't a destination, Eli," she had said, her voice soft, "it's a journey we choose to embark on, every single day." Her words had resonated deeply with him, capturing the essence of what their partnership had become.

This commitment to intentionality permeated every aspect of their lives. It was evident in the way they approached their work, not just as a series of tasks, but as a shared endeavor that required their collective strengths and mutual respect. When planning the sanctuary's expansion, for instance, Eli's pragmatic foresight in resource allocation and logistical planning was seamlessly integrated with Mara's vision for enhanced educational programs and the creation of a more immersive, nature-connected experience for visitors. They didn't simply delegate; they collaborated, engaging in rigorous discussions, weighing options, and always, always, ensuring that their decisions aligned with their shared values and their overarching vision. This deliberate process, though sometimes time-consuming, fostered a deeper understanding of each other's perspectives and solidified their trust in their combined abilities. It was a testament to their belief that their partnership was not about individual achievement, but about shared success.

Beyond the professional realm, their intentionality extended to the intimate landscape of their personal lives. They had learned the importance of carving out dedicated time for each other, even amidst the demands of their busy schedules. This wasn't always grand gestures; often, it was as simple as setting aside their work an hour earlier to share a pot of tea on the porch, or dedicating Sunday afternoons to exploring hidden coves along the coastline, without any agenda other than to simply be present with one another. They understood that in the constant ebb and flow of daily life, it was crucial to create deliberate moments of connection, to actively nurture the bond that held them together. They actively practiced open communication, creating a safe space where vulnerability was not just accepted, but encouraged. There were no unspoken grievances, no assumptions left to fester. Instead, they approached their conversations with a genuine desire to understand, to empathize, and to find solutions that honored both their individual needs and their shared aspirations.

Eli remembered a particular instance when this intentionality had been tested. A particularly challenging winter had strained their resources, and a series of unexpected animal arrivals had placed immense pressure on their already stretched capacity. Eli, accustomed to problem-solving on his own, had found himself wrestling with a sense of isolation and responsibility. Mara, sensing his quiet burden, had gently, but firmly, drawn him into a conversation. She hadn't offered platitudes or easy answers. Instead, she had simply sat with him, listened to his anxieties without judgment, and then offered her own perspective, not as a solution, but as a shared understanding. "We are a team, Eli," she had said, her hand resting reassuringly on his. "Whatever challenges we face, we face them together. Your strength is my strength, and my support is yours." It was this quiet reaffirmation of their partnership, this deliberate act of shared vulnerability, that had lightened his load and reminded him that they were not just partners in their work, but partners in life.

Their commitment to each other was not a passive state of being, but an active, ongoing choice. They understood that love, in its most profound and enduring form, required conscious effort. It meant actively listening when the other spoke, even when tired or preoccupied. It meant offering support without being asked, anticipating needs, and celebrating each other's successes, no matter how small. It meant offering forgiveness freely when mistakes were made, understanding that perfection was an illusion, but growth and grace were attainable realities. They had cultivated a language of love that went beyond words – a shared glance that conveyed volumes, a gentle touch that offered solace, a quiet presence that spoke of unwavering support. This deep, unspoken understanding was the result of years of intentional cultivation, of choosing to see each other, to truly know each other, and to love each other more fully with each passing day.

The sanctuary, once a symbol of Eli's personal journey towards healing and purpose, had evolved into a tangible manifestation of their shared dreams and their enduring commitment. The expansion of their facilities, the development of new educational programs, the increasing number of volunteers drawn to their mission – all of it was a testament to their collaborative spirit. They had intentionally built a community around their shared values, a network of support that extended far beyond the boundaries of the sanctuary itself. This wasn't merely about rescue and rehabilitation; it was about fostering a deeper connection with the natural world, about inspiring a sense of stewardship, and about demonstrating, through their own lives, the power of intentional living.

Eli often marveled at the depth of their connection. It wasn't built on grand pronouncements or dramatic declarations, but on the quiet accumulation of shared moments, of mutual respect, and of an unwavering belief in each other. He saw how Mara's innate empathy and her boundless creativity infused their work with a soulfulness that resonated with everyone they encountered. And he knew that his own steady presence, his analytical mind, and his unwavering dedication provided the stable foundation upon which their shared vision could flourish. They were two halves of a whole, not in the sense of incompleteness, but in the sense of a perfect, harmonious balance, each complementing and strengthening the other. This was the essence of their partnership, defined not by circumstance, but by deliberate, conscious, and enduring choice.

The horizon ahead, once a source of apprehension for Eli, now shimmered with the promise of a future they were actively, intentionally, building together. It was a future filled with the quiet joys of shared sunsets, the gentle rhythm of the tides, and the enduring strength of a love that had learned to thrive not in ease, but in the profound beauty of conscious commitment. They had discovered that the most fulfilling journeys were not those stumbled upon by chance, but those meticulously mapped out with love, respect, and an unwavering dedication to navigating the path, side by side, forever. Their relationship was a testament to the power of intentionality, a quiet, yet powerful, force that shaped their days and illuminated their shared tomorrows.

The concept of "forever" had once seemed abstract, a distant, perhaps unattainable, ideal. But now, for Eli, it was a tangible reality, woven into the fabric of his everyday life with Mara. Their love was not a static monument, but a living, breathing entity that they actively tended to, nurturing its growth with the same care they gave to the most delicate of their rescued seabirds. This intentionality manifested in countless small, yet significant, ways. It was in the morning ritual of coffee shared in comfortable silence, each lost in their own thoughts but deeply aware of the other's presence. It was in the way they instinctively reached for each other's hand during moments of shared joy or quiet contemplation. It was in the deliberate practice of expressing gratitude, not just for grand gestures, but for the mundane acts of kindness that punctuated their days – a perfectly brewed cup of tea, a thoughtful reminder about an upcoming appointment, a comforting hand on his shoulder after a long day.

They had learned to be fiercely protective of their shared space, both physical and emotional. Their home, the sanctuary, was more than just a dwelling; it was a haven, a testament to their shared values and their collective dreams. They had deliberately cultivated an atmosphere of peace and mutual respect within its walls, ensuring that it remained a sanctuary not just for the animals, but for their own relationship. This extended to their communication, where they had established a practice of honest, open dialogue, even when it was difficult. There were no hidden agendas, no assumptions left unchecked. Instead, they approached every conversation with a commitment to understanding, to empathizing, and to finding common ground. This deliberate vulnerability, this willingness to be truly seen by each other, was the cornerstone of their emotional intimacy.

Mara's artistic spirit, which had initially drawn Eli in with its vibrant energy, had also become a source of profound learning for him. He had witnessed firsthand how her creativity was not confined to her art but extended to her approach to life, to problem-solving, and to nurturing relationships. She had a gift for seeing possibilities where others saw only obstacles, for finding beauty in the mundane, and for infusing everyday moments with a sense of wonder. Eli, in turn, offered her a grounded perspective, a pragmatic approach that helped to translate her visionary ideas into tangible realities. They had intentionally cultivated this dynamic, recognizing that their differing strengths were not a source of conflict, but a powerful engine for growth and innovation. It was a conscious choice to lean into each other's uniqueness, to celebrate their differences, and to build something stronger and more beautiful together than either could have achieved alone.

The sanctuary's ongoing success was a constant reminder of the power of their intentional partnership. The expanded rehabilitation facilities, the growing volunteer program, the successful fundraising initiatives – all of it was a direct result of their collaborative efforts. They had intentionally sought out individuals who shared their passion and their commitment, building a team that mirrored the values they held dear. This wasn't simply about expanding their reach; it was about creating a ripple effect, inspiring others to engage with the natural world and to embrace the principles of compassion and stewardship. Eli found immense satisfaction in witnessing the tangible impact of their work, knowing that it was born from a foundation of shared purpose and unwavering dedication.

He often looked at Mara, observing the quiet grace with which she navigated their life, and felt an overwhelming sense of gratitude. Her resilience in the face of challenges, her unwavering optimism, and her deep well of compassion were qualities he had come to cherish and, in many ways, to emulate. He had learned from her that true strength lay not in stoicism or self-reliance, but in the courage to be vulnerable, to ask for help, and to offer unwavering support to those you love. Their relationship was a living testament to this understanding, a continuous cycle of giving and receiving, of lifting each other up and celebrating each other's triumphs.

The horizon stretched before them, not as an unknown abyss, but as a canvas upon which they would continue to paint their shared story. It was a future they approached with a quiet confidence, a deep sense of purpose, and an abiding love that had been forged not by chance, but by the unwavering intention to choose each other, every single day, and to build a life together that was as beautiful and as enduring as the ocean that stretched out before their home. Their partnership was a masterpiece in progress, a testament to the profound beauty and enduring strength found in a love defined by purpose, by passion, and by the intentional, unwavering act of choosing each other, always.

The salty air, once a harbinger of storms and uncertainty, now carried the familiar scent of hope and healing. The rescue center, nestled against the rugged coastline, stood as a testament to the enduring spirit of both its inhabitants and its caretakers. Its sturdy walls, weathered by countless seasons, seemed to absorb the ceaseless rhythm of the waves, a constant reminder of the powerful forces of nature they worked to protect and preserve. For Mara and Eli, the center was no longer just a place of work; it was the very heart of their shared existence, a living, breathing embodiment of their commitment to one another and to the vast, intricate tapestry of marine life.

The days at the sanctuary had fallen into a comforting, yet vibrant, rhythm. Mara, with her characteristic grace, moved through the bustling rehabilitation pools, her hands gentle yet firm as she administered medication or offered words of encouragement to the recovering seals and seabirds. Her laughter, like the call of a distant gull, often echoed through the airy recovery rooms, a sound that seemed to instill a sense of calm in even the most distressed creatures. Eli, his brow furrowed in concentration, could often be found poring over charts and maintenance logs, his quiet dedication a grounding force that ensured the smooth operation of every facet of the center. He possessed an almost innate understanding of the complex systems that kept the facility running, from the intricate filtration systems to the carefully calibrated feeding schedules. Together, they were an unstoppable force, their individual strengths weaving together to create a seamless, effective operation.

Their partnership, forged in the crucible of shared purpose, had become the bedrock of the rescue center's continued mission. It wasn't simply about the daily tasks, the feeding, the cleaning, the veterinary care. It was about the unwavering belief in the sanctity of life, the profound responsibility they felt towards the vulnerable creatures entrusted to their care. This shared ethos permeated every decision, every action. When a particularly ambitious expansion project was proposed – a state-of-the-art marine mammal rehabilitation pool designed to accommodate larger species – it was Mara's visionary appeal to the emotional impact, her ability to paint a picture of hope for rescued dolphins and whales, that ignited the initial spark. Eli, in turn, meticulously mapped out the logistical hurdles, the financial projections, the engineering requirements, transforming Mara's dream into a tangible, achievable reality. Their debates were passionate, often lively, but always rooted in a deep respect for each other's perspectives and a shared commitment to the ultimate goal: providing the best possible care for every animal that crossed their threshold.

The sanctuary had also become a hub for the wider community, a place where the principles of conservation and compassion were not just taught, but actively lived. Mara had poured her artistic talents into creating engaging educational programs for visiting school groups, transforming complex ecological concepts into accessible and inspiring experiences. She designed interactive exhibits that celebrated the resilience of nature, featuring the success stories of animals they had nursed back to health and released. Eli, ever the pragmatist, ensured that these programs were well-resourced and effectively managed, creating volunteer opportunities that allowed community members to actively participate in the sanctuary's mission. The center, under their stewardship, had become more than a rescue facility; it was a vibrant center for environmental awareness, fostering a new generation of stewards for the fragile coastline.

One crisp autumn afternoon, as a particularly fierce storm raged outside, threatening to batter the coastline with its unforgiving fury, the true strength of their combined efforts was put to the test. A pod of stranded pilot whales had been reported struggling in the churning surf, their lives hanging precariously in the balance. The call had come in just as Eli was about to conduct a crucial maintenance check on the backup generators, a task made all the more urgent by the darkening skies and the rising wind. Mara, without hesitation, had gathered her team, her voice steady and reassuring as she outlined the rescue plan, her mind already anticipating the needs of the distressed animals.

Eli, his heart pounding with a familiar mix of adrenaline and responsibility, had swiftly completed the generator checks, ensuring that the sanctuary's life-support systems would remain operational throughout the storm. He then joined Mara on the beach, his powerful frame moving with practiced efficiency as he helped to carefully maneuver the large marine mammals from the water, their sleek bodies heavy and vulnerable against the crashing waves. The operation was a testament to years of practiced teamwork. Eli's strength and precise movements complemented Mara's delicate handling and her calming presence. They worked in near-perfect synchronicity, their focus absolute, their shared understanding transcending the chaos of the storm. Other volunteers, inspired by their dedication, worked tirelessly alongside them, their efforts amplified by the unwavering leadership of Mara and Eli.

The rescue was arduous, fraught with danger from the treacherous waves and the sheer physical exertion. But as they finally managed to guide the last of the pilot whales into a specially prepared, temporary holding pool at the sanctuary, a collective sigh of relief swept through the exhausted team. Mara, her face streaked with saltwater and her hair plastered to her forehead, met Eli's gaze across the dimly lit recovery barn. In that silent exchange, a world of shared accomplishment, of mutual respect, and of profound love passed between them. It was a look that spoke of countless challenges overcome, of a future they were building together, one rescue, one sunrise, one shared moment at a time.

The pilot whale rescue was not an isolated incident; it was a microcosm of the rescue center's continued mission. Each successful rehabilitation, each release back into the vast expanse of the ocean, was a victory celebrated by Mara and Eli, a testament to their unwavering dedication. They had cultivated a culture of resilience within the sanctuary walls, a place where setbacks were met with renewed determination, and where every small success was a cause for quiet celebration. They understood that their work was a marathon, not a sprint, and that the commitment to conservation required sustained effort, unwavering passion, and a deep, abiding love for the natural world.

The physical structure of the rescue center itself seemed to mirror their own journey. The new marine mammal pool, a testament to their ambitious vision, was nearing completion, its sleek lines a stark contrast to the older, more weathered buildings. Yet, even the older structures held their own charm, their history etched into every beam and every stone. Eli had overseen the meticulous renovation of the original clinic building, preserving its original character while upgrading its functionality. Mara had infused the new administrative offices with warmth and personality, using natural materials and incorporating elements of her art to create a space that felt both professional and inviting. The entire facility, from the bustling recovery wards to the quiet research labs, resonated with their shared commitment to excellence and their deep respect for the sanctuary's legacy.

Their shared life at the sanctuary had also fostered a deeper understanding of their own personal growth. Eli, who had once struggled with isolation and a reluctance to rely on others, had learned the profound strength that came from genuine partnership. He found a deep satisfaction in collaborating with Mara, in entrusting her with his own vulnerabilities and in witnessing her unwavering support in return. Mara, in turn, found in Eli a steady anchor, a grounded presence that allowed her to pursue her most ambitious dreams with confidence. Their relationship had become a living embodiment of the sanctuary's ethos – a place of healing, of growth, and of unwavering hope.

The horizon beyond the sanctuary's coastline was a constant reminder of the vastness of the ocean and the myriad creatures they strived to protect. But for Mara and Eli, that horizon also represented a future they were actively, intentionally, building together. The rescue center, a beacon on the rugged shore, was more than just a facility; it was a symbol of their shared purpose, their enduring love, and their unwavering commitment to the vital mission of healing and conservation. As the sun dipped below the waves, casting a warm, golden glow over the water, they stood together, hand in hand, their hearts filled with a quiet contentment, ready to face whatever the tide might bring. The work was far from over, but with each other by their side, and the sanctuary humming with renewed life, they knew they were ready for whatever tomorrow held.

Love, for Mara, had become less of a sudden revelation and more of a persistent, gentle question, whispered on the ebb and flow of their shared days. It was a question that settled into the quiet moments between the calls of distressed gulls and the hum of filtration systems, a question that asked, *"Are you still here? Are you still choosing this? Are you still present?"* And with every sunrise painting the sea in hues of rose and gold, with every successful release back into the vast expanse of blue, and with every quiet evening spent by Eli's side, her answer was a resounding, heartfelt "Yes." It wasn't a singular, monumental affirmation, but a constellation of smaller, deliberate choices, each one a stone laid on the foundation of their shared life.

This understanding had dawned on her not in a singular, blinding flash, but in the cumulative weight of their experiences. It was in the way Eli's hand would find hers as they surveyed the vast stretch of ocean from the observation deck, a silent acknowledgment of their shared responsibility and their deep, unspoken connection. It was in the way she'd catch him watching her, a soft smile playing on his lips as she animatedly explained a new enrichment activity for the seals, his gaze a testament to his unwavering belief in her. These weren't grand declarations, but the quiet affirmations of a love that had grown organically, deeply rooted in the fertile ground of shared purpose and mutual respect.

The analogy of the sea, so ever-present in their lives, had become her guiding metaphor for love. The ocean was not a placid, unchanging entity; it was a dynamic force, constantly shifting, breathing, and responding. There were calm days, where the surface mirrored the sky in serene beauty, and then there were storms, where waves crashed with untamed power, testing the resilience of the shore. Love, she realized, was much the same. It wasn't about maintaining a perpetual state of tranquil bliss, but about navigating those inevitable storms together, about being present and steadfast even when the waters grew rough.

Each day at the rescue center presented its own set of challenges, its own subtle tests of their commitment. A sudden influx of injured seabirds after a particularly harsh winter, a complex medical case that required round-the-clock monitoring, or the ever-present need for funding – these were the daily tides that threatened to pull them in different directions. Yet, time and again, they found themselves standing shoulder to shoulder, their individual strengths complementing each other, their shared dedication a powerful anchor. Eli's meticulous planning and unwavering pragmatism often provided the framework for Mara's passionate advocacy, while Mara's ability to inspire and connect with others helped to rally support for Eli's often complex logistical undertakings.

Their conversations, once focused on the immediate needs of the sanctuary, had naturally expanded to encompass their shared future, not as a distant, abstract concept, but as a tangible, evolving entity. They spoke of dreams that extended beyond the coastline, of a life where their passion for conservation could intertwine with their personal aspirations. Eli, who had once been reticent about his own hopes and desires, now openly shared his ideas for expanding the center's research capabilities, his eyes alight with a quiet enthusiasm that Mara found endlessly endearing. Mara, in turn, found herself articulating her artistic visions with a new clarity, envisioning educational programs that could reach far beyond the sanctuary's physical boundaries.

This evolution wasn't about erasing their individual selves, but about weaving them together more intricately. It was about understanding that their growth was not a solitary pursuit, but a shared journey. When Mara poured her energy into developing a new outreach initiative, Eli was her staunchest supporter, ensuring the resources were in place and the logistical complexities were handled with his characteristic efficiency. When Eli faced a particularly daunting engineering challenge with the new rehabilitation pool, Mara was there, not with technical solutions, but with unwavering encouragement, her belief in his capabilities a silent but powerful force.

The persistent question of love was also about honesty, about the courage to voice unspoken fears and to celebrate quiet triumphs. It was about the willingness to look at each other, even after a long and demanding day, and to say, "I'm here. I see you. And I choose us." This conscious choice, repeated daily, was what transformed a romantic ideal into a lived reality. It was the difference between a promise made in the flush of emotion and a commitment that weathered the passage of time.

Mara often found herself reflecting on the early days of their relationship, the tentative steps they had taken, the uncertainties they had navigated. Now, their connection felt as natural and essential as the rhythm of the tides. They had learned each other's silent cues, understood the unspoken language of a shared glance, and found solace in the simple act of being together in comfortable silence. This was the beauty of a love that had been allowed to grow, to deepen, and to mature, unhurried and authentic.

The horizon, that ever-present line where the sky met the sea, no longer represented an uncertain future, but a shared canvas. It was a reminder that their journey was ongoing, that each day brought new opportunities for connection, for growth, and for love. They weren't searching for a static destination, a perfect ending that would freeze them in time. Instead, they had found their forever in the continuous act of becoming, in the shared horizon of their tomorrows, forever tied to the ebb and flow of the sea, and to the persistent, gentle question of love that they answered, with all their hearts, every single day. Their love was not a sheltered cove, but the open ocean, vast and full of wonder, demanding presence, honesty, and an unwavering commitment to the adventure. And in answering that call, they found a depth of connection and a strength of purpose that resonated with the very heartbeat of the ocean itself.

Glossary

Enrichment **Activity:** Designed to enhance the psychological well-being of animals in human care, enrichment activities provide stimulation and encourage natural behaviors.

Filtration Systems: Essential for maintaining water quality in aquatic environments like rehabilitation pools, these systems remove waste and impurities.

Observation Deck: An elevated platform providing a vantage point for observing marine life and the surrounding environment.